ONE MORE KILL FOR MOTHER

A DI GUTTERIDGE NOVEL

C. R. CLARKE

Troubador Publishing Ltd
Unit E2 Airfield Business Park,
Harrison Road, Market Harborough,
Leicestershire LE16 7UL
Tel: 0116 279 2299
Email: books@troubador.co.uk
Web: www.troubador.co.uk

ISBN 978 1 80514 490 8

British Library Cataloguing in Publication Data.
A catalogue record for this book is available from the British Library.

Printed and bound by CPI Group (UK) Ltd, Croydon, CR0 4YY
Typeset in 10.5pt Adobe Garamond Pro by Troubador Publishing Ltd, Leicester, UK

For

DAVID

For all those who've emboldened me in my endeavors –
them who dared believe me capable of such a daunting
task as penning four novels. Specially my Zoe, whose
unwavering encouragement and staunch fortification of
my fickle confidence often fueled those efforts.
My gratitude goes to you.

WELCOME TO
BOOK #2

A NOTE FROM THE AUTHOR

If you're reading this, chances are you've acquired my book, and for that alone I am genuinely grateful.

The novel you're holding is book #2 in the series, and although I made every effort to ensure that each book can be indulged on their own merits, I would urge you to read book #1 as not only does it introduce you to the main characters, but there are also a number of continuing narratives that would certainly make more sense if ingested in the right order.

Let me say this now, and I'll make no bones about it: what you're holding in your hand is a thoroughly dark book, and in penning it, I not only had to do a significant amount of research into those members of the population less wholesome or harmonious than ourselves, but also allow myself to absorb and 'become' the characters within these pages. Something that can, at times – as any author will tell you – leave you feeling decidedly unwashed.

We, all of us, love a cosy crime thriller, and that includes me. But if that type of novel is to be considered one end of the spectrum, this book resides at the other.

Murder is a wholly horrific proposition, and as uncomfortable a concept to contemplate as any, let alone witness, and I'd be lying if I said that discomfort won't land from time to time when reading this book, as I seek to take you into the mind of our killer, as I also did in book #1, but in this, the sequel, I have to admit I may have tweaked things up to 'eleven'.

But isn't that the joy of literature, and by association, film and television, that we can witness the abhorrent without the inconvenience of peril?

So, once again, thank you for your faith that I can entertain you, and if you've already read one of my other offerings, welcome back...

C. R. Clarke.

PROLOGUE

DETECTIVE INSPECTOR GUTTERIDGE lay curled up into a semi-fetal ball, his anticipant gaze locked on the two-foot parting in the bedroom curtains he'd leaned out from the duvet to effect, watching for the next crackling flash of the electrical storm that had been raging for the last hour, or at least, the last hour that he was aware of, having been rudely awoken from his sleep by a deep, guttural boom that had rattled the windows in their frames.

He pondered how easy it must have been for his ancestors to believe in the gods they assigned to such awe-invoking events – gods that must have given their simpler lives such direction and meaning. Direction and meaning he often felt was missing from his own life.

The gap in the curtains suddenly ignited to the intermittent stutter of pupil-shocking fury, back lighting the sputtering tracks of rain cascading down the glass.

Gutteridge counted again. 'One, one thousand. Two, one thousand. Three, one thousand. Four, one thousand. Five, one thou—' *Boom!* The whole night shook, punctuated by two more staccato flashes to cement his awe, and for one fleeting moment, it could be believed that it was daytime outside, and not 02:27 in the morning as the blinding numbers of his bedside clock indicated.

He could hear the steady, regular breaths of his wife, Eve, in slumber, lying behind him, oblivious to the ferocious spectacle broiling outside.

Gutteridge allowed himself a smile. 'That girl could sleep through a war,' he mumbled into the fizzing silence.

Another flash incinerated the sky, shorter this time, but brighter, looking like the muzzle flash of Kieran O'Leary's captive bolt gun as the piston fired up through the soft flesh beneath his jaw, punching skull fragments into his corrupted mind.

O'Leary's last words replayed in his memory. '*Please… forgive me for what I have done!*' he'd said, his expression so lost, so defeated, so *remorseful…*

Gutteridge blinked it away, pondering the notion that if someone in a lab coat with a large enough brain came up with a way to drag and drop such memories into a delete file – some Scientology-style 'auditor' – would he choose to utilise it, knowing full well that such experiences shaped the people we are, and the people we're destined to become?

Eve stirred, shifting onto her other side, muttering something unintelligible to Gutteridge's limited knowledge of Polish, Eve's mother tongue.

Gutteridge wondered what she'd said, contemplating grabbing the English to Polish dictionary that had now taken up permanent residence in his bedside drawer.

'*Homary sa tutaj?*' he began muttering over and over so as to not forget it, but knowing full well he didn't have it in him to stir enough to switch on the light, open the drawer, rifle for the book, search out the words, blah, blah, whatever. So the words eventually petered away into silence and, once again, quiet reigned supreme.

Another stuttering flash shocked his eyes. Another vision of O'Leary, a vectoring fan of atomised blood spraying from his gurning mouth as he dropped to the floor, and of Eve – his dearest, lovely Eve – taped into a chair at the side of it all, spattered in O'Leary's blood, eyes alight with shock, fear and disbelief…

Gutteridge rose, motivated by a desire to break from such repugnant memories and a growing need to pee, ambling his aching limbs towards the en suite.

He'd become somewhat of a gym bunny of late, partly motivated by a desire to stay healthy, and partly by a need to vent the pressure of the despair for his previous life – pounding iron and leather turning out to be an effective way to 'audit' his inner demons. But he enjoyed the ache, that day after, the day after soreness that sang of progress.

He wandered into the echoing familiarity of the shower room, fumbling around in the dark, feeling for the cord to the light switch. He pulled it, and with a very different kind of flash, a face that seemed to him to be looking more like his father's with every passing day appeared in the mirror above the sink. He took a moment to absorb it, studying the few, localised signs of age that it now displayed, but knowing from the compliments of others within his sphere of trusted opinions that he was faring well on the aging front.

Gutteridge sidestepped his reflection to relieve himself, spinning on the hot tap to allow the water time to get to temperature, using the gurgling of the plughole to mask any sounds and keep it dignified. He considered not flushing; both him and Eve having long ago agreed that anything liquid can remain until the morning, so as to not risk waking the other. But he figured if Eve could sleep through a storm as ferocious as the one raging outside, she could certainly sleep through a flush, and he leaned on the handle.

His vertebrae crunched like sand in mechanics as he rolled his neck, hands fidgeting in the hot water. His gaze eventually landed back on his reflection. 'Hello again, Father,' he quipped.

As he spun the taps off again and shook his hands dry, Gutteridge's wandering attention gravitated to a small bottle of talcum powder perched inconspicuously high upon the cabinet, his frowning eyes locking on its undoubtable presence in the room as he quietly dried his hands on the towel.

He stretched up and took it down, careful not to dislodge any of the skyline of product bottles surrounding it, squeezing the periphery of the perforated lid with his fingers until it popped, revealing the contents.

He peered inside at a concoction of ground chalk mixed with grains of rice, sporadically shaking the bottle to irritate the contents until a flat, rectangular packet appeared like a crooked headstone.

He reached a curious finger inside and dragged it up the side of the container until he could pinch it from the lip, and placed the bottle down again.

Gutteridge blew the light dusting of powder off his find like an archeologist, revealing a neatly folded wrap of cocaine that had been expertly encased in clingfilm alongside a packet of silica gel to help regulate the moisture. Two grams – the good stuff, not that stamped-on shit that had been cut to death with speed and caffeine.

Kieran O'Leary's forlorn face came to Gutteridge again, followed by the face of Cynthia – his ex-wife – slaughtered merely for having the presence of forethought to choose Gutteridge as her life partner. His mood sank once again, along with his insides, contemplating opening his hidden secret, placed there by him years ago to help combat the panic that having none in the house inflicted on a mind that craved its nose burning high. That time he'd been actively trying to kick the habit, and until now, he'd forgotten it was even there.

His fingers began gingerly tugging at the clingfilm, carefully unwrapping the flat, plump little parcel of mischief – a one-way ticket to a hellish night of heightened paranoia and crippling self-awareness, where every creak and pop from the bones of the old house imprisoning his inability to abstain would become the creeping footsteps of something unseen with nefarious intentions, where every lingering look from those around you would become the truth-searching stares of people who *know* you're back on it again, the loser that you are, unable to handle life's torments with the dignity and grace it warrants.

'Fuck you,' he whispered, in a moment of strength, and of sanity, dropping his discovery into the toilet and belligerently tipping the contents of the bottle in after it. He thrust hard on the flush to eject it from his life.

He breathed a deep sigh of ultimate relief, and smiled, feeling pride in his strength, in his ardour, pulling images of the woman asleep next door to the fore. His *new* drug: tall, long-limbed, and beautiful in a way very few could hold a candle to. A drug whose active ingredient was her body, soft-edged and undeniably feminine; but firm to the touch and toned. Mile-high legs that rippled when she strode through the world she commanded. Her stomach, flat and defined, had become almost an obsession to Gutteridge and his inflamed fascination, and his infuriated despair.

'My Eve,' he muttered, feeling the craving for coke dissipate into a lake of his very fondest memories of this new life. 'My lovely, beautiful, Eve…'

ONE

2011

'IS EVERYTHING ALRIGHT, MISS?' asked the concerned fifty-something managing the bar of the Lake Vyrnwy Hotel — a sprawling, faux-Tudor building with prominent Swiss overtones nestled deep in the hills of Powys that seemed to lord over the huge expanse of water stretched out before it.

It was New Year's Eve, and the reclusive female sitting at the bar, folded in on herself, had dropped six neat shots of vodka in less than half an hour, and it *hadn't* gone unnoticed.

She sat in contemplation of her dwindling options, eyes reddened from silently weeping, coming to terms with a decision she'd reluctantly been forced to make.

'Miss?' the manager reiterated, 'are you okay? Are you resident? Do you have a room here tonight?'

The woman lifted glassy eyes to meet the manager's concerned gaze. 'Yes,' she lied, 'I erm… yes.'

The manager allowed his inflating concerns to show in his face as a precursor to softening the suggestion he was about to make – and did he *recognise* this woman?

1

'I'm really not sure it would be wise for you to have any more, at least not for a little while.'

But the woman rose from her seat before he could finish. 'I'm done anyway,' she said, as she unsteadily unhooked her bag from the back of the stool. 'I'm going to go up to my room now.'

'Can I help in any way?' the manager asked. 'What room are you in?'

But the woman ignored his blatant attempts at fishing, and with a forced, insincere smile, turned to make her way towards the door that led into the foyer. She sidled through animated pockets of irreverent revellers, serenaded by the murmur of standard banter and intermittent bursts of unrestrained laughter that appeared to mock her mood.

She exited the bar and wandered past the staircase that climbed to the guest bedrooms, heading towards the main exit at the rear of the building. Two middle-aged men flanked the door, exchanging news of their lives.

'Excuse me,' said the woman.

'*Hellllo!*' said the man to the right, propping up the frame of the door with a provocative raise of the brow. 'You're not leaving us so soon are you?'

His companion laughed.

The man to the right continued, fuelled by excessive quantities of alcohol. 'If I said I love you, would you stay a while and keep me company?'

The companion laughed again at his obnoxious colleague's ponderous attempts at charm.

The woman kept her face averted, not wishing to be recognised. 'Can you just let me past, please,' she insisted.

Reluctantly, the man stepped aside, feigning hurt, opening the door with an exaggerated bow to ridicule her desire to be left alone.

The woman sidled through the pungent aroma of his inebriated breath and pressure of his stare, and stepped out into the frigid night air. Her own breath turned white as she considered the sky, cloudless and charcoal black. Jewels of stars began to resolve in her widening vision as she made for her car – a silver Mercedes SL sat abandoned on the side of the lane that snaked to the overcrowded carpark.

She fumbled for the keys in her bag, popping the door and dropping inside the chilled interior, turning a look out of the side window to check she hadn't been followed.

A Jack Russell Terrier pawed at her arrival and padded expectantly in the passenger seat beside her, watching the woman intently. The animal could sense the hopelessness emanating off its master's wilting ardour, her joy-starved cheeks glistening with films of dried tears, kicking the light polluting the crisp, night air that bled from the hotel ahead. Her fight was gone, and there was nothing left to do.

She fumbled the keys into the ignition and fired up the engine, contemplating turning on the heating, but decided against it, hitting the button for the air-con instead to acclimatise herself to the cold in readiness.

She turned right at the bottom of the lane onto the road that encircled the lake, deciding to avoid the narrow road that traversed the slate-stone dam on the southern side of the shore and the fender-bending opportunities that went hand-in-hand with navigating it.

The narrow road meandered through tall spires of Douglas Fir that seemed to reach for the heavens like the pillars of a cathedral. Sporadic glimpses of the still waters glistened in the moonlight on the left, the ground carpeted in thick blankets of grass and moss that popped in the halogen glow of the car's sweeping headlights.

The woman began to dry-sob for her situation, and the animal could sense the last remaining dregs of hope that had been evaporating off its owner for weeks leave the car, and she seemed to sag into reluctant acceptance of a destiny that appeared inevitable.

New tears came, rehydrating those that had run before, cascading from eyes reddened from hours, days, weeks of weeping. Had she failed as a mother? Had she not tried her hardest, done the very best she could with her need to balance work with home-life?

She hoovered past a waterfall on her right, then across a small, grey, slate-stone bridge, and began to scan the swinging horizon for the remote, roadside parking area she was seeking.

Rows of staggered masts penned in by a wave of white-painted fencing suddenly appeared in the headlights ahead, and she turned the nose of the Mercedes into the clearing a short way past and shut the engine off.

She sat in silence with her regrets for a time, listening to the rhythmical ticking of the cooling engine, then, taking a faltering breath, she popped the door of the car and rose into the skin-burning chill.

The dog followed, hopping off the seat onto the frosted tarmac. It had been here before for walks – it recognised the scent of the surrounding conifers – but it looked confused to be here when the sky was charcoal-black and sunless.

The woman drifted off again, peering out into the night. She was in her early sixties, mid-length hair and smartly dressed in a tweed trouser suit designed for office life, but the clothes looked unkempt and in need of a wash; her pallid complexion coated in a cursory layer of makeup that looked to have been applied more out of habit than personal pride. But despite the tiredness that now masked her very existence, she still managed to be the elegant woman she always was, wearing her advancing

4

years with grace and a certain level of dignity, however jaded. A dignity that had brought her to this point in time, and to this decision.

Raucous laughter drifted across the water from the hotel that was now on the far side of the lake, pulling the woman out of her daydream – the exaggerated merriment an audible contradiction to her own, polluted feelings.

She turned her attention back to the car, the rear parcel shelf stacked with newspapers, most displaying the headline: 'MASTERSON ON THE RUN!'

She sucked in a staccato sob, but clenched hard to halt its insistent flow. She wiped her eyes dry again on the sleeve of her jacket, smearing her eye makeup, then wandered around to the back of the car and popped the boot with her fob.

It swung open to the hiss of the struts, revealing a long-handled bag filled to the brim with gravel, topped with a solitary roll of duct tape. She lifted the holdall clear of the boot with a grunt, hoisting it onto her emaciated shoulder and dropping the keys in the boot.

The woman struggled along the unlit lane, across a brutalist, slate-stone overflow bridge, and continued until she saw the gloss-painted fencing to the canoe rental paddock.

Upturned fibreglass boat hulls loomed from the dark, shielded by the fog, looking like drifting icebergs in the hanging mist as she stumbled past the lot, unsteadied by the weight of her burden.

The gates to the paddock were shut and firmly padlocked. With a grunt, the woman shrugged the bag over to the far side of the railings and dropped it on the other side. Unsteadily, she climbed over and re-shouldered the holdall, then made her way down the shingled path towards the water's edge.

The dog had been following, but the woman hadn't

noticed, far too engrossed in her own iron resolve. It wove its tiny body through the railings to join her, trotting off to sniff for evidence of other dogs.

The woman continued her struggle down the trail, her unsuitable choice of footwear slipping on layers of shale.

Trees and bushes seemed to emerge from the dark. She could smell the water as she neared the shoreline: fresh, clean, invigorating, amalgamating with the woody scents of the evergreen pines that peppered the entire landscape, carried down by the sinking, frigid air and filling the basin of the valley.

She could see the glistening shoreline ahead, a greyscale vista rippling in the light of the moon. The few patches of grass she'd negotiated were slick with dew, soaking her shoes and chilling her feet, but she couldn't bring herself to care.

The woman reached the shore and the concrete slipway that emerged from the liquid blackness, looking more like ink than water. With a grunt, she dumped the bag of rocks onto the ground.

She tried to muster awe within her for the moonlit beauty of the view ahead, but she felt empty, and couldn't. Things were different now – sullied, stained, defiled, and could never be the same again.

Another burst of unrestrained laughter drifted across the lake from the hotel ahead. Her stomach folded in on her pain. Oh, how she wished – wished she could have done things differently. Shown more love, perhaps? No… that wasn't it.

She sagged under the pressure of her failure as a mother, and spun a look to the grassy bank behind her. She sat, dragging the bag in closer.

Taking the roll of tape from the holdall, she began winding it tightly around the ankles of her trouser suit, illuminated by the moonlight reflecting off the water – calm and still, like a mill-pond.

She tore the last strip of tape off the roll, placed it aside and stood again. Her whole demeanour was wan and defeated; she looked and felt empty, starved of happiness.

She unfastened the belt and button of her trousers, and lowered them to the ground. The midnight air bit at her skin with the teeth of winter and stung to the pain of her nakedness as she stooped and began methodically scooping handfuls of gravel from the bag into the crotch of the pants, filling the bucket of cloth between her feet. She began to cry again, tears of regret splashing off the stones as she scooped, and filled, and wept.

The bag empty and tossed aside, she grabbed the waistband of the trousers and stood. With a ceramic hiss, the gravel ran into the legs, dammed by the duct-tape bindings. She could feel the pressure against her legs as she refastened the belt, ignoring the stabbing pain scything through her ankles.

The dog had returned and been watching its owner's actions with head-twisting curiosity. It barked at her new routine, sensing it wrong, but the woman failed to hear it – alive only to her own muted resolve.

She shuffled down the bank towards the black-painted boathouse, then spun to face the lake, stopping just shy of the lick of the water's edge.

Shouted numbers counting from ten down to one began to drift on the wind from the hotel on the opposite shore, followed by the roaring hiss of fireworks fizzing heavenward into the skies surrounding the lake.

The woman paused momentarily to witness the cracks, pops and bangs illuminating the onyx ceiling high above her, soaring from every surrounding village and town, exciting the horizon, feeling the thud of each explosion deep in her sorrowful chest.

Her eyes returned to the still waters, now mirroring the

eruptions of colour being sent skyward to celebrate the advent of another year. But alas, not for her, not now, not ever…

Reluctant feet began shuffling into the brim of the lake, sending arcing ripples expanding from her wanton corruption of serenity, and kept walking, stumbling under the weight of the ballast with each determined step.

Her skin stung to the rising waterline washing up her body as she shuffled down the slipway, cutting her breaths short, until they melded with the stuttered sobs that were now all she had left of anything resembling an emotion.

The water reached her thighs, her waist, her chest… the breasts that had gladly fed that tiny little life. A life that would flourish only to destroy her own. She ploughed on, the water climbing past her shoulders, her neck, her jaw, licking at the lips of her gasping mouth.

She turned her face up to the moon and kept shuffling, toes reaching for the feeling of concrete and shale beneath each tentative step.

The dog's tail had long ago ceased wagging and it just stood, watching, whining – its companion in life vanishing from its sight and from its life.

The woman paused momentarily from her iron resolve, her upturned face now the only thing still visible from the distant shoreline, like a Venetian mask afloat on the water's surface, considering the watching moon.

She was now numb to the cold, as she'd become numb to life. She never imagined – when she'd first held that perfect, beautiful, innocent little life in her grateful arms all those years ago – that things would end this way.

One, final tear curled from an eye that had seen enough and bled into the lake she was gifting her life to. She took a last, determined stride into the black, liquid resolution to an existence turned sour, vanishing from the dog's sight, allowing its life-extinguishing flow to fill her lungs with rivulets of death.

She watched the night sky through the swirling lens of the water inches above her face, her white, ghostly visage peering from within the shadows of the lake, a new-found ability to feel calm rising through her like a frozen wave.

The swimming stars in her vision began to settle, as her body – like the water – fell still, and she began to die. Receding, waning, sinking away from a life she was no longer interested in living, and she felt surprised – as she succumbed to her actions – that she sensed herself smiling.

TWO

DS KEATON attempted to look proudly maternal for the crescent of interested well-wishers glad of a momentary distraction from their cases, coo-ing and ahh-ing at the tiny life looking up at their mixed attempts to draw the child's leapfrogging attention.

But Keaton's electric-blue eyes were locked on DI Gutteridge, watching to see if he noticed the baby boy lying in the carry-cot before him, mirroring his considerable interest, had the same chestnut eyes as his own; with the same milky-chocolate flecks emanating from the coronas that gave the child's fascinated gaze a muted brilliance comparable to his own.

The eye shape was a match, too – the way the sweep of the lids met at the lacrimal caruncle and dove to points towards their respective noses. To *her*, it was plain to see – as plain as the button nose on the baby's innocent face. But would *Gutteridge* notice?

In her mind, men rarely absorbed such details – that form of interest seemed to be the domain of the female of the species. But was he not a detective, attuned to noticing attributes and characteristics, and had he not commented on the beauty of her own electric-blue eyes on the night they allowed themselves a moment of abandonment, resulting in the mess she now found herself in and was so desperately trying to hide?

She'd told him it was another's – a one-night stand during an uncharacteristically absent spell of her birth control regime – in reality, the very real reason why this child now existed. But was she *really* that good of a liar to hide that the baby was *his*?

'He's beautiful, Jane,' Gutteridge said, sounding distant and pensive, seeming to forget they weren't alone, his eyes locked on the kicking life beaming up at him.

Was that a flicker of doubt she saw in Gutteridge's face? Of recognition, or suspicion? Should she tell him? Threaten to ruin the wedded-bliss that had recently put such spring into his whole demeanour? His wife was a goddess after all: tall, handsome, loving – how could she possibly hope to compete.

Sure, she was, herself, considered a beauty, but as jaw-droppingly gorgeous as Ewelina Kaminska? Correction, Ewelina *Gutteridge* – and there-in lay the problem. He was happy, now. After a life turned sour, he was happy. And Jane *loved* him – enough to trade her own happiness for his, even if it meant raising the child without the comfort and convenience of a father-figure.

Gutteridge's attention drifted back into the room, like he'd woken from a daydream. 'He's gorgeous, Jane. Just like his mother,' he said, before his muted smile flickered. 'So when are you coming back to work? *Are* you coming back to work?'

'Why? Have you missed me?' she replied, with a wry smile.

'Fuck me, yeah. *Sorry!*' he snapped, darting an apologetic look in the direction of the baby.

Keaton laughed. 'Don't worry, I don't think he can comprehend swear words. Not just yet anyway.'

Gutteridge rolled his eyes at the looseness of his tongue. 'Sorry, Jane... I guess I'm not used to being around kids.

Me and—' He paused, stumbling on his words. 'Me and...
Cynthia, never managed to have children, not before... you
know...' He paused again, unable to force his lips to form the
words: *before she was murdered.*

Keaton extended a compassionate hand and placed it on
Gutteridge's knee. She'd only found out that Gutteridge had
previously been married a little over a year ago, just as the
O'Leary case had reached its violent and bloody conclusion.

Cynthia had been discovered by Gutteridge, sitting in a
high-backed, winged seat at their home. Her hands had been
nailed to the armrests, her feet to the floor; her eyes removed
from their sockets and placed on her lap, looking in the
direction of his arrival through the front door.

There had been a note pinned to her chest. It had simply
read:

*You ruined my life, so I'm ruining yours. Is that so very
wrong? JM*

Jerry Masterson – the serial killer, dramatically referred to
by the world's press as 'The Shropshire Ripper' – had slaughtered
Gutteridge's wife to punish him for having the audacity to work
out that *he* was the culprit of the twelve-victim killing spree that
had consumed three years of Gutteridge's life. She was – as far as
it had been known – his final victim, and he'd never been jailed.

It was assumed he'd committed suicide, or else gone to
ground in some far-flung country, and Gloucester Constabulary
periodically scanned the world's press for cases that might
match his peculiarly warped MO, but so far, to no avail.

'I can't imagine how you feel,' Keaton said.

He strained a smile. 'No... it *was* a mess, a *total* fucking
mess! For *everyone* involved,' he said, flicking another apologetic
look in the child's direction.

He perched himself on the lip of one of the desks and took a look about for unwanted ears, lowering his voice to a more furtive level, feeling an uncharacteristic desire to speak about what amounted to the most painful time of his life. He took a preparatory breath, and Keaton listened.

'After it had all come out and became a nationwide manhunt, Jerry Masterson's mother took her own life out of the sheer shame and indignity of it all, drowning herself in a lake in Wales. His brother – Terry – moved away from the area, ostracised for simply being related to the monster, and we – me and Cynthia – never got to have our... our... *b-baby*.'

Gutteridge briefly crumbled, but managed, with much effort, to pull it back together. He regathered himself and took a breath... 'She was pregnant, see – a pregnancy I didn't actually find out about until *after* the autopsy. I guess that should officially take his body-count to thirteen. A fitting number, don't you think,' he said, forcing an ironic chuckle, but with tears threatening to rupture from his ducts and embarrass him.

Keaton's brow buckled as she watched him struggle to fight through his torment. She reached out and gave his hand a compassionate squeeze.

I could give him that child, she thought, *he's right there, in front of him, watching him, in desperate need of a father – a father like him!*

Her lips parted, pawing at the air, threatening to spill the beans, open that inconvenient can of life-changing worms. *I could tell him, now, and he could hold it, nurture it, and he could be happy! We, could be happy!*

But saner thoughts prevailed, and she drowned the idea in a sea of reality. 'In a week,' she said.

Gutteridge's brows furrowed and he emerged from his pained memories. 'What?'

'A week. I'm starting back next week. You asked me when I'm back.'

Gutteridge frowned again, flicking a confused look in the direction of the child.

Keaton smiled. 'My sister and mother are going to share baby-sitting duties. My sister has a child of her own,' she explained, 'so it's no real upheaval to add another.'

She twisted a smile at the child. 'I love the little tyke, but if I don't get back to work soon, I'll go insane!' She tilted a look in Gutteridge's direction. 'Why? Don't you want me back?'

He coloured, strangely offended by the suggestion. '*Christ*, yes!' he hissed, still maintaining the clandestine levels of their conversation. 'Koperek's lovely an' all, but she's driving me nuts. So *please*, for the love of all that's holy, come back and save me from her incessant yammering about boys and clothes and bloody pop-music!'

Keaton smirked, then softly laughed. 'Well, okay then. But only if you're absolutely sure you want me around.'

Gutteridge held her stare, his empathy clear to those beautiful, electric-blue eyes, and smiled. 'Yes… I want you around.'

THREE

HEAVILY LINED EYES that were no strangers to anguish watched as the receptionist at the far end of the waiting area shuffled her papers, his mind divided, contemplating the two possible paths his life was about to be forced along.

He distracted himself with thoughts of whether the forty-something busying herself with filing and phone-answering duties was attractive or not. She had a slightly ratty face, a romanesque nose, and the folds beneath her brow cloaked her upper lids – but somehow, it worked, and he came to the conclusion that she was oddly beautiful, and in a way that would grow on you over time and you wouldn't easily tire of. In fact, if he stared at the creature for very much longer, he might fall in love with the woman.

He dropped his eyes and pondered the phone call he'd received.

It must be bad, he thought, *else, they'd have told me the results, there and then. Wouldn't they? Didn't they only call you in if what they had to say was bad? Unethical to give such news in any other way but directly to your horrified face?*

The metallic buzz of the internal phone dragged the man back into the waiting-room. The rat-faced angel answered it, lifting her eyes to meet his. She nodded for the phone, and replaced the handset. 'Terrence Masterson? Dr Caine will see you now.'

She semi-stood from her seat to greet his tentative approach, leaning over the polished teak countertop, swinging a paddled hand towards the door directly across the corridor and to the right.

Her breasts pressed against the varnish of the wood, forcing her already crowded cleavage to lift into the core of her plunging neckline.

Masterson allowed his attention to drift to the soft pillows of product-moistened skin as a distraction and stirred below at the sight. Her skin was smooth, pliant, but taut, and looked to be doughy to the touch – and he imagined it glistening with the ethereal iridescence of viscera. He waited until her eyes averted and discretely adjusted the resulting erection.

He knocked on the door, expecting to hear 'come in', or 'enter', but instead, he heard footsteps approach from the other side. The door swung open to reveal a face attempting to look respectful, but without the error of displaying optimism.

Masterson's stomach sank to his pelvis and his legs turned to overcooked pasta.

'Mr Masterson. T-Terrence. Please. Come in. Take a seat,' the consultant said, stepping aside by way of invitation. He was young for a consultant, and didn't yet appear to be fully hardened to the task of delivering shitty news.

Masterson complied. 'It's Terry… Only my mother used the name Terrence,' he said, as he hesitantly lowered himself into the buttoned, leatherette seat facing the cluttered desk. The folds in the upholstery reminded him of the rat-faced angel's breasts and his hand gravitated to the plush texture beneath his thighs.

The consultant took his seat opposite, forcing a smile, and

Masterson could see him toying with the idea of wheeling his own seat around the table to face him, but he seemed to change his mind, remaining where he was.

He wants detachment, Masterson thought. *It must be bad.*

'So, *Terry*... how have you been?' the consultant asked, sounding comedically jaunty in the core of the awkwardness and clinical stench of the room.

'Am I going to die?' Masterson responded.

The consultant looked shocked by the question, like he'd received a hard slap across the cheek. He stuttered in the moment.

'I'd rather just know. I don't need no bullshit to smooth the way,' Masterson added. 'I'm no stranger to death.'

The consultant took a moment to adjust to the new air of blatant honesty and inhaled a calming breath. This was seemingly going to be harder for him than the man sat opposite.

The consultant visibly sagged into the moment, cocking his head to one side. 'I've examined your latest scans and the results of your last blood tests, and the cancer *has* spread.'

Masterson reeled back slightly from the news, and sat in contemplation of its stone-cold relevance. 'How far?' he asked.

'Far enough.'

Masterson shifted in his seat, fingering a fold in the faux-leather breasts. 'How long?'

'That depends.'

'On what?'

'On whether you want chemotherapy to prolong your time, or if you just want to let it take its course, enjoy the time you have left relatively free of hospital involvement?'

Masterson sagged again. 'And there's no way... the chemotherapy, might—'

'—No,' the consultant said, cutting him off, not allowing hope to take an undeserved hold. Despite the nature of the

17

news he had to convey, he was enjoying this new avenue of honesty. It made things so much easier than the usual pussy-footing awkwardness he was used to having to negotiate. 'I'm afraid it's gone too far, it's already spread to your—'

Masterson lifted a hand to stop him. 'I'd rather not know,' he said, exhaling an unsteady breath. 'How long? If I don't have chemo, how long?'

A pause. 'Six months. Maybe eight? A year if you're lucky.'

Masterson closed his eyes, brushing his finger one last time through the cleavage of the seat, and stood.

The consultant stood with him, mirroring his movements. 'We'll provide you with medication to manage the pain, when it comes. And we will – of course – do all we can to make you as comfortable as possible.'

Masterson strained to summon a heartfelt smile of appreciation for the consultant's honesty, and extended a hand to shake.

The consultant took it. 'I'm so sorry,' he said.

'Is what it is,' Masterson responded, turning to make for the door. He opened it a sliver and paused… 'Will I be able to function normally?' he asked over his shoulder.

'For the most part.'

Masterson smiled, this time genuinely. 'Good,' he muttered, under his breath. 'I intend to go out with somewhat of a bang!' He paused in his thoughts, hanging by the door. 'Again, thank you… and goodbye.'

The consultant took a half-step towards Masterson's departure. 'Well? Of course, I *will* be seeing you again?'

Masterson grinned, peering out at the receptionist through the crack in the door.

The face of his brother, and the name 'Jerry' popped into his thoughts – a name that hadn't been in his life for the best part of a decade. 'I wouldn't bank on it,' he said. 'I have things to do, and someone to see. Someone I haven't seen in a very, *very* long time.'

A belligerent, almost mischievous smile stretched wide across his face. 'If I'm going out, Doctor, I'm going out on my own terms.'

FOUR

EWELINA GUTTERIDGE sat and watched her husband silently redistributing pierogi around his plate, without any of it ever reaching his mouth.

He seemed distracted tonight, and for the first time since their marriage twelve months ago she felt alone in the house.

'A penny for them?' she said, with a compassionate tilt of the head.

But Gutteridge didn't hear her, his attention robbed by thoughts of how much Keaton's offspring looked like photos of him as a child.

'Pat…?'

He broke from his musings, coaxed out by the soft tones of his wife's Polish accent. 'Hm?'

'Do you feel like sharing?' she asked.

He waved the notion off with a smile, as if the ideas barrelling through his swelling sense of unease didn't have the potential to fuck up his whole existence. 'It's fine, love. Sorry. Just something at work, and not for here,' he muttered, defusing the moment with a half-smile.

He sat, eyes drinking her in, allowing the shimmer of her deep mauve lipstick and the sweep of her feline eyes to distract him from his worries. 'I'm sorry, sweetheart.' He smiled, reaching out to take her hand in his. 'Why don't you tell me about your day?'

But she held onto her concerns, not allowing the conversation to deviate. 'I've not seen you like this, not for a long time, not since—' She paused, dragging forth memories of the O'Leary case. 'Not since... you were hunting down... you know...'

Gutteridge lifted a polite hand into the core of the conversation. 'Let's not go there,' he said, his eyes momentarily flicking a look up to where, just fourteen months ago, Eve had stitches in her scalp, caused by the ramming of the business end of a captive bolt pistol against the delicate skin of her cranium. That time she'd been one-pound-per-square-inch of trigger-pressure away from being euthanised.

Gutteridge recalled rushing to her aid, thumbing the blood from her sweat-soaked hairline, and how she'd shaken like a captive bird in his thankful embrace as he freed her from the dining chair that Kieran O'Leary had taped her to.

Unreserved compassion welled through him at the memory and he fell in love with the woman all over again, rounding the table to deliver a heartfelt kiss to the scars she now wore proudly on the crest of her otherwise perfect head. She closed her eyes to accept it, clutching a hand to her sternum.

Gutteridge's fingers gently cupped her delicate jawline and lifted her face to meet his, her painted lips parting as he gazed down at her, longing and fondness softening his watching eyes. She loved him, and not just because he'd saved her life, but because he was a man worthy of love.

But there was a strange sadness she could sense buried deep within him that she felt from time to time. A sadness that made him meek and vulnerable; a vulnerability that brought the latent mother in Eve to the fore and she just wanted to hold him, console him, pull him into her bosom to let him know he wasn't alone.

She allowed her gaze to drop away, averting her attention, toying with the idea of raising a subject she'd been attempting to broach for well over a week, ever since she'd found a photo album hidden away in the loft space.

Is this a good time? she wondered. *But is there ever a good time, one that could be considered ideal?*

Her mouth crimped ruefully. 'Sit,' she said. 'Please. I have something I wish to talk about.'

Gutteridge couldn't hide the concern in his eyes. 'What is it, sweetheart? W-What's wrong?'

'Please,' she said, paddling her hand towards his chair. 'Just sit, for me.'

Intrigued, he acquiesced, gingerly lowering his frame back onto his seat.

Eve stood, moving her chair in closer, and sat directly facing him. She took his hands in hers and peered into him, her eyes full of questions.

'Do you remember, a couple of weeks back, I worked frrrom home?'

Gutteridge sat in contemplation of the question, then nodded. 'Yes. What of it?'

'Well, I took the chance – while you weren't here – to clear away some of my crrrap that's been clogging up the spare room ever since we got married and I first moved in.'

'...Okay...?' he said, a dip of suspicion in his voice.

'So, I put much of it in the loft, the stuff I knew I wouldn't be needing. Thing is, while I was up there, I found something... something I suspect you might *not* have wanted me to see.'

Gutteridge's quizzical frown briefly darkened, then brightened in realisation. 'Oh! You mean... *shit!* he said, looking like he'd been caught in a lie. 'I... I can explain...'

'Shhhh,' she said with a wilting brow, giving his hands a gentle squeeze. 'It's fine. I'm not angry. We all have a past, and that *includes* me.'

Gutteridge's gaze fell away. 'I know, but I really should have said something. I should really have told you.'

Ewelina shrugged. 'Well. Tell me now. You're my husband – and unless you're about to tell me you offed her for the insurance money, nothing you can say is going to stop me loving you.'

Her words brought Gutteridge's eyes back into the conversation. He looked remorseful. 'I know, but… I should have said something. But it's not easy. It's difficult for me…'

Her brows knitted. 'Why? Did she *leave* you?'

His eyes dropped again and he almost laughed at how in error her assumption was. 'If only… God, if only… I could have lived with that.'

Another squeeze of the hands. 'Then tell me.'

His head hung low; he looked defeated, his breaths long and deliberate, wondering how best to interject knowledge he *knew* he should already have presented.

He erupted from his seat. 'Wait here,' he said. 'I won't be a sec.'

He made off in the direction of the front door, slipping his shoes on and stepping out into the biting night air.

Eve watched, wondering where he could be going. She heard the garage doors open, the click of the light switch and sounds of rifling through the walls, then the doors closing again.

A moment later, Gutteridge stepped back into the hallway, kicking off his shoes and making his way back into the dining room.

He had another album under his arm, and Eve could see age-yellowed newspaper clippings projecting from its pages. 'What's that?' she asked, genuinely interested as he sat again.

He pushed their plates aside and gently placed the album on the table, resting his hands upon it. '*This*, is every newspaper cutting there was regarding a part of my life I sorely wish had never happened. But it did, and here we are...'

After a beat, he gingerly opened the leather-bound cover, and spun it to face his wife.

She leaned in cautiously, and began to scan the scattering of articles tiling the pages:

'A SECOND BODY DISCOVERED!'

'THE SHROPSHIRE RIPPER STRIKES AGAIN!'

'BODY # 3! IS ANYONE SAFE?'

'A FOURTH BODY: POLICE MAKE
A DESPERATE PLEA FOR POSSIBLE
WITNESSES.'

Gutteridge leaned across and turned to the middle pages, where the headlines continued:

'JERRY MASTERSON NAMED AS
SHROPSHIRE RIPPER!'

'MASTERSON ON THE RUN, POLICE
BUNGLE ARREST!'

'MASTERSON GONE TO GROUND,
WORLDWIDE MANHUNT ENSUES!'

Eve read the cuttings with interest, twisting her gaze this way and that, until Gutteridge leaned across again and turned to the very last page. It fell open on a solitary article:

'LEAD DETECTIVE ON MASTERSON CASE DISCOVERS MUTILATED REMAINS OF WIFE ON RETURN HOME!'

Eve took a moment to absorb the words, then her whole face gasped to the realisation, her hands lifting to cover her appalled expression. '*O mój Boże!*' she said, reverting to her mother tongue, nearly retching the words out onto the table. 'You… *f-f-f-found* her?'

A pause, then a tight, rueful nod laced with ultimate sadness.

Eve held the look, her eyes glistening with sorrow for the man she loved. She shook her head in denial, hands still covering her mouth. 'How… *how* do you survive something like that?'

He shrugged. 'Maybe you don't? It haunts me constantly.'

'Jesus!' she slurred, finally allowing her hands to drop away, revealing a face alight with empathy. 'Oh my God! You…?' Her eyes revisited the pages, re-reading the headline. 'Now I underrrstand what it is, this thing I see in you,' she said, her Polish accent now singing strong and defined. 'I wish you had told me, but… I underrrstand why you didn't.'

Gutteridge looked sick to his stomach and fearful. 'Would it have changed anything? Might you *not* have married me?'

She loosed a sorrowful smile beneath a brow wilting with compassion. 'Of courrrse I would have married you. I love you, you dickhead.'

Gutteridge allowed a laugh to quell his inner sadness. 'I love you too, Eve… you asshole…'

She joined in the mirth, turning a last look at the headline pasted into the album, then slowly, she closed it… 'We should keep this safe, in the loft, next to the album of your wedding day. You might get foxing on the pages if you leave it in the garage.'

Gutteridge smirked, then chuckled.

Eve shook her head, her brow pinching quizzically. 'What is it? What did I say?'

Gutteridge fondly laughed. 'How the fuck does someone from Poland know the word "foxing"?'

FIVE

MASTERSON'S HUNTING GAZE scanned the tired but ornate frontage of the three-storey Victorian semi facing him, before he turned to take in the street it presided over.

The road seemed suitably busy – certainly, busy enough that no one would take any notice of his everyday comings and goings. It appeared to be free from prying eyes – just the way it had looked on the street map app on his phone.

The building had a look of faded grandeur, with tall bay windows overlooking the front garden which had largely been gravelled over for extra parking.

A row of slender conifers separated it from the adjoining plot, with a low-level wall engulfed in thick bushes and a gate at the curb end for privacy. On the face of it at least, it seemed ideal for his needs.

'So, Mr Masterson, what do you think?' asked the agent, in a slightly forced, chirrupy voice.

'Call me Terry,' Masterson said, his tone deep and matter-of-fact, his eyes never leaving the house.

He eventually allowed his attention to drift to the estate agent hovering off to one side. The girl was young, youthfully pretty, wearing a corporate suit that had been tailored to accentuate her considerable curves. Masterson's scrutiny sank to take in a pair of well-turned ankles that would have made the Victorians the house had originally been built for foam at the mouths with lust. Her legs rose from stilettoed shoes that forced her calves into sublime fists of muscle. It was a cold morning, making her skin look pallid and strangely blue. Masterson could almost imagine those legs lying on a mortician's slab.

'So, *Terry*,' she clucked. 'My colleague was saying you're moving to the area? Is that a Clwyd or a Powys accent I'm hearing?'

Masterson lifted frowning eyes to meet the girl's interested gaze. 'Close,' he said, his brows knitting. 'I currently live in Derbyshire, but it's probably a Shropshire accent you're hearing – a small village near Shrewsbury.' He twisted a fascinated look her way, inviting elaboration.

She laughed. 'I studied languages. Did my PhD on regional dialects – not that I'm making a whole lot of use of it renting out properties,' she giggled. 'Perhaps moving further north nearer to Yorkshire's more coarse dialect has hardened your native tongue, making it somehow sound more Welsh?'

Masterson thought about her theorising, then allowed himself a smile. 'Maybe… interesting,' he said. 'That's really good.'

'So, what brings you to Gloucester? Friends, family? A change of scenery?'

'Business.'

'Oh, what business are you in?'

Masterson inhaled a frustrated breath, agitated at the incessant questioning. 'Look. I just want a place to rent for a year. I have *things* I need to do, *people* I need to see. Personal business. You understand.'

The girl took the hint, smiling through her mild embarrassment. 'I'm sorry,' she muttered. 'Everyone at the office says I talk too much. I'm just interested in people, I guess.'

Masterson allowed his agitated front to soften. 'That's okay. I suppose *I* talk too little – I just don't have answers to all of your questions. At least, not answers I'd be wise to give without fear of police intervention,' he said, punctuating his answer with a grin and a cheeky wink.

The girl giggled, shrugging with a twee smile as she turned to the house, keys in hand, paper fob spinning in the wind.

She sauntered up the steps to the porch-covered doorway, the swing of her thighs pulling tight against the restriction of the black, pencil line skirt that clung to her body like a second skin, drawing Masterson's attention up the steps with her.

His eyes were glued to the seductive roll of her hips, the way they rocked to the rhythm of her walk. He wanted to take them in his large hands, feel the softness of her obliques against the balls of his thumbs. Smell her neck, her shoulders, the deep-dive of those cupid's-bow trapezius muscles. This girl obviously hit the gym on a regular basis and he wondered what her sweat would taste like – salty? Sweet? Both? Was she strong? She looked it. But strong enough to put up a good fight?

'After you Mr—' she paused, '*Terry*,' she said, stepping back to invite him to pass through.

He obliged, lumbering up the steps to the door, sidling through the cloud of scent that hung around her taught, elegant frame. He grinned. '*Mr* Terry?'

She shook her head in mock embarrassment. 'I meant, Terry.'

His grin became a smile, and then a soft laugh. He liked this girl. She was funny, and amiable. Alas, so amiable, he *wanted* her.

The name 'Jerry' came to him again. *Jerry*, he thought, *why did you have to dispose of Jerry? Is it time to unleash the beast? To honour his legacy?*

'And where do *you* live?' Masterson asked, turning from the dimly lit hallway to face the adolescent light of the girl's relative innocence. 'I mean, what's considered a *nice* area around here?'

'I actually live quite close, just one road along in fact,' she said, leaning back out of the door and indicating a direction with an elegant sweep of her hand. 'It's a nice enough area, on the whole. I share an apartment with two other girls. Flat 2, Wolseley Lodge – just along there on Wolseley Road. If you *did* decide you liked the place,' she said, dressing her eyes around the hallway, 'then we'd be neighbours.' Again, she lifted twee shoulders to her perfect ears – small and porcelain, like a china doll.

Why did you have to go and deny Jerry? Masterson thought again, his avarous gaze ingesting the ideal proportions of the creature stood before him. *He'd have gone for this one, she's just his type.* But he already knew the answer to *that* one – because he'd *had* to.

'It said unfurnished in the ad,' Masterson queried, continuing further into the hallway, 'but the agent I spoke to – Jackie, is it? She said there were a few pieces kicking around that I'd be welcome to use.'

'Yep,' said the girl, consulting her faux-leather folder. 'It's down here somewhere… Here we go. It says there's a chest of drawers and a dressing table in one of the spare rooms, an antique wardrobe in the main bedroom, and an oak dining table in the kitchen – all in good order.'

Masterson watched the girl's fake lashes flicker and flinch as she consulted her notes. Her eyes looked so alive, so temperate and attentive. Would they look as bewitching if the girl were dead? *More* bewitching, perhaps? Wide-open windows to where a soul once lived. He stirred below.

The girl snapped her folder closed again. 'But if you didn't want them here, we could arrange to have them removed.'

'Nah. That's okay. Save me the need to completely empty my home of belongings while I'm down here.'

'So... you still have another property?'

'Yes. The one in Derbyshire. Buxton, to be exact.'

'Ooooh, you lucky thing. I love Buxton. I've only been twice, but it's a beautiful town. Do they still have that tap thing in the street that you can get free mineral water from?'

Masterson wandered into the living room. 'Indeed they do.'

'Wahhh. I think that's fab. What a perk.'

Masterson spun in the core of the room to drink it in. It had the slightly musty smell of decrepitude, but it looked to be in good order, tastefully decorated in suitably period styling befitting of the building's age. Masterson lowered his eyes again to take in the chirpy English rose. 'And what's *your* name?'

She smiled wide at the attention. 'Kaylie. My name's Kaylie. It's Gaelic. It means beautiful, or graceful? Or something like that. Presumptuous to assume your child will turn out to be attractive, don't you think.'

Masterson sniggered. 'I guess so... you *did,* though.'

The girl flushed crimson. 'Oh... I'm... thank you.'

Masterson spun a smile towards her gratitude as he wandered through into the kitchen. ''S'okay.' He smiled, nonchalantly brushing his fingers along the countertops. 'Tell me, *Kaylie*, what would the owner, or indeed *you*, be needing in the way of paperwork? I tend to be quite a private person, see.'

She opened her folder again. 'The usual. We would need some sort of reference, three months of bank statements, a security deposit, and the first—'

Masterson politely cut her short. 'How about if I just paid an entire year up front, cut through all the crap. Would that suffice?'

The girl's eyes widened. 'Um, I guess so. I'd have to make a phone call of course, but I can't see anyone having a problem with that.' She lowered her voice theatrically to a more clandestine level, like the place was bugged. 'Between you and me, I know the owner's been trying to let this place for quite some time. There's nothing wrong with it an' all. It's a very nice place. It's just a bit too large and expensive for most who are looking to rent. It's also quite far from the centre of town, certainly too far to walk. Makes it harder to let, so I reckon – if you made that offer – they'd snap your hand off.'

'Well then, let's make that offer.'

The girl beamed, chuckling through her words. 'Ho-kay. I'll just make a quick call to the owner. Oh! Don't you need to see the rest of the house, first?'

Masterson shrugged. 'Is it pretty much the same as it is down here?'

'It is. The same kind of order, *and* decor.'

'In that case, no. I am fully trusting of young Kaylie's judgment on that front.'

The girl turned coy and smiled wide, blinking her gratitude with a humble grin. Through the thirsting eyes of his own forced abstinence, she was *beyond* beautiful.

Masterson drifted from the moment, becoming lost in his musings and the flawless sheen of the girl's incandescent eyes – emerald green and jewel-like. Eyes so full of verve they ignited his soul.

What would they look like, pleading up at him for mercy? Dulling, mattified, filming over as her life ebbed away, losing focus as her fight, her reluctance, her ardour was relentlessly snuffed from existence?

'Are you okay?' asked the girl with concern, stepping towards him and reaching out a compassionate hand. 'You looked like you were having a moment there.'

Masterson reemerged from his fantasies. 'W-What?'

'You… are you okay? You seemed – I don't know – a bit out of it? Are you alright?'

'Oh… yes. I'm fine. I was just thinking about my mother.'

'*Your* mother? Oh… is she ill?'

'Noooo. N-No. She, um… she died, years ago, for reasons…' He winced an anaemic smile. 'Someone else's fault, see. Someone I've never forgiven.' He softly smiled. 'Certain events in life are hard to let go of, don't you find?'

The girl thought about his words, then nodded. 'They can be, I suppose. I guess I'm not really old enough to have developed any real grudges, yet.'

Masterson smiled at her unexpected wisdom. 'You're probably right… Anyway. You don't want to be hearing about all *that* crap.'

The girl broke from the moment with a smile. 'I'll make that call. Why don't you take a look around the rest of the property, make absolutely certain you're happy with it?'

'Okay. Thank you, *Kaylie*.' Masterson gave the beating of the girl's exaggerated lashes one last perverted glance as she looked at her phone, then turned to make his way upstairs…

Kaylie, he pondered. *K-a-y-l-i-e*. He liked this girl: the name, the body, the swing of the hips, the swing of her thighs. And the eyes. *Those* eyes… incandescent flames of vibrant youth, scorching his desires. Fires of life that existed only to be extinguished, and he felt sure – as his stomach flipped and rolled to thoughts of his perverted imaginings – that *she* would be the one.

He took his phone from his pocket, prompted by seemingly favourable sounds emanating from the hallway below, scrolled to a pre-saved number for a local removal company, and hit call.

SIX

'**H**ANDS UP! DROP YOUR WEAPON!' came a voice from somewhere close behind. 'The possession of a woman with looks that lethal is illegal in this county!'

Eve and Gutteridge broke their nonchalant saunter through the Quays Shopping Centre and turned to discover DS Keaton rushing to catch up, techno pushchair and companion in tow, her face alight with mischief.

The companion's face had unquestionable similarities to Keaton's, though not as pretty, and Gutteridge had to assume that this was the sister he'd not yet met.

'Oh, hi,' he smirked, exchanging looks between the two faces beaming up at him, before settling on Keaton's. 'I should really be arresting *you* for making such a lame joke,' said Gutteridge with a grin, before redirecting his obvious joy at seeing his partner outside of the confines of work in the direction of the companion. 'And you must be Hollie?' he asked.

The companion nodded curiously, surprised to hear her name peel from his lips, unprompted. 'I am. Nice to finally meet you,' she said. 'I've heard a lot about you.'

'And *I've* heard a lot about *you*. The majority of it good.'

The girls laughed.

'You're apparently the reason I've got my partner back?' he said, flicking a look in Keaton's direction.

'I guess you could say that. I've always been the babysitter of the family,' beamed Hollie, who seemed to be fighting an impulse to gawp at Eve.

Gutteridge turned to follow her gaze until both their attentions were focused on the slender beauty hovering by his side. 'This is my wife, Eve.'

'I guessed that much,' said Hollie. 'Jane described you to me, but you're *way* more beautiful than I ever imagined.'

Keaton shuffled in mild discomfort at her sister's adulating.

'Thank you,' smiled Eve, reluctantly, embarrassed by the flattery, but as an ex-escort, she was used to being fawned over simply for the way she looked.

She clocked the sister darting looks to her scalp, and fought the urge to lift a hand to cover her battle-scars. The scars themselves weren't visible, so she knew the looks could only have been fuelled by gossip and rumour. But the scarring *beneath* her skin remained, and that was something that still warranted significant effort to cope with.

'Is this him?' asked Eve, breaking from her simmering insecurities with a turn to Keaton, twisting a theatrically inquisitive look towards the pram.

Keaton smiled, warmly, and nodded.

'May I look?'

'Of course. Please,' said Keaton.

Eve's protracted elegance rounded the hood of the pushchair and she lined her smile up with the child's. She clutched a hand to her breast-bone and leaned in. 'Hello there little man...' she sang. 'Well. Would you look at you. Aren't *you* the gorgeous thing, just like your mother,' she said, turning a genuine smile up to meet Keaton's hunting gaze.

Keaton watched, waiting… waiting for the moment that Eve saw her husband's face reflected in the child's, but the moment never arrived.

She looked to Gutteridge, who seemed to have the exact same expectant look in his own eyes.

Does he know? she wondered, *know this child is his?* It wasn't hard to imagine he did, simply by the dreading looks she saw in his expression.

Keaton leaned her bubbling paranoia in and pulled the blanket higher around the baby's face. 'It's chilly today,' she said with a nervous laugh. 'I have to remind myself to keep him covered up.'

Eve leaned back to make way, then stepped in again to help tuck him in. 'He's gorgeous, Jane. You must be very prrroud of him.'

Keaton turned a nervous smile up towards the 6'1" in heels angelic obstacle to the child having a father-figure in its life, and thanked her for her kindness.

'We were actually about to go and have a quick bite to eat,' said Gutteridge. 'Would you ladies care to join us?'

Before Keaton could kindly reject the offer, Hollie piped in and cordially accepted, and with no opportunity presenting itself to deliver a protesting elbow to Hollie's ribs to correct it, they were soon on their way to Zizzi, a standard chain Italian, but no one could deny the food there was good.

The restaurant's interior had an ingrained aroma of parmigiana and basil woven through its fabric, with rustic, mismatched decor that gave the space an open, contemporary feel – obviously contriving to recreate Tuscany's air of calm and tranquillity.

They were shown to an end table near the till-station where there was room for the stroller. They sat and were dealt menus.

'Can I take an order for drinks while you're choosing?' asked the waitress, a gothic twenty-something attempting not to look socially awkward. Gutteridge's guess was that she was a student trying to earn a little extra money for partying at the weekends.

'White wine for me, please,' chirped Keaton, her sister nodding enthusiastic solidarity for the choice. 'Pinot,' she added.

'Sure,' said the waitress. 'Large?'

Keaton and Hollie exchanged looks, then nodded in unison. 'Oh, go on then, but only if you insist,' said Keaton, willingly accepting the shameless upsell.

Gutteridge lifted a soft smile to meet the girl's sweeping gaze. 'Just tea for me, please, with milk.'

Eve watched him, contemplating her husband's choice, then lifted a look to the girl. '*And* me. Earl Grey if you've got it, with lemon.'

Gutteridge extended a compassionate hand and placed it gently on his wife's arm. 'Have wine, too, if you like, love.'

Eve spun a look of calm alliance towards the offer, rejecting it with an understanding smile. 'I'm fine, honey. I actually quite fancy a cup of tea,' she insisted, placing her hand atop his and giving it a gentle squeeze with her slender fingers, her manicured nails painted black to match her hair and her lips making Gutteridge suddenly want her. The tranquil look of understanding in her eyes burned through him, and his love for the woman once again spiked.

Gutteridge had turned to drink and cocaine for a period in his life, tormented by the memories of discovering his first wife's mutilated remains. There had been much talk of it between the pair of them of late – ever since Eve revealed that she'd discovered the wedding album, and as a result, the moments where Eve abstained as a show of solidarity were becoming more frequent, only serving to cement Gutteridge's love and admiration for the angel by his side.

'King prawn linguine,' barked Hollie with an odd kind of triumph, clapping the menu down on the table in celebration of her decisiveness.

Keaton scanned the options, flipping the card several times over. Gutteridge noticed that she seemed to be counting subconsciously with her lips.

'I'm just going to have a pizza. Margherita,' she said.

Her sister leaned in and discretely whispered something, and Gutteridge was sure he heard: 'Have whatever you fancy. I can pay.'

But Keaton kindly rejected the offer with a back-foot smile. 'I'm fine, but thank you,' she mouthed.

Gutteridge aimed a look towards the pushchair, to the single-parent baby sleeping soundly amid the hum of the restaurant.

The denial finally left him. He *knew* Keaton wasn't the type to give herself to anyone: no one-night stands with strangers of indeterminate morals or lineage. The child four-feet away from his crumbling repudiation was his, and despite his attempts to ignore the fact, he knew it to be true.

He allowed his eyelids to close around the problem, around memories of their shared night of intimacy. The night they abandoned their adherence to the realities of life and relinquished control of their bodies to feed the desires of each other's wanton disregard for prudence.

He could almost taste her sweat again as he remembered kissing the butter-soft skin around her flexing midriff, serenaded by groans of pleasure and pregnant anticipation that his mouth was mere inches from committing the ultimate act of shared intimacy. Oh, how her body bowed in spasm to the outrage, laying itself bare to the pleasures of the flesh as his tentative tongue caressed her tender loins. An insistent tug on his unruly hair; her pert, pillowy lips on his as she exhaled into him a clarion call to the thrusting violation of her widening crotch, her rolling eyes alight with the flames of the swirling, turbulent fires of decadence. A single moment of unashamed madness, and a tiny life created.

He opened his eyes again. Keaton was looking directly at him, vague, intermittent flickers of a regret-filled smile attempting to cut through the mask of remorse.

'I won't be a sec,' Gutteridge said, standing from his seat. 'When the girl comes, love, could you please order me the ravioli. I have a quick call I need to make. It'll only take a minute.'

Eve looked mildly perplexed, but nodded. 'Okay, honey.'

Gutteridge took his phone from his pocket and made for the exit, pretending to scroll through his list of contacts.

Once out of the door he mimed dabbing the screen, lifting the device to his ear. He nonchalantly sauntered past the windows until he was sure he was clear of interested eyes, then broke into a relaxed sprint in the direction of the nest of cashpoints at the far end of the main shopping area.

Gutteridge arrived, surprised at how little he was panting. He'd been hitting the gym plenty of late, driven by what he would like to believe was concern for his own physical wellbeing, but in reality was more likely to be a desire to redress the disparity of having 5'10" of physical perfection constantly by your side. And besides, since meeting Eve, he'd been gradually succumbing to the erotic charms of the more toned, gym physique she undeniably possessed, and wanted to make an effort to address the imbalance.

He already had his card at the ready and slid it into the mouth of the machine. He knew he could withdraw up to £1000 on this, his premier card, and tapped in '500' when prompted, then pocketed the ejected stack of notes.

He turned and trotted a short distance to the card shop and darted inside.

He quickly grabbed a random card and envelope from the rack without looking at it, then stepped up to the counter.

The man behind the till had been watching. He looked down at the offering, frowning smiling eyes at his choice.

'For my darling eighty-year-old wife?' he said, holding the card up to show him.

Gutteridge had to laugh. 'I only need the envelope,' he said, 'and I'm in a bit of a hurry.'

The attendant grinned and stooped below the counter, reappearing brandishing an envelope. 'On the house,' he said, handing it over. 'We always have some left over. I don't know why? Maybe people shoplift cards but neglect to take the envelopes?'

Gutteridge smiled broadly at the gesture, shooting a look at his now redundant choice.

'Don't worry about that, I'll put it back for you,' said the attendant. 'It's been pretty slow today.'

Gutteridge took the envelope with a smile and a knowing nod, and thanked the man, backing towards the door. 'Cheers fella.'

Sprinting back towards Zizzi, he slipped the wad of notes into the envelope and sealed it with a lick.

He slowed to a relaxed saunter as he drew near, taking deep, deliberate breaths to calm his racing pulse. He paused momentarily to take a look at his reflection in an adjoining window, straightened his hair and stowed the cash in his pocket, before taking out his phone and resuming the charade he was on a call.

'Everything alright?' asked Eve as he took his seat again.

'Fine, love. It didn't turn out to be quite so important.'

'You were gone a long time for something that wasn't "quite so important",' said Eve.

'What was it, then?' asked Keaton.

'Oh, just some new leads on the Mark Evans case, but nothing particularly groundbreaking. Nothing that's really going to help solve it any quicker.'

'Like what?' Keaton asked with a frown.

'Tomorrow,' he said. 'It's Sunday. I'm not talking shop on a Sunday, not if I'm not on the clock.'

Keaton's brows furrowed – this wasn't how things usually went.

Gutteridge flashed hardened eyes at Keaton's reaction as a hint to let it go. Reluctantly, she acquiesced. The food finally arrived and plates were dealt to eager hands.

'It's been lovely to finally meet you, Hollie,' said Gutteridge, as he leaned into the pushchair to consider the slumbering baby. Taking care not to wake the child, he carefully rearranged the blankets that swaddled the tiny life as the three ladies jostled with coats and bags, checking makeup in mirrors.

'You really didn't need to pay,' said Keaton, 'but thank you. That was really nice of you.'

Gutteridge turned a smile up from the pram towards the gratitude. 'My pleasure.'

'Yes. Thank you,' added Hollie. 'Next time, my shout.'

'Yes,' piped in Eve, 'we should do this again. It's been so lovely talking to you both, and to finally meet *him*,' she added, turning a fond-filled look in the direction of the pushchair.

Gutteridge looked quizzical and smirked as he finally stood from attending to the baby. 'I've just realised something,' he grinned. 'We don't know what he's called? You've never told us, and none of us have even thought to ask,' he added, looking around the circle of burgeoning friendships.

41

Keaton dropped a pensive look to the floor, frowned, then chuckled. 'No. I haven't, have I?'

'No-ho. You haven't.'

'Blimey. What a div!' She smiled. 'Anyway. It's Joshua. I decided to call him Joshua. It was my father's middle name.'

'Joshua...' repeated Gutteridge, considering if the name fitted the child he was looking down at, the one that looked so much like him. He decided it did. 'I like it. Joshua – good choice.'

SEVEN

'**H**ELLO NEIGHBOUR,' sang a voice from nowhere, soft and strangely familiar.

'Who's that?' came the echoing response from the interior of the white, Luton box-truck.

'It's me, Mr Masterson. It's Kaylie.'

Kaylie Wyatt edged past a tail-lift fully laden with a life's worth of furniture, and presented herself in a break between two stacks of boxes.

Masterson didn't instantly recognise the girl stood before him, and then it clicked. 'Ahh. Yes. Kaylie. I remember you. How are you doing?' he asked. But of course he remembered her – he'd thought of little else since the first time he'd encountered the creature, and the emotion at seeing her again could only be described as joy – even *if* that joy was corrupted by sexual aberrance. 'You look so different out of your corporate garb,' he said, 'but I certainly recognise that lovely smile.'

She laughed, coyly, loosing one of her famous shrugs.

She wore a white, cotton summer dress printed with vivid red flower-heads printed its length that popped in the midday sun – they looked, Masterson thought, akin to blunt-force trauma blood-spatter.

The lightweight cloth of the mid-thigh hemline danced in the wind to the tune of late summer, with delicate, bootlace straps hooked over her slight but toned shoulders. She had a sports bag slung over her back.

'I've been down the gym,' she said, indicating a vague direction where with a nonchalant lift of the elbow. 'It was so nice out, I decided to walk back.' She turned a look to the house behind. 'So, you took the place?' she asked, more out of politeness than interest, because of course, *she'd* had to finalise the paperwork.

Masterson ceased what he was doing, placing the stapled pages of his inventory down on a box and sidled through the city-skyline of belongings towards the visitor. 'Come in a mo,' he said. 'You can give me the female opinion I so desperately need on my furniture layout.'

Kaylie sniggered, dismissively. 'I wouldn't ask me, I'm a complete duffer at that sort of thing.'

'That makes two of us,' Masterson smiled, as he dropped off the tail-lift and ambled towards the house, urging her to follow with a carefree toss of the head. 'Come on,' he insisted, 'you can give me your opinion anyway. Two wrongs might just make a right.'

Kaylie laughed again, and followed. She found Masterson to be funny and light-hearted. Her father was the same, and it was a trait she found attractive in a man. If only Masterson wasn't twice her age.

Masterson stopped shy of the steps that led to the door and invited Kaylie to pass through with a gentlemanly bow, and she accepted with a suitably thespianic curtsey in response.

Masterson's eyes watched her float past from beneath the hood of his brow, his leering gaze following her every tread as her legs – toned from hours of pounding cast iron – rippled like those of a thoroughbred racehorse.

Her calves looked different out of heels. Still the sublime fillets of muscle that they were, but less hard-edged, less fist-like. He was becoming obsessed with the way they moved.

The shadow of her flat, tight obliques showed through the paper-thin cloth of her dress, looking like a belt wrapping her minuscule waist in the cast of the midday sun.

Masterson wanted to bite them, to take them in his teeth, to feel their firmness resisting through the blades of his incisors.

Kaylie twisted back to see if he was following.

His eyes snapped up to meet hers as he smiled up at her, ambling to join her with as carefree a saunter as he could muster. But his eyes dropped away again, irresistibly drawn down by the sight of her flat, defined abs twisting as she turned to watch him. They rose and fell to the pressure of her diaphragm as she breathed – a taut ribbon of healthy muscle fibre wrapping a perfect body, and Masterson desperately wanted to 'do the job' there and then.

No! He thought. *This was not the plan. You've got to stick to the plan.* But his desire for the female four feet from his depraved obsessing seemed to be trying to argue the toss. Was this love, or lust? Or simply the perverted musings of a voyeur, viewing the girl in the same way an onanist views pornography?

Emerald eyes smiled at him as he ascended the steps to join her side. He sidled past and led the way into the lounge.

'You see, I don't know whether to position the settee facing the window, or the fireplace?' he bemoaned.

Kaylie wandered into the core of the room, and one at a time, began crouching, as though sitting in both positions – being the observer, seeing which felt 'right' to her younger sensibilities.

Her dress rode up her thighs as she crouched, quadriceps flexing with the effort of holding the squat.

Masterson stared at the velveteen sheen of the perfect

skin cladding her legs, like French silk stockings: soft, sinewy, rippling with sublime perfection.

His ability to resist was crumbling. He had a plan, and this girl was *definitely* at the core of it, but could that plan be *adjusted*?

Kaylie stood and repositioned herself to the 'fireplace' option and crouched again, imagining it aglow with the incandescent warmth of smouldering coals, tongues of flame licking at the air.

Masterson took a hesitant step towards her. She had her back to him. He could rush her now and deliver a knee to the back of her skull before she even knew what was happening. She'd be down, out, and his! He stepped in further, hesitating.

What the fuck would you do with her here? he pondered. *This was not the fucking plan! You've come to this place for a reason – retribution. Remember – Jerry! You have to remember – Jerry!*

Kaylie flicked her hair from the left side of her face to reconsider the window, exposing the nape of her neck, drawing his lusting eyes to its perceived fragility.

Just one swift, sharp blow, and she'd be down. You could have her, smell her, bite her, taste her, eat her! he thought.

He stepped closer still, fingers curling into a fist.

Kaylie frowned, pouting at her own indecision, the glistening ridge of her cerise-painted lips catching the sunlight that illuminated the bay windows.

Masterson's eyes gravitated to the seductive sweep of their exaggerated profile. Were they speaking? Forming words? Talking to him? He wondered, or was he confused by the hallucinations of his excited mind?

He observed her lips from within the shimmering haze of his amplified fantasies. '*Do it! Do it now!*' the lips seemed to be saying. '*I want this. I want you. Have me! Kiss me. Kill meeeeee…*'

'Fireplace!' barked Kaylie, standing again and smoothing her dress with a deft brush of the hands.

Masterson stumbled from his dream-state, staggering back from the looming figure. He managed to catch himself before she could turn to see him, and he resumed the act. 'Okay,' he said, dragging himself back into the real world. 'That's actually the side I was thinking myself. Fireplace it is, then!'

He smiled, turning his attention to the door that led into the kitchen. He erupted from his musings and made his way towards it. 'I'd offer you tea or coffee, but I'm pretty sure I've checked every box now, and I can't seem to find where I've packed the kettle.'

He reached the centre of the kitchen and spun to face his guest, examining the contents of an open crate sat next to him. He pretended not to see the kettle, teabags, coffee, sugar and mugs housed within it, before closing the lid with counterfeit despair, shrugging with apparent annoyance.

'That's okay,' said Kaylie. 'Thanks for the offer though. I'm sure it'll turn up, eventually.'

Masterson huffed in mock annoyance, looking about his unpacked belongings. 'I sure hope so. I've been gagging for a brew all morning. Thirsty work, this.'

Kaylie joined in looking about the kitchen, then her face lit up. 'Tell you what. Why don't you slide the stuff that's on the tail-lift back in the truck and lock it up, then you can pop around to mine. *I* can make *you* tea, give you a bit of a break? It's only a short way up the road.'

'Noooo,' Masterson said, 'I couldn't possibly trouble you like that. And I'm sure your flatmates would simply *love* you if you turned up with some rando.'

'*Rando?*' giggled Kaylie, surprised he knew such a modern term, smirking with amusement. 'Look at you, down with the kids!' she added, loosing a laugh that was laced with fondness.

'Anyway, it wouldn't be a problem, none of them are in at the moment. I'm pretty sure Maddie said she's got lectures for most of the day, and Jane doesn't knock off work until 5:30.'

Masterson gave another exaggerated look about the room, before giving her an appreciative look – one that he'd rehearsed a thousand times in the mirror. 'Well. If you're sure. I wouldn't want to be a pain, but at the same time, I *am* in peril of expiring from thirst.'

'Done!' She barked with triumph. 'Come on then, let's get this busy man rehydrated.'

Masterson snapped the padlock on the clasp of the tailgate, before trotting up the steps of the house to lock the door. 'Oh!' he said, holding a finger in the air. 'Hang on a mo. I'll just get my bag, it has all my important stuff in it. Can't be too careful.'

He trotted up the steps and strode inside with conviction, leaving Kaylie stood on the driveway with her hand held to her forehead like a sun visor, awaiting his reemergence.

Masterson rushed through the entrance hall into the kitchen and grabbed his rucksack, unzipping the main compartment and tipping its contents out onto the kitchen island.

He grabbed his keys and wallet from the detritus and tossed them back in, then lunged to one side to glance down the corridor to check he hadn't been followed. He seemed to be alone still, and couldn't hear footsteps climbing the steps to the door.

He turned his attention back to a box marked 'BITS AND PIECES' that had travelled with him in the cab of the truck. He grabbed a fruit knife from the counter and began frantically slicing at the duct tape sealing it.

Another cautionary glance towards the door – still no one. He was beginning to sweat.

He sliced through the final strip of tape, liberating the

contents and tossed the knife, peeling back the flaps. He fumbled through the contents of the box, drawing out a folded rag and a bottle of chloroform, transferring them to the rucksack. He also bagged a scalpel handle and a pack of No.26 blades, along with a hammer, nails, pump-spray bottle filled with concentrated acetic acid, nitrile gloves, zip ties, and finally a pre-prepared note. This last item was carefully sealed in a zip-lock bag, together with a solitary hat-pin that had once belonged to his mother.

He took a calming breath, wiping his beaded brow dry on a tea-towel, and with bag in hand, he made for the door...

'How long have you lived here?' Masterson asked, as Kaylie turned the key in the lock.

He'd been especially vigilant the whole way there, even though he was out of practice, and was pretty sure no one had observed him following the short distance they'd travelled to the apartment.

But at the same time, Kaylie looked so striking in that dress that surely any passing motorist would almost certainly have noticed her, especially the males and what he would refer to as 'the butch women'. But would they have noticed him? *Probably not*, he thought. In comparison, his clothes were screamingly dour and visually, must certainly have pushed him into the background.

'Only about a year,' replied Kaylie. 'I did my PhD at Oxford and that's where my folks live, so I lived at home while I was studying.' She withdrew the key, inviting him in by stepping aside.

Masterson sidled through, his heart racing. He hadn't done anything like this for a very, very long time. This was *Jerry's* legacy...

Kaylie dumped her bag by the entrance and led the way

down the door-lined corridor, escorting her guest through to the kitchen at the farthest end.

His gaze was locked on the serpentine sweep of her back: upright, firm, with a seductive curve at the base of the spine.

'These are actually much bigger than they look from the outside,' said Masterson, pulling his eyes away and addressing the space with distracted interest, but without really seeing any of it. The act was on, and he needed to put her at ease.

'They are!' agreed Kaylie. 'That's why I took the place. Tea? Coffee?' she asked over her shoulder as she filled the kettle, clapping it back on its base and slapping it on.

'Tea, please,' Masterson said, smiling, 'with one sugar.' He began looking for opportunities – how would he do this? The chloroform? Or just take her down with a blow?

'One perfectly brewed cup of tea coming right up,' she announced, retrieving two mugs from the drainer. 'So, have you managed to have a look around yet? Do you like the area?'

Masterson placed his bag down by his feet, unzipping the main compartment a little way.

He took a look around to assess the lay of the land. The kitchen was modern in comparison to his own tastes – sharp, clean, and tidy. A sea of chrome and Formica.

The floor was tiled, and he figured the grout would be impossible to clean if he got blood in it. But what did *he* care? He was already dying. What could they do to him that was any worse than that?

'I've had a quick look around,' he said, 'it seems nice enough.'

'Here you go,' chirped Kaylie, turning to hand over a steaming mug. She smiled up at him as he took it.

Her eyes burned through him, flickering, flinching; her seductive blink revealing those crystal-clear green gemstones. His stomach folded. He smiled. Those eyes. Those pleading eyes.

50

'Can I use your bathroom?' he asked, straining to break free from the moment.

'Of course, it's just through there,' she said, stepping into him and turning her head towards the corridor. She extended a knifed hand to indicate where. 'First door along. You can't miss it.'

Her scent hit his nose, like oranges, but more floral. It infested him like a kiss.

Masterson placed his mug on the side, stooping to grab his bag, and with a smile, made for the cloakroom.

Kaylie returned to the sink, deciding to wash the breakfast things left behind from the morning rush...

'Everything alright, Terry?' asked Kaylie, finally managing to recall his Christian name, prompted by the sharp *clack* of the lock and the creaking of the hinges that she *still* hadn't gotten around to oiling.

She wiped a sponge around the lip of the last pan left to clean, swilled it under the tap and placed it on the drainer. She shook her hands dry, looking about for the towel.

An arm suddenly grabbed her firmly around the waist, while another hand clamped a rag across her mouth.

The chemical stench hit her like a slap, filling her head. She swooned to the fumes inside her mind, eyes rolling.

She shook her head violently. The cloth shifted, no longer covering her nose, just her horrified expression.

Kaylie attempted to scream through the fibres, kicking and twisting, trying to free herself, but whoever it was that was arresting her was strong. *Very* strong!

She sucked in air through flaring nostrils, drawing in more fumes from the cloth. Her lids flickered and the room began to spin in her swimming vision.

She attempted to hold her breath, but the physical exertion

of fighting her aggressor was using up all of the oxygen in her system, and she desperately needed to breathe.

Masterson was losing his grip on the girl – she was stronger than her diminutive proportions would have suggested, despite the built nature of her physique.

He stumbled back, nearly losing his grip on the girl, then straining to lift her off her feet, he allowed himself to fall forwards, slamming the girl's stomach against the unforgiving edge of the countertop.

A blunt, simpering breath blew through the rag as Masterson's considerable bodyweight folded Kaylie in two, but, to his dismay, she didn't succumb to the blow.

'*Shit!*' Masterson spat. '*Shit! Shit!*' It had worked on another of his victims, knocking all the fight out of her, but this girl was strong and was now in danger of breaking loose.

He continued to lean into her, feeling himself begin to panic inside, thrusting his considerable bodyweight down against her, trying to force her to inhale. His panicked hand fought to reposition the cloth until it covered her nose again, and he leaned in harder.

Kaylie fought to stay conscious, tensing her gut for all she was worth. She took three desperate, shallow breaths to fuel her efforts, but they were laced with chemical sleep, asphyxiating her airways.

Her mind swam with distorting questions as to why this was happening, then she began to drown in the answers, her consciousness plummeted away from the temperate reassurance of lucidity like a skydiver with no ripcord and, with a whimper, she fell limp.

EIGHT

THE ATMOSPHERE IN GUTTERIDGE'S Saab felt strained and had done all morning – something remaining unsaid contaminating the air of the cabin.

Gutteridge sat silently at the wheel, negotiating the roads, whilst Keaton stared straight ahead as though suffering the aftermath of an argument they hadn't had.

Casework had been effective at distracting the both of them, but, now complete, you could cut the pregnant air with a knife.

'Are we going to talk about this, or are we going to just carry on pretending that nothing happened?' said Keaton, attempting to open the conversation.

Gutteridge fought not to react. He was regretting his impulsive actions but, at the same time, he knew them to be right and proper.

'It *was* you, wasn't it?' she said.

'Was me, what?'

'*Please*, Pat, don't play dumb. I arrived home after we met and found an envelope with 500 quid in it, hidden under the baby's bedding. It can *only* have been you. *You* tucked him in. So *why*?'

Gutteridge slumped from his denialist position, holding his silence for a mile or two, then indicated to pull into a lay-by a short way ahead... He parked and shut the engine off, and sat in contemplation of his situation, wondering just how blunt and forthright to be.

'Is it mine?' he asked, his voice a whisper – meek, fearful.

'Is what yours?'

'Please, don't *you* play dumb. I'm not blind – the *baby*. Is it mine? Is it... *ours*?'

Keaton looked mortified by the question, then dropped her gaze to her lap. She wasn't prepared for this level of honesty, so why had she felt compelled to force it?

'Yes,' she whispered into the deathly silence.

Gutteridge sat, head turned, just staring at her, mouth agape, feeling decidedly out-of-body. '*Fuck!*' he breathed.

Keaton huffed an ironic laugh. 'I know.'

Gutteridge sank back in his seat and turned his attention to the traffic fizzing past his side window. 'What do we do?'

Keaton rose from her cloud of regret. 'What do you mean? We do nothing.'

Gutteridge swung his attention back to her. Their eyes met, both close to weeping. 'What do you mean, nothing?'

'I mean, nothing. I raise my – *our* – son, and you carry on as you are. You have a beautiful wife who loves you, and *you* love her. You *need* her, and I'm not out to do anything to fuck that up.'

'But—'

'*No*, Pat. *I* made the decision not to terminate the pregnancy, so *I'll* wear the consequences.'

Gutteridge reeled in muted anger at the situation. 'I can't just fucking ignore the fact that you're raising my son! That would make me a monster!'

'No it wouldn't. How many sons and daughters do you

think there are in the world that have fathers who know nothing of their existence? Plenty! One more won't make a blind bit of difference.'

'But *I* know, *that's* the difference!'

Keaton fell silent again, mystified gaze returning to her lap, looking lost and dejected. 'You're so utterly happy at the moment, Pat. Do you think I don't see it? I'm not going to be responsible for destroying that, for destroying what you two have together. You love her, I see it. And she *adores* you, *worships* you even.'

Gutteridge held the silence. 'I *do* love her, and yes, she loves me, and I'd be a fool to want that to end. But I'd also be lying if I said I didn't have feelings akin to love for you. At least love enough to care, and to give a shit.'

Keaton's throat strained to stifle the sob that threatened to choke from her lungs at hearing the word 'love' peel from his lips in reference to her.

Gutteridge rocked in his seat in frustration. 'What the fuck do we do, Jane? What do *I* do?'

'I don't know,' she wept.

Gutteridge spun in his seat to face her again, dousing the flames of his frustration, and as if by telepathy, Jane Keaton rolled into his waiting embrace.

He rested his chin on her head and stared out of the side window, feeling her shake as she cried away her pain. He could smell her hair, he buried his nose in its familiar scent. It took him back to their one, reckless night of abandonment.

'I can at least continue to give you money to help. I *have* to help.' Gutteridge finally broke the embrace with a final, heartfelt kiss to Keaton's forehead, and lowered soft but serious eyes to address the meek vulnerability showing in her face. 'How do we play this?' he asked.

Keaton shrugged like a scolded child, then permitted

herself to laugh at the absurdity of it all. 'I really don't know…'
She held his gaze, interested pupils flicking from eye to eye,
searching for truth and meaning in Gutteridge's expression.
'Do you *want* to meet him? *Properly* I mean? Hold him,
knowing he's yours?'

Gutteridge didn't avert his gaze, but did seem to sink away
from the moment, looking lost and despondent. 'I don't know,'
he whispered. 'I mean – yes, of course. But at the same time,
I'm not so sure. It would make things final – *official* – and I'm
not certain that I'm quite ready for that.' He mewed the words
from the far-off place he'd receded into.

He finally returned to the moment, and looked deep into
Keaton's eyes. 'Is that so terrible?'

She lifted a hand to his flushing cheek, and caressed it with
her thumb. 'No, it's understandable. I get it.'

Gutteridge frowned. 'How about I carry on helping you
out, and we'll see where life takes us?'

Keaton huffed a smile of compassion, punctuating her
consent with a single kiss to his bewildered lips. 'Deal,' she
whispered. 'Why don't we do just that.'

He sighed. 'It won't be easy,' he said. 'Will we be able to
carry on our day-to-day lives, with – *this* – hanging over us?'

She popped an almost imperceptible, but carefree shrug.
'Why don't we just try?'

Gutteridge softly smiled, more for the easing of the pressure
than anything meaningful. 'Okay.'

Ewelina gate-crashed his thoughts, her attenuated limbs
stretching open to please him. Part of him wanted her, there
and then, but was it to cement his love? Or to pacify his
frustrations? Did he actually love her? Or did he just lust after
her? Cerebral, or carnal?

It crushed him to question what they had. He replayed key
moments they had shared together, and reflected on the warm

understanding she displayed towards him on a daily basis. No – it *was* love, he was sure of it. But the eroticism and salaciousness was such a prominent component of their alliance it made it easy to dismiss such moments of fidelity and tenderness.

'Come on then, shit-stick,' Keaton said. 'Let's get back to it.'

Gutteridge laughed. 'Okay, toss-pot.'

Keaton twisted to grab her seatbelt and paused. 'Why don't you pop over one night after work… say hello to the little guy? He has your eyes, you know.'

'I know,' said Gutteridge. 'I can't believe the whole bloody world hasn't noticed.'

Keaton laughed, clipping the buckle into its socket. 'McDonalds, on me?' she asked, before sniggering. 'Actually… I could use some of that money you gave me, so really, it'll be on you.'

Gutteridge grinned. 'Go on then.'

'Oh!' she added, 'that money? I bought myself a nice Vendula clutch-bag with some of it. I hope you don't mind?'

Gutteridge laughed, out loud this time, and fired up the engine. 'Gold-digging harlot!' he quipped, as he swung the car around in the road to head back into town.

NINE

THE NUMBER TEN BUS from the centre of Gloucester seemed to hiss in protest at having to interrupt its soporific progress as it pulled into the stop on Barnwood Road.

The doors fizzed open and a tall, self-assured girl dropped onto the waiting pavement, turning a wave of gratitude back to the driver. 'Laters, Pete,' she warbled, as she quelled her hurried trot to something more akin to an urgent stride, lifting a final, parting wave towards the bus' departure.

She'd endured an entire day of lectures and felt in desperate need of a shower and some 'me time' back at the flat to reset her equilibrium.

The sun made a final appearance through the patchwork of late-afternoon cloud to mark the end of the day. The girl turned her face up to meet its blinding glare, feeling the warmth pricking at the tenderness and youth of her skin.

She was tall and long-limbed in a way rivals would describe as lanky, but with an awkward elegance to her gait dictated by her height. Blonde, chestnut-streaked hair flowed in the breeze behind her urgency as she replayed key points from the day's learning which she considered warranted absorption and possible further research.

She finally reached the pedestrian walkway that led to Wolseley Road and the complex of apartments she now called home. Despite sharing the flat with two other girls, the feeling of freedom she felt at no longer being under the scrutinising gaze of her parents felt like the end of a jail sentence to one who'd – for so long – craved her own personal space, and it wasn't difficult to pretend she now lived alone.

She turned in through the gates to the carpark, scanning the smattering of vehicles to see who was home. She saw a silver Renault Clio she recognised, smiled, and hurried her walk.

The main door buzzed like an petulant wasp as she touched her fob to the reader, complaining of her arrival. Her flat, soft-shoed footsteps echoed throughout the utilitarian entrance hallway.

Her long fingers slid the brass key into the lock of her apartment with a judder, and she shouldered the door aside. 'Kaylie?' she sang. 'Are you in?' But there was no reply. 'Kaylie…?'

She shrugged the hoodie off her weary shoulders, hooking it up behind the door, and spied a familiar white sports bag at her feet. 'Kaylie?'

The girl made her way towards the living room. There was an unpleasant smell infesting the air that made her top lip curl in protest – an aroma like vinegar, but with something else far more repulsive underlying its eye-watering stench. Something carnivorous, something organic?

She tracked the fetid odour into the living room, rounding the open door. Her eyes hardened, snapping to something out of place – something grotesque, something that seemed to have been purposefully positioned centre of the room for effect.

She stumbled back, a low, guttural moan leaving her retching mouth as she absorbed the surreal sight offending her eyes, before they rolled up under her fluttering lids, and she sank to the ground…

*

The tall girl woke, her limbs randomly stacked beneath her like a collapsed mannequin, knees stinging to the unnatural stretch.

Her ashen face winced at the pain as she unfurled herself, not instantly remembering what had happened, or where she was. She blinked exaggeratedly to clear her scrambled vision, just as the acidic, butchers-block stench hit her nose again, sweet and metallic like a meat-locker.

Her swimming vision slowly cleared and she was once again forced to behold a sight that she hadn't fully comprehended before, but that would remain with her for the rest of her days.

A stomach full of revulsion boiled over and ejected from her nauseated mouth, splashing onto her lap. Her flatmate's eyes seemed to be watching her torment from the centre of the room. She fought to remain conscious whilst trying to comprehend the jarring deviation from normality that she was being forced to bear witness to – because those dry, emerald eyes were no longer in her flatmate's pretty head; they were now three feet from the sockets they had been expertly removed from and carefully placed upon her lap.

Her panicked arms began flailing wildly for any means of escape, clawing at the carpet, struggling to motivate the new arrival away from the depraved spectacle of death now contaminating her life. Her manic, staring pupils locked their focus on the door at the far end of the corridor, her only means of escape.

Were those nail heads she'd seen protruding from the backs of Kaylie's hands? And through her feet? And could whoever it was that possessed such a callous disregard for human life as to perform such a repugnant act still be there, in the flat, *with* her?

Her breaths became urgent, hoarse cries of desperation as she crawled for the door, palms thumping on the carpet. A lifted hand, an outstretched arm, her wildly grasping fingers fumbling for the feeling of handle. A twist, a frantic pull, and the door swung open to reveal her other flatmate, stood holding her key out in readiness.

The tall girl's imploring eyes lifted to meet the confused expression looking down at her. She was shaking, her eyes wide in their slick, reddened sockets, pleading up at her friend's sudden arrival.

Her desperate, staccato breaths finally cracked and became a shrill scream of lamentation for her desecrated innocence. 'K-K-Kayliiiiiiiiiiiie!' she screamed, into what had revealed itself to be a sick, evil world, ribbons of drool running from her grimacing mouth.

'What is it, Maddie? W-W-What's happened?' insisted the friend, sinking to her knees in an attempt to console.

'K-Kaylie!' she wailed again. 'Sh-sh-she's d-d-deeeead!'

The flatmate slowly lifted her horrified gaze to peer into the unlit corridor of the apartment, the meat-locker stench now hitting her nose. She fumbled in her pocket for her phone and quickly woke the screen.

TEN

'**WHAT THE HELL'S GOING ON?!**' griped Gutteridge. 'I'm duty SOI on this shift, so why haven't we been called in?'

'Christ knows?' said Keaton, who was hurriedly inputting the address they'd heard over the radio into Google Maps. 'W-o-l-s-e-l-e-y R-o-a-d. Never heard of it,' she said, hitting search. 'Shit!' she spat. 'It's just up the road here, off Barnwood.'

'How far?'

'A mile. Maybe less? Hang on,' she said, spreading her fingers against the image and studying the map. 'It seems to be pedestrian-only at the Barnwood end. We'll have to go around the back way. Turn up Elmbridge, then it's first on the left.'

Gutteridge nailed the throttle and indicated to turn onto Barnwood Road. 'What's Bryant playing at?' he said.

'Does he think you're on leave or something?'

'*No*, he doesn't! We discussed shifts only the other day.'

Keaton shrugged her cluelessness, watching the road ahead unwind. 'Turn here,' she barked, pointing to a junction, 'then hook a left.'

The headlights swept into Wolseley Road, illuminating the houses like a hunting searchlight. They could see the sharp reflection of blue flashing lights cascading off the windows lining the street.

'Suspicious death… wonder what that means?' asked Keaton.

'I guess we're about to find out.'

A police cordon loomed into view as they negotiated the final bend that took them back towards Barnwood Road. A uniformed officer approached their arrival, the flat of his hand held out towards them.

Gutteridge slowed and lowered his side window, presenting his Warrant card. 'Detective Inspector Gutteridge,' he announced.

But the officer seemed to recognise both him and his name, looking strangely surprised by his sudden arrival. The officer appeared utterly thrown by Gutteridge's presence, darting a worried look in the direction of the cluster of police cars that were gathered at the far end of the cul-de-sac.

'Erm… Can you hold on here a second, sir? I just need to radio this in.' He turned his back to the car to create distance, and began speaking softly into his collar.

'Oh, fuck this,' spat Gutteridge, throwing the car into gear and snaking through the barricade, making for the commotion ahead.

'Sir! Please, wait!' shouted the cop, who was trotting after his departure.

Gutteridge spied a space a hundred yards ahead, and aimed the nose of the Saab towards it. He hit the brakes, foot thrumming to the rumble of the anti-lock.

He and Keaton popped the doors and rose into the soft, dusk light and biting air of a cloudless evening.

Neighbours in comfortable clothing not usually seen outside of bin-day stood in doorways, wrapped in dressing gowns and watching events unfold, wondering what could have happened to disrupt their otherwise mundane lives. Some had crossed the street to consolidate their clandestine huddles with other neighbours they knew as more than mere passing acquaintances, trading theories, one calling out to Gutteridge by name.

He was famous in the area now, ever since the post-storm fanfare of the O'Leary case, with a glowing op-ed written by Kerry Marston about him and his illustrious career gracing the pages of *The Echo*, drawing widespread attention from the nationals who felt inclined to buy the piece and also run the story. He'd been news, and the department had gladly ridden the coattails of his celebrity. So why was he being passed over now?

With vehemence, Gutteridge strode towards the apartment block that seemed to be the hub of the broiling activity. Even in sensible shoes, Keaton struggled to keep up.

He flashed his ID to other officers who didn't need to see it to know who he was, all with the same mortified looks on their faces that he was even there.

At least three of the officers turned after he'd swept past and took to their radios, seeming to pass on news of his imminent arrival.

DCI Bryant suddenly appeared through the main entrance of the apartment block, looking about nervously. He clocked Gutteridge and hurried to intercept his arrival.

'Pat! Old friend. No! This one's not for you,' he said, breaking into a trot to cut him off.

Gutteridge stopped shy of the barricade of Bryant's outstretched arms, his knitted brows darkening. 'What's this all about? *I'm* duty SOI today, why am I being passed over?'

He leaned to one side to glance past Bryant's shoulder towards the entrance. He caught the eye of one of the uniforms watching, who seemed to wince an awkward, regretful smile.

His attention returned to Bryant, whose barricading arms had softened, and now looked almost like the opener to an embrace.

'*Please*, Pat. You have to trust me on this. This one's not for you.'

'*Why*? Do I know them? The victim? Or is it victims?'

'Victim,' Bryant said, finally allowing his arms to lower a little, 'and no, I don't think so. It's not that.'

'What is it then?' Gutteridge asked. He was becoming frustrated by the cloak-and-dagger cryptic feeding of information.

'It's something else, old friend, something I don't want you seeing.'

Gutteridge leaned another look towards the entrance, his interest now well and truly spiked. Bryant's arms raised again in response.

'Okay. Well, what about Jane?' Gutteridge asked, stepping aside and turning to take in Keaton, who had been hovering in the sidelines the whole time.

Bryant followed the line of Gutteridge's gaze to consider the waiting DS. 'I guess she could stay and assist the team I already have on the case. I just can't have *you* involved,' he explained.

Bryant turned back to face Gutteridge, who was no longer there. He spun towards the block of flats just in time to see Gutteridge's back disappearing inside.

'*Fuck!*' Bryant spat, turning to chase him down. 'Pat! No!'

Keaton tentatively followed the commotion, observing Bryant as he thundered into the building.

She could hear Gutteridge's name being shouted over and over at the top of desperate lungs, echoing around the passageways, and then it stopped... All had gone disconcertingly quiet. She hurried her walk, following the line of officers who were all facing in the direction of the excitement until she came to an open door to one of the apartments. She flashed her ID as a matter of course, stepping tentatively inside.

It was eerily quiet. One of the WPCs manning the corridor ahead of her had her hand held to her mouth, her attention turned to one of the adjoining doorways as though witnessing something life-changing.

Keaton sidled through and saw Gutteridge standing static, barely inside the door, his eyes locked on something inside. Bryant's hand was resting lightly on his shoulder, and she wondered why he wasn't tearing her partner a new arsehole? Gutteridge's face seemed almost emotionless, but with a confounded flicker of grief and repudiation saddening his unblinking eyes.

Keaton's pulse quickened. She sidestepped the open doorway to join the throng and see what was arresting Gutteridge's attention. Bryant turned a look towards her arrival, his face appealing to hers.

As though mimicking the WPC she'd just passed, Keaton's hands raised to her open mouth in response to the sight that greeted her. Gustav Hoegen was stood to one side, gloved and suited, a pillar box of concern visible from behind his mask as he hovered in the background, observing Gutteridge's torment.

There was the body of a young girl on display dead centre of the living room, her white summer dress with poppy print sodden with tides of coagulating blood that had drained from her empty sockets, which had once framed eyes now neatly placed upon her lap.

There was another pool of blood beneath the seat that she'd been nailed to, and Keaton could just make out what looked like calf muscles that had been surgically removed.

Keaton came over bilious; she knew what this was. Gutteridge had described this exact same scene to her just once in their entire time together, and the name that came to her was 'Cynthia'.

Gutteridge rocked on his heels as he considered the reality of his very worst, recurring nightmares made flesh, absorbing every hideous detail. Everything seemed the same – almost a facsimile – except this wasn't his old home in Shropshire, and this *wasn't* his deceased wife, Cynthia. This was some seemingly random girl at some seemingly random location in Gloucester. Nothing felt real.

His mortified eyes lowered. There *was* a difference. The feet had been nailed to the chair, whereas his wife's had been nailed to the floorboards. But *these* floors were made of concrete, and that would account for the difference in MO.

The calves – that was different, too, but hardly new. Victim No.3's calves had been removed, and as was clear from the physique of the corpse sat facing him, she'd also been a gym bunny.

He realised he was fighting the impulse to scream at the top of his lungs by being analytical – but did that make him cold-hearted? Or was it simply stone-walling denial?

He became aware of Bryant's hand still resting upon his shoulder when it delivered a comforting squeeze. '*Do* you know her?' he asked.

A shake of the head. 'No. I mean, I don't think so. It's hard to tell…' he said, his voice unsteady. 'Her name?'

'Kaylie Wyatt.'

Gutteridge fought not to look relieved, and shook a remorseful head. 'No. No, I don't know her.'

'Come on then,' said Bryant. 'Let's get you out of here.'

'No, wait!' said Gutteridge. 'The note,' he added, lifting his chin towards the corpse. 'I've got a horrible feeling it's for me.'

Tentatively, he stepped out from under Bryant's consoling hand and approached the body. He could see a Victorian hat-pin protruding from the body, skewering a note to one of the victim's breasts – just like the one he'd found on his wife's body, the one that had read:

You ruined my life, so now I'm ruining yours. Is that so very wrong?
JM

He stepped in closer, complaining eyes stinging from the fumes of the acetic acid rising from the corpse.

A memory of Cynthia – laughing, smiling, dancing in the sun's luminous rays at a summer barbecue in their garden back in Shropshire – flashed into his thoughts.

Hoegen respectfully handed him a pair of gloves. He pulled them on and leaned over the edge of the puddle of blood to carefully remove the note. He handed the pin to Hoegen's waiting hands. Hoegen bagged it.

Gutteridge stepped back two paces, eyes locked on the folded note, looking so much like the one he'd found pinned to his wife over a decade ago. It transported him back to the horrifying moment that his life ended.

He took an unsteady breath, and with his fingertips, carefully opened it…

Hello, Gutteridge, is this like old times? I read about you in the papers from time to time, you're quite the celebrity these days.

Want to know how I'm doing? Well, I'll tell you – our mother committed suicide because of you, because of your interference, because of your actions.

Due to you and your ilk, I lost everyone I have ever loved – so now, I'm going to 'adjust' everyone you've ever loved. Is that so very wrong?
M

Gutteridge's stomach knotted as he ran the message through his mind several times over. Was this a copycat, or the real deal?

He could hear Bryant behind his shoulders gloving up, and swung his arm behind him to pass the note to other interested hands. Bryant took it in his fingertips, and began ingesting it.

Gutteridge stepped up to the victim again and crouched to bring his eyes to face level. He could see – even through the congealing mask of blood and ocular fluid – that this girl was once attractive, with a prettiness to her features exclusive to the young. That was certainly a match to Jerry Masterson's MO. All twelve victims – including Gutteridge's wife – had been what could politely be called 'lookers', sending a wave of panic throughout Shropshire and its neighbouring counties affecting those narcissistic or self-aware enough to consider themselves *beautiful*, and the pickings at nightclubs and bars had become decidedly thin for hot-blooded males seeking perfection during those times, and it remained that way until Gutteridge had solved the case and Masterson had fled.

Gutteridge sidestepped the pool of blood to examine the trauma to the calves. They'd been removed, and with something sharp.

'A knife?' he asked Hoegen, who was still stood back on the sidelines, watching events unfold and thinking Gutteridge was handling all of this extremely well, better than expected.

'A scalpel, I believe,' Hoegen said. 'Peri-mortem, judging by the extensive levels of blood loss,' he added, in his soft, Dutch accent. 'If I was to go out on a limb, I'd say he used a No.26 blade. You can tell by the depth of the cut attained with each swipe of the knife. It leaves a kind of stepped surface, and from that, you can see the blade was straight, not curved or recurved – and the cutting face long. Certainly longer than a 10A. So as I say, that leads me to believe it was probably a No.26.'

Gutteridge considered the stark similarities to the cold-case he'd had nothing to do with for over a decade. Was The Shropshire Ripper back for a repeat performance? Everything seemed to fit, except the note – it ended 'M'. The one pinned to his wife had ended 'JM'. Was that relevant?

'I want to head the case,' Gutteridge said.

'No!' Bryant snapped. 'Conflict of interest.'

'That's bullshit! We don't even know if this was Jerry Masterson. It could just be a copycat, a *fan*. Either way, no one in this division knows more about the case than I do. I want to head the team. I'm not conflicted, I just want whoever did this, caught.'

He finally stood and turned to face Bryant. 'Unless, that is, you want Gloucester to wear the same humiliation Shropshire division did for amassing a twelve body-bag hoard that clogged up the mortuary for years before he was rumbled?'

Bryant contemplated Gutteridge's reasoning and the ethics of even letting Gutteridge in, let alone head the team, given his personal history and involvement in the case. His wife *was* one of the victims after all – but that was twelve years ago now, didn't that passage of time alone create ethical distance?

'Alright, you're on the case. But if I see cracks forming, I'm taking you off.'

Gutteridge nodded. 'Understood, sir.'

Bryant momentarily considered if he'd just made a huge mistake, but decided to let his decision stand. 'What would you suggest the team does first?'

Gutteridge had already been pondering that very question. 'I would send DS Keaton to interview Terrence Masterson, see what he has to say. I'd always assumed Jerry was dead, but if he *isn't*, maybe Terrence Masterson has been in contact with him at some point. Despite the things Jerry did and the way it fucked up Terrence's life, I always got the impression they were sort of close.'

Bryant considered the suggestion. 'Why don't you go?'

'I need to be here, to set things up. Besides, I don't think Terrence Masterson likes me all that much. Their mother drowned herself after it had all come out and I got the impression Terrence somehow blamed me for that, and anyway, I remember he liked the girls, and Keaton's looks could do a lot to loosen his tongue. If that isn't wrong to say in this day and age.'

Keaton finally piped in, popping a subtle, but carefree shrug. 'Whatever you think would work to help catch this guy, chief.'

Gutteridge turned to take in the scene again, absorbing the relevance apparent in the horrifying details. '*I* won't go making this personal,' he muttered, 'but whoever the fuck did this sure as hell wants to!'

ELEVEN

KERRY MARSTON lifted a wave to Candy on reception as she crossed *The Echo*'s foyer and made for the lifts. The day had been a long one, with very little of interest to write about.

She pondered how much she missed the buzz of London journalism – political intrigue; celebrity scandal; police corruption and high-end crime. Plenty for a hungry hack to get her razor-sharp teeth into.

The Echo's news desk hadn't been the same since the O'Leary case had drawn to its bloody conclusion and she found herself almost wishing for another psychopath to come along and at least give her something vaguely interesting to write about.

A polite bell rang out to end the silence and the doors to the lift rumbled open. 'Well, at least *they're* working again,' she muttered, in rebuke of the building's notorious unreliability.

The tick-tack of her heels resonated around the concrete pillars of the multi-storey carpark, as she scanned the designated spaces for her car. She saw it fifty yards ahead and sped up her walk.

It was growing dark. She checked her watch – it was 20:19 and the shops were now shut.

The usually overcrowded carpark looked eerie in its stark and emptied state, the lightless sky just visible outside, giving way to the localised glow of streetlights.

'Kerry Marston?' asked an inquisitive voice from somewhere behind her urgent walk, but the unnatural echo of the space meant she couldn't pinpoint exactly from where.

She spun to find the voice. A man approached from shadow, stooping apologetically. 'I'm sorry,' he said, with a humble, almost ambivalent smile. 'We've only met the once. You interviewed me… It was a while ago now, so you might not remember, I mean, why *would* you. But I thought it was you across the way, so I decided to come over and say a quick hello.'

The man – tall, strongly built, with neat but heavy beard growth, and strangely handsome for someone so obviously carrying years – extended a meek hand to shake.

Marston forced an anaemic smile to mask her annoyance, and swapped her bags over to her other hand to reciprocate the gesture.

The man took the offering, then instantly clamped her delicate fingers tightly in his vice-like grip and yanked her towards him.

Marston grimaced and folded in on the pain, barking a yelping scream that resonated around the unforgiving facets of the concrete pillars. She stumbled forwards, her ankle folding on her heel.

The stranger extended his other hand inside the flap of her jacket and Marston felt something hard being thrust up under her ribcage – sharp, pronged, metallic. 50,000 volts suddenly fired through her body like a fizzing punch to the gut. She stiffened like a board and toppled into the man's waiting arms like a felled chimney-stack. The spine-curling crackle ceased, and with a whimper, Marston fell limp.

She let out a dazed groan as she was spun around like a rag-doll, a folded elbow hooking her neck, dragging her towards the open door of a waiting car. A muscular hand clamped the base of her skull and pushed down hard, cutting off the blood supply to her brain.

Marston's head swelled from the pressure and she became frantic, her kicking feet skidding on the concrete, trying to find purchase. Darkness encroached the periphery of her clouding vision; a gurgling breath escaping her compressed lips. The pressure increased, relentless, unwavering, until her hands fell away from the persistent arm and slapped against the concrete. She blacked out…

*

'Wake up,' a dispassionate voice said, softly-spoken but cold, almost caressing the words. 'I said, *wake up*.'

Kerry Marston groaned awake, flowing in and out of lucidity, unaware of what or where she was.

She inhaled a deep breath to wake her lungs, wincing at the tentacles of pain coiling deep inside her diaphragm from where she'd been zapped.

Something flat suddenly connected sharply with her cheekbone, the stinging pain spreading across her face like a brush-fire, engulfing her stunned expression, shocking her awake.

'*Wake up!*' barked the voice again, sounding impatient.

Marston tried to lift her hands to cup the pain, but they were held fast. She became aware of a tightness across her shoulders and around her wrists, and she realised her hands had been tied somewhere behind her. She was sitting, at least that's how it felt. She began to squirm, then instantly stopped, screaming through the fibres of the rag that had been taped into her mouth.

Her eyelids fluttered to the agony, saliva flooding her jaw to a very different pain. Mucus bubbled from her nostrils as she retched at the agony. Her lids eventually relaxed their squint and opened, taking a moment to clear and pull the scene before her into focus.

Marston's horrified eyes widened at the sight of her naked thighs nailed to the chair she was in, webs of blood leeching from the wounds. Surrounding the large, coin-like nail heads were what looked to be bite marks, *human* bite marks, some inflicted with sufficient force to draw blood.

Her rufescent stare hardened. She screamed into the rag again, hoping it would wake her from the nightmare she was living.

An impatient hand appeared from nowhere and grabbed her beneath her jaw, lifting her face. Her twitching eyes met her assailant's. It was the man from the carpark.

The carpark! She finally remembered. *The stranger, the assault, the taser – and now, this.*

Marston blinked away the pain-induced tears fogging her vision to get a clearer view of the man. She recognised him from somewhere a long way in her past, but from where?

Then the words she heard at the multi-storey reran through her mind. '*We've only met the once. You interviewed me…*' Then it hit her: *this* was one of the Masterson boys? *Terry*? He'd had a beard – a beard she recalled he'd purposefully grown thicker to help disguise his identity. Wise after news of his brother's crimes first hit the newsstands and life as he knew it had turned to shit.

Masterson clocked the look of recognition in the twitching pupils peering back at him. 'Yeeees. You do recognise me, don't you? You were with the *Daily Mirror* then – a "roving reporter", isn't that what it's called? Sent out to harass people like me just for having the audacity to do what they do.' Masterson smiled, almost grinning. 'And now here we are, together again, over a decade later. Can you guess why it is that you're here yet?'

Marston peered back at him, trying to decipher his intentions. She shook her head.

He huffed a dismissive smirk, as if he didn't believe her claim of ignorance. 'You're here, because of *this*,' he said, attempting to tether his stewing anger, teeth grinding his considerable contempt. He was holding up a copy of *The Echo*, carefully folded open at an article she'd penned about DI Gutteridge's life and career.

'You're here, because of your fucking fawning, drivelling, grovelling worship of this... this... *man!* he spat. 'The man – may I remind you – who killed my mother. Who killed *our* mother!'

Kerry Marston's eyes began to plead, her muffled words filtering through the cloth clamped between her teeth, begging for mercy and understanding. She began to shake her head frantically, rejecting her situation, more muffled words warming the makeshift gag.

Masterson turned and cupped a mocking ear towards her efforts in jest. 'I'm sorry, I can't hear you? You'll have to speak up.'

Marston fell silent again, and sat back, silenced by the ridicule, but with eyes still pleading for mercy that she wasn't sure would come.

Masterson twisted his right shoulder down and grabbed something off the floor.

'Now, I'm going to take the gag out, so we can converse, *civilly*,' he said, levelling his eyes with hers. '*If* you try to call out, I'll swing this through your teeth,' he said, lifting a three-pound lump-hammer into the core of his threat, 'and I'll keep swinging, until all that remains of your face is a swollen bag of teeth and bone fragments, and the only way *anyone* will ever know the resulting detritus was once *you*, is by swabbing the remains I had the audacity to dump on the steps of the police station. Do you understand me? Nod if you understand me.'

Marston took a moment to absorb the severity of the threat, and nodded.

Masterson's mouth twitched with an almost imperceptible smile and he placed the hammer back on the ground between Marston's feet.

As he leaned in to remove the tape from her mouth, Marston took the opportunity to absorb her surroundings, searching for clues as to where she might be so that she may relay them to the police, *once* her ordeal was over. That's when she noticed the clear plastic sheeting lining the entire room, like it had been prepared by a clean-up team in readiness for a mafia hit.

There was a chintz settee sitting directly facing her beneath the Visqueen, looking jarringly normal in light of what was occurring. The settee looked recently to have been sat in – the sheeting puckered from the weight of a body, with what looked like lanced flower-heads scattered around the periphery of the indentation.

She blinked the tears away again to clear her vision and realised that they were in fact balled-up sheets of kitchen paper and began to convulse inside at the thought that she – in her captive, unconscious state – had been the pornography.

She felt a tug on her mouth and stiffened her lips as the tape was peeled from her face. She could see faint traces of lipstick on the tacky side as it was lifted away, but much less than she would have expected to see, always being one to lay it on fairly thick. That's when she noticed the faintest smear of terracotta pink across Masterson's beard-growth, and across the back of his right hand. He'd apparently been kissing her while she was out!

She nearly retched at the thought, then began wondering why any of this was happening. Had Jerry Masterson's brother been cut from the same cloth all along? They *were* similar in many ways, that she *could* remember.

She inadvertently tried to shift in the seat again, sending blinding waves of pain searing through her legs and up her spine.

Bile pumped from her gagging mouth and splashed onto the rubescent skin surrounding the nail heads, mixing with the ribbons of stigmata blood cascading onto the seat.

Masterson's hand clapped across her mouth to stifle her cries. '*Shhh*,' he hissed, bringing his mouth close to her ear. 'I said, no noise,' he whispered, wagging a finger in front of her face like a teacher scolding a petulant pupil.

He straightened again, and began pacing the room in front of his guest, eyes turned down to the newspaper still in his hand.

'I've marked a passage of particular interest,' he said. 'Would you like me read it to you to refresh your memory?' But Masterson didn't wait for a response, he just cleared his throat theatrically, parading the room like a university lecturer, article held aloft. '"Detective Inspector Gutteridge first rose to prominence, or some might even say, fame, within both the force *and* the public eye when he single-handedly linked the Shropshire Ripper murders to Jerry Masterson. Many of his colleagues at that time were reluctant to share his belief that the evidence indicated Masterson to be the most likely suspect, tying their allegiances to a very different mast. It was possibly this lack of consensus that, in all likelihood, led to the arrest being bungled, leading to Masterson's subsequent release on a legal technicality, just hours before he then went on the run and was never seen again. But the killing spree ceased and lives not directly affected could return to relative normality, and it is still a widely held belief within the force that Jerry Masterson is in all likelihood no longer of this earth, even though no body or evidence of his death has, to this day, ever been found."'

Masterson's brow puckered, and he turned the paper theatrically in his fingers, as though unable to find something he was expecting to see. 'So… where's the other part? The part about my mother being hounded by *you* fuckers, all feeding off the undeserved fanfare and toadying adulation of Gutteridge and his ilk until she was no longer able to handle the limelight and drowned herself in Vyrnwy Lake? Where's that part?'

Although her mouth was now uncovered, Marston couldn't find the words to speak. Unable to read Masterson's intentions, she feared prodding the hornet's nest. 'I don't know what I'm supposed to say?'

The hate and resentment spread fast across Masterson's face. He thundered towards her, tossing the scrunched up article aside, livid hands grasping her shoulders, rocking her back in the seat.

The nail heads tugged at her thighs with the inertia. More bile climbed her throat at the pain.

'You're supposed to speak the fucking *truth*!' he spat, seething at her perceived ignorance. 'That because of Gutteridge's unreasonable interfering, and *your* incessant badgering, she had no other choice left open to her than to wander into a lake and fucking drown herself!'

Marston recoiled from the anger emanating off Masterson. 'But, your brother,' she whispered.

'My fucking brother had to die for his part in all of this! For abandoning his duties as a son and leaving her at the mercy of the likes of *you*!' His face contorted with rage, lip curling hard into his flaring nostrils. His weeping eyes burned with malice. 'He was as guilty of her death as you, and for that, he had to die!'

Panic flooded Marston's body and she began to struggle. '*Patriiiiiick!*' she screeched. 'Oh *please*, dear God in heaven, Patrick, help *meeeeeee!*'

The mention of Gutteridge's name seemed to pacify Masterson's anger, which dissolved into his surprise. His stance softened. 'Patrick? Pat-rick?' he repeated. Masterson held Marston's stare which was swimming with confusion, then after a beat, he reeled back, allowing himself a smile.

A soft, wide grin of realisation birthed from his anger. 'Of course, you *know* him. You and him are friends. Of *course* you are.' His eyes returned to hers, peering deep, looking for truth in her jittering pupils. 'Have a thing together, did you? *Lovers*, were you?'

Marston's eyes and lids flinched, then averted at the mention of the word, 'lovers'.

'Oh… oh, you did.' He loosed a knowing smile, unable to hide the joy from showing in his face. 'This is *sooooo* much better than I could ever of have hoped for.' He began to laugh, the irony warming his undeserving soul, before he quelled it, looking deep into Marston's confused gaze with hunting eyes.

'Do you want to know why I'm here, in Gloucester? I *bet* you've been wondering…' He placed his hands on the armrests, and leaned into Kerry Marston's terrified expression. 'I'm here to deprive Gutteridge of anyone he's ever loved. To remove them from his world one by one, to return the favour he did for me. You understand?' He smiled what seemed to be a genuine smile. 'I was actually going to kill you just for the fun of it, because of what you were complicit in doing. But now, your death will have *so* much more meaning,' he said, his words turning Marston's glazed expression to terror.

He leaned back again, levelling his stare. 'You *do* know who I am, don't you? You *have* worked it out?'

Kerry Marston began to weep again, and nodded.

Masterson crouched down before her, looking up at her tear-drenched mask of fear and confoundedness. 'I detest you,' he slurred, lifting a hand to caress her forehead. 'Which is a shame, because you're actually really rather attractive under that aging, hack exterior. And your lips – *mmmmm*, those lips – they tasted *so* good, like strawberries and cream.' His brows raised, playfully. 'I even considered keeping them, as a trophy, you understand?'

He brushed her lips with the pad of his thumb, turning wistful. 'My type like trophies,' he mumbled, looking lost in his own musing, before his face suddenly brightened. 'Oh! Which reminds me.'

He twisted down again, lifting a spray bottle from the floor and giving it a healthy shake. He began pumping its contents onto her face, the caustic smell of bleach hitting her nose like a punch and she began to choke.

Then the burning started – her skin, her eyes, her tongue. She began to rock in her seat as the pumping continued, howling her anguish, ignoring the pain scything through her legs. She screamed as her skin began to fizzle, bleeding eyes stinging.

Masterson rose from his crouch like a kraken, hammer in hand. 'I thought I told you to make no sound,' he said, before smirking, darting the briefest of looks toward the bay window. 'Luckily for *them*, I think my new neighbours are out.'

He considered the weight of the hammer with a few light tosses, then spun his attention back to Kerry Marston through the corner of his mischievous eyes.

He widened his stance in preparation and presented the head of the hammer to Marston's gritted teeth and the peeling skin of her boiling lips, then drew his arm back, taking aim…

'After all those years disrespecting the privacy of others,' he frothed, 'it's finally time for *you*, to become the news.'

Marston squirmed in desperation, hands tugging desperately at her restraints, face boiling, gagging on the fumes of her own cooking skin. She screamed a scream that could animate the dead, howling Gutteridge's name at the top of her burning lungs.

Masterson tensed his limbs, transferring his sizeable weight to his back foot, and with a grunt, swung the implement low and hard.

It landed with a flat, dull thud that spattered his gurning face, and the screaming stopped. The pleading stopped. The life stopped. And his lonely, twisted world – such that it was – fell silent again.

TWELVE

GUTTERIDGE pulled into a lay-by, unable to hold back the grief from surfacing any longer.

He'd dropped Keaton off at the station to collect her car, but very little had passed between them since leaving the crime scene, both stunned by the events of the night.

He grasped the leather-bound wheel and squeezed so hard his fingers ached and his knuckles cracked, curling in on his pain, as he heaved great sobs for his rekindled memories and the nightmare of his previous life.

He strained against the suffocating heartache as he felt a decade of tears cascade down his face. The years of effort attempting to deny the past to clear a view to a happier future crashed down around him like the walls of Jericho.

He also shed a tear for the bright, young life that had been needlessly snuffed from existence simply to send him a message, and spent a lonely hour letting his sorrows flow like a river of misery… Gutteridge finally settled into some strange, stagnant form of torpor, a fluid, swimming sense of detachment, tear-ducts dry and emotions spent.

His phone chimed loud in the wake of his grieving. He turned a demoralised look towards the device lying on the passenger seat beside him, seeing it was from Keaton just before the screen went to sleep again. He thought about turning it off, beginning to find life a little overcrowded.

Gutteridge took a tissue from the packet in the pocket of the door and dried his eyes. He took up the phone and opened Keaton's message.

I hope you're alright. As brave a face as you were putting on it, I could tell you weren't. Call me if you need anything. Jane. x

He read it again twice over, then powered down the device. He turned the key in the ignition, pulled away, and headed for home…

*

The front door of Gutteridge's cottage crept open as he parked the Saab. Eve presented herself in the opening, still decked out in her corporate garb fit for office life. She looked concerned but knowing, her solicitous eyes waiting to greet his arrival.

Gutteridge rose into the cold arms of night. His brow furrowed. Eve looked far from uninformed.

'Come in,' she said. 'Come out of the cold. I've been waiting forrr you. I've been worried.'

'Worried?' Gutteridge said.

She offered a sorrowful smile. 'Jane called me,' she said. 'We exchanged numbers that day at the restaurant. She told me what happened.'

Gutteridge wavered slightly at the news that *he* was a font of gossip, and felt the tears threatening to make a repeat appearance. But he took two deliberate gulps to swallow them back and reset his equilibrium, then wandered towards his waiting wife.

Eve opened her arms to entice him in. 'Come on. Come here. Come to me,' she said.

He accepted the bait, locking the car and climbing the steps to face her.

She engulfed him in her pitying embrace, pulling him into her bosom like a consoling mother, placing a kiss atop his bowed head.

'I'm so sorry,' she said, 'I can't know how you feel, but I'm here to trrry.'

Gutteridge wept...

Despite being presented with food usually considered a firm favourite, Gutteridge appeared unable to contemplate anything as prosaic as eating.

Eve just sat quietly opposite, observing him with concern, like a psychologist assessing a new case.

With his untouched plate of food pushed aside and apologies given, she began looking for an 'in'.

'Was it the same?' she asked – her genteel voice evaporating the silence, drawing Gutteridge up from the pit of his grief-hole.

'What?'

Eve softened her front... 'The girl – the one that was killed... Was it the same as before? In the same way, b-by the same person, maybe?'

Gutteridge looked both perplexed and irritated by the question. 'Erm? I don't— Yes. I think so.'

Eve wilted, regretting what she now perceived to be her clumsy attempt at empathy. 'Sorry,' she said. 'I guess I shouldn't be asking.' She shuffled in her seat, backing away from the meat of the conversation. 'That was insensitive. I know, this really has nothing to do with me.'

Gutteridge looked even more irritated by the response

than the probing, before realising that *he* was the fuel of his own irritation. He allowed his temper to thaw.

'No, love. It's… it's *me* who should be apologising, not you. You have nothing to apologise for. You're my wife – of course it's your business.'

He turned a distant, pensive look away towards the spitting flames of the log fire. 'It's just a shock, seeing that again, after all the years of effort trying to push it away until it was nothing more than a bad memory. Almost as if I'd dreamt it.' He turned back to drink in Eve's concern. 'Do you understand?'

She gave an empathic smile, and nodded. 'Yes. I underrrstand.'

Gutteridge attempted a half-smile that, in the scheme of things, felt inappropriate. He pushed his seat back from the table, his arm outstretched by way of an invitation. 'Come here,' he said.

Eve contemplated the invitation, and the manner in which it was delivered.

She stood, clad in a short, black, pencil skirt that hung shy of her delicate knees, limitless legs sheathed in silk extending from the hem, punctuated with classically delicate, stiletto heels, her favourite style of shoe. An ice-white blouse completed the ensemble, unbuttoned to her sternum. To Gutteridge, she was the ultimate sight for tired eyes, statuesque and regal, Amazonian, even, and it hadn't gone unnoticed. Just what Gutteridge needed to distract his mind from what had been a horrible day.

She sidled around the table, perching herself on his waiting knee. He wrapped her minute waist in his grateful arms and gave her a hug loaded with appreciation, and just held her, nose buried deep in her scent.

'It's been a hell of a day,' he said by way of a hint, nuzzling his nose deep in her hair.

86

'If... there's anything I can do to help?' Eve asked.

He lingered, lost in her scent, contemplating her invitation. His eyes finally left her neck to deliver a look she understood – a look she'd seen many times before, a look she knew meant he wanted to drown his frustrations in a sea of lust and eroticism. Or was it more accurate to say – take them out on her sexually?

One and the same, she thought, *just different interpretations of the same act.*

She knew him to be a man of honour: kind, caring and loving. But also knew him to be a slave to his passions, and at that moment in time, she was happy to be a vessel for his fire. After all, she *did* love the man, finding his innate masculinity supremely alluring.

With a discerning smile, she rose to check the living-room curtains were shut tight, striding to the window on spiring legs, stretching up and grasping the drapes, snapping them together a couple of times to ensure their efficiency at obstructing prying eyes, then turned her attention back into the room.

Gutteridge was already on his feet and sauntering across to join her, thirsting eyes flicking from one rousing detail to the next. From thighs to knees to waist to calves to cleavage to neck to eyes to lips... Strong arms reached involuntarily for what they desired to caress; hands and fingers craving the feeling of skin on muscle on flawless bone-structure.

Eve's hands and attention fell away, lithe fingers unhooking his belt and twisting buttons free of their restraints.

Gutteridge observed the concentration in her face as she worked to free him from the prison of his uniform, lashes flitting and flinching to the tune of her focus.

He felt the pop as the pressure of cloth was released, and Eve's eyes rose again momentarily to accept his telepathic appreciation, before she spun like an adagio dancer, parting her feet on pin-straight legs that towered from her heels like the pillars of a cathedral – slender, toned, slight but muscular.

She bent at the waist and extended her arms out to the sides in cruciform, grasping the back of the couch, crimson nails clawing at the cloth.

She could sense the confounded hesitation mere inches behind her wordless invitation. 'Rip them,' she said, rolling her hips back in encouragement. 'Just tear them off me.'

The unrelenting hem of her skirt cut across her long, sinewy thighs as she rocked her feet further apart, urging him to appropriate her gift.

Gutteridge gently cupped her waist, thumbs lifting the cloth of her blouse clear of her satin skin. He bowed his face down to caress the small of her back with his cheek, feeling the cables of muscle either side of her flexing spine pulse through his lips. He kissed her back, her spine, her obliques, inhaling the saccharine scent of her skin, then slid his hands down her stilettoed spires of heaven to unveil the gifted distraction to a day turned sour.

Eve felt the drag of her skirt being drawn up around her midriff, flexing the small of her back in response, presenting herself. She was already wet, throbbing, full to the touch.

Strong, determined fingers hooked beneath the top of her tights, winding themselves around the sheer fabric in readiness, feeling their velveteen sheen through his fingertips.

Gutteridge turned uncharacteristically superior eyes down to absorb the sight of Eve's overlapping coils of onyx hair spilling down the perfect sweep of her back, using his broiling lust to vent the frustration from his aching heart – like the kraken it had become, feeling it surge, tight through his body, arms and fingers fizzing with the need to unload his vexation at having to relive and replay – like the stuck record it had become – the pain and humiliation of a moment in time of another man's orchestration. A moment in time that refused to allow him to take back control of his emotions, as his insistent hands tensed, solidified, then parted like the Dead Sea at the behest of Moses, tearing the cloth of Eve's clothing like parchment with the force of his anger and resentment, exposing all his drooling, leering, ebullient lust desired as he thrust his anger deep inside the love of his life, always there for him, without fail, without question or complaint, her lissom neck and serpentine spine writhing to the relentless, jarring, rhythmical violation of what she claimed was his, and *only* his, gifted as a token of her commitment to his happiness and contentment as her chosen companion in life. A life that at that very moment seemed to Gutteridge to be filled only with pain and indignity as he drove himself deeper and faster and harder and…

He stopped. Taking a breath. Pausing from the moment. Sensing inside the monster he'd become. Woken from his rage by the muted, barked sounds of affliction and torment that had been forced from Eve's grimacing mouth – an audible silver bullet to his slavering lycanthrope.

His hands – clamping her minuscule waist, thumbs almost touching – relaxed their insistent grip, as he felt the aberration rising within him.

Eve sagged, head lolloping forwards onto the cushions.

'Oh, *Jesus*,' he slurred. 'I'm so sorry,' he said, sliding a tentatively apologetic hand forwards to caress the small of her back. 'I… I didn't… mean—'

Eve swung an arm behind her back to silence him, taking his hand in hers and giving it a reassuring squeeze. 'Shhhhhh,' she insisted. 'Just use me.'

Gutteridge shook his head in silent response, denying the beast within that he knew had surfaced and was feeding off his torment.

'I'm not here to use you,' he said. 'I'm here to *love* you… I just… I don't know what came over me.'

Eve rocked back, pushing onto him, cementing her intentions; affirming *his* intentions. 'Then love me,' she said, sounding meek, but in control. 'I want this. I *need* this,' she said, rolling her face a quarter turn until her blood-red lips were visible to his questionable motives. 'Don't you think these things affect me, too, make *me* insecure?' she whispered. 'Well... they do. So take me, *please* me. Sometimes the best way to tackle a fire is to let it burn itself out.'

Gutteridge allowed a sad but compassionate smile to warm his features. Her mollifying words melted his rage and embarrassment in the flames of their honesty.

He withdrew himself, hooking his hands beneath Eve's outstretched arms and pulled her up straight until her back was tight against his chest.

He brushed aside her hair and delivered a kiss to her neck with all the softness of a landing hover fly.

Her apprehension thawed, relinquishing its grip on her limbs, and she reclined into the attention.

Gutteridge's lips left her neck and moved to her ear. 'No one on this earth could make me as happy as you do,' he whispered. 'I truly don't deserve you.'

Eve spun in his embrace, prompted by his consolatory words and pressed an emphatic kiss to his lips. She read the stoop in his gait and hooked her arms around his muscular neck, swinging her legs clear of the polished oak floor and into the grasp of his waiting hands.

He carried her featherlight frame with ease to the hearth rug and gently lowered her onto her back. Eve unfurled her body like a flower in bloom, skilfully removing her skirt and unbuttoning her blouse, regifting herself in the new light of his affection.

Faced with the vision of Eve lying prone before him – warmed by the licking heat of the flames, his rage muted by feelings of love and devotion – Gutteridge accepted the offer...

*

Gutteridge woke to the sound of an engine roaring and the ceramic hiss of spattering gravel. 'Prick!' he muttered into the mellow light of dawn, bending his eyes to the side to check the time. It was still early and the bed felt warm, Eve lying by his side, still sound asleep, a look of contentment on her face that sang of happy dreams.

The events of the previous night felt strangely distant and unreal, like a nightmare that had evaporated into the light of a new dawn.

It amazed Gutteridge the level of commotion Eve could manage to sleep through – things that would wake him in a second, and as he watched her lying beside him – limbs scattered to the nine winds – he felt the slightest twinge of jealousy that he wasn't capable of the same.

Although it was still relatively dark – the curtains illuminated by a sun that was just beginning to peek above the chilled horizon – he could still make out the majesty of Eve's body, soft light kissing the peaks and highlights of her exquisite construction.

He could see her breathing, the hypnotic heartbeat of her diaphragm concaved into her flawless ribcage, the rise and fall of the rhythm of her sleep mesmerising to his thirsting eyes.

He extended a curious hand and cupped her belly, a belly not yet compromised by the ravages of pregnancy, her skin feeling like a breath from God's own lips – tight but butter soft.

Gutteridge allowed his palm to ride up the crater of her stomach at rest, feeling the slow reciprocating rhythm of her slumber through the heel of his hand. Her pert breasts lay flat and neat, her arms high, hands resting on the pillow either side of a face aglow with quiet contentment – a face not displaying any apparent repercussions of the previous night's trauma.

His eyes wandered to intercostal muscles that flexed like fingers cupping something precious, observing the expansion and contraction of a body in repose, finding eroticism in the witnessing of the mechanics of life – a life he loved, a life he cherished.

'Are you having fun there?' asked a voice: soft, Slavic, playful.

Gutteridge visibly started. Eve was watching him with amused eyes and a subtle, knowing smile that warmed her morning face.

He thought about removing his voyeuristic fingers, but an elongating stretch of the torso invited them to remain and continue their exploration.

Gutteridge loosed a smile and relaxed into the invitation, allowing his hand to glide back down her midriff to her belly.

Eve's eyes slowly closed and her lips parted; inhaling a breath in response to the sensation of his touch.

He cupped her abdomen in his muscular hand and caressed it with his thumb, wondering what a kick from a developing child would feel like through the undulating wall of toned perfection.

Thoughts turned to his son... his fatherless son. Was he asleep; or was he keeping his mother awake? The dearest, darling, other, very *different* love of his life.

Gutteridge waited for the moment where thoughts of his brood killed his passion, but the moment never came. He remained hard and erect, his groin pulsating with the desire to fuck the exquisite creature lying beside him.

He often wondered about his ability to detach feelings of love from a moment of lust – how he allowed that lust to reign unabated, temporarily objectifying the focus of his desires, the way he knew – in reality – most men could. But still... he pondered if such an ability was an indicator of a sociopathic mind. But would a sociopath have struggled for twelve years the way *he* had with the death of his first wife? The answer – he had to conclude – must be 'no'.

A hand grasped Gutteridge's – shocking him out of his musings – and carried it down to the valley between Eve's spreading legs, manipulating his middle and fore fingers clear of the rest and introducing them to an erect clitoris.

Eve's body embowed in spasm and she exhaled a lungful of breath under the pressure of his touch. His fingers parted, curled inwards, and began stirring the temperate moisture of a body primed for copulation.

A groan of pleasure escaped Eve's lips as she stiffened under the force of his attention, writhing to the familiarity of his stroke. Covetous eyes watched as he orchestrated her pleasure like a conductor: his fingers the baton, his intimate knowledge of her body and its pleasure centres his notation, pulled along by the persistence of the moment, aware of the fascinated animal he'd gradually been becoming since their perfect wedding day, allowing his desires – and, dare he say it, perversions – room to flourish unabated. He had explored his wife's impeccable construction, scrutinising her every detail, discovered what worked for her, while obsessing over what worked for him.

Eve's neck lengthened and she rolled her face to the headboard, as she shook and shuddered and barked an untethered cry that filled the room and Gutteridge's ears whilst she coiled beneath his attentive hand.

The shudder and the clamour continued to intensify, incinerating the early-morning calm, crashing through the ceiling at the summit of Eve's unbridled pleasure, before slowly, it subsided, spiralling away to a breathless simper of relief...

But Eve's cries were instantly replaced by another scream that lit the air outside the cottage, decapitating the moment.

Gutteridge quaked at the sound, withdrawing his hand

and leaping from the bed. He strode to the window and parted the curtains to look, the scream having now become the whimpering sobs of someone apparently fractured by terror.

It was darker outside than the glow of the drapes would have suggested, but Gutteridge could still make out the shadow of a woman with a dog, torch in hand, cowering in the middle of the street outside of their home.

The figure noticed him at the window and seemed to be contemplating running. But then she seemed to sense Gutteridge's confusion, and just lifted an uncertain arm and pointed towards the front of the cottage.

Gutteridge pressed his face against the glass, twisting his gaze down to see what the figure was attempting to guide his attention to, but whatever it was sat outside of his limited field of vision.

He suddenly remembered he was naked, but neither he nor the woman seemed to care.

He lifted a hand to the woman, instructing her to wait. She nodded, her demeanour wholly and visibly negative. She looked petrified and Gutteridge's stomach squirmed at the thought of what may have caused such a reaction.

He withdrew from sight to throw on some clothes.

Eve was already dressed. 'What is it?' she asked.

'I don't know. Something. There's a dog walker outside pointing towards the house. I *think* I recognise her, she lives just up the road here, but it's too dark to be sure.'

He swiped his jeans off the chair, slipping them on and grabbing his T-shirt.

Eve rushed from the room. Gutteridge could hear her hurrying downstairs and making for the front door. He finished threading himself into his top as he heard the clack of the locks and the door creep open…

Eve cried out in horror – a sick, putrid, guttural scream that filled the house and shook Gutteridge to his very core. It was a sound like nothing he'd ever heard expel from Eve's lips before, not even when she'd been cowering beneath Kieran O'Leary's captive bolt pistol, awaiting the inescapable conclusion to her life.

Gutteridge thundered across the landing and sprinted downstairs, past Eve who was now sitting on the floor of the hallway, shuffling back from something outside that he could just make out had been bound to the left-hand pillar of the portico that covered the entrance to the cottage.

He slowed, stooping to place a comforting hand on Eve's shoulder as he passed her, his eyes locked on the new addition to their home. He could feel her shaking through his fingers – a very different shake to the one from a few minutes earlier.

He stepped tentatively outside, the cold air hitting him like a slap and he shivered, clocking the woman in the street who was now recognisable beneath a rapidly brightening sky.

Gutteridge stepped cautiously around the mass of whatever it was that was bound to the pillar, trying to make it out in the misty luminescence of dawn.

His eyes gradually adjusted to the low-level light and he could see it was a body, lashed to the post with rope, looking like a scene from Homer's *Odysseus and the Sirens*.

He withdrew his phone from the pocket of his jeans, switching on the torch function, and crouching down, stooped to see the face of whoever it was.

He shuddered in horror and stumbled backwards, nearly falling. Where a face should have been, there was only a hole – a gelatinous crater lined with shattered bone fragments, all set within a lining of congealed blood. Then he noticed the note. *Another* note. Pinned to the chest in readiness for his arrival.

He spun his phone's torchlight around and threw a disbelieving look through the door to Eve. She was now

95

cowering against the far wall, biting the side of her hands, petrified eyes looking straight at his.

He turned back and carefully removed the folded slip of paper from the chest of the victim, and taking an unsteady, anxious breath, opened it...

Oops! I've done it again! My bad – as the kids say.

I believe you two have met? In fact, I distinctly got the impression you even had history together, oh how utterly sweet life can be! She screamed your name, you know, screamed your name, just before I brought an end to her ability to ruin any more lives. How quaint. How touching. How utterly satisfying...

Are you feeling my pain yet? I wonder who I should take next?
M

Gutteridge's eyes instantly turned to Eve, still cowering in the corner of the hallway, curled into a petrified ball like a relic from Pompeii. His mind turned to one all-consuming thought – *get her away from here!*

Gutteridge turned back to the body, his tortured gaze absorbing the blood-spattered details: the smart, tweed suit; the close-cut, manicured nails; the ring-encrusted fingers that lacked a wedding band to complete the set; and the watch – the Baume et Mercier Classima automatic that he knew he'd seen before, and that he *certainly* recognised. This body, it belonged to Kerry Marston.

'It's Kerry Marston,' he whispered, his voice reedy and unsteady. 'She's a reporter. Oh dear God!'

He suddenly remembered the audience, and spun a look to the woman in the street who'd now been joined by a man whose attentive actions towards the dog-walker suggested he was her husband, or partner. 'Did you call it in to the police?' Gutteridge asked.

She nodded, holding her phone up as if it were some kind of evidence of her actions, but the vocal response came from the man by her shoulder. 'She did. They're on their way, now.'

Gutteridge nodded, contemplating the moment. Two deaths in as many days, and all reeking of Jerry Masterson. 'Dear God in heaven!' he slurred into the morning chill. 'He's back… and he's here!'

THIRTEEN

Gutteridge thundered down the M6 at the wheel of Keaton's Renault Megane, ten percent of his attention on the road ahead, the other ninety on the rear view mirror, allowing his paranoia to flourish to keep him sharp and alert.

Eve sat in silence in the passenger seat beside him, wondering just how she should be feeling. She was there only at the insistence of Gutteridge, but at the same time, she knew his reasoning made perfect sense.

Eve began to wonder if life with Gutteridge was always going to be this way, always *this* unstable. 'Exciting' was the word she was attempting to utilise, just to make it more palatable a proposition to contemplate.

Gutteridge had messaged Keaton on WhatsApp to make sure the details of his plan were encrypted, just in case Jerry Masterson – or whoever it was that was doing such a convincing job of copycatting his MO – somehow had access to his tech.

He'd driven around Gloucester for the best part of an hour with Eve and her hastily packed possessions in tow, until he was as sure as he could be that they weren't being followed. He'd arranged a rendezvous at a pre-arranged destination with Keaton – an underground carpark on the west side of town.

They'd covertly swapped vehicles away from prying eyes before Gutteridge set off again, for a very different assignation he'd been forced to hastily arrange. A favour he was owed and was finally cashing in on.

The Renault was eating up the journey in a way that surprised Gutteridge, having always had a disregard for French-built cars.

Keaton was somewhere on the same stretch of highway at the wheel of his Saab, DC Koperek by her side, making their way up to the small town of Buxton in Derbyshire to interview Terrence Masterson – Jerry Masterson's long-suffering brother.

The boys in technical had tracked down Terrence Masterson's mobile number, and he'd agreed to meet Keaton at his Buxton home later in the afternoon.

*

Tired, but as certain as he could be that they hadn't been followed, Gutteridge finally arrived at the sleepy village of Knutsford in the affluent county of Cheshire. He swung the nose of the Renault into the driveway of Toby Jackson's sprawling, nouveau riche property.

He turned a thin-lipped, regretful smile to Eve. 'Are you going to be okay?'

Eve paused to consider the question. They'd hardly exchanged a word the whole way there. She strained a smile to alleviate her husband's obvious concerns, and nodded. 'Of course. I'll be fine.' A lie, because she still had the image of the body dumped at the doorstep of their pretty little home emblazoned on her mind – the arrival of the police, the blue flashing lights, the CSI team picking around the shattered remains of what used to be a person. It was all too similar to her memories of the O'Leary case and she had to fight hard for it not to show.

The door to the picture-postcard barn conversion crept open as Gutteridge pulled in alongside Jackson's lime-green Lamborghini and shut the engine off. The car fell silent, amplifying the awkwardness.

Jackson appeared in the opening, but resisted lifting a hand to wave to the new arrivals. This wasn't a social visit – he knew that much by the tone of the call he'd received.

His Polish wife, Asha – a statuesque appendage to Jackson's enviable life – appeared in the doorway beside him, looping her arm through his, looking every inch like the newlyweds that now they were. Once again – like it had the very first time he'd visited Knutsford during the O'Leary case – it hit Gutteridge just how alike Eve and the angel watching from the doorway were. He was reminded that the Polish vision greeting their arrival was the very reason he and Eve were now an item.

It was Asha's uncanny similarity to Eve that had first prompted Gutteridge to contact his own Polish muse after a period of time starved of her company. And now, over a year on, they were husband and wife.

He loved her and didn't want to lose her – that's why they were here. Their marriage – such that it was after the traumatic events of that morning – would have to be put on hold, at least for now.

Gutteridge gave Eve's hand a fond squeeze, before popping the door and rising into the calming breath of the afternoon breeze.

'Pat,' Jackson called with a lift of the chin from the doorway, by way of greeting. 'Good to see ya.'

Gutteridge attempted a smile, but it felt weird and tortured on his face, like a mask worn to cover his inner anguish.

'Hey, Toby. Good to see you, too,' Gutteridge replied,

'Asha,' he added, nodding a greeting to the angel of the northwest holding Jackson's arm.

He'd been spending a lot of time at Jackson's over the past six months, helping develop a new app to add to Toby's ever-expanding empire of downloadables, and they'd become firm friends during the process, at least, Gutteridge felt it was a friendship, and nothing Jackson did gave him cause to think it was otherwise.

Asha slinked around Jackson's shoulder and crossed the gravel to greet Gutteridge, ever the hostess.

She wrapped her arms around his broad shoulders in what felt like slow motion, her long limbs giving her movements an ethereal elegance like she was floating underwater, swamping him in the warmth of her embrace.

'It's nice to see you,' she said into his ear, her voice almost a whisper.

She peeled off after holding the hug for what felt like a beat too long, then turned and made for Eve, who was now out of the car and smiling across at her. Asha repeated the greeting, and the two began swapping pleasantries in their mother tongue.

Gutteridge recognised some of the words. Since their wedding, he'd been attempting to learn the basics, but his knowledge didn't yet extend far enough to be able to discern what was passing between them. But by the smiles and facial caressing, he knew the words to be amiable.

Asha gathered them both up by looping her arms through theirs. 'Come on you two. Come with me,' she said, escorting them to the doorway, all three stepping in time like a scene from *The Wizard Of Oz*. 'Come and tell us what this is all about.'

There was a heavy oak portico – similar to the one at Gutteridge's cottage – covering the entrance, and Gutteridge saw Eve visibly recoil from the left-hand pillar as she passed beneath it, turning her face away and shutting her eyes.

Gutteridge feared her ever being able to feel comfortable in their home again, their quaint, perfect little home, but at the same time – after her terrifying encounter with O'Leary – he knew her to be as strong and resilient a woman as he'd ever encountered.

As he sauntered up the steps to the door, Gutteridge spun a look past his left shoulder at what appeared to be another vehicle lurking beneath a cover on the far side of the Lamborghini. It was almost as low and wide as the Huracan, and he wondered what particular brand of licence-loser lay in wait beneath the shroud.

He turned his attention back to the door. Jackson was observing his curiosity with a distinct smile twitching at the corners of his lips.

'What's under there?' Gutteridge asked, indicating the new addition with a toss of the head.

'Oh. Nothing. Just another car,' Jackson said, his wry smile growing wryer. 'I'll show it to you, later…'

Toby Jackson dealt drinks to grateful hands and took to his seat. 'So tell me, what's happened?' he asked from the opposite side of the dining table, leaning into the question, genuine concern tugging at his brows. 'Just by the tone of your call I could tell it was bad.'

Asha sat down next to him and looped his arm, mimicking his concern. Eve sat uneasily by her husband's side, happy to let him do the explaining.

Gutteridge gave a clueless sigh as an ice-breaker, pondering where to begin… He fought through his reluctance and took a stab at it. 'While you and me were developing our app, I *must* – at some point – have mentioned one of my old cases? The one that got away?'

Jackson paused for effect and to gather his memories, then nodded. 'You mean the Masterson case?'

Gutteridge requited the nod. 'Yes. The Masterson case.'

'You *did* speak of it. What about it?' Jackson asked.

Gutteridge turned to look at Eve, as if seeking permission to speak of her part in the ordeal. Eve winced an uncertain smile of consent, and he turned his attention back to the fascinated faces watching his tortured attempts at an explanation.

Another pause. 'That case – Jerry Masterson, The Shropshire Ripper – I... *we*, think he might be back, but now he's in Gloucester.' He sighed and sagged. 'He's killed two already, or at least, two that we know of.'

Two shocked faces looked on.

Gutteridge continued. 'The first was a stranger, a young girl, murdered just to get my attention. But the other... the other is, *was*, someone I knew.'

'Someone you knew... Who?' asked Asha.

'Her name was Kerry Marston. She was a reporter, for *The Echo*. I knew her. Knew her pretty well.'

'*Jesus*, Pat!' Jackson hissed.

Eve gave Gutteridge an urging look. He nodded, and sighed.

He continued. 'But that's not all,' he said. 'Her body – Kerry Marston's – was dumped at our house this morning. She'd been bound to one of the pillars of the entrance portico. And there was a note pinned to her chest. A note left intentionally for me.'

'A note?' Asha interjected. 'What did it say?'

Gutteridge took a calming sip of his tea and contemplated the looseness of his tongue. 'I really shouldn't be saying too much at this stage. I've probably said too much already. It's an active case, you understand.'

Jackson tried to mask his disappointment. He'd grown

to care for the two troubled faces sat awkwardly opposite his inflating interest, but this was the most exciting thing he'd encountered since Kieran O'Leary. O'Leary The Spatchcock Killer – had invaded the very house they were all sat in, holding a knife to Asha's defenceless neck just fourteen months previous, before she'd managed to free herself of her restraints, secure a weapon, and fire a single shot that blew through the flat of O'Leary's pleading hand as a thank you for the indignity and humiliation he'd inflicted on the couple, before he'd fled, running into the night, naked save for the clingfilm wrapping he'd applied to thwart the efforts of any subsequent forensics team.

Jackson attempted to push his fizzing intrigue and the thousand questions that sat poised on his tongue to the back of his mind, alive to how inappropriate – under the circumstances – they would be to present.

'So how can I help?' Jackson asked. 'How can *we*, help? What is it you need, my friend? Whatever it is, it's yours.'

Gutteridge turned another look past his shoulder to Eve, drinking in the awkward, back-foot demeanour that met his gaze.

'Can Eve stay with you for a while? Up here, away from Gloucester,' he asked. 'I hate to be a burden, but…'

Jackson peered at Gutteridge in contemplation of his request, attempting to decipher the reasoning. 'Well, of *course*… Of *course* she can stay… But *why?*'

Gutteridge sagged. 'Because Masterson – or whoever it is who's doing such a great job of mimicking his particular brand of insanity – says he, *they*, are going to kill everyone I've ever cared for.' Another look to Eve. 'Anyone I've ever loved…'

Eve attempted a compassionate smile that failed to land, before Gutteridge's attention returned to Jackson's concerned face. 'Revenge killings, you understand. He means to hurt me.'

'*Holy shit!*' slurred Asha, swinging her grey eyes to the side to absorb the mixed look of fear and dejection on Eve's face.

Asha leaned forwards and extended an arm, taking Eve's hand in hers and giving it a squeeze of Slavic solidarity. 'You're very welcome to stay here as long as you like.'

Eve strained an unconvincing smile that still managed to be laced with gratitude and sincerity. '*Dziękuję,*' she said, her voice now little more than a whisper.

'Are *you* staying, too?' Jackson interjected, looking strangely and unexpectedly hopeful.

'No. I've got to get back. Someone needs to catch this psycho.'

Jackson looked visibly disappointed, which warmed Gutteridge's aching soul, before nodding his understanding. 'What about tonight?'

Again, Gutteridge shook a regretful head. "Fraid not. I have to drive back to Gloucester, pretty much straight away...' He seemed to slouch in resignation at the situation he found himself in. 'I'm the one heading up this mess, so it'll be an early start tomorrow.'

Jackson smiled ruefully, flicking a look to Eve. 'We understand. And don't worry, we'll take good care of her.'

Gutteridge winced a joyless smile. 'Thank you, Toby, Asha...'

Jackson spent a moment absorbing the gratitude flavouring the air, before his eyes flitted in the direction of the entrance hallway.

He wondered if this was really a good time, or if it might almost be seen as inappropriate. But Gutteridge looked in need of a lift, they *both* did, so he made a decision he hoped wouldn't backfire.

'Do you have a moment before your leave?' Jackson said. 'There's something I have to show you, something that might help take the sting out of the day.'

Both Gutteridge and Eve exchanged looks of intrigue at

Jackson's cryptic line of questioning. 'Well, yeah. I can give you a few minutes. What is it?'

Asha understood the gist of her husband's encrypted intentions and fizzled at the knowledge of where the conversation was heading.

She and Jackson exchanged looks, then erupted into appropriately reserved, but near child-like excitement.

'Follow me,' Jackson said, barely able to contain himself. 'You both look like you could use some good news.'

He and Asha leapt from their seats and made for the main entrance, waving encouragement for the visitors to follow.

They'd rehearsed this moment and knew each other's roles inside out, and although the timing definitely didn't feel ideal, they felt their 'audience' was in need of a lift, and would react well to their performance.

Eve and Gutteridge rose from the table, gingerly acquiescing, thrown by the sudden change in mood.

Jackson led the procession out of the main door to the front of the house. The sun was out and burning bright, painting the world and all within it a subtle shade of tangerine.

In comparison to the grey light of the morning's events, everything suddenly felt optimistic in the temperate light of the day and the core of Jackson's adolescent buoyancy. The repugnant traumas of the morning felt light years away from the reality that was. Even the air they breathed was scented by the honeysuckle that entwined the pillars of the portico and everything felt light, airy and sanguine.

Jackson led them across the crunching gravel to the garages. He stopped shy of the cars and turned to face them.

'So, our app – *Inspect. Detect. Collect.* has been doing rather well. *Unbelievably* well, in fact, and I'm pleased to say you'll soon be getting the first of many six-monthly royalty cheques as evidence of just *how* well!'

Asha wanted to laugh, well versed – since meeting Jackson – in the experiencing of life-changing moments, imagining the look on Gutteridge's face the moment he draws the cheque from the envelope it'll eventually arrive in. But the situation dictated she arrest her excitement, and attempt to keep things calm and respectful.

'Thing is,' Jackson continued, 'I wanted to say thank you for all of your efforts. A *gift*. Something I know you've been wanting. I certainly wouldn't've been able to produce the app without you and that amazing brain of yours, and for that, I'm grateful.'

Gutteridge could see Asha was close to bursting, but fighting hard to subdue it.

Jackson continued. 'I've seen the way you look at my car and I know how much you liked it when you took it out for a drive. So to say thank you, I got you one of these.'

He turned, and stooped to grab the corner of the sheet covering the vehicle that Gutteridge had clocked on their arrival, whipping it back to reveal what Gutteridge recognised to be a Ferrari F430 in gleaming Rosso paint.

The horrors of the day momentarily evaporated, and Gutteridge even felt compelled to allow himself a smile, despite it feeling wrong in light of the recent death of someone who – in this odious reality – had been way more than an acquaintance.

Jackson continued. 'Now, I know – given everything you've just described – this isn't an ideal time, but I figure, with a job like yours, when is it *ever* going to be an ideal time?'

Gutteridge smirked at the truth in Jackson's words. 'Toby. It's amazing!' he said, allowing himself a moment to languish in the dream-come-true-moment. A perfect antidote to the nightmare he was presently living. 'I mean. I don't know what to say. It's… It's amazing!'

Eve unstuck her feet from the gravel and sauntered over to

the blood-red creation sat crouched on the driveway, looking every bit like an animal stalking its prey. She brushed the car's exquisite lines with her long fingers as she circled it, absorbing its aggressively penned, exaggerated curves. '*To jest piękne*,' she muttered.

Asha smiled. 'It is, and it's all yours,' she said. 'I just wish we were handing it to you under different circumstances.'

Gutteridge turned a muted but genuine smile towards Asha's words. 'That's life, I guess. Doesn't prevent this from being a bit of a dreamy moment. A *nice* moment, I mean, it's a bloody *Ferrari*, I've always wanted one, ever since I was a kid. But are you *sure*?'

'I couldn't be surer,' said Jackson, his response immediate and in no need of contemplation. 'You know,' he continued, 'the way the downloads and the analytics are looking, you might even be able to retire... Leave this job that seems to me to be the font of all of your problems.'

Gutteridge let that thought percolate, feeling Eve's eyes watching him for a reaction to a suggestion he was almost certain she'd find desirable. 'Retire...' he murmured, as if the word was redundant to a life like his. He sniggered. 'Who knows... Maybe.'

'Anyway,' Jackson clucked. 'I'll get it shipped to yours as soon as a transporter becomes available.'

Jackson's words woke Gutteridge from his dream-like state, reality stepping back in to deliver a kick to the only good thing that had happened to him since his wedding day.

'You might have to leave it a week,' he explained. 'Our house is effectively a crime scene, until the CSI team have finished their sweep and it's been officially released.'

Jackson slouched in solidarity, and blinked. 'No problem, brother, just text when it's released, and I'll organise it. Anyway, come on, let's get Eve installed in one of the guest bedrooms.'

He looked to Asha who, by now, was stood on Eve's shoulder, also admiring the car. 'The one overlooking the south gardens?' he suggested.

Asha broke from the moment of shared admiration to consider his suggestion. 'Yes. I think so,' she agreed – knowing that the room adjoining that one was the one Gutteridge and Keaton had shared on their night of intimacy, and figuring it appropriate that Eve sleep in a bed where *that* hadn't happened. 'That one would be just perrrfect.'

Jackson moved towards the Renault and popped the boot, his demeanour purposefully jaunty in an attempt to lift the mood. 'Are all these bags yours?' he asked Eve.

She smiled at the welcome attention. 'Yes, and there's one more on the back seat, but I can grab that.'

He loaded himself with cases and turned to Gutteridge. 'I'll go and get Eve settled in – why don't you have a look around your new toy?' He turned a smile across at Eve. 'Come on, you. You follow me,' he chirped, before setting off in the direction of the house.

Eve followed a beat behind, tucking her hair behind her ear and turning a coy smile back at Gutteridge as she climbed the steps.

Asha watched them leave, hovering until they were out of sight and she was sure it would remain that way, before grabbing Gutteridge's hand and towing him past his new toy into the second doorway of the paddock of garages.

Gutteridge stumbled in behind her, surprised both by her actions and her willowy strength.

The space was lined floor-to-ceiling with motoring memorabilia from every perceivable decade: Ferrari and Lamborghini flags; F1 steering wheels peppered with knobs and buttons; vintage fuel cans; tin signage from yesteryear; wheels; helmets; framed overalls.

Asha led him to the back corner with an insistent pull towards a fully stocked Snap-On tool chest, far away from the entrance and out of sight of the house. She backed him into the corner and stopped, turning to front him, but said nothing. Her hunting eyes looked deep into his, face a picture of worry. He wondered what she could possibly be searching for, what she was expecting to find in his own expression?

With two, deep, urgent breaths, she finally broke her silence. 'Are you in danger?' she said, her voice soft but laced with concern, lifting a solitary hand to cup his cheek.

Gutteridge was taken aback by the unprompted display of tenderness, nearly recoiling from the touch. But he didn't, and was surprised to find himself leaning into it.

He'd developed what could politely be called 'a thing' for this woman, since the first time he'd met her during the O'Leary case. A shared, unspoken bond that simmered beneath the surface ever since that first encounter. But now, faced with danger, once again, it was resurfacing.

Gutteridge shook his head. 'I don't know? I guess so...'

Asha's caressing hand enveloped his cheek, and he could feel the tenderness emanating from her fingertips.

'Then stay here. With us. Away frrrom danger.'

Gutteridge smiled weakly through the worries he *himself* had been denying. 'Asha. I can't... I wish I could.'

An unexpected tear erupted from the corner of her eye and careened down her cheek. A tear apparently shed for him. A tear that warmed his aching heart.

'Then prrromise me you'll be careful.'

Gutteridge winced a confused but genuine smile, lifting a finger to clear the droplet from the delicate sweep of her jaw. 'I promise.'

Asha turned her ear towards the door, seemingly listening for the crunch of approaching footsteps.

110

Gutteridge gazed at her profile, straight-lined and elegant. The long, flat bridge of her nose and the way it cut back and dropped to the prominent ridge of her upper lip, breathtaking in its subtle simplicity.

Satisfied that there was no one approaching, Asha turned her attention back to Gutteridge, a concerned expression returning to her face that was now just inches from his own.

Her hand was still on his cheek, but it felt so natural he hadn't noticed. The other one raised to mirror it. She entered his desires with her penetrating gaze – tentative and apprehensive.

'If anything should happen to you...' she whispered, before – after a beat – leaning in and pressing her lips against his – soft, velvet pillows of affection bonding to his soul, and all the care and passion she'd held for this man over the preceding months migrated into his body from hers, carried in on a wave of unexpected passion that soaked through him like a sinking mist, both of them growing high on the stolen moment.

Their lips finally parted, but they both lingered in the aftermath, letting it sink in.

Gutteridge felt like he'd had full, untethered sex with the woman who was now stood assessing his reaction, her sensuous grey irises flitting from one confused eye to the other, looking to see if her moment of abandonment would backfire.

She drew in a breath, seeming unsure, but also like she was actively seeking an opportunity to tell all. 'I couldn't stand it if you got hurt,' she muttered, the look of pain in her expression so unexpected. 'And if I'm honest with myself, I think... I...'

Gutteridge cut her off. 'Shhhh. Don't say it,' he whispered, brushing the backs of his fingers across her face. A smile. A knowing blink. 'Why don't we just feel it... *know* it... but leave it unsaid.'

Another small tear broke rank. She smiled at his words and

at the knowledge that she wasn't alone in this, the corners of her lips quivering with frustrated joy. She nodded. 'Okay...'

The sound of crunching footsteps and chirpy banter drifted through the open door.

Gutteridge stooped to quickly clear away Asha's tears with his thumb, taking a moment to assess his handiwork. 'There,' he said, smiling. 'Beautiful.'

He leaned in and deposited a kiss on her cheek before quickly turning and pulling open one of the drawers of the tool chest.

'Blimey!' he barked. 'He's got all the gear hasn't he,' he said, just as Jackson and Eve sauntered in from the blinding sunlight. 'Oh. *There* you are,' Gutteridge clucked. 'What the hell have you both been doing? I was beginning to suspect infidelity!'

Asha couldn't help but snort at his blatant cheek like an amused child – his often dry and witty humour the one thing she wished Toby had a little more of.

'Didn't you know?' said Jackson, engulfing Eve's shoulder in a pally embrace. 'This has been going on for weeks, months even. You're not going to arrest me, are you?'

Gutteridge smirked. 'There isn't a jail cell large enough for your ego.'

Jackson let out a laugh that filled the garage, before dousing it, and turning respectfully mournful. 'Is everything going to be alright?'

Gutteridge softly closed his lids and nodded. 'It'll be fine... *I'll* be fine.'

'We hope so,' Asha added, smiling ruefully up at him, exchanging telepathic confirmation of what had just passed between them.

Jackson extended an invitational arm towards his wife. 'Shall we? Leave these two lovebirds alone. Let them say their goodbyes?'

Reluctantly, Asha floated away from Gutteridge's side, her grey, feline eyes looking back at him.

Gutteridge could see the loss and longing in her stare, desperately hoping the others couldn't. He turned back to the tool cabinet to shut the drawer, stealing the chance to wipe his mouth clear of evidence of a kiss that he wasn't even sure had happened.

He turned back just as Eve arrived by his side, taking Asha's place. Her tumbling black hair popped in the sunlight behind her shoulders, casting her face in back-lit shadow, illuminating her features like the ethereal glow of an eclipsing moon.

Sultry eyes cut through his swimming guilt. She flicked a momentary glance to the blood-red Ferrari sitting on the driveway behind her. 'Almost makes it all worth it, doesn't it?' she said, returning her admiring glance back to her husband. She laughed, if a little forced. 'You have a Ferrari!'

Gutteridge flashed brows and joined in the levitous mirth. 'I know. Doesn't feel real. Didn't see that coming! And it's *we…* *we* have a Ferrari.'

Eve flicked a second look behind her, but this time more in the direction of the house. 'She likes you, you know – Asha. I see it in the way she looks at you.'

Gutteridge forced an amused frown, shaking his head in mock bewilderment. Eve shrugged at the apparent doubt in his response, her face contemplative. 'She's very beautiful. Do I have anything to worry about?'

Gutteridge knew that denial of the statement would smack of insincerity, so chuckled in solidarity of her opinion. 'She sure *is* beautiful. They don't come much more beautiful than Asha.'

Eve's face dropped, wounded by his response.

Gutteridge quelled the frivolity in his reply and coloured serious. 'But they do come *as* beautiful, and when you marry

113

that to feelings of love, that beauty intensifies,' he said, gently hooking her delicate jaw with his finger and lifting her eyes to meet his. 'Nothing on this earth could overshadow you. Not even *that* Ferrari,' he joked, darting his eyes towards the new addition to their life. 'But I'll certainly heed the warning. I couldn't handle *two* Polish princesses chasing me around the countryside.'

Eve smiled at his words, and leaned in to kiss him.

Gutteridge feared Eve tasting Asha on his lips. He'd been licking them to try to dilute the evidence of his wrongdoing, but his wife tasted so good in the light of the loneliness he knew he was going to feel at her absence, he threw caution to the wind and wrapped himself around her slight frame to absorb the feeling and flavours of her love and devotion.

The familiar taste of her favourite brand of lipstick mixed with the tang of her breath, filled his lungs with an erotic tincture that boiled his blood, and he wanted to hoist her onto the bench top behind him and fuck her until she screamed out to the world they commanded.

Eve drew in a chestful of breath through her flaring nostrils and broke from the kiss. She held her husband's face in her delicate hands and peered into him, telepathically transmitting all the emotions she had, has, and will ever feel for him through eyes alight with the flames of devotion.

'You'd better get going,' she said, straightening his collar and thumbing his lips clear of evidence she dearly wanted him inside her, but this was not the time, *or* the place, and she would have to ignore the fact that Gutteridge's clothes were laced with Dior Eden-Roc — £350 a bottle and Asha's favourite scent.

They ambled over to the Ferrari and stopped to consider it. It finally hit home to Gutteridge that it was his. 'Holy shit!' he muttered. 'We have a Ferrari.'

Eve laughed, the terrors of the morning now seeming

almost like a distant memory. But she knew they weren't, and would always exist in her very worst nightmares, with Kieran O'Leary and his captive bolt pistol never too far behind.

FOURTEEN

'LEFT AT THE JUNCTION, then follow the road around to the right,' DC Koperek said, consulting her phone. 'Not too much further now.'

DS Keaton scanned the staggered rows of gritstone brick houses lining the streets. Although stained dark grey from decades of existing in a bustling town, they still managed to look quaint and idyllic.

'Interesting place,' Keaton said. 'There's an area in the centre built to mimic a pier with a promenade – like you're at the seaside. I guess it's a remnant from the Victorian era?'

Koperek leaned into the windscreen and joined in the admiration. 'I wish we had time to pay *that* a visit, sounds fun. It seems like a nice area. As remote as it is, I think I could happily live here.'

Keaton sniggered, considering the multitude of downsides to city living. 'Me too,' she agreed.

'Oh, take a left!' Koperek barked, returning her attention to her phone.

Keaton swung the nose of the Saab into a side street.

'Sorry, too busy gawping,' Koperek mewed. 'It's just a mile up here on the right.'

Keaton nodded, turning mute and pensive. She was about to meet the brother of a notorious serial killer, and she suddenly felt exposed and decidedly vulnerable at not having Gutteridge by her side.

'So, tell me again, why am I here instead of Gutteridge?' Koperek asked, as if able to hear Keaton's thoughts. 'I know you've told me already, but I didn't really take it in, too busy checking the route.'

Keaton inhaled a breath and raised delicate brows in contemplation of the explanation she herself was given.

'Two reasons: firstly, after what happened this morning, Gutteridge is transporting Eve away from danger, to some out of the way, secret location that he hasn't even told *me* about.'

'He hasn't told *you*?'

'Nope.'

Koperek let that sink in. 'Understandable, I suppose, given what a shameless gossip you are,' Koperek joked. 'And the other reason?'

'Because apparently, Terrence Masterson doesn't hold Gutteridge in very high regard. Bizarrely, he blames Pat for the death of his mother.'

'He blames *Gutteridge*? Why? What's he supposed to have done?'

Keaton shrugged. 'Well, she apparently committed suicide after it all surfaced that her son was The Shropshire Ripper.'

'Don't see how that can have been Gutteridge's fault?'

'Nor can anyone else, including me, but you know how people can be. Gutteridge also said this guy likes the girls, so thought sending you and me, us being – according to Gutteridge – the 'lookers' of the squad, might just help in our quest to loosen his tongue.'

Koperek's face crumpled in mild protest. 'A bit sexist, isn't it?'

Keaton's shoulders hopped another noncommittal shrug. 'Maybe? Or perhaps it's purely the best and most efficient way to get the case solved quicker?'

Koperek see-sawed an acknowledging head. 'You might be right. Anyway, what are we trying to extract from this guy?'

'The main thing we're trying to find out is if Terrence Masterson has had any contact with his brother since he went to ground. That would confirm he's still with us, and at least go some way to ruling out a copy cat.'

'But hasn't it been over a decade? If he *was* still alive, how has he never been caught?'

Another clueless shrug. 'Gutteridge says it'd always been assumed that Jerry Masterson had committed suicide, and that his body has simply never been discovered.'

'The bodies of suicides always turn up,' scoffed Koperek.

'Not necessarily. What if the remains had been picked apart by wildlife before anyone had a chance to find them? Or what if Masterson knew of a cave, or an old abandoned bunker, or a waste pipe, or threw himself off a boat in the middle of an ocean? The possibilities are endless.'

Koperek turned her attention out of the side window, reflecting on Keaton's reasoning. 'I suppose so. Still seems weak.'

Keaton laughed. 'I know. I might actually agree with you. Just playing devil's advocate.'

Koperek smirked, before turning animated. 'Stop! This is it,' she said, indicating a mid-terraced house sat high on a bank on the right.

Keaton leaned a look up at the house as they cruised by, then pulled in to a space twenty yards further on and shut the engine off.

This certainly didn't *look* like the home of the brother of a notorious serial killer, but what was that supposed to look like anyway? Purposefully morose? Suitably gloomy? A black-light beacon to warn the world that beneath this roof lives a man who had the audacity to spring forth from the same womb as someone who slaughtered twelve women?

Keaton was well aware that she would have to push any of her own prejudices aside, that here lives a man who blames Gutteridge for his mother's death – she had to walk through that door with an analytical mind tuned only to gathering information. Not an easy task when the subject of the accusation is not only your partner, but also the father of your child – and when you add the confused and questionable feelings of love into the equation!

Keaton spun her attention back to Koperek. 'So, we have to tread carefully. It isn't out in the public domain yet, that his brother might be killing again.'

'Understood,' Koperek said with an exaggerated nod.

'Besides, it's possible that no one in the area knows this guy's identity. That's why he moved here from Shropshire in the first place, to start over again. So no talking to neighbours. Let's treat this like it's a standard, periodic reopening of an old, unsolved case, and that we're simply going over old ground with fresh eyes to see if we can't discover new leads.'

Again, Koperek nodded.

'Come on then. Let's get this done. Grab this fucker's ankles and see what we can shake from his pockets.'

Koperek laughed. 'Aye, aye, boss.'

After two choruses of what – in the scheme of things – felt like inappropriately melodic chimes of the bell, the door crept open, revealing an unexpectedly impressive man clad in corduroy pants and a light cotton T-shirt.

The sunlight from behind their shoulders caught the hairs of his close-cut beard. They could see him attempting to smile through his obvious annoyance at being disturbed.

'Mr Masterson?' Keaton asked, but knowing her assumption to be likely based on grainy newspaper photos she'd seen previously and Gutteridge's own description.

'Indeed,' came the reply. Masterson's eyes seemed to sparkle at the sight of the two attractive females stood on his doorstep, then appeared to snap from his musings as if disconcerted by his own neglect of the basic rules of etiquette. 'Why don't you both come in?'

He stepped aside by way of invitation, letting them pass, his gaze following their polite acceptance of the offer.

Keaton could feel Terrence Masterson's eyes upon her, wondering if that should trouble her, or not?

Masterson shut the door behind them. 'Go through into the living room,' he said, wafting a nonchalant hand towards a door on the left.

Keaton led the way, stepping into a room that was sparsely decorated with a single armchair and two balloon-backed dining chairs positioned directly facing it.

Keaton turned a curious look back at Masterson.

'You've come at a bad time if you want to be comfortable,' he chuckled. 'I'm just in the process of redecorating the whole place. I've only just had house clearers in two days ago taking all the old tat away, and the new stuff doesn't arrive for another week.' His eyes turned distant and thoughtful. 'We all need a change sometimes, don't we?'

Keaton popped a contemplative smile, her thoughts turning to her son. 'I guess so.'

Masterson reemerged from his introspection, and lowered his large frame into the armchair, extending an arm that invited the visitors to join him.

Keaton and Koperek followed his lead, taking out pads and pens as they sat, shuffling to get comfortable.

'So, what's this all about?' Masterson asked, flicking his

attention between the two faces examining him. 'As if I couldn't guess.'

Koperek turned a look to Keaton, establishing *her* as the lead for the interview. Masterson took the hint, and locked his eyes on Keaton's.

Keaton held a granite stare directed at Masterson, contemplating his manner. *What did he mean by, 'as if I couldn't guess'? Did he know something? Or was it simply a reference to this being about the 'same old case, same old questions'?* she wondered.

She couldn't risk asking, because then he'd *realise* there was a specific reason for their 120-mile trek across the countryside of England – something *more*, something *greater*, something *new*.

'We're simply going over cold cases to reassess the evidence, to see if it leads us down any new paths that were missed. I'm sure we've all been here before.'

Masterson laughed, ironically. 'Indeed we have. Tea?' he asked, preparing to stand. 'Before we get fully into it?'

'No, thank you,' Keaton said, smiling weakly at the offer, avoiding the very real risk of being poisoned. 'We're fine.'

Masterson sank back into his seat and settled again.

Keaton took a moment to explain that anything he said would be admissible as evidence, whilst at the same time trying to play it down to keep the conversation casual. She then consulted her scribbled notes.

'If I could just start by asking – and I'd like to stress, I've been instructed to advise that you wouldn't be in any trouble if the answer came back as a "yes", but since your brother went on the run, have you had any contact with him? Any contact at all, either directly or through a third party?'

Masterson held his flat, mannequin stare at Keaton, the only perceptible movement being a flicker at the corners of his mouth – a knowing, mocking smile that threatened to betray his poker face. He lifted his chin from the core of his contemplation of Keaton's intentions to deliver his well-rehearsed answer. 'No, I haven't.' His eyes pinched back at her, intrigued. 'But if I had, do you *really* think I'd be dumb enough to sit here and persecute myself?'

'That depends,' Keaton said, 'on whether you've got anything to hide.'

Masterson smirked again, seeming to find amusement in their corporate facades. He lifted a deliberately flamboyant hand to his mouth and coughed theatrically through a tunnel of fingers in readiness to deliver his reply. 'No. I have not had any contact with my brother.' His response was curt, sarcastic, and mocking of the seriousness of the question.

Keaton closed her pad and stowed the pencil in its slip, a move she'd learned from Gutteridge. A move that seemed to project an air of heightening seriousness, whilst also suggesting that what was about to pass between both parties was off the record – which, of course, it wasn't.

'Do you *agree* with what your brother did?' Keaton asked. 'Because from where *I'm* sitting, it seems you do?'

Masterson smiled again, an amused smile, a contemplative smile. Then his face turned stern, adamant and solemn. 'What my brother did was unforgivable. Unforgivable and worthy of a death-sentence.'

Keaton considered the response. '*Is* he dead?' she asked.

Masterson leaned forward in his seat, resting his elbows on his knees. Keaton had to resist recoiling from this new closeness.

'Jerry Masterson killed twelve people,' he began.

'Twelve *women*,' Keaton corrected. Masterson's continual use of the third person not going unnoticed – she assumed to put distance between himself and his brother's actions.

Masterson's eyes flashed with irritation. 'Okay… twelve *women*. Is it *your* belief that their deaths were undeserved and that the victims themselves were in any way blameless?'

Keaton had to check she'd heard him right. 'Well, of course.'

'Why?' Masterson replied, without pause.

'What?'

'*Why*? What mechanism are you using to judge that?'

Keaton shot him a deliberately scolding look. 'What mechanism am I using to judge whether the murder of twelve innocent girls was wrong? Are you being serious?'

Masterson leaned in further, Keaton recoiling from his advancing wall of intimidation. 'I've never been more serious in my life, and for your information, no one's innocent.'

Keaton stuttered under the pressure of the moment and the surrealism of the exchange. She wished Gutteridge was there to interject and shut Masterson down with one of his famous, life-learned snippets of wisdom, but he wasn't – she was alone in this.

'Because it's wrong?' a voice added from somewhere else in the room. It was Koperek. In the haze of Masterson's hostility, Keaton had forgotten she was even there.

Masterson redirected his attention to the new contributor. 'Ahh, it speaks,' he hissed, sarcastically. 'Welcome to the party.'

Koperek and Keaton exchanged glances. They looked and felt out of their depth.

Koperek stiffened her resolve again. 'I said, because it's wrong.'

Masterson shrugged and reclined in his chair like the conceited emperor that, in his own mind, he was. 'What *is* "wrong"?' he asked.

'The opposite of right,' Keaton snapped.

Masterson turned his eyes back to Keaton, considering her response. 'And what *is* "right"?' He sat forward again. 'Isn't it all relative? Isn't that the reality that we're all supposed to feign ignorance of?'

The two detectives exchanged glances again.

Masterson continued, now completely immersed in his own discourse. '*Everything's* relative – an endless stream of comparisons of one thing against everything else.' He shuffled in his seat, bedding in for his sermon. 'Did God not supposedly create Adam and Eve in his image, and then gift them paradise to live in, but at the behest of his unreasonable rules and intolerable restrictions? A questionable gift for his supposed kindness in creating them with a propensity to yield to temptation – before placing them next to a tree laden with apples and saying "eat no apples". But what *is* paradise? Without the means or opportunity to compare it to anything else, it doesn't exist as anything other than itself. You can't know heaven, if first, you haven't experienced hell.'

'And your point is…?' Keaton asked, her gaze hard and unyielding.

'The point *is*, if you don't know *right*, how can you – with any level of accuracy – be expected to judge *wrong*?'

Keaton frowned, giving the comment time to percolate. 'That doesn't mean anything.'

Masterson reclined again, pausing for effect. 'Do you think that when an alligator clamps its jaws around the windpipe of a wildebeest, it considers if its actions are right or wrong? Good or bad? Godly or ungodly? Or do you think, maybe, it's just doing what comes naturally to it, in order to survive?'

'Your brother didn't do what he did to survive. He did what he did because he was *perverted*,' Koperek snapped.

Masterson looked briefly offended at the interruption, before visibly pulling back from his annoyance. 'Hungry, perverted. What's the difference?'

Keaton stepped in again. 'The difference *is*, you *need* to kill when you're hungry.'

'Well I suggest the evidence would *seem* to indicate that you *need* to kill when you're perverted.'

Keaton caught herself smiling, almost enjoying this back and forth. 'At the end of the day, isn't this a justification argument?'

'Clarify?'

'The alligator is *justified* in succumbing to actions that are motivated by hunger, Jerry Masterson isn't... *wasn't*... justified in killing simply to feed a sexual perversion.'

Masterson sat in what felt to Keaton like inappropriately comfortable silence for a while, the mechanics of his mind just perceptible behind his unforgiving gaze. 'Feed... hunger... all words from the same pot, wouldn't you say?'

Koperek joined the debate again. 'I thought you just said that what your brother did was worthy of a death sentence? So why this needless arguing about a point you *seem* to claim we agree on?'

'Awww, don't spoil my fun,' Masterson smarmed, pouting at her complaining like a ridiculing juvenile.

Keaton steeled herself, loading her tongue with a bullet of a question. 'Did you ever assist your brother in the killings?'

Keaton's directness hit Masterson like a punch. He reeled back from the question with a belly laugh that filled the empty void between them, startling both detectives.

'Is that what you've come here with? Is that *really* all you've got?' He leaned in again, his nose now only inches from Keaton's. 'Write this down,' he said, flicking a cursory glance down at her pad. 'Jerry Masterson killed twelve people; Terrence Masterson wasn't involved. Okay?'

He leaned out of the huddle again, and gave an obviated look about the room. 'Where is Gutteridge, anyway? Why is *he* not here?'

'Because you said on the phone that you didn't want to see his "sanctimonious fucking face",' Keaton answered.

Masterson chuckled, then switched to austere. 'And since

125

when did Gutteridge do *anything* simply because it was requested? If he had, he'd have gone and fucked himself long ago.'

Keaton shrugged. 'Maybe he's mellowing in his advancing years.'

The words, 'advancing years' brought thoughts of the cancer that was eating him from the inside out to Masterson's mind. 'And how is the tosser – leading a happy life?'

Keaton and Koperek shuffled, swapping awkward glances, memories of the body dumped at his Gloucester home strong in their thoughts.

Masterson narrowed his eyes, his lower lids licking at his irises. 'And what was behind *that* look?' he frowned, supping on the unease infesting the room. His eyes pinched. 'What's going on here? Has something happened? Is that why you've suddenly materialised?' He reclined again, contemplating their awkward manner. His brows flickered, then solidified. 'You said "*isn't*".'

'What?'

'You said, "Jerry *isn't* justified", then quickly changed it to *wasn't*. Is Jerry active again? Is *that* what's happening?' A look of bright, cold, realisation spread across his face like a wildfire. 'He is! Isn't he? He's active again. *That's* why you're here. Right?'

The silence that met the question answered it. '*Myyy* God. What's he done now?'

'You're asking like you *know* he's still alive,' Keaton said.

'And *you're* acting like you suspect he *is*,' Masterson responded.

Screaming silence filled the room again. 'Go on,' Masterson prodded. 'What's he done?'

'You know very well we can't go into details like that, not at this stage.'

'But it's bad, isn't it?' he asked, looking strangely excited by the prospect.

Keaton flashed brows. 'You could say that.'

'Bodies?'

A pause from Keaton. 'Two.'

'Who?'

'Can't say,' Keaton muttered.

Silence engulfed the fizzing atmosphere again.

A smell hit Keaton's nose, a smell that had first landed the moment she walked through the door. A strange, oily sweetness that she couldn't quite place. Not wholly unpleasant, just unnatural in such a setting and indicative of decay. Looking about the place – sparse, but well kept – it didn't seem likely that it was the musty smell of long-term neglect.

'So, two bodies have surfaced?' Masterson said, looking distant, his booming voice making Keaton lurch from her musing. 'What leads you to believe it was my brother?'

Keaton dragged her attention back into the room. 'If I tell you, I want you to promise it goes no further than these four walls.'

Masterson nodded. 'Not a problem. No one in this town knows who I am, or the cunt I'm related to, and I'd much prefer it to stay that way.'

Keaton fell silent for a beat, trying to judge Masterson's reliability.

She decided to throw caution to the wind. 'Two things lead us to suspect your brother: the MO, and notes left at the scene,' she said.

Masterson's eyes crimped quizzically. 'Addressed to who?'

A pause. 'Detective Gutteridge.'

Masterson giggled like an excited child. 'Jerry was always the vindictive one.'

Koperek's eyes darkened. 'I'm glad you find the deaths of two innocent women amusing.'

Masterson ceased laughing, turning pensive and reflective,

almost philosophical in his manner. 'When you've lived with this for as long as *I* have, you learn simply to laugh to dam all the other emotions.'

That smell emerged again, tickling the membrane at the back of Keaton's nose. 'Mr Masterson, would it be at all possible to use your bathroom?' Keaton asked. 'It's not our usual protocol, but the drive here was a long one—'

Masterson lifted a hand to cut her off. 'Of course. It's just upstairs on the right. You can't miss it.'

Keaton stood. 'Thank you.' She smiled, handing her notes to Koperek, indicating some questions of lesser importance. 'Why don't you carry on with these, and I'll be as quick as I can.'

Keaton crossed the room to the door as Masterson watched, transfixed by the slender, almost Mucha-esque sweep of her hips, and the way the pants of her trouser suit cupped her glutes so tightly that he could see every muscular oscillation that powered her seductive walk.

'Do you work out?' Masterson asked.

Keaton stopped shy of the door and turned to face the remark... 'What?'

'You... Do you work out? You're in *fantastic* shape.'

Koperek leaned back out of the line of fire of the exchange, and spun glances between the two in the room with her, feeling like neither of them was alive to her presence. A fly on the wall, so to speak.

'I'm not sure how that's relevant, but *yes*, I work out, about four times a week.'

Masterson winced a smile that, on the face of it, looked passive, but Keaton could sense a sliding air of sexual aggression emanating off him.

'You look good,' he said, his wandering eyes scanning her stomach, her breasts, the fitted shirt that clung tight around her waist. 'I just think hard work and dedication should be applauded.' He grinned an empty grin, and Keaton left the room…

'What the *fuck*,' Keaton hissed under her breath as she made for the stairs. They creaked under the load of her featherweight footsteps, whilst her curious eyes scanned the surprisingly empty space, looking for signs that this house was, or ever had been, lived in.

As she climbed the treads, the landing area up ahead hoved into view at eye-level.

Keaton's gaze swept the floor for evidence of dust rings and the walls for sun-bleached paint-fade – anything that might indicate that furniture had once graced this house.

The smell came again – stronger, sweeter. The kind of smell that a nose could become accustomed to over time, but still, one that could be considered unpalatable and certainly alien to what's normal to find in a home.

She stepped onto the landing and saw the bathroom to her right. She leaned an ear back towards the stairwell again to listen. She could hear Koperek's voice – forthright and efficient.

Keaton spun in the space, sniffing the air. The smell seemed to be getting stronger as she moved further along the landing.

She stepped softly, opening and closing the door to the bathroom with an obvious *bang* as she passed it.

There was a bedroom ahead – a single bed the only thing in the entire room. She leaned in and sniffed, but the scent here seemed weaker.

There was another door hanging ajar to her left and she stepped quietly through it. It was dark; the single window in the far corner of the room had its curtains pulled shut. She felt around the wall by the door until her fingers found a switch, flicking it on.

A single, insipid bulb flashed awake, illuminating a

dumping ground for miscellaneous belongings from times been and gone. The smell seemed much stronger in here: saccharine, organic, unpleasant.

Keaton lunged gingerly into the space, stepping softly, scanning for anything that might emit such an unpalatable odour. There was a large, wooden blanket box in the opposite corner by the window. She threaded herself carefully through the islands of junk and crouched. Carefully, she opened the lid, expecting to find something unpleasant that would make her recoil and wretch, but nothing – just old clothes and a random selection of hand tools.

She quietly closed it and stood again, darting a look back towards the door, listening for any tell-tale creak from the stairs, but all was quiet, she was still alone.

Then something in her peripheral vision caught her attention – a stain on the ceiling that looked to have been hurriedly painted over, an oblong smut on the purity of the paintwork like grease and oil soaking into the plaster.

Keaton crossed the room and stepped in to look closer. She rifled through her pockets while her eyes remained glued to the stain, and found a petrol receipt.

She stretched up on tip-toes and swiped it a few times against the plaster until there was a nice, thumbprint-sized grease spot soaking the fibres of the paper.

She resisted carrying it to her nose, instead folding it in on itself a few times and slipping it back into her pocket, wiping her fingers clean on her trousers.

The smell was much stronger here, putting her gag reflexes on high alert. Keaton outstretched her arms and positioned herself directly beneath the stain, which seemed slightly longer than the reach of her fingertips – about the length of a man… Her mind turned to one thought, and one thought alone – *get the fuck away from here!*

She quickly pulled her phone from her pocket, unlocked it and tapped the camera function. She was surprised to find that her hands were shaking. She stepped back and took a few photos, then looked around and saw an A4 refill pad lying atop some boxes. She tore off a blank page, licked it, and stuck it on the wall near the stain for size reference.

She fired off a few more shots for good measure and pocketed her phone, making for the door after quickly peeling the A4 sheet off the wall and stuffing it in her back pocket.

Keaton walked gingerly across the landing to the bathroom, quietly opening the door, slipping through it and nudging it shut behind her.

She inhaled a deep, deliberate breath, feeling the sick inducing quiver of her diaphragm in her chest. She exhaled the sensation away, and spun on the taps, washing her hands as clean as she could without the luxury of soap.

She assessed herself in the mirror... 'It could be anything,' she muttered, 'anything at all.' But she couldn't reason away that smell – light, pungent, but definitely alien. Maybe not the unholy stench of a freshly decomposing body, but something that sent alarm bells ringing in the deepest, primordial recesses of her psyche.

Her attention returned to the mirror. She spent a moment straightening herself and regaining her composure, before stretching out an arm and flushing the toilet.

She opened the door to make her way back downstairs to rejoin the others, drawing the phone from her pocket again and opening the settings menu. She scrolled to sound options, ring volume, and moved the slider on the screen ever so slightly with her thumb.

Her phone rang out, fracturing the silence. She let it sing for two bars before closing the menu and pretending to answer it. 'Keaton,' she said as she thumped down the staircase. 'Yes,

131

sir… Okay,' she said to no one. 'Copy that. We're just finishing up here. We'll be on our way now.' She feigned swiping the phone off even though no one was watching to see it, jogging down the last few steps and turning into the living room.

Two faces with questioning looks turned to observe her arrival.

'That was Bryant,' she announced as matter-of-factly as she could. 'We need to get going.'

Koperek's face was a picture of confusion, still only halfway through the list of questions. Keaton shot her a look that spoke volumes, and Koperek took the hint, stifling her curiosity and stowing her pad and pen.

'We're sorry about this, Mr Masterson – we'll have to terminate the interview. Something's come up.'

Masterson stood, his brows knitting in confusion. 'That's a shame. I was beginning to enjoy having company about the house, and such pretty faces to talk to.' He gave a smile beneath eyes that were hard and focused. 'And let's have none of this "Mr Masterson" nonsense. Call me Terry.'

'I'll stick with Mr Masterson, if that's alright with you.' Keaton smiled, coldly, stooping to gather her things. She could feel Masterson's eyes upon her again, watching, leering, absorbing the individual details of her body.

Masterson's ogling gaze was transfixed on Keaton's latissimus muscles, watching them pulse beneath the drum-skin tightness of the cloth of her shirt, spellbound by the way they hugged so close to her ribcage, only fanning where they drew level with her scapula and blending with the seductive sweep of her shoulders. It was like she'd been sculpted by Bernini's very own hands.

It was happening again – the 'Jerry' gene – an unquenchable, all-consuming desire to drag his tastebuds the length of the sweat-glazed valley of this woman's back. To feel the flexing undulations of her spine through the flat of his tongue, before sinking his teeth into the crunching fibres of her neck, just to hear the rapturous, soprano shrill of reluctant ecstasy filling his ears. Then with insistent, unrelenting pressure to her trachea, orchestrate her silence.

'We'll contact you if we need to speak again,' Keaton said, standing to face Masterson.

He seemed shocked to suddenly hear her voice, even stumbling back from her words. 'Are you okay?' she asked.

Masterson shook the moment away. 'Sorry,' he smiled. 'Miles away there. Yeah, sure. Just call if you need anything.'

Keaton twisted back to check if Koperek was ready, Masterson using the opportunity to snap eyes to her obliques, wound tight against her minuscule waist, looking firm and hard to the touch – a touch he craved to reach for.

'Got everything?' Keaton asked.

Koperek nodded.

Masterson edged past Keaton to escort the visitors to the door, cupping an opportunistic hand against the base of her spine as he sidled through.

'As I said, if you need me again, just call,' he smiled, covertly adjusting his erection as he reached the door. He twisted the latch and unveiled the now inclement weather outside.

Suddenly a pain shot through his body like a bolt from the blue, emanating from the spot where the doctors had mostly been focusing their scanning efforts. The cancer was making its next move, its next gambit, working its way slowly towards its endgame. But as quickly as it had come, the pain seemed to pass – a stinging love-letter from disease to remind him of its presence in his life.

'Are you okay?' Keaton asked, her face a picture of concern.

Masterson nodded and delivered a pained smile. 'I'm fine, just a twinge,' he said, smiling the moment away. He stretched it out, taking a breath, allowing a moment for his body to recover. He leaned a furtive look outside through the open door and could see there was no one around.

With the cancer knocking at the metaphorical door, he considered going for broke – slamming the door shut and locking it, then turning and taking these two down with sharp, snapping blows to the temple, or a knee to the gut. Then he could relive the old days, the *good* old days, the best days. Have his fun, knowing that nothing anyone could do to him would be any worse than the undignified death he was already facing.

But this lead detective, she looked strong. She worked out, and as much as he now obsessed over that body type, he had to remember the last time he'd nearly fallen foul of the inherent strength that exists within a physique such as this, and as big and strong as he undeniably was, there would be two of them to contend with.

'Drive safe,' he said, finally stepping aside.

The detectives stepped past into the rain, turning back to face him. 'Thank you for your time, Mr Masterson. We'll be in touch.'

Masterson nodded, delivering a half-smile. 'Call me, anytime. You have my number,' he said, smiling for the parting guests. 'I'm sure you'll be seeing *me* again,' he added, directing his words more to Keaton.

He watched from beneath the hood of his heavy brow as the detectives negotiated the steps down to the pavement, before slowly closing the door. He drew his phone from his pocket, and with a splintering, ceramic *crunch*, folded it in half.

*

'What the fuck was that all about?' Koperek spat as they pulled out of the parking space.

Keaton sat in awkward silence, negotiating the narrow streets, staring out of the windscreen but looking every bit as though she wasn't seeing the road ahead, as though driving on autopilot.

Koperek leaned forward in her seat, trying to force herself into Keaton's field of vision. 'DS Keaton…? *Jane?*'

Keaton reemerged from her trance, looking lost and clueless. 'Oh my God,' she slurred. 'I… I think there's a body in there.'

Koperek stiffened in her seat. 'You what?'

'A body. I think I found a body.'

Koperek looked stunned. 'A body? W-Where?'

'Up in the loft. I think it's up in the loft.'

'The *loft?* You didn't go up in the loft, did you?'

Keaton shook her head in frustration. '*No.* No I didn't. I just saw a stain on the ceiling. A stain about the size and shape of a man!'

Koperek held a wide, but mildly disbelieving stare. 'Then why aren't we arresting this guy?'

'*Because*, I'm not sure. It might be a leaking tank or something. And besides, I had no permission to search the house.'

'So what makes you think it's a body?'

Keaton turned to look at Koperek with 'are-you-serious' eyes. 'Didn't you smell it – that horrible, sickly stench in there?'

Koperek's face crimped with doubt. 'It smelled a bit, but not like a body?'

Keaton allowed her attention to return to the road ahead. Maybe Koperek was right. Maybe she was letting her imagination run away with her.

Then she suddenly remembered. 'I took a sample, it's in my pocket,' she said, rolling onto her hip and extracting the receipt from her pocket.

She checked the mirrors, pulling the Saab over to the side of the road and hopped out, popping the boot and rummaging through Gutteridge's kit for a sample bag.

'I'll let Carl take a look at this,' she muttered to herself, as she swiped the jiffy bag closed, 'see if I really *am* imagining things…'

FIFTEEN

WHAT HAD ALWAYS SEEMED to Gutteridge to be the rather bizarrely named Lord High Constable of England restaurant in the city's Quays district was heaving with way more people than he would ever have expected to be confronted by on a weekday.

He entered the door, his eyes scanning the sea of faces for one he recognised.

Keaton's hand rose from the river of heads like a struggling swimmer and waved at him frantically. He smiled in recognition of her efforts, and began negotiating his way through the tables to save her from drowning in her desperation for companionship.

'Hey,' he said with a heartfelt smile, finally arriving at the table reserved for two. 'Sorry I'm a bit late. I've been preparing for tomorrow morning's briefing.'

He sat and shuffled to get comfortable, skinning his jacket from his back and hooking it over his seat.

The waitress arrived just as his attention returned to Keaton's smiling but oddly concerned face. 'Oh. Hi. Um...' he said, pressured into contemplating his thirst, clocking Keaton was already in possession of a glass of white wine. Pinot, he assumed.

'Just tea for me, please,' he said with an amiable smile.

The waitress beamed, nodded, handed him a menu and turned to leave.

Gutteridge finally settled and allowed himself a moment to consider Keaton's appearance. Her eye makeup was grey and smoky; her small, pert lips popping from the canvas of her alabaster skin in deep maroon. To the eye's of his forced loneliness, she looked very lovely. 'So, how are you?' he asked.

Keaton's head see-sawed her undeniable indecision as to her *own* opinion on that front.

'What is it?' Gutteridge asked with a frown. 'You sounded – I don't know – troubled on the phone. What happened up there? How was it? How was *he*?'

Keaton huffed and gave an ironic smirk that failed to project levity. 'Two answers,' she replied. 'Crushingly normal, and really fucking weird!'

'Weird? In what way, weird?'

Keaton drifted away into her memories of the encounter. 'I don't know... on the one hand, he was almost charming, *gentlemanly* even. And then at some point during the whole thing, he flipped. Flipped into something that made the both of us fucking uncomfortable.'

'Mmm. Yeah,' Gutteridge mumbled, pondering the decade-old memories of his own, previous encounters with Terrence. 'He always did have that Masterson *strangeness* gene. How's he looking these days?'

Keaton popped a shrug. 'I don't know, I don't *really* know how he looked before. I've only ever seen him in low-res newspaper clippings. But he's big, hefty. A bit like that guy over there,' she said, lowering her voice to a whisper and lifting her chin towards a clean-cut man being shown to a table adjacent to their own. 'Except Masterson has a beard, of course.'

Gutteridge discretely turned to look towards the man's

broad back. 'That's kind of what he looked like before,' he muttered. 'Wide, stocky, a big build. So he still has the beard, does he?'

He turned back to face Keaton's concerned front. 'He's always had that, but he grew it much heavier to try and hide his identity. His brother was also on the large side. Big. Broad in the shoulder. Naturally muscular, like a builder.' He huffed a disquieting laugh. 'His victims never stood a chance.'

The waitress arrived brandishing a tray laden with all of the components needed to make tea, and dealt them onto the table. 'Have you had enough time to choose yet?' she asked.

'Can I have the steak and kidney pudding, please, with mash,' Keaton said, sitting back and smiling up at the waitress.

Gutteridge flicked a glance down at the menu in his hands that he hadn't even looked at yet. 'I'll erm… I'll have the same. Actually, no. Do you still do the chicken salad?'

'We do.'

'I'll have that then please, with chips.'

Another parting smile, and once again, they were alone.

'So, come on then,' Gutteridge said. 'Something shook you up there. You sounded troubled on the phone. So what is it you wanted to speak about?'

Keaton reflected on her worries. 'I don't know what to do.'

Gutteridge cocked a curious eye. 'What do you mean? About what?'

Keaton exhaled a lungful of her frustrations and leaned into the conversation, looking furtively about for unwanted eavesdroppers before continuing. 'I know this guy's been through a lot, so I don't want to do anything that might risk upsetting the apple cart, or draw attention to the anonymity he's so obviously spent considerable time and effort establishing.'

Gutteridge's brow fluttered, trying to read the unsettled expression colouring Keaton's soft, feminine features. 'What exactly *did* happen up there? Something's really bothered you, I can tell.'

Keaton locked her gaze with his. She took a breath in readiness. 'I think there's a body in the loft.'

His eyes flashed at her words. 'A body? Who's loft?'

'Terrence Masterson's.'

Another flash of the eyes. A doubting frown. 'You saw a body?'

Keaton waved the question away before he'd finished asking it. 'No. Not directly.'

Another frown, almost laced with ridicule. 'So, what do you mean?'

Keaton twisted in her seat to retrieve her phone from her bag and swiped the screen to unlock it. She scrolled for a moment then turned the screen to face Gutteridge, just as the waitress arrived with their food. Keaton snatched the phone away again, clamping it to her chest to cloak the image.

'Chicken salad for you, sir, and the pudding for you.' The girl took a moment to meticulously square the plates, then forced a grin. 'Would either of you like any sauces?'

Keaton shook the offer away. Gutteridge considered his plate, then mirrored the rejection.

'Well, enjoy your meals,' the waitress beamed, turning to leave and snaking away through the tables like a downhill skier.

'So, this body you suspect was in the loft, but didn't *actually* see. You were about to show me something?'

Keaton unclamped the phone from her chest again, revealing a low-cut blouse that framed a cleavage exaggerated by motherhood. Gutteridge fought to drag his attention away from the draw of her lustrous flesh. With the absence of Eve and her Amazonian physique in his life, he felt his lust for Keaton beginning to simmer again.

Keaton spun a nonchalant look about the restaurant,

before passing the phone to Gutteridge. 'While we were at Masterson's, I noticed *that*,' she whispered, pointing her pinky at the screen. 'There was a sickly sweet aroma infesting the whole house – something slight, but organic, so I feigned a need to pee to take a look around, and *that* was on the ceiling of one of the upstairs bedrooms.'

Gutteridge studied the image, flicking a berating look in Keaton's direction. 'You looked around, without a warrant?'

'Yes, I *know*… but if I legitimately went to use the toilet, then saw *that*, wouldn't that fall within the remit of "in plain sight"?'

Gutteridge raised doubtful brows, allowing his attention to return to the image. 'I wouldn't like to argue that with a competent lawyer,' he muttered, before leaning into the screen. 'What exactly is it I'm looking at?'

'It's a stain, on the ceiling, like grease. The piece of paper you can see on the wall is an A4 sheet I placed there for scale. But I measured it against my arm-span, and it looked to be about the size and shape of a body – and if I'm right, I'd say a *man's* body.'

Gutteridge's attention remained glued to the screen.

'There *are* other pictures,' Keaton explained. 'Just swipe either side of that one.'

Gutteridge did so, spanning his fingers against the screen to zoom in, assessing Keaton's doubtful assumptions.

Keaton craned her pinky in again. 'See here, too. He's hurriedly painted over the stain to try to hide it, but you can see whatever it is has leeched through again. Why would he do that?'

Gutteridge shrugged. 'Wouldn't you do that over *any* stain that appeared, simply just because it's unsightly?' he suggested.

Keaton's shoulders sagged, she had to concede the notion. 'But what *else* would make a stain like that?'

'Now that's where you've got me,' Gutteridge replied. 'If it *was* something like water, from an overflowing tank or something, it would eventually dry out and you'd be able to paint over it. But that would also probably have made the plaster, or plasterboard sag, and *this* isn't sagging.' He leaned into the picture again. 'No, this is something that's remained moist, like oil, or grease.'

Keaton cocked her head inquisitively. 'Or fluids from a melted body?' she suggested.

Gutteridge's eyes lifted from the phone to meet hers. 'Or indeed, fluids from a melted body.' His eyes narrowed. 'And you say there was a smell?'

'Yes, sweet, but distinctly acrid. A smell that I think was once unpleasant enough to pollute the fabric of the entire building, but that has dispersed over time, and it was strongest *right* beneath that,' she said, indicating her phone.

They sat in silence for a beat to consider the ramifications, the murmur of the restaurant an ambient hum in the background of their shared contemplation.

Gutteridge broke the silence. 'I'll talk to a judge, try and swing a warrant. And tomorrow – after the briefing – you contact Derbyshire Constabulary, make them aware of our suspicions and establish a liaise to be present for a search.'

'*If* we can get a warrant?'

'Oh, I'll get a warrant,' he assured her. 'Everyone's freaking over this shit resurfacing. Anything I request that might help to end it quicker, trust me, they'll hand over on a silver platter.' Gutteridge smiled and nodded his approval.

'So, you don't think I'm being ridiculous?'

Gutteridge sniggered. 'You might be – but if you are, now *I* am too.'

Keaton laughed.

'Come on, let's eat,' Gutteridge said, forcing a temperate

smile to thaw the tension. 'Else yours'll get cold, and mine'll get warm.'

Keaton smirked again, allowing her attention to drift to her plate of mash, scooping her fork into its buttery perfection. Gutteridge also harpooned a mouthful of leaves and wrapped himself around them. The crunch of the salad filled his head as he watched the viscid meniscus of Keaton's mauve lipstick tear as her lips parted to accept the offering, using her elfin beauty as a distraction from the case.

His stomach rolled, the same way it had the first time he'd kissed the sensuous mouth sat opposite. He had to wonder… his marriage was a supremely happy one, and his wife, the goddess of all goddesses. But he still had feelings for the bright, lovable life sat facing him, who was, after all, the mother of his child, and nothing he'd tried so far seemed to be able to douse those flames.

'I've been meaning to ask, if I may?' said Keaton between mouthfuls, lowering her voice to a near whisper. 'Where exactly have you ensconced Eve?'

Gutteridge used the time it took to empty his mouth to decide how best to answer. He swallowed and ducked into the conversation again. 'Do you not think it best that I don't tell you? That I don't tell *anyone*, to ensure there's no way that, whoever this killer is, could find out?'

Keaton frowned. 'How would they find out?'

Gutteridge turned serious. 'If this *is* Masterson, *Jerry* Masterson, and someone was in possession of information he wanted, he would get it.'

'How?' Keaton frowned.

Gutteridge quietly lowered his fork to his plate, and his voice to a more clandestine level, leaning in to close the gap between them.

Keaton's scent hit his nose like a caress from a loving hand,

and he wanted to kiss her, there and then. To press his mouth against hers and imbibe the affection from her lips. But there were serious issues to discuss.

'Victim number four,' he said, leaning on his elbows. 'Joan Speare, from Cheshire, she was a dancer – films, television, stage. She was abducted, missing for two weeks, then her body was discovered with her legs removed, taken as some kind of trophy. I remember seeing pictures of her on stage and she'd had the most incredible legs – long, slender, toned – and it was obvious that Masterson, at some point in history, must have coveted them, until he claimed them for his own.'

Keaton visibly winced.

Gutteridge continued. 'When the autopsy was performed, post- and peri-mortem bleeding indicated he'd amputated them *whilst* she was still alive, with toxicology results showing nothing vaguely anaesthetic in her system. She'd actually pulled so hard against the wire restraints shackling her wrists during the process they'd sliced through to her bone.' He sat back. 'He must have stood by and watched her bleed to death from the wounds, which – fortunately – wouldn't have taken long.'

He held serious eyes directed at Keaton. 'You don't think a man like that could extract anything from anyone? A man able to ignore screams for pity, for mercy? No, trust me, you're better off not knowing.'

Keaton swallowed back her revulsion and nodded quietly, before her thoughts turned to Gutteridge's slaughtered wife. She imagined what could have been if it had been *her* wearing that wedding band.

Gutteridge could read her thoughts from her repulsed expression. 'And yes,' he said, 'Cynthia was also still alive when...' he paused to compose himself. 'When he did what he did.'

'Jesus, Pat... I'm so sorry...' she said. She considered

144

extending a compassionate hand to grasp his, but remembered they were out in public.

The look of loss and remorse that coloured Gutteridge's normally happy expression crushed Keaton's pounding heart, and all thoughts turned to the unaccepted gift she'd given him, a potential replacement for the child she recently discovered he'd lost.

She took a deep breath, unsteadied by pity and solicitude, and steeled herself. 'Would you like to pop over to mine after we're done here and meet Joshua?'

Her words dragged Gutteridge back from the brink. 'Meet Joshua?'

Keaton nodded, her painted lips wincing a succession of uncertain smiles. 'Yes, meet him. Maybe even hold him? But, you wouldn't have to, if you didn't feel ready for that.'

Gutteridge's mind turned to Ewelina. His lovely, beautiful, wonderful Ewelina, and the mounting cache of secrets he now seemed to be keeping from her. Secrets which, he assumed – like his insatiable need for female attention – were the result of the unusual levels of trauma he'd had to face in his life.

'Okay,' he agreed. 'Why don't we do that.'

*

Gutteridge peered into the cot that had been gently placed before him, gazing at the kicking life within. Joshua looked back at him with alert, penny-bright, chestnut eyes, like he had before – but this time, it was different. This time, he knew for sure that here lies a life which had sprung forth from his loins, from *Keaton's* loins, from *their* loins.

'Would you like to hold him?' Keaton asked, wondering if the question was presented too soon.

Gutteridge considered the three feet of air between him

145

and the child, three feet of detachment, of denial, of what was beginning to feel like rejection. 'Yes,' he whispered. 'I… I would.'

Keaton bundled the baby up in the blankets surrounding it, and passed him over to Gutteridge's waiting arms.

Gutteridge appeared nervous. 'I'm not sure what to do? I've… I've never held a child before.'

Keaton laughed. 'Nor had I, until the first time I did,' she chuckled. 'Try not to think about it too much. Just do what feels natural. If it's comfortable for you, it'll probably be comfortable for him. You just have to remember to support his head, okay?'

Gutteridge nodded like a clueless child, opening his arms to accept the bundle, looking prepared but undeniably awkward.

Keaton giggled as she manoeuvred the baby towards him.

'Don't be laughing at me,' Gutteridge griped, but his rebuke just made Keaton laugh even harder.

She placed the bundle into his open arms and he enveloped it.

The baby instantly fell silent and still, save for his legs that pushed into the crook of his elbow, big eyes locking their attention on Gutteridge's looming face.

'Hi, little fella,' he said.

The child reacted to the baritone rumble of his voice with a smile that both lit the room and warmed his soul.

Keaton stepped back to seal the moment, tilting a fond-filled gaze towards the two most important men in her life.

Gutteridge let the awkwardness settle, then melt away, and before long, nothing else existed but him and the tiny face watching his morphing reactions.

Keaton crossed her arms in front of her chest, a metaphorical hug for those she watched. Gutteridge may have looked screamingly out of place in her suburban semi, but did he look so out of place in the moment? She thought not, and her jealousy – such that it was – of Eve and her situation boiled to the surface once again, like it had every day, of every week, of every month since the wedding…

But she had no animosity towards Eve – in fact, she'd grown to love the woman, in an odd, convoluted kind of way. She just wished she was standing where Eve was, arm-in-arm with the man stood holding her son. Holding *his* son… their son.

'Do you think you'll ever tell her?' Keaton asked. But Gutteridge was too engrossed in the angelic face beaming up at him that he didn't notice.

'Pat?' she repeated. 'Do you think you'll ever tell her?'

Gutteridge finally broke from his trance. 'What?'

Keaton took a half step back, for reasons she wasn't sure of. 'I was just wondering, Eve, do you think you'd ever tell Eve?'

Gutteridge's whole demeanour flinched, stiffened, then slowly softened again. His breaths turned shallow. 'I'm not sure… I…' He glanced at the child again. 'If there was a way I could, and I knew she wouldn't leave me, then yes, I would. In a New York minute, I would. I just don't want to risk losing her.'

His words shattered her hopes, her desires, her ideals – as wholly unrealistic as she knew they were in the real world. She felt like she'd been punched square in the pit of her stomach, and she wanted to fold around the fist of reality and retch – but one look at the child held in the embrace of his strong arms, and she felt compelled to fight the feeling away again.

For now, at least, he was here, holding Joshua and seeming ready to be involved, and in the world that was, that was a very healthy beginning to any child's life, and for that, she at least had to allow herself to feel blessed.

SIXTEEN

PAMELA SCANLAN rose unsteadily from her table of friends amidst the ambient murmur of conversation echoing around the interior of The Armoury pub in Shrewsbury.

It was her favourite haunt, with its inviting décor and book-lined walls that seemed to be contriving to look like a scene from *The League of Extraordinary Gentlemen*. But it was growing late – she'd had a couple over what she knew she could comfortably handle and she found herself hankering for the cosseting warmth of the Edwardian sleigh bed she'd recently purchased.

She fought back the insistent onslaught of requests to 'stay for just one more', hugged and cheek-pecked her goodbyes, then meandered to the door on three-inch heeled, knee-length boots that – seven cocktails on – felt decidedly more precarious than they had at the beginning of the night.

She caught sight of a man from the corner of her eye who'd been propping up the bar for the majority of the evening. He downed the last of his drink, before gallantly striding to the door to open it in readiness for her arrival.

'Please,' he said and smiled, extending a gracious arm. 'After you…'

She paused to study him. He was clean-cut, tall, with a

large frame, and she took a few moments to decide if he was to be considered handsome or not.

He looked to be on the older side of ideal, but then again – despite her continued ability to draw male attention – she had to remind herself that she was no longer the spring chicken that once she was. But he had a friendly face, with a playful glint dancing behind his gleaming blue eyes.

'Thank you,' she smiled, bowing graciously, stepping through the draughty entrance into the night.

The sky was a cloudless blanket of stars that were still visible through the town's hazing aura of light pollution.

She heard the door bang shut fifteen feet behind the tick-tack of her heels, and footsteps trotting to catch up with her. She tried to resist turning to face whoever was approaching, but failed, looking around nervously.

'I'm sorry,' said the stranger, breathing hard and slowing to a walk. 'I didn't mean to scare you – it's just I'm pretty sure you and I have met before?'

She stopped, her expression one of intrigue as she turned to face the man. 'I don't think so,' she said, her brows popping a succession of quizzical frowns, examining the energised face before her. 'Maybe I just look like someone you know. I've had that before.'

The man's brow furrowed. 'No. I'm *certain* it was you. I couldn't mistake such a pretty face.'

The woman blushed.

'Your name's Pamela, right?'

The woman's face brightened at the sound of her own name. 'Erm, yes, it is.'

The man smiled warmly, making his imposing proportions appear slightly less intimidating.

'It *was* a long time ago now,' he said. 'You may have married since, but wasn't your surname *Scanlan*?'

She laughed, and smiled at the irony. 'It still is,' she chuckled, turning mildly but theatrically regretful. 'I seem to have a penchant for choosing terrible men.'

The stranger joined in the mirth. 'I'm sorry for that,' he said and smiled. 'Just know it's not for anything wanting on the physical front, you still look fantastic.'

Pamela blushed again. 'Oh, um… thank you.'

'Are you going this way, too?' he asked, indicating the path running parallel to the river.

'I am.'

'Do you mind if I tag along, keep you safe from midnight marauders?' he quipped, lifting jazz-hands in the air to simulate peril.

She laughed. 'Of course. Please. Some company would be nice and you're right, it *is* quiet tonight.'

They began sauntering in rhythm, considering the ground before them. 'So tell me again, where is it that you know me from?' she said, turning a smile towards him. 'Admittedly,' she added, 'it is my *usual* custom to bullshit if I don't recognise someone from my past, you know, to try to style my way through it – but I'm too sloshed for that today.'

The man laughed. 'That's alright. I guess life in general would be a whole lot simpler if we could all be a bit more honest with each other about the realities of the world we inhabit, huh?'

'Wouldn't it just,' she barked with an inappropriate level of mirth, turning a convivial smile to warm the side of his face.

They ambled some more… 'So go on then, whereabouts in our parallel paths through this wonderful life we live did you and I collide?' she reiterated.

The man glanced across at her quizzical expression. 'You *used* to date someone I knew in passing.'

Another intrigued smile floated his way. 'Who was that, then?' she asked. 'As I just said, there have been so many.'

The man laughed again. 'He was a copper, a detective... Patrick Gutteridge?'

The woman's progress slowed to a near crawl, distracted by the force of a name from her past, before she made an effort to speed up again.

'Oh my word!' she said. 'Now there's a name...' She seemed to sink away into her rolodex of memories. 'Patrick Gutteridge,' she muttered. 'All the girls liked Patrick. Do you ever see him?'

The man see-sawed a strangely indecisive nod. 'On occasion.'

Her brows knitted. She slowed again. 'But... hang on, didn't he move to Gloucester division? Wasn't he involved in that awful O'Leary case?'

'That's actually where I last saw him,' the man said. 'In Gloucester.'

'Really,' she responded, slightly taken aback. 'And how is he these days?'

'Not a lot different. He's married now, to some pretty Polish thing.'

'Oh...' she said, forcing a smile that failed to convince, her movements growing animated to cloak her jealousy. 'And where exactly did *we* meet? Can you remember?'

The man smirked. 'Of *course* I remember, how could I forget a life-changing moment like meeting you.'

She smiled again and blushed.

'Yeah.' He grinned. 'We met just a couple of minutes ago, back there,' he said, indicating somewhere far behind with a carefree toss of the head. 'Don't you remember?'

The woman laughed, but the deadpan look on the face peering back at her soon doused her frivolity.

The air between them suddenly turned uncomfortable and peculiar. 'What do you mean?'

The man turned the briefest of looks behind him. 'We met, back there, just now. Admittedly, I *have* spent the majority of the night observing you with your friends, so I kind of know more about you than you'd probably feel comfortable with. And of course, I read that piece that was in the papers many years ago about the relationship you and Gutteridge had together. That time when he became famous because he apparently solved The Shropshire Ripper case, causing my dear mother to take her own life.'

She ceased walking, trying to untangle the stranger's words, turning nervous looks back towards the pub. It seemed far away now and there was no one else in sight, and she was wearing boots designed more for drawing the lusting eyes of men than for running.

'Wh-who *are* you?' she said. 'I-I don't know you at all, do I?'

He spun around to face her birthing doubts and stepped towards her – her stumbling retreat halted by the riverside railings. His hands were doing something at the periphery of her vision, but she didn't dare to look away from his face that looked unnervingly serene but full of enmity.

'No, you don't know me,' he said, grinning. 'But trust me, you *will*.'

His features suddenly hardened and a hand thrust forwards towards her face, something pale and out of focus held in his fingers.

Before she could react, she felt the fingers of another hand wrapping her neck, pulling her face into a folded cloth. She tried to scream through the fibres, her lungs swelling to the back pressure of her impeded cries for help.

She clawed at the stranger's wrists with nails designed more for looks than for self-preservation, before the chemical stench replaced her breath, filling her lungs and her head with an indomitable desire to sleep.

Her flickering vision muddied and rolled to the star-filled sky, feeling her rocking ankles folding on the heels, her legs buckling beneath her. In a heartbeat, all went black…

SEVENTEEN

GUTTERIDGE ADDRESSED THE ROOM of attentive detectives, feeling socially naked at not having DCI Bryant present on his shoulder.

He huffed the deepest of sighs laced with regret for the situation he found himself in as the opener for the meeting.

'Well, here we are again,' he said. 'Two bodies in and no sign of it stopping any time soon.'

He turned mournful eyes down to the notes held in his hand, taking pains to choose his words with care.

'We're all aware that this city has witnessed its fair share of criminal activity over the years, but I'm sure it's also fair to say that these recent events can be considered out of character, *even* for a city that can be as contentious as Gloucester.'

A murmur of solidarity filled the room, seeming to qualify his opinion. He consulted his notes again, looking through them rather than at them.

'DCI Bryant is over with the magistrate as we speak, securing a search warrant for Terrence Masterson's Buxton residence. DS Keaton has also contacted Derbyshire Constabulary and established a liaise for the search. Their details are on the notes you have in your hands.'

The uncomfortable silence was disrupted by the shuffling of stapled A4 sheets of paper.

'DS Keaton and DC Koperek made the long drive to Masterson's home to assess Masterson's level of awareness of the case, and to try and discover if he, at any point in time, has had contact with his missing brother.'

Gutteridge turned a preparatory look to Keaton. She nodded.

'As most of you will be aware by now, while they were there, DS Keaton thought she observed what she believes could be evidence of the existence of a body on the premises. I think it's better if that information comes directly from her mouth.' He stepped aside and paddled an invitational arm. 'DS Keaton?'

Keaton stood, gathering the notes she knew she wouldn't be needing, her relative lack of experience causing her to have thoroughly prepared for the meeting.

She exchanged a muted smile with the father of her child and turned to address the room of interested faces.

'As DI Gutteridge was saying, myself and DC Koperek drove to Buxton in Derbyshire to interview Terrence Masterson. While we were at Masterson's property, it not only became obvious that he knew more than he was officially letting on, but there was also a strange odour infesting the whole property – an odour I *believe* he'd grown so accustomed to over time that he was no longer aware of it.'

She frowned. 'It was an odour hard to describe, something sickly sweet, but undeniably pungent, and *definitely* organic. A faded stench of decay that I believe had been muted by the passage of time. So during the interview, I feigned a need to use the bathroom in order to see if the scent was also present upstairs, which it was. Not only that, it was noticeably stronger. I ducked my head into one of the rooms where the scent seemed strongest, and found what *seemed* to be the stain of what I *believe* to be a body on the ceiling above the entrance to that room.'

Keaton consulted her notes, flipping to the second sheet of her scribblings.

'I took a quick sample, that I'm *sure* the more astute of you here might realise was bordering on unethical. Nevertheless, Carl McNamara in pathology has examined the sample and it is now also his belief that my assumption has legs. He believes – as I do – that the substance soaking the ceiling could be fats and oils from a melted, or decomposing corpse. However, he also concluded that the fluids – having filtered through the contaminating fibres of the plaster – are no longer "clean" enough to perform a dependable DNA test. Both DI Gutteridge – as SIO, and DCI Bryant have deemed our findings to be of enough interest to warrant further investigation, and that is why DCI Bryant is with the magistrate as we speak, generating the appropriate paperwork for a search.'

She turned another subtle smile back to Gutteridge to indicate the end of her report. He nodded his approval.

'Does anybody have any questions for DS Keaton?' Gutteridge said, stepping in to join her side.

McWilliams raised his hand. 'Aye. It's just a procedural one,' he said, his bawling Glaswegian accent filling the air in the room. 'As we're attemptin' to raise a warrant based on evidence obtained by an illegal search, won't that make our findings inadmissible in a court of law?'

Keaton raised her brows in acknowledgement. 'It is our *current* belief that as I made the discovery during movements through the building that I'd been given permission for – combined with the presence of the unusual odour – that my discovery falls within the remit of "in plain sight".'

McWilliams reeled back in his seat, smirking his doubts. 'That's a bit sketchy, to say the least.'

Gutteridge stepped in. 'We're well aware of that, but our legal team has given us their consent to move forward with this.'

Gutteridge swung an invitational arm to Keaton to take to her seat again. 'Thank you, Jane.'

He consulted his own printouts, flicking to a page marked with a Post-It note. Pages detailing the autopsy findings of Kerry Marston's mutilated remains.

'Can you please all turn to page five of the case notes, where you will see the preliminary findings of Kerry Marston's autopsy,' he asked the room. Again, the air erupted with the sounds of shuffling paper.

'Carl McNamara oversaw the autopsy, assisted by Gustav Hoegen. Carl also explained that due to his current workload, these are not the full and final results of what will eventually be a more thorough examination, and they are to be taken as such.'

Gutteridge had to strain to push his emotions aside. Try and forget the prior relationship that he and the victim had shared. A relationship that – as far as he knew – none of the team watching knew anything of.

'The victim's body – as you are aware, most of you having attended the crime scene – had been subjected to such a savage level of damage that it made definitive visual identification virtually impossible.'

A hand went up. It was McWilliams again. 'I've been meaning to ask that. You *seemed* pretty certain of the identity of the victim during the initial investigation, despite – as you're sayin' – there being no ID present on the body. How on earth would you have been able to establish that?'

McWilliams presented the question with a knowing, accusatory tone that unnerved Gutteridge. Out of all the detectives in the room, he knew McWilliams to be the only one who'd voiced concerns about Gutteridge's possible conflicts of interest. The rest of the team seemed more understanding of the case's exceptional circumstances, and, as such, appeared to be behind his efforts.

'Three ways. Her watch, her hair, and her jewellery.' Gutteridge fired back.

McWilliams frowned, almost mocking. 'The hair I get, but how on earth would you know anything about her watch and her jewellery?'

Gutteridge wasn't in the mood to get into an unproductive haranguing match in front of a room full of colleagues. He didn't know what McWilliams' agenda was in questioning him, but right now, he didn't care.

'*Because*, both DS Keaton and I interviewed Kerry Marston during the O'Leary case – an interview that I believe *you* actually organised – and while there, I noticed the unusual design of her droplet earrings, and clocked the brand and design of her rare and expensive watch. You know, the way we're trained to as detectives.'

A wave of muted laughter circled the room, and McWilliams leaned his reddened face back out of the conflict.

Gutteridge fell still and silent, save for the growling stare he dressed about the room. 'Does anyone else here see a problem with me heading this team? *Me*, the only person here who knows anything of import regarding this case. *Me*, the only person connected the original investigation. *Me*, the person who first figured this fucking mess out and initially brought an end to the mindless killings?'

A murmur of resounding support warmed the air, lancing McWilliams' dubious motivations in questioning the arrangement.

'Okay then, your support is much appreciated.' He darted a look to McWilliams, who seemed to want to melt through his seat.

158

'As I was saying before I was interrupted… the level of violence inflicted on Kerry Marston is unprecedented in all but the most vicious of cases that *I* have ever been made aware of! The primary weapon is believed to be a lump or sledge hammer. The blunt-force trauma impact wounds were found to have a soft-edged, but decidedly square imprint, and the level of damage inflicted with each impact would suggest the implement had considerable weight, and was swung with sizeable force.'

He turned to another sheet. 'What skin remained untouched by traumatic force showed signs of chemical burning and, from the vapours present and the damage visible not only to the skin but to the surrounding clothing, it would suggest bleach was used in an attempt to destroy any surface evidence.'

DS Banks raised a hand. 'Is there a theory as to why the change in MO? Wasn't it acetic acid that was used on Kaylie Wyatt to perform the same task?'

'It was,' Gutteridge confirmed. 'All I can say is that, during the original case, Jerry Masterson's MO was never set in stone, to the point that we *initially* suspected multiple perpetrators may have been involved. Now, whether this was to keep those on the case guessing, or because he enjoyed trying different ways to mutilate his victims, we'll probably never know. But the fact that there *are* differences, fits the MO of who we – at this present moment in time – suspect is committing these atrocities.'

Parker's hand lifted from the throng. 'We've all read the history files, but what can you tell us personally about Jerry Masterson. *If*, indeed, this *is* Jerry Masterson?'

Gutteridge lowered his eyes from the sea of watching faces and shut them, immersing himself into that dark part of his memory he'd long ago partitioned off in order to protect his sanity.

'Jerry Masterson is no respecter of life. I doubt he has ever looked on *anyone* in all his years as the sum of their parts. He sees people – especially the females of our species – purely as machines. *Organic* machines. Machines that are aware of their surroundings, of themselves. Machines that can be messed with, toyed with, dismantled and destroyed. To him, women are a collection of individual parts with an awareness of self. With fear, with dread, with a desire to live, a desire that – in his damaged mind – he can *influence*, and for nothing more or less than his own depraved, sexual gratification.'

He opened his eyes again and looked about the room. 'After he fled, we discovered literally hundreds of publications at his Shropshire property on the subject of anatomy: books, magazines, journals, forensic manuals – all amassed over time like an avid collector, barely a page left free of... shall we say, *organic* matter.'

The room shuffled with unease.

'Understand this,' Gutteridge added. 'Jerry Masterson is as dangerous a man as ever walked this earth. He's heartless and sadistic, and in ways, and at a level rarely encountered. If this *is* him, God help anyone he sets his sights on. Because to him, women are toys to be investigated, explored, tampered with until they no longer function, and he'll be gazing deep into their dying souls with unblinking eyes, enjoying the fruits of his labour as the light leaves their eyes...'

The whole room continued to shift silently within an expanding air of discomfort.

Gutteridge erupted from the moment, tossing his folded sheets on the desk ahead of him. 'So let's catch him, once and for all,' he said, flicking a berating look in the direction of McWilliams. McWilliams blinked and nodded in response.

Gutteridge took a breath, exiting memories of his past and resetting himself. 'As last time, DC Koperek will be our data logger for the HOLMES system, and as usual, I'll be seeing you all one at a time throughout the day to discuss your initial roles. This team worked well last time, so I'm reluctant to change too much. Does anyone here have any questions?'

The room remained silent, still reeling in discomfort.

'Okay then, let's do our best work…'

EIGHTEEN

THE CLOUDED TUNNELS of Pamela Scanlan's swirling consciousness transitioned from the swimming unreality of dreams, to the nightmare of lucidity, and she suddenly became aware of a tightness across her chest. A difficulty drawing breath that felt constrained and unnatural.

A series of jolts shook her whole body awake and she gradually reemerged into the real world like a birthing child, her parting lids unveiling the true horror of her situation.

She was looking at a broad chest that was leaning into her, obscuring her view, ears stinging to the fizzing rip of duct tape just inches from her head.

The chest eventually cleared her vision, revealing the stranger from the bar. 'W-what's happening? W-where are we? What are you doing?' she slurred, still feeling groggy.

The man twisted down to peer into her perturbed expression. She tried to move, but she was fastened to something solid. She could feel bars against her back, some sort of parallel framework, her skin stinging from the cold.

'Oh – hello there. So you've decided to join the party, have you?' the stranger said, delivering an empty smile – a smile that almost instantly turned to mock regret. 'Aww, but I'm so sorry,

I'm not quite ready for you just yet, and I can't have you crying out for help, not while I still have preparations to make. That wouldn't be beneficial to my plans at all.'

The woman began to blind panic. 'Please!' she wept. 'I don't know what you want from me, o-or what it is that I've done? But whatever it is, I'm sorry!'

A sweeping gust of cold air brushed up her body and across her face. She realised she was outside. It was dark, and she could just make out the open door of a panel van from the corner of her eye.

The stranger spent a moment examining the confounded expression looking back at him, before placing his hand around her neck. He peered with what seemed to be fascination into her dancing pupils, looking strangely expectant.

'I'll be seeing you again real soon, okay? Just hang in there for me.' He smiled, almost grinning. 'You've been sleeping for a day already, I'm sure a few hours longer won't do you any harm.'

His fingers suddenly tightened around her neck and the thump of her racing heartbeat leapt to her throat, dammed by the stranger's relentless grasp.

Her eyes bulged from the pressure. She tried to scream, but nothing came out. She tugged desperately at the restraints, her vision clouding over, fingers of darkness crawling across the fascinated expression observing her torment with such diseased excitement. Growing increasingly frantic, she tried to shake her head in an attempt to dislodge the insistent grip clamping down on her carotid artery. Colours began fading to black and white – the stranger's greyscale face watching her succumb with-head twisting curiosity.

The curtains of unconsciousness began to close again on the stage of her worst nightmares, bringing an end to the scene. A forced intermission before the final act played out…

'Pamelaaaaa…' a voice hissed, into her floating self-awareness, calm, breathy, mildly taunting. 'Wakey-wakey. Your party's ready for you now.'

She fluttered awake again, feeling groggy and nauseous, swirling within a crumbling sense of indignity.

She could taste the aftermath of the seven strawberry daiquiris consumed before life took a wrong turn, coating the back of her throat – a throat that felt bruised deep within the fibres of her neck.

Her vision finally settled. She was looking out over a midnight scene, the organic smell of damp grass and wet foliage burning her nostrils.

She seemed to be on some sort of tall, bridge-like structure, looking out over an unlit road thirty feet below that appeared to be unfrequented by traffic.

She shuddered at the cold and her lack of comprehension as to why *any* of this was happening. How had the train of her life jumped tracks so suddenly to this moment?

'W-W-W-Where am I?' she stammered. 'I-I don't understand? What is going on?'

She turned an exploratory look down towards the tightness across her breasts, seeing bands of duct tape wrapping her body – her waist, her thighs, her chest – binding her to something unseen behind. She became aware of the bars again, digging in to her back, the frame of something arresting her ability to move.

The cold breeze bit at her skin and, peering around, she realised that she was naked save for her black, knee-length boots.

'Yes,' the stranger said, as he stood watching her flustering within her cloud of confusion. 'I… erm… I couldn't bring myself to remove those. They – how should we say – *do* it for me,' he said, grinning like a demon. He broke from his leering and wandered away out of sight.

She began to weep again, shaking her head violently with frustration, rejecting the severity of a situation she wasn't even sure was real. Inconsolable tears of fear and bewilderment ran free, filling her grimacing mouth.

'I don't understand. Why are you doing this? Where are we? Why am I here?' She began to hyperventilate.

The stranger was somewhere behind her pleading, outside of her confused, restricted field of vision. She could hear him rummaging through what sounded like a bag.

'You're *here*, to fulfil your role as collateral damage,' his disembodied voice said. 'You're going to be famous you know, in *aaaaall* the newspapers. Your fifteen minutes of fame – as Mr Warhol would so succinctly have put it.'

He reappeared in her shaking line of vision. 'As for *where* you are. You're currently sitting on Edstone Aqueduct, but I'm sure someone as vapid and self-absorbed as you undoubtedly are wouldn't have heard of anything as historically interesting as Edstone Aqueduct.'

He smirked derisively and began nonchalantly uncoiling a pre-prepared roll of wire. 'This aqueduct on which you are perched so precariously was actually one of the earliest-known prefabricated structures, built roughly 200 years ago now. It spans almost 500 feet. Crazy, huh?'

He wrapped one end of the wire around the railings spanning the bridge, coiling it tightly around itself before tugging on it several times to check it held firm.

He turned again to address his guest. 'I've always had an interest in history, *and* engineering, even as a child,' he said, looking reflective. '*I* have history,' he added, 'did you know that? For instance, did you know that your ex lover boy – DI

Gutteridge – drove my mother to commit suicide, depriving me and my brother of her excellent company and – some might even say – her calming influence?' He smiled ruefully, his eyes wandering and distant. He allowed his attention to return to his guest. 'Of course you don't. Why would you?'

The stranger turned back to the task in hand, tossing the role of piano wire over the side of the aqueduct, keeping hold of the other, clean-cut end. He stepped in and began wrapping it around the neck of his guest, twisting it around itself multiple times to fasten it as he had on the railings.

The woman's reddened eyes hardened. She began to panic at the feeling of wire against her throat, frantically lunging against the duct-tape bindings arresting her freedom.

'Heaven help *meeeeee*…!' she screeched to the obsidian sky, rocking against her restraints, ignoring the scything pain of the bars hammering into her back. 'Pleeease! Oh Jesus Christ, will somebody *help meeeee*!'

The stranger stepped away from the clamour, retrieving something else from the bag, and returned. He raised ridiculing brows. 'No one can hear you, you know. We're miles away from anyone who remotely gives a shit,' he said, calmly surveying the midnight silhouette of the surrounding horizon. 'So there's no reason to continue embarrassing yourself like this, now, is there?'

The man turned strangely mournful. 'Shame, really, having to use you this way,' he said, looking oddly regretful, examining the tormented features of her tear-drenched face. The corners of his mouth twitched almost imperceptibly with something vaguely resembling remorse. 'In a different life, maybe you and I might have gotten along.' The forced remorse then morphed into an almost jaunty, brow-raised smile. 'We may even have had a fling? Who knows. Parallel realities. Parallel lives.' His smile turned pensive and soft. 'And that face. Ah, such a *lovely* face you have,' he muttered, stroking the back of his hand against her glistening cheek; a disjointed moment of tenderness that seemed out of character.

Her pupils tremored in their crimson sockets, jaw dripping with terror.

'By the way. My name, it's Masterson. I'm sure – as a Shropshire lass – you'll recognise it. As names go, it's really rather famous. Or perhaps it would be more accurate to say, *infamous*…'

The woman's eyes widened at the mention of his name. She quaked, feeling like she'd died already.

Masterson reached an arm around to retrieve something from his back pocket. 'Better not forget this,' he said, displaying a folded note and what looked to be an antique hat-pin. 'This is for lover boy,' he said, placing the note against her sternum before stabbing the pin through it.

The woman screamed through the stinging pain, and kept screaming, rocking violently in the nucleus of her humiliation.

Masterson disappeared behind her as she continued the fruitless attempts to be heard, wailing to the heavens to be saved by some unseen God – a God too heartless to leave their ivory tower and intervene.

Suddenly, her whole body was tilted back and she began rolling towards the railings on the sack truck she'd been taped to. A voice presented itself in her ear. She could feel Masterson's breath on her neck.

'I'll be keeping your head by the way,' he whispered. 'It's far too pretty a memento to relinquish. I hope that's okay with you? Oh,' he added, 'and I've devised a devilishly interesting way to remove it – twenty feet of piano wire and gravity-based solution… ingenious really, even if I say so myself. Saves me the trouble of messing around with knives.'

The hot breath left her ear and with a grunt, Masterson heaved the sack truck onto the railings.

The woman's vocal chords ripped to the harmonic of her screams for mercy that she now realised had never existed, filling the treetops and the crowning night sky with her desperation, her head shaking in denial of a destiny that was no longer within her sphere of influence.

'Sometimes, it's the prettiest flowers that need dead-heading,' Masterson said, before one, determined push sent the sack truck arcing over the railings, the cold tarmac below rushing up to meet its fall.

With a jolt that shook the whole bridge, the wire snapped tight, decapitating her screams as the sack truck clattered against the road's unforgiving surface.

The buckled remains of the trolly and the headless body settled, baptised by a sinking cloud of atomised blood, and silence once again returned to a land not used to such sights.

NINETEEN

'**D**CI WAINWRIGHT, this is my colleague, DS Keaton,' Gutteridge said.

The six-feet-five of slender, middle-aged man bowed his slightly gaunt and chiseled features down to meet Keaton's, extending a hand into the core of the introduction. 'Pleased to meet you, DS Keaton. I understand it's you who initially raised this as a possible concern?'

'It is, sir,' she replied, shaking the outstretched offering.

'Well, we'll do what we can to help.' The detective smiled before his brows raised. 'I feel like I already know you both; I think most of us in this division do. We all followed the O'Leary case with interest up here. Nice work putting an end to *that* mess so quickly. Such cases can have a tendency to linger.'

The two guest detectives smiled their appreciation.

'Indeed they can,' Gutteridge agreed.

Wainwright gave Keaton her hand back. 'To be honest, if it wasn't for your success with that case, we might not have been quite so accommodating in assisting you. You have to know that the basis for this search is pretty weak.'

'Indeed we do,' Gutteridge said. 'But Jane's... DS *Keaton's* hunches have a tendency to have legs.'

The tower of a man smiled down at Keaton. 'I imagine they do. Well, we at Derbyshire CID are here to assist in any way we can.' He turned to address Gutteridge directly. 'We'll be in control of entering the property, of course, but then you'll have control of the scene – that's assuming there *is* a scene.'

*

A flurry of marked and unmarked squad-cars quietly pulled into spaces shy of Masterson's home.

Gutteridge shut the engine off and checked his watch. It was 5:26 am. He turned to face Keaton. 'Ready?'

'Yes,' she said, taking a deep, pacifying breath, her stomach churning at the possibility that her suspicions may have been erroneous.

Gutteridge could see the concern in her face. 'Don't worry,' he said. 'If this ends up bootless, it's on me.'

She smiled, touching a hand to his knee.

'Come on then,' he said. 'The raid's set for 5:30. Let's do this.'

Tightly coordinated clusters of uniformed officers in tactical dress snaked through the warren of lanes and passageways leading to Masterson's property, taking up positions that effectively cut off all routes and means of possible escape.

Gutteridge, Keaton and Wainwright quietly climbed the steps to the door, alert eyes scanning the windows for signs of movement. They followed close behind the entry team – a three-man train of officers wearing stab jackets and with a 'Rammit' in tow in case they needed to effect a more 'imperative' entry solution.

They all spied the doorbell Keaton had described and Wainwright stepped through the throng, presenting an ear to the hinge side of the door and extending a finger to press the button. He heard the chimes ring out throughout the house and hung still, listening…

'Nothing,' he said. 'I can't hear anything.'

Gutteridge straddled a privet hedge, which bordered a small patch of grass displaying – what he judged to be – at least a fortnight's worth of growth. He peered through the bay window of the living room.

'Can you see anyone?' Keaton whispered.

Gutteridge shook his head. 'No. Nothing.'

Wainwright pressed the bell a few more times, dropping to his knee and stooping his gangly frame to peer through the letterbox.

He scanned his eyes around what he deemed to be a space looking unusually barren for an apparently occupied dwelling.

The smell Keaton had described hit his nose. It seemed especially pungent in contrast to the freshness of the crisp, morning air.

He presented his mouth to the letterbox. 'Terrence Masterson? Derbyshire Police. Open the door. We have a warrant to search your property.' His eyes returned to the oblong window to someone else's life and waited in silence for the sight or sound of movement. None came…

Wainwright struggled to his feet again and stepped back. 'Right, put it through,' he said, waving a knifed hand towards the door.

The two officers wielding the ram stepped in, eyeing the locations of the main locks on the door, looking for weak points, adopting wide stances in readiness.

'I think he's moved out,' a voice said, drifting from the opposite side of the dividing wall to the next property.

All six officers turned to face the source of the voice. There was a short, slender man looking to be in his late seventies, watching their activities with neck-craning interest.

171

His face – indeed, his whole physique – was subtly gaunt, grey, thinning hair blowing in the breeze, clad head-to-toe in plaid pyjamas and a dressing gown.

Gutteridge stepped up and crouched by the wall to bring their eyes level. 'Hello, sir. We're police officers, did you say you believe he no longer lives here?'

The man nodded, looking decidedly certain of his words. 'Yes. Well, I believe so. He had a van here – oh, it must have been a couple of weeks back now, at least? He was loading his furniture into it.'

Keaton joined Gutteridge's side. 'Are you referring to Terrence Masterson?'

The man's face showed the briefest of looks of surprise. 'Well, we didn't know his name was Masterson. We only know him as Terry, so… I guess so?' He looked around at the crescent of faces. 'There was no one else living here with him.'

Keaton stepped in closer. 'I was here with another officer just a few days ago, and he was here then.'

The man looked surprised, and more than a little perplexed. 'Oh! We – my wife and I, that is, she's inside – haven't seen him in ages.' The man craned a look towards Masterson's front door. 'We never spoke much, you know. I guess some people just value their privacy, but we would always see him around, tending to the garden, popping in and out. But as I say, we haven't laid eyes on him for at least a couple of weeks.'

Keaton turned pensive, her brows knitting, then she sank to the realisation of clues that may have passed her by. 'It was all bullshit,' she muttered.

'What was?' Gutteridge asked.

Keaton exhaled an exasperated sigh. 'He told us some baloney about modernising his home, saying he'd not long had house clearers in to make way for new furniture that hadn't arrived yet.'

The neighbour piped in again. 'He's never had house clearers in. We'd have seen that.'

Gutteridge dropped his eyes to the ground, contemplating the options. 'And you're *sure* he's left?' he asked the neighbour.

The old man nodded. 'It certainly looked like it. He loaded an awful lot of stuff into that van he had.'

'And how big was it, this van?' Keaton asked.

'Big,' the man said. 'I mean, I'm saying a van, but it was more like a box truck.'

Gutteridge turned to look up at Keaton. 'He might have travelled back that day just to meet with you guys. That could be why he arranged for the meeting to be so late in the afternoon, to give him time to get up here.'

'Why do that?' Keaton asked.

'To hide the fact that he no longer lives here. It's the only explanation that fits everything you told us – otherwise, why the lie about having house clearers in?'

'*Fuck!*' Keaton spat.

'But the question is, *why*? Why the desire to hide the fact that he's no longer living at this address, and does that tally with events in Gloucester?'

Gutteridge suddenly stood again, startling Keaton. 'Let's get inside,' he said. 'Something doesn't feel right.'

The neighbour shuffled in closer, extending a hesitant hand towards the front of the house. 'I don't know if they are still there, but I did once hear him cursing to himself late one night that he'd left his house keys wherever it was he'd just come from – then I saw him through the window taking a spare set from the gas meter box over there, at the side of the door.'

Wainwright's eyes followed the direction of the neighbour's outstretched finger, until he spied a plastic meter box faded light brown by the sun. He stooped and tugged at the lid but it was locked.

173

'Here, sir,' said one of the entry team, unfolding a set of pliers from a multi-tool and handing them over.

Wainwright clamped the triangular locking pin and twisted it, lifting the lid clear and tossing it aside. He peered into the snake pit of pipes and spiderwebs, seeing a folded sandwich bag pushed into the farthest corner.

He tentatively reached his repulsed fingers into the gossamer netting to retrieve the bag. It jangled.

'Got them,' he barked, with an air of triumph, handing back the tool and shaking the cluster of keys into his hand.

'What's he done?' the neighbour asked, who had now been joined by his wife who was stood watching from the open door.

'Oh, it's really nothing, sir. He's just helping us with our enquiries,' Gutteridge said with a smile, attempting to waylay their concern. 'But thank you for your assistance, it is much appreciated,' he added, just as Wainwright turned the key in the lock.

'We're in!' Wainwright said, gingerly opening the door. 'Terrence Masterson?' he called into the echoing space. 'This is the police! If you're in here, you need to come out and keep your hands where we can see them.'

The three officers who made up the entry team erupted into action, sidling past the lead detectives and expertly negotiating the warren of rooms and corridors with shouts of 'kitchen, clear. Living room, clear.' Booted footsteps thundered up the stairs to a fanfare of further shouts of, 'Show yourself!'

Gutteridge wandered into the living room and stood, considering the triangle of seats that sat in the centre of the space. Keaton joined him.

'Is this all that was here?' he asked.

Keaton nodded, looking sheepish. 'I should have known something wasn't right.'

Gutteridge shrugged. 'No you shouldn't. You didn't at that point in time have any reason to suspect he was lying.'

Wainwright stepped in to join them. 'The house is clear. There's no one home.'

Gutteridge turned and nodded. 'Thank you, sir. Okay, Jane. Whereabouts is this stain of yours?'

TWENTY

GUTTERIDGE LEANED A HESITANT LOOK into the bedroom Keaton had indicated to be the location of the images on her phone. It was the only room with a notable amount of possessions still left in it – the rest of the house looking abandoned.

He turned his eyes to look at the ceiling above him. Keaton leaned in and flicked on the light switch with the end of her pen, to avoid smudging any possible prints.

Gutteridge's phone began to vibrate in his pocket. He'd set it on silent for the sake of the raid. He withdrew it from his pocket and swiped to answer. 'Gutteridge?' He nodded for the voice on the other end. 'ETA?' he asked. 'Okay. We're inside now. He wasn't home and I don't think he's likely to be any time soon, but I'll explain more when you get here. See you when you arrive.'

He lowered the phone from his ear and swiped it off. 'Carl's about thirty-five minutes away,' he said to Keaton, then turned to address Wainwright. 'Our Home Office Head of Forensics,' he explained.

He allowed his attention to return to the ceiling, to the oblong stain directly above him. The smell was indeed stronger in this particular room, and he found himself drawing the same conclusions as Keaton.

'There's a hatch out here,' Wainwright said, pointing to a panel in the ceiling at the farthest end of the landing.

'I'll go and get some ladders from the truck,' one of the officers said, trotting away down the stairs.

'You've got a good team there,' Gutteridge said.

Wainwright smiled with gratitude for the compliment. 'Indeed I do.'

Moments later, the sound of booted footsteps approached again, accompanied by the clatter of aluminium. 'Here you go, sir.'

Gutteridge received the ladders with an appreciative smile, snapping them open and positioning them beneath the hatch. He took a breath, unsure of what they were about to uncover.

'Any bets?' he asked the crescent of watching faces.

Keaton's shoulders hopped a shrug. 'A body. Male.'

'A leaking tank,' Wainwright offered, almost sounding ludicrously hopeful.

Gutteridge began climbing the aluminium stairway to hell towards the answer.

'What about you?' Wainwright asked.

Gutteridge reached the hatch, lifting an edge and blowing to clear the curtain of falling dust.

An acrid smell hit the membrane at the back of his nose. Gutteridge snorted and turned an apprehensive look down towards the question. 'Having had history with this family, I'm with DS Keaton. It's a body.'

He carefully lifted the hatch clear of the hole and handed it down. Wainwright took it, propping it up against the wall.

'We should dust that for prints,' Gutteridge said, before popping his head through the opening and peering around suspiciously like a paranoid meerkat.

'Sir?' one of the officers watching from the sidelines said, stepping in with a weapons-grade torch and handing it up. 'Just press the button once, or it'll start flashing.'

Gutteridge took it and nodded, his expression crumpling in response to the smell. Not the fetid, gut-churning stench of a recently rotted corpse – more the lingering, unpleasant scent of time-served decay.

He thumbed the torch on and shone it around the loft space. The disk of light meandered over random islands of junk from a life lived, with roof timbers decorated with strands of cobweb bunting wafting in the rising heat and the residual breeze weaving through the tiles.

'The floor looks to be partially boarded over,' Gutteridge said. 'I'm going up.'

He climbed to the top rung of the ladder, Wainwright stepping in to hold them steady. He placed the torch to one side and struggled into the hole.

The ridge height was just tall enough to stand in. He brushed himself off, directing the beam towards the location of the stain. There was a mound visible between two of the rafters – something that looked to have been hurriedly covered over with fibreglass insulation.

Gutteridge painted the light around the rest of the loft space, seeing an area where he believed the insulation may have been taken from.

'So what have you been hiding up here?' he said into the strange air of seclusion that being in the space alone was creating.

He straddled some boxes to take a closer look, blowing the drifting cobwebs and the fumbling cellar spiders away from his face. The smell, although still subtle, was much stronger here.

He took a pair of nitrile gloves from his back pocket and

pulled them on, his eyes remaining locked on Masterson's secret.

DCI Wainwright's head popped through the hatch like a whack-a-mole. 'Found anything?' he asked.

'I don't know. I'm about to find out.'

Hesitantly, he reached in, pinching a slab of insulation in his reluctant fingers and lifting it away… His guts churned and he recoiled from his find.

'It's a body!' he called, covering his mouth with his arm, taking a moment to gather himself, painting the disk of light around the desiccated, skeletal remains of someone, liberally peppered with dry larvae husks.

Wainwright struggled into the space to join him, his long legs striding over the box barricade with ease.

'Holy shit!' he slurred. 'Your colleague's hunch was right.' He leaned further in to examine the remains. 'They look old!'

'Indeed,' Gutteridge responded, straightening to consider their find.

He took another look about the loft space. 'I can't tell how long these have been here, but it's a long time. *Years* I'd say.' Gutteridge turned to face the remains again. 'My guess is that whoever this is was killed and hidden here during the summer months of whatever year it may have been. Sometime in June, July or August, perhaps.'

'Your reasoning?' Wainwright asked.

'Well, we obviously have some grave wax leakage from the fats that have decomposed, but there's also evidence of partial mummification,' he said, moving the torch beam along the length of the body. 'If it was hot up here, combined with the draught we can feel, might account for that. Perfect conditions for mummification.'

'Makes sense,' Wainwright agreed.

'But I'm sure Carl will be able to tie that down to something more definitive.'

*

Carl reached his double-gloved hand in to remove the last slab of insulation, Hoegen carefully taking it from him and bagging it.

Keaton appeared through the hatch. 'Here you go,' she said, handing up LED battery lamps.

Gutteridge took them and began hanging them around the space. Gustav Hoegen took up his camera and proceeded to fire off shots of the scene, making sure to tread carefully. The bright pop of the flash shocked the already unnerved sensibilities stood on the sidelines, watching.

'I don't understand,' Gutteridge said. 'Is this one of *Jerry's* victims? One we missed?'

'Can you just take some photos of this?' Carl instructed Hoegen, leaning back to clear the view.

'There's something here,' Carl proclaimed, pausing a moment for Hoegen to finish firing off a few shots for their records, before carefully removing something from the rotted remains and twisting to hand whatever it was back to Gutteridge.

It was a folded handkerchief that seemed to be enveloping something small and rectangular, looking like waxed cloth from having soaked up the liquefaction.

'It was sitting on the sternum, beneath the hands,' Carl explained. 'They'd been arranged in a kind of criss-cross pattern in front of the chest, like a mummy, looking almost ceremonial in its posture, and *that* was beneath them.'

Gutteridge carefully took it from him.

'And you don't have to be too careful,' Carl added. 'These

180

remains are at least seven or eight years old, maybe even older? So there's no way I'd be able to get usable DNA off *that* gunk. Oh, and Keaton was right – whoever this is was a man.'

Gutteridge spied an old side table near the hatch and moved across to it, carefully placing the find on its dusty surface and began carefully opening it with his fingertips. Wainwright and Keaton leaned in to watch.

The desiccated remnants of putrefied flesh crumbled like dry soil as the cloth was opened like a grotesque flower. Inside was what looked like a wallet. Gutteridge unstuck it from its shroud and gently opened it…

'I think I can just see a monogram on the hanky,' Keaton exclaimed.

'Can you make it out?' Gutteridge asked.

Keaton reached in and gingerly lifted the crusty handkerchief to eye level, studying the monogram in the glow of the lamp that hung behind her right shoulder. She wheeled it in her fingers. 'Yes,' she said. 'It says… J-A-M… Jam?'

Gutteridge withdrew a bank card from the wallet with a featherlight grip, lifting it into the light. His whole face dropped as he read the name. 'Jeremy Anthony Masterson… *Jesus Christ*,' Gutteridge slurred, turning to look across at the mummified remains. 'I think this is Jerry Masterson!'

His phone began to buzz in his pocket. He stood to retrieve it. 'It's Bryant,' he said, prodding the screen. 'Sir?'

Keaton lowered the handkerchief and tried to listen in.

'*What!* Where?' Gutteridge snapped, his face a picture of concern. 'Dear God in heaven…' he muttered. 'And do they know who she is yet?' His expression muddied. 'Her head? What about it?'

Keaton observed Gutteridge's catalogue of morphing expressions.

'P-Pamela Scanlan!' He repeated, his eyes flashing in

recognition of the name. He saddened and seemed to slump like a deflating tyre. 'Yes, I... I knew her, a long time ago now, but I knew her,' he said, looking demoralised. He took a moment to gather himself. 'Okay, sir. Can you ping me an address and a contact, and we'll drop over as soon as we've finished up here. It's kind of on our way back.' He continued listening, the device clamped loosely to his ear, his head bowed. 'Yes, sir, we did, and it *is* a body. I'll explain more later, we're right in the middle of it.' He listened some more. 'Okay, you too. Bye, sir.'

He lowered the phone from his ear, looking wounded and dejected.

'What is it?' Keaton asked.

'Another victim, last night, in Warwickshire...' He turned distant and appeared starved of hope.

'You said Pamela – who's Pamela?' Keaton ventured.

Gutteridge breathed a sigh lacking in hope. 'The victim – her name was Pamela Scanlan,' he said. 'She was an old flame of mine...'

Keaton's stomach knotted and she hesitated in the moment before replying. 'Oh fuck,' she sighed. 'I'm so very sorry.'

All attentions then turned to the corpse. 'So if *this* is Jerry Masterson,' Carl began, 'if *this* is The Shropshire Ripper, then who the hell is committing these murders?'

Gutteridge drifted away on another, different train of thought. Suddenly his mind dawned on a repugnant truth. 'It's Terry!' he said. 'It's his brother, Terry!'

TWENTY-ONE

'ADDRESS?' Keaton asked, her voice soft spoken and understanding.

'University Hospital, Coventry,' Gutteridge replied.

Keaton quietly tapped it into Google Maps, then slipped her phone into the cradle. The phone instructed them to proceed east then turn right at the next junction.

'About an hour-fifty,' Keaton said, twisting to grab her belt. 'Are you okay?'

Gutteridge considered if he was or not, fully aware that if he appeared to those around him to be moved by recent events, he would likely be taken off the case for conflict of interest, and for whatever reason, he didn't want that to happen. Besides, the notes pinned to each victim dictated his involvement, and that was something that no one – not even Bryant – could ignore.

But if he *was* going to be involved, by desire or by design, he wanted to be firmly at the helm of the investigation team.

He strained an unconvincing smile. 'I'm fine, I'll be fine.'

He turned the key in the ignition, the engine fired up and they pulled away.

Gutteridge trotted across the road from the carpark towards the University Hospital building with Keaton following a beat behind, traversing an area of light-coloured paving that felt weirdly optimistic underfoot in light of the events of the week.

The building ahead was shaped like a cylinder, reminding Gutteridge of the old BBC Television Centre building in London's Shepherds Bush district, which he'd once visited on a tour.

The reception desk was bow-fronted to mimic the building's exterior. Gutteridge's approach was met with a smile. 'Can I help you?' the plump receptionist beamed, looking at ease in her job and comfortable in her own skin.

'We're here to see a Doctor Cobb in Pathology,' he explained, 'he's expecting us. DI Gutteridge, and this is my colleague, DS Keaton.'

Keaton hung in the background, looking around the vast expanse of the reception area. The perimeter was peppered with newsagents and convenience kiosks, with a restaurant located at the very back of the wide open space. It felt more like a shopping centre than a hospital. People milled around – some in clothes, some in nightgowns – trying to look unconcerned about their reasons for being in this particular building.

The plump, bow-fronted receptionist, who looked to have been designed to mirror the plump, bow-fronted reception desk she manned, struggled to her feet and leaned over the countertop. She paddled a hand towards the far side of the room.

'Take one of the lifts through there to the fourth floor, then follow signs for Pathology. You'll come to another reception desk. I'll call ahead and let Dr Cobb know you're here. He'll meet you there and escort you both in.'

Gutteridge smiled for her easy manner, thanking her as he and Keaton made for the lifts.

Exiting the lift, they meandered through the warren of corridors until they eventually spied the second reception area ahead. A lab-coated man was perched on the edge of the desk forcing a carefree manner – he appeared to be chatting up the pretty girl sat behind it, swivelling in her seat in the core of the attention.

Her false-lashed eyes and red, painted lips turned from whatever form of conversation it was the pair were having to face the new arrivals.

The girl's vibrant choice of lipstick reminded Gutteridge of Eve, a colour that perfectly suited his wife's pale complexion. He missed her – her touch, her scent, her smile. That *body*…

The man in the lab coat rocked from his perch and rounded the desk to greet the visitors, turning suitably corporate and sullen, though strangely animated. 'DI Gutteridge?'

'Indeed,' Gutteridge replied, extending a curious hand for the man to shake. 'Dr Cobb, I'm assuming?'

Cobb took the offering and gave it a healthy shake. 'Yes. I'm Dr Cobb. It's a very great pleasure to meet you both.'

Gutteridge's brow puckered at both the levity and perceived familiarity of the greeting, suddenly remembering Keaton was in tow. 'This is my colleague, DS—'

'DS Keaton,' Cobb cut in. 'I know who you are. I've seen your picture many times in the newspapers.'

Gutteridge frowned, delivering a bemused smile.

'Oh!' Cobb laughed. 'We all followed the O'Leary case up here. You two are kind of celebrities around the lab.'

Gutteridge attempted to smile despite his aversion at having to be there. 'We seem to be getting that a lot these days,' he said, flicking a glance back over his shoulder towards Keaton.

Cobb laughed again, then remembered the circumstances for their visit, and worked to quell it.

'Here are your passes,' Cobb said, turning to receive them from his red-lipped muse sat behind his efforts to be charming.

The guests put them on.

'Would you like to follow me?'

The laboratory was the usual fayre of white-painted walls with a neat row of gleaming autopsy tables at its centre, kicking the stark, checkerboard lighting above. The wall on the far side of the room featured a number of polished mortuary refrigerator doors.

Another man in dark blue scrubs and surgical clogs was sliding a body out of one of the coolers and onto a cadaver gurney. He wheeled it to one of the tables, where he and Cobb muscled it into the tray. The man in scrubs then returned to the cooler and retrieved an opaque plastic container, and respectfully placed it on an adjoining table.

Gutteridge – for whatever reason – found himself averting his gaze, trying to find anything of interest within the uncluttered space with which to distract himself. A distant memory momentarily attempted to cleave its way through his artificial attempts at preoccupation – of Pamela Scanlan, fresh-faced and beaming from the adjoining seat of the Nemesis ride at Alton Towers, laughing through her fears and holding his hand so tightly that he could almost still feel her petrified grip through his fingers.

She was the first woman he'd ever truly loved, lessons learned that a kiss from one who holds your heart has the power to move the earth beneath your feet. It had been an adoring union, the experience forever permeating his soul.

Now, once again, he was close to her, but under dramatically different circumstances.

Cobb stood by the table, purposefully blocking the remains, an air of awkwardness colouring his demeanour. He waited for the visitors to cross the room and join him.

Cobb cleared his throat. 'It's, erm… it's my understanding you *knew* the victim?'

'Indeed,' Gutteridge said, reading the conflicted feelings emanating off Cobb. 'Listen,' he said, sighing. 'We both know – in a text-book world – that I shouldn't really be on this case. But we also know that I don't have a choice. So I need you to try and see past that, for the sake of the potential victims we're attempting to save.'

Cobb's lips winced a thin but understanding smile, nodding his comprehension of the unconventional circumstances. 'How much detail?' he asked.

'Don't hold back,' Gutteridge said. 'I'm good.'

Another nod. 'Okay…'

Cobb stepped aside, and Gutteridge's eyes widened at the sight. He had to work hard to stop himself from staggering, recognising the small, butterfly tattoo on the left shoulder of the headless corpse – a tattoo *he'd* paid for.

'*P-Pam!*' he blurted, lifting a hand to his mouth to stifle the reaction.

Cobb stepped forward to hide the remains again.

'*No*,' Gutteridge insisted. 'I'm… I'm okay.'

Keaton stepped through to take up the reins, giving Gutteridge the time he needed to reset.

The body of what looked to be a female in her late thirties lay in the tray, head missing, the skin flanking the decapitation partially cut but more torn towards the back of the neck.

Two vertebrae of the spine protruded from the open wound, and Keaton had to swallow back the taste of the sandwich she'd hurriedly eaten in the car on the journey down.

'Do we know what did this?' she asked, indicating the clean-cut region of the throat.

Cobb turned a look to the assistant who was hanging in

187

the background, who dutifully retrieved a roll of wire from another box and carried it across.

'This,' Cobb said, taking the wire and presenting it. 'It's 20SWG piano wire. Less than a millimetre thick. About 350-400lbs breaking strain.'

The confusion showed on Keaton's face. 'How?'

Cobb turned a look of uncertainty in the direction of Gutteridge. Gutteridge stepped in closer. 'Please... Go ahead. I'm good.'

Cobb felt decidedly uncomfortable, but at the insistence of Gutteridge, he continued. 'The answer to your question is, *inertia*... One end had been attached to the railings of the viaduct, the other, around the victim's neck.'

He paused, noting that Gutteridge was still looking mostly together and suitably resolute. He carried on, but trod carefully, one concerned eye remaining locked on Gutteridge.

'Whoever did this, then pushed... pushed her off... off the...' he tailed off, but the room understood.

Keaton cocked her head and gave a compassionate look to where the head should have been, then lifted her gaze towards the opaque container. 'Is *that* it... in there?' she asked.

'Is that what in where?' Cobb asked.

'The head. In the box?'

Cobb followed her gaze to the container, then returned his attention to Keaton, shaking a regretful head. 'No. Those are just her belongings, and anything else gathered as evidence,' he said, tapping the container. 'The head was – *is* – missing, and I think whoever did this must have taken it from the scene. It appears they kept it.'

Keaton grunted. '*Jesus!*'

Cobb's attention returned to the table. '*This* much of her was found lying in the road that runs beneath the viaduct by a motorist who was driving to his job as a night watchman, so we can gauge her time of death with quite some level of accuracy. We think it must have been around 12:45 am.

'Was she alive – you know, when this happened?' Gutteridge asked, looking oddly hopeful, feeling the guilt of her innocent blood on his hands, slaughtered simply because of their prior association.

Cobb sensed the hope in Gutteridge's voice. He sagged and nodded. 'I'm afraid so. She'd been taped to a sack truck, presumably to make transporting her to the location easier. The spread of the blood at the scene and the size of the droplets would suggest the presence of arterial pressure.'

Gutteridge's stomach sank.

'Oh!' Cobb barked, holding a triumphant finger in the air. 'I also found traces of mild dermatitic irritation and chemical burning around the clavicular region at the top of her chest, possibly from exposure to drips of chloroform? But we'll need the toxicology report to confirm that of course.'

He then leaned in and used his pinky to indicate areas of what little neck remained. 'I also found deep-tissue bruising to the sides of her throat, concentrated around the area of her carotid arteries. Thumb and finger print in size, *and* shape.' He lifted his eyes to meet Gutteridge's. 'I think she'd literally been "pinched" unconscious at some point by what must be the very strong hand of whoever did this. I'm not sure why, to silence her perhaps? Sadistic really, cruel, heartless. But whoever this was is strong, so almost definitely a man.'

Gutteridge still seemed lost in his swimming guilt. 'So… is there a chance – *any* chance – that she was unconscious when this happened? You know, with the chloroform rash and the bruising to her neck?'

Cobb knew the rash didn't – to him – look recent, and the bruising seemed substantially peri-mortem in its colouration, but decided to lie. 'It's possible.' He wandered over to the container of belongings and bagged evidence. 'There was also a note pinned to her sternum,' he said, retrieving a bag from the box. 'It's addressed to you, which I've been led to understand follows a pattern? Would you like to read it?'

Gutteridge took a long, preparatory breath and held out his hand. 'Please.'

Cobb un-bagged the note and handed it over, looking on with interest. 'We did try passing a light through it, but we couldn't make out too much. We left it for you to open.'

'We appreciate that,' Gutteridge whispered, his gaze fixated on the envelope, observing the spatters of dried blood splashed across his name.

'We've already processed the outside and found nothing, but if you could try and be careful with the contents,' Cobb added.

Gutteridge nodded. 'Of course.'

Cobb's assistant stepped in and offered Gutteridge a scalpel. He took it, and sliced the envelope open, handing the implement back and withdrew the note with his gloved fingertips. Gingerly, he thumbed it open…

You're probably looking at this note, while I'm looking at this girl's lovely head. Pretty thing, tastes nice. Such pretty lips.

Are you feeling it yet? My pain? The pain that you caused?

You only have yourself to blame – you had it coming and it'll keep coming, until, like me, you have no one left to care for.

Your suffering has become my legacy – a life of misery you'll inherit from me. I have risen from the depths of my despair to become your cancer.

Reap the illness, for soon, that is all that shall remain.
M

Gutteridge suddenly felt alone in all of this, a veil of seclusion descending around his grief and his inflating feelings of inadequacy.

He decided to combat it by sharing the contents of the note with the interested faces looking on, witnessing his mounting anguish, reading it aloud for the room.

The circle of colleagues stood motionless, listening, absorbing the literary insanity floated off the note.

Cobb held his stare for a time after Gutteridge finished. 'Now I get it,' he said. 'This is personal – to him *and* to you, right?'

'Right,' Gutteridge confirmed.

Cobb's gaze turned quizzical. 'When I spoke to your boss – DCI Bryant? He made noises that sounded very much to me like this might be The Shropshire Ripper?'

Gutteridge replayed the morning's events through his mind. 'This stays in here, okay?' he said.

Cobb nodded. 'Of course.'

Gutteridge turned to give the usual look at Keaton for her opinion. She shrugged and nodded.

His eyes returned to Cobb. 'At this moment in time, it is our belief that just a few hours ago, we found the remains of Jerry Masterson – The Shropshire Ripper – hidden in the loft space of his brother's Buxton residence.'

Cobb's face washed over, confused. 'So, who's doing this then?' he said, swinging a momentary look down to the corpse at his left elbow.

'His brother,' Gutteridge said. 'We think it's his brother. We think it's Terry.'

TWENTY-TWO

KEATON SAT IN THE passenger seat of the Saab watching Gutteridge milling around the carpark on his phone. He glanced at his watch and said something to whoever was on the other end of the line, then turned to look towards the car, smiling his apologies for the delay and continuing the conversation.

Keaton sat in the cosseting, womblike silence of the cabin, pondering the day's events. Once again – like during the O'Leary case of over a year ago – she was experiencing moments where nothing felt real. A subconscious disconnect from the realities of a world that seemed to have turned surreal – one that had her using all she'd learned during her psychology degree to self-diagnose her fluctuating emotions.

The mere thought that she'd stood in the same space as what remained of one of history's most infamous serial killers felt unreal enough, but in addition to that, she'd been sat in the same room as the person they *now* suspected of committing some of the most heinous and sadistic murders *she'd* ever heard of – let alone been involved in trying to solve.

Gutteridge looked to be wrapping up the call, his back and

forth pacing slowing to a saunter, head lifting from the meat of the conversation.

He tapped the phone off and trotted to the car, popping open the door and dropping inside.

'Who was that?' Keaton asked.

'Hm? Oh, Bryant. I gave him an update, and I made another call afterwards. Listen,' he said. 'I've okayed it with the chief, but would you mind if we do two things while we're up this way?'

'Like what?' Keaton asked, intrigued.

'That depends,' he replied. 'Is there any reason you need to get back to yours tonight?'

Keaton gave the question some consideration… 'Well, Joshua's with my sister – I guess she could look after him for just one night. He usually sleeps through these days, he's very good. Why?'

'Because, while we're up this way and I can feel certain we haven't been followed, I'd like to visit my mother. Our shift would have ended by the time we got back, what with the early start we both had, so… you know.'

'Your mother? I didn't know she was still alive. You've never really spoken of her.'

Gutteridge attempted to shrug it off, fighting the feelings of guilt that sporadically resurfaced. 'I know. Well, you know how it is. We get so busy that I tend to forget she even exists. Shitty son, huh?'

'No,' Keaton said. 'We can all be guilty of those sorts of things. Anyway, where is she?'

'A care home, near Nottingham.'

'*Nottingham*! What the hell's she doing in Nottingham?'

Gutteridge sat back in the seat and rolled his eyes. 'Before she met and married my father – who *is* dead – that's the area she originally came from – the area she grew up in. I have extended family there, too. Family I've lost touch with a bit over the years. Shame, really.'

Keaton pondered his situation. 'Well, if you've cleared it with Bryant, I *guess* it's okay. But you said two things – and what's this about not making it home?'

Gutteridge took a moment to consider his answer. 'Well, if you drive a relatively short way west from Nottingham, you eventually arrive at Knutsford.'

Keaton had to expend a few moments to recall where in her recent history that place name featured... then it landed. 'You mean... Toby Jackson's place?' The silence that met the question answered it. 'Why would you want to go there? I know you've become friends and all, but...' Then it dawned on her. '*Ahhhhh*... Is that where Eve is?'

'It is,' Gutteridge said, frowning. 'I know this *thing* – this *situation* – between you and I is a bit of a mess, and you know I want to be there for you, *and* for Joshua.'

'I do,' Keaton responded.

'Thing is... I *do* miss Eve. I miss her being around, miss her voice, her company. You know?'

Keaton reached out and placed an understanding hand on his. 'I know, I know. So, was that the other call you made, to Jackson?'

Gutteridge nodded, looking strangely like a naughty child caught in a fib.

'And are they okay with us just turning up?'

'They are. They actually seemed really excited about it, especially Asha. She's always talking about you.'

Keaton smirked. 'Is she? And you – are *you* okay with me being there? That *is* where you and I... you know,' she said, being deliberately vague.

The guilty look returned to Gutteridge's demeanour. 'Do you regret it?'

Keaton huffed a soft laugh. 'The truth? No,' she smiled. 'I don't. You've given me the child I'd always denied that I wanted, and I know it's a bit of a mess, but I wouldn't want anyone else to be the father but you.'

Gutteridge turned to her with a look steeped in concern.

'I *didn't* mean it like that,' she assured him. 'I know that we – you and I – could never be. If you want me to be frank and base about it, I'm talking genetically.'

Gutteridge allowed himself to laugh. 'Sperm bank now, am I?'

Keaton came over serious. 'No, not at all.' She took a moment to arrange her emotions. 'The truth?' she muttered. 'The *real* truth is, I wish you and I *could* be a thing. I'd be lying if I said I didn't love you and I think you know that. But I'm happy raising your child, and as long as I get to spend my days with you, it'll help keep the heartbreak at bay.'

Gutteridge held a concrete stare directed at Keaton, her confession breaking his heart. 'But…'

'Shhhh,' she insisted. 'Don't. It's not important. I'm happy – happy that *you're* happy, and happy that I now have a child. Your child.' She gave the hand she realised she was still holding a squeeze. 'Just be there for me. That's all I ask.'

*

Gutteridge turned the nose of the Saab in through the entrance of Radcliffe Manor House Care Home that forked off Wharf Lane, a narrow track flanked by impressive walls adorned with brickwork patination.

Keaton could see sporadic glimpses of a grand old building through the trees that lined the gravel driveway, her interest serenaded by the crunch of the tyres.

'It's huge!' Keaton said.

'It *is* a pretty sizeable place,' he agreed. 'The building's listed. Posh or what.'

'What on earth must *that* be costing a month?'

Gutteridge smirked. 'Plenty,' he said, as he hunted for a parking space with a view. 'My folks have never been short of a penny or two. Another windfall to land some day.'

He pulled into a space overlooking the impressive gardens and shut the engine off.

'*Another* windfall? What was the other one?' Keaton asked.

Gutteridge cursed the looseness of his tongue, then rolled a smugly ironic look her way. 'If I tell you, you must promise to keep it to yourself. I mean, *really* promise.'

Keaton considered the ramifications of purposefully denying herself an opportunity for gossip. 'Okay,' she agreed, begrudgingly.

'You know that app I've been helping Toby Jackson to develop?'

'Yeah. What about it?'

'Well, according to him, it's gone ballistic – I apparently have the first of many clinically obese royalty cheques winging its way to my letterbox for my efforts.'

'You're shitting me?'

'Nope! Straight up. Oh and as a thank you, I'm now also the proud owner of a gleaming red Ferrari!'

'What? A *Ferrari*! How?'

'Jackson presented it to me as a thank you the last time I saw him.' He suddenly succumbed to a wave of crippling guilt, and it showed on his face.

'What's wrong?' Keaton asked.

Gutteridge let go a sigh that was flavoured with a discernible amount of frustration. 'The last time I saw Jackson and Asha, was after we'd discovered the body of Kerry Marston. Now, it's Patricia Scanlan. Both dead because of me.'

Keaton watched him crumble. 'It's not *you* who killed them.'

Gutteridge deflated like a punctured tyre. 'No. It's only *because* of me.'

'That's bullshit and you know it.'

Gutteridge's cheek winced with doubt. 'I know. Still, I'm finding it hard these days to feel happy and grateful for the positives in my life, such as they are.'

Keaton softened. 'I know. I get it, but you should. This guy – whoever he is – is doing the wrong things for the wrongest of reasons, and chances are, if it wasn't you who triggered him, it would be someone, or something, else.'

Gutteridge smiled at her attempts to dignify his potential to feel contentment. 'Thank you, Jane,' he said.

He broke from the awkwardness and opened the door. 'I'll be as quick as I can,' he said. 'I'd bring you in, but the dementia has sunk its teeth into her of late and the staff say strange faces can confuse her. She barely remembers *me*.'

'That's fine. Take as long as you like, I'll still be here.' She leaned across, pulled him in and deposited a kiss on his cheek. 'Go and see your mum, and give her a hug for me. Spend as much time with her as you like. Most of all, be happy – remember that you're going to be seeing the mother of all women tonight,' she said, flashing her brows suggestively.

Gutteridge smiled. 'I've actually spent all day with one of those…'

*

Gutteridge sidled up to the reception desk, embarrassed by the amount of time that had elapsed since his last visit and feeling somewhat on the back foot.

He recognised the man in his thirties sat behind the

197

counter. He was busy filling in some kind of duty log, having not yet realised Gutteridge was there.

Gutteridge coughed, politely.

'Oh. Hey!' the man beamed, taking the briefest of moments to place the face smiling down at him. His expression suddenly brightened with some form of recognition. 'Patrick! Mr Gutteridge. How have you been keeping?'

The attendant's name finally came to him. 'I'm very well thank you, Martin. Good to see you. How's she been?' Gutteridge asked, flicking a cursory look in the direction of the suites.

The slightly hippyish attendant pumped an exaggeratedly ruminative nod in response. 'Yeeeaaahhh, she's been good, man.' He leaned a look back through the open door behind him – more for effect than for anything practical. 'I think she's still in the day room, looking out of her favourite window.'

'And the… erm, the dementia?'

The attendant see-sawed a noncommittal nod in response. 'She has her good days, and bad, of course.'

Gutteridge smiled, unable to decide if that somehow – in some warped way – this made him feel less guilty. If his mother increasingly having a tendency to forget he'd even visited would somehow absolve him of blame for the times where he hadn't?

'Can I go through and see her?'

'Of course,' the attendant chirped. 'I'll get Andrea. *Andrea!*' he called out, to somewhere behind his shoulder. 'She'll take you through.'

'Are we still doing the mask thing?'

The attendant held out some sort of jazz hand rejection of Gutteridge's question. 'Nooo – we stopped all that nonsense ages ago.'

A young, heavy-hipped girl with an attentive nature and an awkward, rolling gait weaved through the reception and rounded the counter. 'Would you like to follow me?' she smiled.

*

Gutteridge wandered through the gauntlet of scattered bodies, some dozing, some with pensive stares, looking every bit to him like a junkyard for lives that have outlived their usefulness. A veritable sea of faces looking thoughtful of the dreams they'd never fulfilled and the things they dearly wished they'd done differently.

A halo of white hair in front of one of the windows lit his way, like a burning bush sent by God to illuminate his path to being a better son.

The carer politely leaned her face into the messaging angel's field of view. 'Margaret, there is someone here to see you,' she mewed, gently spinning the woman's wheelchair to face into the room.

'Hi, Mum,' Gutteridge whispered, crouching down to bring their eyes level.

He was shocked by the changes he saw in her face and the fragility of her limbs. He attempted to recall exactly how long it had been since his last visit, but couldn't.

'You're looking well, Mum,' he lied.

The care worker peeled away with a temperate smile. 'I'll leave you two alone. I'll make you both a cup of tea.'

'Thank you,' Gutteridge smiled, astounded that she'd apparently remembered he only drank tea, knowing they usually would offer guests and visitors the option of coffee, too.

Gutteridge returned his attention to the old lady who was now peering at him with her sepia eyes, their whites yellow, colour faded by time. The faintest look of recognition eventually tugged at her wrinkled lids.

'It's me, Mum. It's Patrick. Your son...?'

The old woman's brow furrowed, then slowly brightened. 'Patrick?'

The joy and relief in Gutteridge's face lit the air between them. 'Yes, Mum. It's me, I've come up to see you.'

'Here,' a voice behind him said, as the carer gingerly slid a seat towards him.

'Thank you,' Gutteridge beamed, positioning the offering directly in front of the woman who'd done such a fine job of raising him and lowering his apologetic frame into it.

A hand, clad in paper-thin skin, suddenly reached out and wrapped itself around his. He could feel the tremble of her failing nervous system transmit through her featherlight grip. 'Where's George?' the old woman asked, looking around, appearing lost and bewildered.

Gutteridge's brow flickered, trying to recall anyone of importance in either his or his mother's life named George. 'Who's George?' he asked. 'We don't know any George, do we?'

His mother's face gradually washed over a picture of confusion and doubt, looking lost and dismayed by his response.

Gutteridge's heart cracked at the sight. 'Oh, sorry, yeah. Of course. George... George couldn't make it, Mum,' he said, placing a hand atop hers. 'But he sends his love, and told me to say he misses you, dearly.'

His mother's elated face beamed, her hand delivering a succession of fluttering clenches to his own.

'Here's some tea,' announced the care worker, dragging the smaller of a nest of side tables into the core of their reunion. 'I'll put it here for you,' she said, delivering the cups onto saucers. 'And there's some sugar and biscuits,' she added, before departing with an understanding smile...

Gutteridge sat in a cubical of the men's restroom, reeling within his guilt and sadness, tears cascading down his crumpled face. He tried to counter the images of the shadow his mother had become with his fondest memories of when she was young, vibrant and – in the eyes of the love of a child – beautiful. Those years when she was still somebody – a person of value in a world that she improved simply by existing within it.

He sat for what felt like a day, crying his guilt away, mourning the passing of someone not yet dead, letting his tears wash away the regret he knew was showing in his face.

Eventually, he unfurled a handful of sheets from the roll by his shoulder and dabbed his face dry – nothing left within him to shed.

'Just throw yourself into your work,' he muttered, his voice echoing around the hard, tiled walls – his long-standing mantra for times such as these. 'Just throw yourself into your work…'

TWENTY-THREE

DESPITE OVER A YEAR having elapsed since Jane Keaton had last visited Toby and Asha Jackson's impressive home, she recognised its gravelled approach and the impressive aspect of the timber-framed frontage and its riot of glazing with surprising clarity.

The conversation during the entire journey there had been case related, regurgitating the facts and details to court clarity and coherence, which for Gutteridge had helped to appease the guilt that undeniably existed in allowing something as mundane as 'life' to contaminate their working day. There was a killer to catch, but their mental wellbeing undeniably deserved, and it could be argued, *needed*, consideration.

'Back here again,' Gutteridge said, trying to channel the perception of the woman sat to his left, because of course, *he'd* been back plenty of times himself, since.

'It's much bigger than I remember,' Keaton chirped, leaning looks out of all the windows.

The front door opened and Eve hoved into view to greet their arrival. Despite the weather growing cold – the winter months now fast approaching – she'd seen fit to clad her svelte figure in a red summer dress for the occasion, her impossibly long legs rising from what she would refer to as 'strappy sandals'.

'Good lord,' Keaton said without moving her lips. 'How the hell is anyone supposed to compete with *that*?'

Gutteridge allowed himself a titter to mask the effervescent fizz in his belly that the sight of his statuesque wife was stirring. A sight that their day of death only made him hungrier for.

'She's not all that,' he quipped.

'Fuck you,' Keaton snapped, jabbing an elbow into his side. They both shared a moment of laughter.

Keaton let out an audible gasp as something to her left caught her eye. 'That's not it?'

Gutteridge flicked a glance towards whatever it was that had hooked her attention. His Ferrari was sitting pride of place outside of the block of stables. 'That's it,' he said.

'Oh my God! No way!' she slurred, before turning her attention back into the cabin.

She twisted her back hard up against the door, theatrically and purposefully attempting to create distance between her and her partner, looking him up and down. 'You're now about twice as attractive as you were twenty seconds ago.'

Gutteridge laughed at the slur as he parked the car and pulled the handbrake on. 'Sod you,' he chuckled.

'*No. I mean* it.'

'You shallow, puddle of a woman,' he clucked, still grinning.

Keaton leaned a look past him out of his side window. 'I think there's someone who's keen to see you,' she muttered.

Gutteridge followed the line of her gaze and found Eve, standing back from the car at a respectful distance, padding about, awaiting his emergence.

She looked like a beacon of hope in a world turned dark in her ruby-red dress – a gift to eyes that had seen too much of the horrors of mankind of late.

'Go. Go get her,' Keaton said. 'I'm not saying I'm that way inclined, but quite frankly, looking the way *she* does and after the day we've had – if *you* don't, *I* probably will!'

*

Ewelina led Gutteridge by the hand towards her temporary accommodation, towing him through the billowing clouds of scent that trailed from her willowy neck. The taste of a delectable dinner was still in their mouths, a desire to be alone in their hearts.

Gutteridge reached out an involuntary hand to stroke the obsidian hair tumbling down her back. It felt strangely like the first time he'd ever touched any part of her; the absence of her company seemed to both reset and reignite his appreciation of *who* and *what* she was.

Eve dragged him through the door to her bedroom and flicked it shut behind them with an almost impatient hand, then turned to face him. Her liquid grey eyes burned into him, their feline sweep searching for clues to his wellbeing. She caressed his cheek with her long, graceful fingers. 'I've missed you, Patrick,' she exhaled, her accent singing softly Polish, her glossed lips, painted red to match the dress, flinching a succession of genuine smiles, but flavoured with the mildest of hints of concern. 'I've been so worried, so very worried,' she added.

But before Gutteridge could respond, she slid her hands from his flushing cheeks to the back of his neck and pulled his lips to hers, exhaling a chestful of love, relief and desire into his lungs – something she'd learned over time stoked his fires. Her breath tasted sweet as it washed through him, rinsing away the canker of loneliness which her absence had been feeding.

Inwardly, he gathered the more repugnant memories of the

case together – those sick and twisted results of Masterson's damaged psyche – and placed them in the part of his mind that he'd long ago partitioned off to protect his sanity, locking them away from the possibility of contaminating such a deliciously hungry moment.

Gutteridge felt the muscles of his lower back tense as Eve lifted her spidery legs clear of the floor and coiled them around him. He carried her across to the heavy oak desk in the corner, reaching his arms around her to grab it and drag it away from the wall. He swiped it clear of the detritus of life and deposited the angel enveloping his trembling excitement upon it.

Her lithe fingers were already unthreading his belt and undoing his buttons, untethering his swelling appreciation of her timeless beauty.

Gutteridge muscled the hem of her dress from beneath Eve's pert behind and drew it up her body, unveiling a midriff that looked even more toned than he was usually presented with from what he assumed must be daily access to Jackson's personal gym.

'Oh my days!' he exhaled, his eyes drinking in the trim, defined results of her considerable efforts – the flexing of her core muscles mesmerising to eyes that seemed only to have witnessed death of late. Eyes that Ewelina *knew* had become obsessed with that particular region of her extravagant body. His fingers gravitated to her stomach, powerless to resist the flat, taut, Lilliputian ribbon of muscle so very firm to the touch.

Eve watched him investigating her with tentative hands, attempting to read his wants, his desires, the hunger broiling behind his lusting eyes. She leaned her weight back purposefully to solidify her core and so doing, validate his desire to touch her – and attest her desire to *be* touched.

He placed his palms flat against the toned, undulant slab of perfection, drawn in, his groin swelling to the feeling of hand-on-skin, his dilating pupils drinking in the fruits of her training as his gaze drifted from one erotic trigger to the next.

A diaphragm – stimulated by nervous expectation – heaved from beneath Eve's perfectly formed ribcage. Gutteridge placed his hand against it, feeling her breathing through the grasp of his intoxicated fingers.

He glanced down, she'd had nothing on beneath the dress. She parted her tender thighs: stimulated, lubricated, ready to accept him. Gutteridge stepped in, inserting his lust...

Eve's eyes fluttered shut and she groaned to the gods, with each and every penetration expelling the breath from her tremulous lungs.

Gutteridge's hypnotised gaze remained locked on the ribbon of muscle beneath his reprising rhythm, perfectly framed by the blood-red cloth of the rucked-up dress, his perverted thoughts further catalysed by the lilting cries of pleasure being driven from Eve's glistening lips.

Her elated face suddenly rocked forwards, her eyes wide and yearning. 'K-kiss me!' she stammered.

Gutteridge peered deep, into the arabic sweep of her lids, happy to acquiesce. He leaned in and pressed his open mouth against hers, driving himself in deeper, exchanging a shared, guttural breath until no oxygen remained and the world around them began to swim in a partially lucid sea of depleting reality. He smiled inside at the feeling.

With a grunt, Eve thrust his mouth off hers before she swooned, but her insistent stare remained locked on his, fuelled by the sensation. Gutteridge could see her toying with the spark of an idea behind those glistening, grey eyes. 'Grab my throat,' she said. 'When I cum.'

Gutteridge's rhythm slowed, his brows crimping at what seemed to him to be such an out of character request. But he'd read about this, in a book he had back at the house, so *knew* it to be 'a thing'. But never before had he encountered it in a real-world setting and it took him aback. Then he had to wonder, if she'd found it, this book, and read it?

'What?' he breathed.

Her expression turned hard and insistent. 'I said, take hold of my throat, and make it difficult for me to breathe, w-when I'm cumming.'

Her face suddenly fell away again, her body beginning to shudder. She presented her neck into the focus of his uncertainty, long and slight, her wet, gleaming lips biting at the air.

Gutteridge briefly wavered, hesitating. Then, pulled along by the moment, he unleashed the inner pervert he knew to be in every man, allowing it to thrive – if only to please his wife and perhaps, unload some of the burden of those multitude of incidents that had frustrated his life up until then, clasping a hesitant hand to her delicate neck.

Eve exhaled a whimpering cry laced with some skewed, nefarious form of joy to the skies, the shudder of her perfect body intensifying to the sensation of the pressure enveloping her throat.

Gutteridge gradually grew curious, gently tightening his grip, his fingers wincing with uncertainty.

'Harder!' Eve barked, though now sounding equally hesitant, equally unsure, but wholly invested. 'A bit harder, until it's difficult for me to breathe.'

Another frown and for the briefest of moments, Gutteridge faltered again, then, gingerly, he began clamping her throat tighter until her simpering cries began to stifle.

Her liquid grey eyes rolled in rhythm of their hips moving as one, the elated, joy in her face aglow with the most impure form of euphoria.

Eve's body went into spasm, a coiling spine arching her

back, thrusting that slender wall of abdominal perfection towards Gutteridge and his hypnotised eyes.

He thrust himself in deeper, intensifying the spasm, dragged along by this master-and-servant game they now seemed to be enacting, playing her body like the instrument of pleasure it had become. He reached his free hand in to grasp her sweat-lacquered stomach, lost in a turbulent storm of erotic depravity.

Gutteridge now also felt fully invested in the twisted moment they were sharing, comprehending Eve's new variety of corrupted desires with telepathic accuracy. He dragged his fingers the length of her medial ridge, through her sacral chakra, towards her swollen groin and her alert clitoris, unleashing a stifled, simpering cry from Eve's gasping lips that ignited the air around them.

Gutteridge's body finally succumbed to the sights, sounds and sensations, his libido boiling over, releasing the pressure of his mounting lust to a shared cacophony of base cries and contorting limbs. With a final triumphant bark, they both fell limp.

Gutteridge hung awkwardly in the aftermath of the 'event', sweat dripping from his nose onto Eve's heaving torso, unsure of exactly how he should be feeling.

He removed his fingers from her neck and cupped her recherché ribcage in his hands, scrutinising – with ultimate fascination – its expansion and contraction. He couldn't help but wonder if this was how the Mastersons of the world viewed *their* physical stimuli – the muses, the obsessions, the potential wellsprings for their twisted trophies. The comparison suddenly made him deeply uncomfortable, causing him to relax his inquisitive grip on his wife's spent body.

That recurrent feeling that he'd allowed too much of his inner 'Masterson' loose for the world to witness resurfaced again, engulfing his assuredness, egged on by the outwardly angelic but – what he briefly perceived to be – the inwardly corrupted fallen angel lying beneath his glazed expression.

Eve lay panting, her body prone and spent. 'No more,' she blurted, her mouth gulping for air that never seemed enough. 'Please… no more.'

Gutteridge extended a compassionate hand and placed it softly to the side of her face, his thumb caressing the defined ridge of her pawing lips.

Eve placed her hand atop his, rolling her cheek hard into the cradle of his tender caress. 'God, I love you!' she stammered. Four simple words that hit Gutteridge like a punch; a declaration made that landed hard, sending waves of warmth and compassion thundering through his trembling muscles like lava.

And *there* it was, the difference – his reaction. The one thing he knew that set the likes of him and Masterson apart: his empathy, his tenderness, his careening, often out-of-control ability to love and *feel* loved. Gutteridge somehow felt clean again, absolved of blame, washed clear of the grime and feculent of their foray into mild perversion.

Nevertheless, he was painfully aware he'd allowed that naturally sensual side of his nature – one that had always existed – a free reign to thrive and proliferate. Undoubtedly, a reaction to the pressures he was currently having to endure, but he'd felt them beginning to snowball and run away with him, causing his struggling inability to handle the pressure to feed thoughts and desires that he was beginning to feel deeply uncomfortable with. But were such thoughts not considered normal? Or at least, normal enough to render that discomfort unfounded?

'W-what brought that on?' he stuttered, curious, his ardour still quaking to the rush of his loins.

Eve tittered like a naughty child, her smile – a gift from heaven – returning to a face incandescent with pleasure.

'I thought I'd like to try it,' she said, her voice breathy. 'And I thought, if I'm not going to be seeing you for a while, I wanted it to be memorable.' Her head tilted to her shoulder, her aqueous grey eyes turning to look up at him. 'Why? Did you not enjoy it?'

Gutteridge *still* felt unsure of how he should be feeling.

Eve lifted his hand from her cheek and placed it flat on her sweat-jewelled stomach, pulling it into the crater of her concave ribcage. 'Hm?' she asked again, flashing brows and smiling knowingly, seeming to both approbate and validate the focus of, what to him, was beginning to feel like a fetish.

Gutteridge relaxed out of his uncertainty and allowed himself a nervous laugh to quell his reticence.

He could feel her racing heartbeat pulse through his palm, enjoying feeling the mechanics of what – in the eyes of his unquenchable love – was a body without peer. A body that belonged to and motivated the woman he'd grown to adore, and with such style and grace that it regularly took his breath away.

'Yes,' he mewed. 'I enjoyed it. Very much.'

She smiled at his welcome reaction. 'In that case, perhaps we can do it again sometime?' she said, dragging his hand the length of her stomach. 'We all have a "thing", you know – I've known yours for some time. And now, I guess you know mine.'

She loosed a second smile, this time appearing slightly more reluctant. 'All I ask is that you prrromise you'll never hurt me,' she added, carrying his hand to her cheek again, before her delicate brows raised playfully, and she cocked her head. 'Well,' she said, shrugging. 'Perhaps just a little…'

TWENTY-FOUR

GUTTERIDGE TIPTOED down the polished oak staircase, the cast of dawn light through windows barely bright enough to illuminate his way. The mornings were getting noticeably darker now, the cold, unforgiving embrace of winter fast approaching.

He looked and listened for signs of Keaton, having mutually agreed on 05:30 to be an ideal time to leave to travel back south. He checked his watch again – it was now 05:08, then he heard sounds emanating from the kitchen, and wandered down the hallway towards it, pulled along by the light bleeding from the open doorway and the drifting aroma of frying bacon.

Gutteridge rounded the door and was surprised to find all 5'9" of Asha Jackson stood at the hob, conducting the components of a cooked breakfast.

She turned to greet his arrival. 'Morning,' she beamed.

'What on earth possessed you to get up at this ungodly hour?' he whispered, sauntering into the hub of the activity.

'I got up to see you both off,' she said, her voice sounding inappropriately chirpy for such an antisocial time of day. 'Toby has an important meeting today with some possible investors,

211

so I insisted he stayed in bed. But it's been lovely seeing Jane again – and *you*, of course.'

She leaned her cheek towards him by way of a request for a morning kiss, and Gutteridge's innate fascination for the woman was happy to oblige, delivering a soft peck to the side of her face.

'Blimey,' he said, inspecting the collection of pots and pans sat simmering on the stove, 'you've got it all going on, haven't you.'

He returned his attention to Asha. 'And *you*. You're already dressed, and made up?'

'Can't have the world seeing how hideous I am under all this slap and finery,' she joked.

'Yeah, yeah,' he responded, mocking the statement. 'A supremely ugly woman.'

She laughed, but it *did* somehow seem jarring and unnatural to Gutteridge to see someone as chic and vogue as Asha Jackson doing anything as utilitarian as cooking. But he got the exact same feelings whenever he saw Eve cook or clean and would often joke that it was like seeing an angel taking a dump.

Asha began stirring the pan of beans and allowed herself an inquisitive smirk. 'Am I going to discover Eve's body when I go upstairs?'

Gutteridge's brow knitted at the statement. 'What do you mean?'

A mischievous glint excited her eyes. 'You sounded like you were murdering her last night,' she chuckled, then baulked at her remiss reference to 'murder' – taboo considering everything that had been happening recently. But Gutteridge didn't seem to have noticed, so she let it lie without apology.

Gutteridge came over embarrassed. 'Oh… I'm sorry. We were… you know…'

212

'Don't you dare apologise,' she snapped. 'If a girl needs fucking, she needs fucking.'

Again, the word 'fucking' emanating from someone so angelic sounded wholly alien – almost as alien as being asked to choke as elegant and delicate a flower as his wife.

'Can I ask you a question?' said Gutteridge, casting a furtive look down the hallway to check they were still alone.

'Of course.'

'It's a tad personal,' he added.

'Go forrr it,' she replied in her Polish, matter-of-fact voice, never one to be fazed by words. 'I think we can consider ourselves more than frrriends at this point – haven't we *always* been frank and open with each other, even frrrom day one?'

Gutteridge smiled at the declaration, acknowledging the truth in the statement, then took a beat to compile his question. 'Do you, and Toby, of course, ever do anything that could be considered... I don't know... *perverted*? In an erotic sense, I mean?'

A melodramatic, cognisant smile stretched slow and wide across Asha's face. 'Oh, I see. Get a bit – how do you English say – *fruity*, last night, did we?'

Gutteridge shuffled uneasily at the response.

'Of what variety?' she probed, stirring the pan of beans.

'*Variety*?' he replied.

Asha lifted her attention from the stove. 'Yes. What *type* of perversion?' she asked, like they were discussing nothing more controversial than the weather. 'Spanking? Bondage? Mechanical sodomy?' she added, her delivery seeming deliberately forthright to court embarrassment, her playful tongue firmly in her cheek.

Gutteridge turned coy beneath both the pressure of the question and her quizzical stare. Certainly, they'd become friends over the last year – but it still felt like a stretch to be *this* familiar, especially in light of the feelings he undoubtedly had for the woman. The third in the triptych of gorgeous females he inexplicably had attempting to complicate his life.

Asha shook her head and frowned at his perceived reluctance to engage. 'You *know* I'm just messing with you. But at the same time, you're not going to attempt to tell me that a detective from the British police force is unversed in, or even *fazed* by, sexual perversion!' she said. 'I mean, we've *all* read the stories.'

Gutteridge smirked. 'I think that might be the Metropolitan Police you're thinking of.'

Asha returned the smirk. 'So, go on then, what kind?' she reiterated.

Gutteridge steeled himself, ironically, taking a breath. 'I guess you would best describe it as… asphyxiation.'

Asha turned to look his way almost mockingly. 'Is that all?'

'Isn't that enough?'

She continued to stir the pan, then banged the spoon clear on the rim before spinning the gas off. 'Toby sometimes clamps his hand across my mouth when I'm… *you* know.'

'*Really?*'

She laughed again. 'Ye-hes. It heightens the sensation – makes it more intense.' She hopped a nonchalant shrug. 'Nothing too crrrazy you underrrstand, just restrrricting the flow a bit. Makes it… I don't know… otherworldly?'

Gutteridge suddenly felt a little easier about the previous night's activities. 'So you don't think it's weird?'

'Well, if it *is*, I guess that would mean *I* am too!' she chirped. 'As long as you're respectful and don't get too carried away.'

She slipped off her apron and tossed it aside, then turned to front him, leaning her body into his to unnerve him, playfully, the way she knew she could.

Gutteridge stuttered slightly at the closeness.

'It's a shame,' she whispered, looking up at him, toying with his abashment, 'that I'll never get the chance to have you do that to me.'

Gutteridge turned coy, becoming aware of the thump of his heartbeat in his head. His mind turned to new varieties of thought he felt were being seeded and propagated by the activities of the previous night.

Asha's eyes peered into his, looking for anything resembling a requited emotion. Still playing, but at the same time, interested in knowing.

Gutteridge briefly imagined the sultry eyes studying him rolling in rapture, his hand clamped across her beautiful mouth, her chest heaving with the inability to draw breath – all thoughts seemingly fuelled by his wife's midnight request.

Before he realised he'd even done it, his mouth was on hers, pulled along by a turbulent river of desire. To his surprise – like the time in the garages – she didn't pull away.

They shared each other's space for a perceived eternity, tasting each other's skin and relishing the closeness – pondering what might have been in a different reality.

Asha inhaled a lungful of breath through her flaring nostrils, then broke the kiss, crowning the moment with a lingering moan of contentment.

'*Mmmm*, well I guess there's no harm in dreaming,' she said, pausing to absorb the sensuality drenching their stolen moment.

The sound of footsteps approaching from the doorway behind made them snap apart. Actions which – until then – Gutteridge had managed to convince himself were harmless, suddenly felt like the infidelity it was.

'Morning,' Keaton chirped as she entered the room, looking around at the beautifully laid breakfast table, appearing humbled and appreciative of the food that was obviously being prepared just for them.

'Morning, Jane,' Asha sang. 'Please, take a seat. I've made you both something to fuel your detecting efforts.'

'That's really lovely, Asha, but you didn't have to do that!' Keaton said.

'I know, but I did it anyway,' she beamed, acting comedically rebellious, cracking two eggs into a waiting pan and pulling warm dishes from the oven. She began plating up as the visitors took to their seats, facing each other.

'Did you two have a nice night?' Keaton whispered to Gutteridge, raising knowing brows.

Gutteridge shook his head and smiled through his mounting despair. 'Women…' he muttered.

The food was delivered to the grateful guests and Asha floated over to the kettle, filling the three mugs she had prepared in readiness.

*

'Don't be strrrangers!' Asha yelled, lifting a jaunty wave towards the departing car. Eve was stood by her side, her image shrinking away in Gutteridge's rear view mirror, looping Asha's free arm in hers and looking decidedly sad and forlorn to be losing her husband again.

'I've discovered something,' Keaton blurted, fracturing the wistful atmosphere in the cabin. 'And if it wasn't for you rearranging your wife last night, I'd have shown it to you earlier.'

'What is it?' he said, ignoring the flippancy of her comment, lifting one last, parting wave through the side window before turning through the gates onto the main road.

'*This!*' she said, with an air of triumph, carefully drawing a sheet of A4 paper from her bag.

Gutteridge's eyes left the road long enough to glance at it. 'And what is that?'

'Do you remember the photos I took of Terrence Masterson's house, the ones of the stain on the ceiling?'

'Of course.'

'And do you recall the piece of paper I stuck to the wall for scale?'

Again, Gutteridge nodded.

'Well, of course, I took it down after, and I stuffed it in my back pocket.'

'So?' Gutteridge said, struggling to grasp the point.

'Well, I found it again last night, while I was folding my clothes. I noticed the imprint of writing just visible on its surface. Biro tracks left behind from the sheets above that had been written on and torn off. Under the light from my bedside table, I could just make it out.' She drew out two more sheets of A4 from her bag, covered in writing that Gutteridge recognised to be hers.

'So what was on it?'

'Two things – firstly, an inventory of furniture, the kind you'd make if you were moving house.'

Gutteridge's expression brightened. 'Well, I guess that verifies what we now believe. What was the second thing?'

'*This!*' she clucked, holding the paper up towards him. 'It took me a while to discern it from the inventory of furniture it was overlapping, but it appears to be a list of medications.' She turned momentarily pensive. 'My father once had cancer – he survived and everything, but I recognise most of what's here because he was prescribed much of the same.'

She lifted a finger to the middle of the list. 'For example, these here, they're growth blockers. They're prescribed to try and slow the spread of the disease, and everything else on the list is of the same ilk.'

Gutteridge sat in silence for a mile, assessing the possible ramifications and incorporating them into his plans.

'Could you ring around when we arrive back to the station, try and find where his doctor's surgery is?'

Keaton looked smugly animated. 'I've already been online last night and made a list of all the surgeries in the area – but none of them open until 08:00 or 08:30.'

'Okay, good. That's about when we'll get back. Good work.'

'Thanks, chief,' she chirped, settling into the seat for the long haul. She rolled a look in his direction. 'Did it help? Staying over last night?' she asked.

A reminiscent smile spread across Gutteridge's face. 'It did. It helped a lot,' he said, sensing that Keaton was compiling a follow-up question.

'And erm… that Asha. She's very beautiful. Have you and *her*… ever…?' Her question tailed off, but he knew what she was alluding to.

Gutteridge frowned at the question. 'Asha? Why are you asking that?'

Keaton smirked. 'Well, firstly, that *wasn't* a "no". And secondly, when you walk into a stranger's kitchen on some random morning, only to discover your colleague tongue-deep in a kiss with a Polish princess who's name *isn't* Eve, before you have to quickly hurry out again and walk back in, making sure to make more noise the second time around, these questions somehow come to you.'

Gutteridge sagged at the wheel.

Keaton burst into laughter. 'You're amazing!' she barked. 'I don't know how you do it. Part of me wants to say you're just some random bloke, but *I'm* one of the poor sods who's guilty of falling foul of your inexplicable charms!'

Gutteridge reeled with embarrassment. 'I don't know what it is. You'd think I was some bloody oil baron or a multimillionaire playboy. But I'm just some flippin' copper who keeps getting hassled by lovely women who's apparent goal in life is to screw with my emotions!'

Keaton's laughter subsided, leaving only the fondest of smiles in its wake. 'And am *I* one of those lovely women?'

'Yeah!' he blurted. 'You *are*, you're gorgeous – and that's what I don't understand. I mean, just look at me!'

Keaton held her amused stare. 'Don't you sell yourself short,' she said. 'You're really rather handsome, do you know that? But maybe more than that, as a human, you're pretty damned fascinating.' Her smile relaxed slightly. 'Just be careful not to be too accepting of *all* the options that present themselves. We both have first-hand experience of how *that* can go!'

Gutteridge flicked a mildly cynical but appreciative look her way, reciprocating her smile. 'I'll try…'

TWENTY-FIVE

DS JANE KEATON trotted along the warren of corridors towards the incident room, brandishing a torn-off page from her notepad, the air alive with the sounds of her echoing footsteps.

She rounded the door and saw Gutteridge sitting at his desk, cross-scrutinising the case files, alerted to her sudden arrival by the decelerating clack of her heels and the sound of her laboured breathing. Her face looked flushed, pained but elated.

'Everything alright?' he asked, peering over his reading glasses.

She gulped back her exhaustion. 'I need to do more cardio!' she blurted, clutching her side. 'I've just sprinted back from town.' She wandered across to Gutteridge's desk and doubled over, passing him the note with an outstretched arm. 'You need to ring this guy.'

Gutteridge took the offering. 'What is it?'

'It's the number, for a Doctor Caine. He's a consultant at Cavendish Hospital in Buxton.'

Gutteridge sat absorbing the scribblings on the slip of paper with brow-creasing interest to the accompaniment of Keaton's heavy breathing.

He had difficulty deciphering Keaton's handwriting at the best of times, but these notes had been scribbled in somewhat of a hurry – and obviously whilst leaning on something unsuitable for impromptu notetaking. He could just make out the key words: mesothelioma, stage three, rejected an offer of chemo, months not years, and the word 'RECEPTIONIST!' scribbled in all-caps.

He allowed his attention to drift up to Keaton again, who was now stood upright, clutching a stitch in her side.

'What's this part about a receptionist?' he asked, pointing at the note.

Keaton gulped again. 'She works at the hospital, on the desk. She's been missing for nearly three weeks.'

Gutteridge's eyes flashed. 'And this Doctor Caine?'

Another swallow. 'He's the consultant who's been dealing with Terrence Masterson's case. He has cancer, meso… mesothel-something?' she said, jabbing a finger towards the slip of paper. 'It's inoperable… terminal!'

Gutteridge held a fixed stare directed up at Keaton, looking more through her than at her.

'Did he say how long?'

She nodded in response. 'He said months rather than years, and that was as accurate an estimate as he was willing to give me.'

'I'll call him,' Gutteridge said.

Keaton wagged a finger towards the note again. 'That receptionist,' she said. 'Apparently she went missing just three days after Masterson last visited the surgery.'

Gutteridge considered the relevance of this particular snippet of information. 'And this visit, is that when he was informed?'

An exaggerated, knowing nod from Keaton. 'It was.'

Gutteridge sat back from the exchange, feeling like he was sinking through his seat.

'Then he has nothing to lose,' he muttered, his mind dawning on a terrible truth. 'Could this be the Masterson clan's final hurrah?'

*

'No, you've been a big help, sir,' Gutteridge said down the phone. 'We appreciate your time. And please, for now – for the sake of the case – can we try to keep this out of the papers for as long as possible?' Gutteridge nodded for the phone. 'Indeed. That's okay, and again, thank you for your time. Goodbye Mr Caine.'

He quietly replaced the handset. 'He reckons Masterson has around six months left to live, but it could be less,' he muttered. 'It's in his lung, just the one side, the left, but it's spread to surrounding organs and tissue.' He brow darkened. 'But *why?*'

'Why what?' Keaton asked.

Gutteridge's whole aspect seemed to frown. 'I don't know. Why do what he's doing? I mean, I know he somehow blames *me* for his mother taking her own life – they *both* did! But how did I miss that he was cut so close from the same cloth as his brother? He always seemed – I don't know – so much calmer, so much *saner.*' He huffed an ironic laugh. 'Perhaps it's a good thing – Terrence always seemed so much less unhinged than Jerry, so maybe I could talk him down from this. Quell the anger – something that I know could *never* have happened with his psychotic sibling!' He lifted his eyes and saw Keaton watching him. 'It could almost be considered as preferable, in the scheme of things?'

Keaton acknowledged the notion. 'What now?'

Gutteridge suddenly recalled feeling his phone vibrate while he was on the previous call. He swiped it awake again and

222

checked his notifications. 'I've got a missed call,' he said, 'from Carl. He's sent me a message.' He navigated to WhatsApp and opened it, reading the update carefully. 'He's finished the full autopsy on Kerry Marston. Fancy a trip over?'

Keaton considered how Gutteridge must be feeling, seeing all of these past loves meeting such horrifying ends. 'Why not,' she whispered. 'Might help us catch the son of a bitch.'

*

Gutteridge held the door for Keaton to pass through into the acrid, chemical atmosphere of the autopsy room. He was surprised to see DCI Bryant hovering next to Carl – he assumed, awaiting their arrival.

'Sir,' Gutteridge nodded, as he crossed the no-man's-land of clinical, white tiled flooring to witness another of life's impromptu nightmares. 'I didn't realise you were going to be here.'

Bryant had a look of suspicious interest. 'I was in the area, so… you know. I thought I'd tag along,' he said. 'Jane,' he added, nodding acknowledgment of Keaton's presence.

'So, Carl, what do we have?' Gutteridge asked, ignoring Bryant's ambiguous scrutiny. The throng of visitors formed a crescent around the body, as they all attempted to hide their growing unease at what they were about to discover.

'Well, as you know I didn't really have very much to go on. But I *can* – in a formal capacity at least – confirm that this *is* Kerry Marston. We know this from fingerprints that – despite the extent of the chemical burning – were still intact enough to allow printing. I can also confirm that household bleach was used in an attempt to destroy evidence and that it was very effective in doing so. If it wasn't for me being able to obtain, albeit partial, print evidence, I would have had to resort to DNA profiling to get reliable confirmation of *who* this used to be,' he said.

Carl finally lifted the sheet that had respectfully been draped over what remained of Kerry Marston's face. The three new arrivals flinched in unison, rocking back on heels that wanted to turn and walk away. The haemorrhaged blood had now been washed away, revealing the full extent of the damage.

Carl took a moment to absorb their reactions. 'I know, right?' he said, moving his gaze around the triptych of repulsed faces. 'Callous is hardly a strong enough a word to describe this… this…' he began, lost for words. His eyes flashed, allowing the compassion he purposefully blocked a rare moment of freedom. '…This…' he whispered, tilting a sympathetic head as he considered the full extent of the trauma. 'Maybe words strong enough to describe this level of cruelty just don't exist in our language?' he finished.

He took up his clipboard to consult his notes. 'Standard stuff first. Stomach contents showed nothing unusual, salad for lunch, biscuits, traces of cereal – probably breakfast – and a *lot* of coffee.' He flipped to the next sheet. 'Toxicology found traces of ibuprofen and evidence of light cocaine use in her system, but no traces of trichloromethane in either the stomach fluids, blood or urine like in Kaylie Wyatt. But I *did* find *this*,' he said, stepping towards the body and indicating surface bruising at the base of the ribcage with his pen. 'Just here. Two prongs, localised burning, and the bruising goes *deep*.'

He lifted his eyes towards his guests and continued. 'Taser. Probably an older model. Made before the manufacture of such things was more regulated.' He straightened. 'High power, probably around 50,000 volts, but more crucially – as is common with older models – *much* higher amperage.' He watched the surrounding faces with interest. 'May possibly have knocked her out, instantly – and is probably *how* she was abducted.'

Gutteridge was beginning to feel like he was floating above himself, being forced to listen to details of his ex-lover's torment.

Carl took a step to the side and indicated the crater where a face once was. 'And now the elephant in the room,' he muttered. 'I took plenty of photos before clean up and I'll furnish you with copies of those before you leave, but as you can see, whoever did this kept swinging long after the victim had succumbed to the sheer volume of damage visible here – to the point that I would say it suggests at least a certain level of contempt, and dare I say, loathing, towards the victim.'

Bryant's attention was now firmly locked on Gutteridge, watching for signs of the extent of the hurt he must almost certainly be feeling. But if he was, he was handling it with a biblical level of composure – despite there being the briefest of flickers of torment visible behind his stoney facade.

Bryant couldn't help but admire Gutteridge's talent for inner strength and fortitude, learned – he assumed – from the unfair levels of tragedy he'd been forced to face in his life.

Carl moved down the table a step, taking up one of the victim's arms and lifting it into the core of the conversation.

'There are deep, ladder-like impressions embossed into the surface of the victim's skin around the wrists,' he explained, circling the trauma with a gloved finger. He lifted his eyes to the watching faces. 'Zip ties. Strong, industrial grade.' He respectfully lowered the arm again. 'And, similar to the Kaylie Wyatt case, she had been nailed to something – I'd suggest it was a chair. More specifically, the dining variety, judging from the shapes visible in the bruising on her back. I also found minute splinters of pine in the wound-tracts, and she'd been pinned to whatever it was through her thighs *peri*-mortem.'

Gutteridge shifted in discomfort, and Bryant noticed.

Carl continued, oblivious. 'There *are* such things as ten, or twelve-inch nails available on the market,' he explained. 'But they're not exactly what could be considered normal to find in an everyday household. They're more of a specialist item, so you might be able to track an unusual purchase like that? Especially if it's for a smaller amount? Trade have a tendency to buy in bulk.'

Carl leaned across the table and began circling his pinky around the distended bruising on Marston's thighs. 'You can see, here, coin-sized trauma around the puncture wounds, where she had been tugging against the nail heads in desperation, causing circumferential tearing to the skin. I can tell you now, the pain would have been unimaginable.'

Gutteridge shifted with unease for a second time, reeling at the description, and Bryant finally stepped into the fray to cut Carl off.

Gutteridge finally succumbed and lifted his damp, mortified eyes clear of the horror of his ex-lover's mutilated body, gladly accepting of the gift of the forced hiatus.

At first, Carl looked perplexed – almost offended by the interruption to his summarising, then softened as the reality of what had prompted it hit him. He knew he had a tendency to be clinically detached, speaking in his matter-of-fact tongue. 'Oh! I… I'm sorry, Pat… I – I didn't think.'

Gutteridge instantly turned back into the huddle, his face alight with pained but understanding smiles. 'Don't you worry, old friend, you're just doing your job, the way you must if we're to have any chance of catching this guy.'

Carl hovered in his embarrassment, mortified by his lack of thought, then offered up an apologetic hand.

Gutteridge took it and gave it a squeeze. 'Please. Old friend of mine. Carry on…'

Carl flicked a concerned look across to Bryant for guidance. Bryant paused in his scrutiny, then nodded.

Hesitantly, Carl prepared to resume his summary, turning back to Gutteridge, who smiled and also nodded to pacify Carl's guilt. 'Go ahead, please,' Gutteridge mouthed.

Carl took a breath to reset, then presented a tentative hand back into the fray to highlight the trauma around the victim's thighs. After a beat, he continued…

'They weren't quite deep enough to take usable impressions, but as you can see, here, there are multiple bite marks visible surrounding the nail wounds. Deep-tissue abrasions that were exerted with enough force to create surface bleeding.' His eyes lifted to the throng again. 'I found similar wounds on the body of Kaylie Wyatt, mainly around her waistline – the lower latissimus, obliques, abdomen. Notably, all areas of her body that were extremely toned and well defined, which *might* be what turns him on.'

Gutteridge's mind turned to Eve's conical waistline and the undulating band of muscle that drew his *own* latent desires to the fore. Once again, he felt decidedly unclean to have made the connection.

Carl continued. 'We all, to some extent, find particular parts, or areas of the physiques of those of the opposite sex to our own a draw,' he said. 'Regions of a body that – to us – are particularly arousing, to a point where it's easy to imagine we're all alone in that. That it's something peculiar to ourselves. We all, *every* one of us, have certain thoughts, ideas, and stimuli that we'd never dream of sharing with anyone else for fear of being judged. But when it creates a desire to do *this* sort of thing,' he said, indicating the wound-tracts, the abrasions, the chemical burning, the compromised face, 'you know that something has gone *very* wrong with that person at some point during their early life.'

Gutteridge found solace – however slight – in Carl's summation, having himself been party to a sound upbringing. But still…

227

'Have you logged the bite marks?' Gutteridge asked.

'Indeed I have. Photos taken next to size reference are included in the files I've prepared for you, along with clear cell overlays detailing what are *actually* fairly unique incisor, cuspid and bicuspid patination.'

'That's very good, Carl,' Bryant said, sounding almost patronising. 'DI Gutteridge, do you have a moment?' he added, paddling his hand towards the door that led out to the corridor.

Gutteridge had an inkling what was coming and had been rehearsing for such a moment. Carl and Keaton watched as they left the room, staying silent to try to overhear.

Bryant turned looks either way up the corridor to check they were alone, waiting for the doors behind them to finally shut before turning to face Gutteridge. 'I think I should take you off the case.'

'*No!*' Gutteridge objected. 'That's the wrong thing to do, and you know it.'

'I'm not so sure anymore. The cracks, they're beginning to show.'

'Of course they're fucking showing – the body of someone I cared for enough to fuck on a regular basis is lying in there with her face stoved in, and it's probably *because* I fucked her that she's even in there. But would I react any different if I *didn't* know her? If I didn't react at all, that would make me as much of a monster as the sick fuck who did this.'

'Try to see it from my perspective,' Bryant said, attempting not to be phased by Gutteridge's palpable agitation.

'And why don't we all try and see it from *mine*?' Gutteridge shot back in response.

Bryant steeled himself. 'I'm your friend, Pat, but I'm also your boss, so let's try and remember who it is you're talking to.'

Gutteridge allowed himself a moment for the feelings of deep frustration to subside. 'Look. I get it. Conflict of blah

blah, and part of me knows you're right. But I'm so close, *we're* so close. Give me a week, that's all I ask. Just seven days, and if he's not in custody by then, relegate me to some case advisory role.'

Bryant gave the proposal due consideration. 'Okay. You've got two. *Two* weeks, and then – to protect my own interests – I'll have to step in. That's as fair as I can be.'

Gutteridge lowered his hackles, his mouth flinching his gratitude. 'Thank you,' he muttered, feeling humble, but justified. 'I'm going to catch this fucker, and maybe *then*, I'll allow myself a moment to cry for those in there,' he said, flicking a look towards the doors. 'But until that moment arrives, I'm fully focused and holding it together.'

Bryant finally softened, and nodded in comprehension. 'Okay, but you go easy.'

Gutteridge breathed deep and sighed. 'I will,' he mumbled, looking meek. 'Don't worry… I will.' He turned to go back inside and rejoin Keaton.

'And Pat?' Bryant said, halting Gutteridge's departure. 'You and the team go safe – this guy's dangerous.'

Gutteridge gave a pensive, but appreciative smile. 'I know, and we will.'

TWENTY-SIX

DISQUIET REIGNED SUPREME in the car on the way back to the station, but Keaton had been gradually gathering the nerve to interrupt the curfew.

'So what was that about?'

Gutteridge was lost in his thoughts, but slowly reemerged into the drone of the cabin, drawn out by Keaton's genteel voice. 'Hmm?'

'In the corridor, what did Bryant want?' Keaton repeated. 'All we could hear were raised voices.'

Gutteridge inhaled a lungful of deep frustration. 'He was suggesting taking me off the case.'

'*What!*' Keaton hissed, acting like she hadn't herself had the exact same thought. She put on a show of faux solidarity for the sake of their relationship and, perhaps more importantly, the case.

Gutteridge's eyes flashed his own doubts. 'Maybe he's right. Maybe I *am* too close to it all?'

Keaton sat in contemplation of the situation, surprised to find herself coming down on Gutteridge's side. 'No. No, he's not,' she said. 'You're the best man to head this team. You know these Masterson brothers better than anybody else alive. It *should* be you.'

Gutteridge smiled in appreciation for the display of unity.

Keaton's ringtone suddenly filled the cabin. She answered it. 'Keaton.'

She listened intently, turning to look at Gutteridge and mouthing: 'It's DS Banks.'

She listened some more, fully invested in the words drifting from the earpiece. Gutteridge directed a succession of interested looks her way.

'Understood,' she said. 'He's here, next to me. We're just driving back, now. He might have his phone on silent, we've just been to see Carl. Can you send me her details? We'll get right onto it.'

Keaton slowly lowered the phone, looking cautious but strangely energised, a fizz in her belly like someone alighting their first rollercoaster.

'What was that?' Gutteridge asked. 'Did I hear you say it was Banks?'

Keaton was almost smiling as she nodded in response. 'He's received a call from someone he knows – an estate agent.'

'*And?*'

Her phone suddenly chimed, loud and optimistic. She opened WhatsApp and saw DS Banks' thumbnail highlighted. She dabbed it and began absorbing the details. 'Her name's Jade Hewlett, she owns an estate agency in town.' She lifted incandescent eyes from the screen to look at Gutteridge. 'The exact same estate agent Kaylie Wyatt worked for.'

Gutteridge took a moment to make the connection. 'What did she have to say?' he asked, craning a look over to her phone.

'Apparently, she's been searching the web for details about the case, and came across a piece written by some true crime blogger who seems to have put two and two together and come up with "Masterson"!'

Gutteridge's brow darkened. 'But how? We've purposefully been keeping that shit from the papers.'

Keaton hopped a socially realistic shrug in response. 'You know uniform can leak like a sieve. And anyway, that's not the interesting part.'

'Then what is?'

She couldn't hold it in any longer and, as wrong as it felt, she laughed. 'They've recently let a property, leasing it to – wait for it – a *Mr Masterson*!'

'You're fucking *kidding*, right?'

'Nope – and guess which attractive female agent was charged with showing him around the property?'

Gutteridge made the connection and his whole face fell open.

Keaton dropped her phone into the cradle and started the navigation. 'Let's go!' she barked. 'She's expecting us.'

*

A deep, two-toned doorbell chimed, announcing their arrival and causing all attentions in the high street unit to divert towards them.

There was a smartly dressed woman who obviously ran the show, leaning over a colleague's computer studying one of the listings. Surprisingly to Gutteridge – considering her senior position – she looked to still be in her twenties.

The woman clocked the authoritarian appearance of the new arrivals, acknowledging their presence with a knowing flash of the eyes. She straightened, indicating something on the screen to the employee, then flicked a subtle head for the visitors to follow.

She led them discretely through the warren of occupied desks to the back of the space and into what Gutteridge assumed must be her personal office. His attention was locked on her mousy brown hair that was tied into a loose but neat ponytail.

She closed the door to ensure their privacy and turned to formally greet them. 'Hi. I'm Jade Hewlett. You must be DI Gutteridge?'

'Indeed, and this is my colleague, DS Keaton. We appreciate you contacting us.'

Hewlett rounded her desk and offered them seats with a well-rehearsed outstretch of the arm. 'Would you care to sit?'

Gutteridge lowered his large frame into the well-upholstered chair, Keaton taking the one next to it.

'One of our other colleagues – DS Banks – said you called with information about a property you've recently leased?'

Hewlett leaned in and began typing on her computer, then swung the screen around to face the detectives. She paused. 'I guess I don't handle loss too well – especially when it was a life as bright and vibrant as Kaylie's. So I've been taking what some might consider to be an unhealthy level of interest in the case, and I came across *this* website,' she said, tapping an outstretched finger against the screen, her manicured nail ringing bright and glassy.

'It seems to suggest a link between the recent murders and an old case that I'm a bit young to properly remember. But I recognised the name mentioned in the piece, and then recalled Kaylie recently closing a contract with someone of the same name... *Masterson.*'

Both Gutteridge and Keaton exchanged a look, then leaned in to examine the article on the screen.

Gutteridge allowed his attention to drift back to Hewlett. 'You say you're too young to remember. May I ask – out of interest – how young, if it's not too rude?' he said, moving his eyes around the plushly appointed office.

Hewlett smirked, unsurprised by his interest and the resulting question that presented itself. 'I'm twenty-six,' she said with a knowing blink. 'My father was also an estate agent and taught me the ropes from a very early age – and yes, he also helped me to set this place up.'

Gutteridge smiled. 'Still. Pretty impressive.'

'Thank you.'

'Do you have the details of the property that was leased?' Keaton asked, trying to bring the conversation back into line.

Hewlett swung the screen back to face her and began scrolling with her mouse, before swinging it back to face the interested detectives.

'I wasn't sure what was best to do. I'm aware that Masterson isn't exactly a rare name, but nor is it that common, and the coincidence was just too striking to ignore. But at the same time, I don't want a whole army of police officers barrelling into this guy's life based on information *I've* freely given, only to find that he's completely innocent. Does awfully crappy things to your online reviews.'

'We understand that and we'll be sure to be discrete,' Gutteridge assured her. 'But – and please, this stays between us, this name, Terrence,' he said, indicating the screen, his eyes alight, '*is* a name of particular interest.'

Keaton also felt a buzz at seeing the name, but tried her best to hide it, recognising the need to keep things formal. 'However, we understand your position,' she added, 'and we'll be sure to be discrete.'

Keaton began jotting down the details then opened the camera on her phone for good measure, presenting it to the screen. 'May I?'

Hewlett nodded her consent, but for the first time felt a squirm in her gut at the breach of trust she had instigated.

Gutteridge sensed the worry emanating off the woman sat before him. 'Don't fret, we'll tread carefully. Just know that you're doing the right thing.'

'I hope so,' Hewlett said. 'We all dearly miss Kaylie around here.'

Keaton presented her phone to Gutteridge. It was now open on Google Maps, showing the location of the address they'd just been given – it was only 500 yards from the Kaylie Wyatt murder scene.

Gutteridge sighed and felt his insides drop. 'You most certainly *have* done the right thing,' he muttered.

TWENTY-SEVEN

GUTTERIDGE PARKED HIS SAAB on Wolseley Road, just a few yards down from the block of apartments where Kaylie Wyatt's body had been discovered.

He'd been mindful of the promise he'd made to Jade Hewlett, resisting calling in a whole squadron of troops, opting instead to pay the property a discrete visit to assess the lay of the land.

They both rose from the car. 'Let's see just how close this property is to that one,' Gutteridge said, eyeballing the all too familiar complex of apartments on their right.

After a short stroll, still unsure of what they were going to find – or even if they were doing the right thing – they turned the corner at the end of the road, trying to appear as nonchalant as they could despite the buzz of uncertainty coursing through their bodies.

Gutteridge had the Glock 17M he kept hidden in his glove compartment tucked into his waistband, out of sight beneath his jacket.

'If this *does* turn out to be him,' Keaton whispered, 'why's he being so sloppy? I mean, to put your real name on the contract for the house you're leasing. It seems almost ridiculous, doesn't it?'

Gutteridge's brow creased, reluctant to form any kind of opinion. 'Who knows how a mind capable of such sick deeds functions. Plus, we already know he has nothing to lose – and getting hold of fake ID isn't as easy as it's made out to be on the telly.'

In much less than a minute, to their surprise, they were already nearing the property. 'Let's just walk past, first,' Gutteridge whispered, swapping over to the curb side so he could get a clearer view of the house. 'Just pretend you're having a conversation with me and I'll take a look. But keep your face averted – he'd probably recognise *you*, but he hasn't seen me in years.'

They sauntered past, pretending to have a conversation, Gutteridge dressing his considerable interest around all the windows and the surrounding land, until they were behind the thick hedgerows at the curb-end of the property. They stopped.

'Anything?' Keaton asked.

'No. Nothing. It looked kind of empty and there's no vehicle on the drive. But maybe… hmm…' his thoughts tailed away. 'Come on,' he said. 'Let's take a closer look.'

He checked his gun was still there – more for personal assurance than anything else, because his belt was purposefully done up tight, the muzzle digging into his gut, helping to keep it invisible to outside scrutiny.

They both wandered back towards the lightweight, wrought-iron gates that partitioned the property from the world surrounding it. Quietly, they swung them open, trying to avoid making any tell-tale sounds that would alert anyone to their presence.

Both of their attentions were welded to the building's tired exterior, as they looked for any sign of movement beyond the unlit panes of glass.

'I'm shitting myself,' Keaton hissed.

'Just stay close to me, and keep vigilant.'

Gutteridge felt for his pistol again, grasping the handle and thumbing the safety catch a couple of times to establish its location, just in case he had to flick it off in haste.

They finally climbed the short flight of steps that rose to the porch-covered door, after what felt like an age spent traversing the gravel and stone-flagged driveway.

They both split to flank the entrance, keeping clear of the door in case bullets began raining through the panelling.

Gutteridge took a breath and considered knocking, then quickly changed his mind. He dropped to his knee and took out his phone, swiping to open the camera and setting the self-timer to three seconds. He then navigated to phone settings to mute the sound.

He leaned in cautiously and, with one hand, gingerly lifted the letterbox flap. He tapped the shutter icon and presented his phone to the slot. It vibrated three times in his hand before falling still again. He withdrew it, opening the image and examining it closely, but there was nothing to see except a dingy house that seemed devoid of anything resembling human occupation.

Gutteridge stood again. 'Wait here,' he whispered, crossing to the front of the property and ducking below the bay window, outside what he assumed must be the living room. He repeated the routine with his phone again, lifting it above the sill of the window and placing it softly against the glass. Three more vibrations through his fingertips and he crouched to examine the next image.

His eyes hardened at what flashed up on the screen. There was something out of focus, but undeniably wrong in the image – something that he was just able to make out, but that simply didn't sit right in such domestic surroundings.

Keaton was watching from her elevated vantage point as

Gutteridge struggled to his feet again, looking lost, dejected and decidedly shaken. He glanced down at his phone one more time, and after a beat, broke into a sprint up the steps past Keaton. He suddenly seemed entirely focused on some mono-directional, blinkered quest for entry.

He strode across the top landing to the door, abandoning all caution, and with a determined, almost manic lunge that shook Keaton to her core and splintered the locks from their housings, Gutteridge smashed through the entrance and stumbled inside. He seemed to hesitate in his surprise at the fact that he was now inside the house, hovering in the hallway. He finally remembered to take the pistol from his belt.

Keaton stepped through to join him. 'What is it? What did you see?'

But Gutteridge didn't appear to hear her, looking strangely dazed. He finally broke free of the bonds of whatever form of trance he was in, and began shuffling towards the living room, pistol held out before him.

Keaton followed, unnerved by Gutteridge's demeanour, looking with piqued attention around what appeared to be an uninhabited space: the hallway, the kitchen at the far end of the passage, the staircase that rose to the top floors. Shadows of the O'Leary case making a repeat appearance in a mind that had dearly been attempting to forget.

Slowly, they edged in unison into the front room, but were stopped in their tracks by the sight waiting for them. Keaton's legs turned gelatinous and threatened to fold beneath her, the sharp, acidic taste of bile climbing her nauseated throat. Gutteridge almost retched with revulsion and deep-seated frustration onto a floor that he wished would just open up beneath him and swallow him whole. The feelings of déjà vu he'd been experiencing across this entire case now reached another level.

The air they were being forced to breathe was flavoured with that now horribly familiar, butcher's block stench of freshly dissected meat – a perfect olfactory accompaniment to the scene they were presented with.

A blood-soaked settee seemed, once again, to have been deliberately positioned to face their imminent arrival, whilst the limbless torso of an unknown female sat propped in the centre of the cushions, carefully placed to witness their disgust and deep-seated despair.

Her dissected limbs had been folded and draped over the cushion backs to resemble angel's wings, like it was some kind of shrine to the indignity of this unknown woman's desecration. Her breasts appeared also to have been removed, and there was another note pinned to where they once were.

Gutteridge stowed the weapon again, and carefully, stepped in to retrieve it with hands that were shaking.

No, not a loved one, not this time. This one was just for the hell of it. For old time's sake. For shits and giggles, as they say.

She was a receptionist, you know, placed here simply to greet you upon your exultant arrival. That was thoughtful of me, wasn't it?

The next one, though, will be a loved one. Perhaps the most loved of them all? Maybe you'll feel compelled to kill yourself after I present you with her 'adjusted' remains? Wouldn't that be the perfect conclusion to my quest for vengeance.

I'm coming, Gutteridge, make no mistake. So prepare yourself, for my storm will rage with all the ferocity of a slighted god for what you took from me!

M

'It's the missing receptionist, from the hospital,' Gutteridge muttered, broiling inside to the heat of his ignominy. 'Poor fucking thing!' he whispered, unable to look her dead in her blood-starved face. He spied an open handbag sitting on a side table near the back of the room, rising to take a closer look.

It seemed too high-end of a brand for a mere receptionist, seeming to be a Vuitton bucket bag at first glance. He peered inside and saw it was indeed a Vuitton – he could tell by the quality of the stitching and the way the cut edges of the leather had been sealed that it was an original, not some Sunday market knockoff.

He tipped the contents out on the table and fingered through the random detritus of a woman's life: a miniature can of hairspray, makeup, a ring bag, pens, paperclips, a journalist's pad, and a wallet. He thumbed the popper of the latter and it fell open to reveal Kerry Marston's press card. He sagged under the weight of his guilt once again.

'It's Marston's,' he said, turning to face Keaton, who'd been watching from the door. 'Can you please call it in?'

Keaton lifted her phone to her ear. 'I already am…'

TWENTY-EIGHT

KEATON WAS HAVING TO TROT to keep up with her partner, almost breaking into a sprint at one point just to pull level. After nearly three hours where it felt like 'hope' was no longer a word within the dictionary, they were leaving the scene to the mercy of forensics.

Anger and exasperation emanated off Gutteridge like the smouldering heat from a furnace, burning fiercely and in danger of scolding Keaton.

'Look, sir... *Pat!* You can't go letting your emotions show like this, or they'll take you off the case. Take *us* off the case.'

Gutteridge suddenly stopped and turned to face her thankless pleading. 'Maybe they should. Maybe I *shouldn't* be on the case, because when I finally catch up with this cunt, I'm going to fucking eviscerate him!'

Keaton intentionally sagged at his response, displaying mock disappointment for a reaction she nevertheless fully understood. She just needed to try to quell Gutteridge's palpable anger.

'Now you know that kind of talk won't help.'

Gutteridge paced the pavement to vent some of his steam, aided by the compassion in the face pleading across at him.

He eventually stopped, deflated, joining in the sag. He sighed. 'I know, you're right… But what the fuck! How many people are going to die because of me?'

Keaton now took up his batten of anger. 'Now you know very well that none of this is any fault of yours. This prick's skewed reasonings do nothing but place the blame firmly at *his* feet. *Not* yours.' She allowed her insistent front to thaw slightly, tilting an inquisitive head and darting a look to the Saab parked down the street. She had an idea. 'Is your kit in your car?' she asked.

Gutteridge frowned. 'What kit?'

'Gym?'

Gutteridge had to think – working out being the farthest thing from his current train of thought. 'Erm… yes. It is. Why?'

'Because mine's in my locker at the club… I think we're *both* in need of some training time to vent our frustrations. I know *you* are.'

Gutteridge also turned to look at his car, still parked a hundred yards away on Wolseley Road. 'What about Joshua?' he asked, turning back to face her.

'I can make a call to the babysitter. I know she's been a bit short of late, so she'll be glad of an extra hour or two. So how about it?'

Gutteridge considered the proposal. There was no denying it, he felt he could happily unleash himself on a heavy bag for at least a good hour.

'Go on then,' he said. 'You always did make a good case.' He gave an appreciative smile. 'Why not.'

*

Gutteridge was warmed through and ten minutes into demolishing a 90kg bag, his fists loaded with acute frustration.

His shoulders, arms and obliques stung with the lactic fire of exertion, each percussive slap of his gloves against the bag an imagined blow to the cancer-riddled body of Masterson – accentuating each and every snapping punch with a muttered cuss word, spat with heartfelt malice through his gritted teeth.

Keaton momentarily stole his attention when she silently materialised from the changing rooms on the far side of the weights room. She was clad head-to-toe in black, wearing mid-calf-length leggings and a sports bra that showed off all her best attributes. Her hair was tied back in a tight, coiling ponytail that bounced in rhythm with her walk.

She gave a coy smile, tilting her head and offering a furtive wave to complete her ensemble as she – as was always her routine – made her way towards the island of pull-up and dip stations.

Gutteridge allowed his enmity to dissipate along with the relentless delivery of infuriated punches, eventually subsiding into bucolic inactivity, leaning his burning shoulder against the weight of the bag as he watched Keaton saunter the length of the machine-peppered landscape to the cluster of pull-up apparatus. He was fascinated by the naturally seductive roll of her entire physique. A swing in the hips that was not so apparent when hidden beneath the smart, sharply creased cloth of her corporate suit.

He suddenly hankered for that second, more effective, and decidedly more erotic form of grievance outlet, fuelled by the vision of the woman who was now hanging from a pull-up bar and crunching folded knees to her exaggerated chest. But the vessel for *that* particular vice was 120 miles distant, and he knew it to be unwise to drive up there – and he couldn't risk potentially leading Masterson and his twisted hunger for revenge straight to her and her secret location. *God*, his wife, how he dearly missed his wife…

244

He swapped his voyeuristic lean to his left shoulder, gazing past the right side of the bag to where it was less obvious he was watching, and carried on observing the elongated physique of his partner in motion.

Her slight but shapely latissimus muscles popped from the sides of her ribcage, her body stretched long by gravity. She looked strong and firm as her flexing midriff furled slender legs to breasts that sat elevated by arms that were racked to the bar above her, framing her small but beautifully proportioned face, looking just like that single, solitary night they'd gifted themselves to each other.

She flushed with colour at the physical exertion, her sweat-beaded cheeks accentuating the red, waterproof lipstick she wore. Glazed with perspiration, her lips gulped for air to charge her endeavours.

Once again, Gutteridge stirred, like he had so many times before in similar circumstances, feeling a sudden desire to lead her by her willing hand to some quiet, tucked away place and fuck away the deep-seated feelings of failure that he *knew* were eating the both of them from the inside out. Their own metaphorical cancers that their apparent inability to halt the ongoing bloodshed was feeding.

Gutteridge pulled himself back from his daydreaming, surprised to find that Keaton was now stood with her back resting against the machine, hands held flat against her burning midriff, breathing long and heavy, watching him with a look of curious contemplation pinching at her round, blue eyes.

She seemed to be trying to read him like a fairground psychic, observing the inner desires apparent in those spontaneous flinches and flickers of a face that was betraying what he would consider to be the most secret of his innermost perversions – or was it demons?

She continued to observe him from afar, exchanging

searching looks, attempting to assess him using skills learned during her psychology degree – this, combined with an in-depth knowledge of who Gutteridge was, having spent at least ten hours a day in his company.

She waited until her breathing slowed to a rhythm less akin to exhaustion, then turned and grabbed her towel, and began making her way back towards the changing rooms.

Gutteridge watched, curious. She looked about furtively, dabbing her neck dry, checking for unwanted scrutiny from the other patrons peppering the space, before flicking a suggestive head towards Gutteridge, signalling for him to follow.

His brow briefly darkened at the impromptu request, before he acquiesced, lunging from his punch bag perch, removing his gloves and wraps as nonchalantly as he could as he tracked her movements. He followed Keaton past the entrance to the changing rooms, through the swing doors towards the vending-machine-lined rest area, then along a corridor that in his five years of membership he'd never once been down. He made sure to maintain a distance of at least twenty feet between them.

Keaton turned to throw a covert look behind her shoulder, checking that Gutteridge was still following, then presented an ear to a door on the left and quietly knocked. She listened for a beat, then popped the handle and slipped inside.

Gutteridge arrived a beat later and saw a brushed aluminium 'baby change' sign mounted high on the wall at the side of the door. An arm thrust out from the dark of the unlit room and grabbed his vest, dragging him inside.

He heard the clack of the lock and a flick of a switch, and with a flicker, the lights flashed on to reveal Keaton's energised face beaming up at him.

After the briefest of searching, wordless looks up into his requiting eyes, Keaton seemed to burst free of some tethered form of excited energy, and began lowering the baby-change station from its stowed moorings, clipping it in place with all the dexterity of the mother she now was. She thrust down upon it with straight arms to check its reluctance to buckle under load. Satisfied that it wouldn't, she turned back to face the centre of the room and enticed Gutteridge to move in closer with simmering eyes.

He crumbled under the welcome pressure and closed the distance between them, both physically and emotionally. No words were, or *needed* to be, said.

Keaton hopped her pert behind up onto the shelf and raised her arms to coax forth the attention she sought, but Gutteridge seemed more hesitant than the thirsting looks she'd received in the gym would have suggested, and then it clicked.

'I'm fully protected,' she assured him, 'and I have morning-after pills at home. So there's *no* risk – don't think about it, just take me. Don't go letting that lunatic break who you are. I want the Patrick I *know* – the Patrick I *love*.'

She directed a pin-sharp look straight into the skittering uncertainty still visible in his eyes, urging him to relent. 'This stays in here. Okay? In this room, with us, just you and me.'

Gutteridge seemed to emerge from his doubts, drawn out by his ever-growing needs. His growing frustration and the sight of Keaton's Lycra-clad body urging him to commit sin, and he nodded.

Keaton had the hem of his vest in her hands and had drawn up over his head before he could react. She tossed it aside, her eyes snapping to his shoulders, swollen to the pump of relentlessly pounding the thick leather of the punch bag.

Her drooling gaze turned thirsting as she watched her own hands caress the skin and striated spheres that crowned his muscular arms, glistening in the sterile light high above them.

Gutteridge saw the look of yearning in her face, recognising it to be the same as that he sensed sizzling inside himself, finding succour and relief in the relatability of her actions, permitting his own eyes to drop away to his own, personal Valhalla.

Her stomach glimmered in the white light, drawing his beguiled fingers in to caress their provocative undulations.

Keaton clocked the look, feeling his fascination through his touch. 'Is *this* what you want?' she said, grasping the hem of the Lycra and pulling it clear of her stomach. 'Is *this* what you like?'

Gutteridge swallowed, and nodded.

Keaton kicked off her trainers, leaning back, drawing her leggings off her hips. Gutteridge took over and pulled them the rest of the way, closely followed by her thong, which he lifted to his nose – inhaling the elixir of pheromones that soaked the cloth.

Keaton grasped his hand and placed it flat against her lower abdomen, the exact same way Eve had – it was almost like they'd swapped notes on his particular kinks, drawing unexpected thoughts to the fore in Gutteridge's mind of their child.

Her other hand suddenly grabbed him about his jaw, playfully, but insistent. 'Take me!' she snarled, sounding almost impatient, her angelic face now a grimace.

Gutteridge smiled at the perceived savagery of her actions – and at her willingness to let those things that can take such matters to much higher levels the freedom to thrive, turning his thoughts to the last time he and Eve bared more than all. Life imitating life, the way it so often seemed to do.

His eager hand dropped away to tug the drawstring of his pants, while the other mirrored Keaton's action – clamping her small, pretty face in the firm but respectful pinch of his large hand. 'Okay. If that's the way we're playing it.'

She grinned, and Gutteridge leaned in so their mouths could meet, but the action was met by a belligerent hand that almost slapped the attempt away.

'No kissing!' she barked, playing the domineer. 'Don't go making it personal.'

A curious smile came to Gutteridge's face once again, licking at the corners of his mouth. He liked this new mien of roughness – it added a layer of prohibited excitement to the tenderness that already existed.

He stepped in and carefully entered her, once again, feelings of déjà vu never too far away. A grunt rather than a whimper escaped from her parted lips – the only notable difference between his *real*, and this *surrogate* Eve.

He began to stroke inside her, watching as the expression slowly dissolved from her face, until nothing remained but calm, contented gratification.

Keaton began to roll her own hips, synchronising her movements with Gutteridge's steady rhythm and adding new pleasures to his own experience, his own sensations.

Her strong stomach muscles rippled at the new motion, drawing Gutteridge's attention down again. He clapped his right hand flat against her writhing belly to feel the pulsation of their shared efforts, presenting his thumb to her proud clitoris.

Keaton spasmed at the touch, her head lolloping on her lissom neck. That surreal veil of déjà vu lowering around him once again, physical echoes of Eve repeating in his erotically inebriated mind.

Gutteridge could sense Keaton nearing climax and what he mistakenly perceived to be his inner Masterson once again boiling to the fore. He felt an insatiable desire to relive the feeling of ultimate control that Eve had given him before, eyeing Keaton's exposed throat with all the questionable intension of choking her orgasm to new heights, simply for the pleasure of witnessing the outcome.

But did *that* make him the same as Masterson? A *sadist*? A *monster*? He still wasn't sure, but what he *did* know is that it was the action itself that felt the closest to being wrong.

Then he recalled his pacifying conversation with Asha Jackson, as he felt the shudder of ultimate pleasure proceed to thunder through Jane Keaton's racking body. He clamped his hand across her mouth, pressing the soft pad of his palm against her flaring nostrils, and to his surprise, Keaton didn't seem to resist, or react – she just allowed him to impede her airways, her neck bulging in her futile attempts to draw breath.

His own body began to rush and release as Keaton's climax peaked, her stomach curling inwards and crunching down on the confused sensation of weakness and strength. Her mouth gasped behind the cup of his hand, then with a muted cry, she slumped back, eyes rolling, looking distant and detached.

'Fuck!' Gutteridge spat, leaning in. 'Jane? *Jane*!'

'I'm fine,' she gasped, finally catching her breath and taking his hands in hers. 'Don't worry. I'm fine. Jesus, Pat, what was *that*?' she panted. 'That was fucking incredible!'

He watched her reeling in the throws of contentment, *still* unsure of how he himself should be feeling.

'Dear God in heaven...' Keaton exhaled. 'I think I should be paying you for whatever that was,' she joked, before laughing out loud at the curious sensation she'd been subjected to, adrenaline still coursing through her limbs.

She allowed her arms to fall away to her sides, and she flopped. 'I might be needing you to take me home now,' she mumbled, 'I'm a bit, how would you say? Spent!'

Gutteridge finally permitted himself to feel reassured by both Keaton's and Eve's acceptance of his actions – actions, he had to remember, were requested by Eve. He deemed therefore that they must be considered close enough to what's considered normal to be acceptable – however close to the line he suspected they truly were.

He placed a comforting hand on her hip, and smiled. 'Okay,' he whispered. 'I'll take you home.'

*

Gutteridge pulled up outside Keaton's modern semi and pulled on the handbrake. Very few words had been spoken the whole way there, both apparently so surprised – or was it dismayed? – by each other's actions.

'Well, that was, erm… unexpected?' Gutteridge mumbled.

Keaton allowed herself a smirk. 'It was amazing,' she responded, purposefully ignoring the tone of his statement. She was still reeling in the wake of Gutteridge's debauched form of infidelity. 'But it always is with you,' she added, rolling a look from the passenger seat towards him, fully aware they'd overstepped a mark once again.

Gutteridge looked unsure and guilty. '*Always?*' he said. 'Hasn't it only been twice?' His voice and demeanour seemed drenched in self-disappointment. 'But I guess we *have* been kissing a lot, lately – what with everything that's happened between us.' The crippling guilt landed again.

'Look… I know that was a bit insane, but *Jesus* I needed it!'

'So did I, but doesn't that make me a heel?' Gutteridge asked. 'I *am* supposed to be married, now.'

Keaton's eyes turned pitying. 'I guess the textbooks would probably say you are. But you're also human, Pat, so don't let it trouble you too much. It was *me*, okay. I *made* you want me, because *I* wanted you.'

'You didn't make me do anything!'

Keaton smirked in jest. 'Really? You don't think a woman has the same amount of power and control as a man does? *More* even.' She attempted to smile, but it felt inappropriate, so relaxed it. 'I wanted that. I wanted *you*, the father of my

251

child, so I made it happen. So blame me, okay – you're just a man, after all.'

Gutteridge reached across, squeezing her knee and sniggering, before forcing himself to turn regretful again. 'We can't keep doing this, though.'

Keaton slouched, recognising the truth in his words. 'I know. As much as that pains me… I know,' she agreed, before turning chipper to try to lighten the atmosphere. 'But *you* – you have your very own killer body at home to please *you*. Where am I going to get my own, personal, matching set of muscular arms?'

Gutteridge chuckled, allowing his spirits to lift from the pit of his despair. 'You always did know how to make me laugh,' he muttered. 'Thank you…' he added, smiling.

Keaton sucked in a lungful of air to extricate herself from the awkwardness. 'Well, I'd better relieve this babysitter before she calls child services on me.'

Gutteridge laughed again. 'Okay, go on. I'll see you at the station, tomorrow.'

Keaton leaned in and placed a kiss on his cheek, accenting it with a cheeky wink. 'I've learned a few new things about you tonight,' she quipped, delivering two jaunty slaps to her washboard stomach and grinning knowingly, before popping the door and rising into the cold embrace of night.

Gutteridge sniggered. 'Well, goodnight, sweetheart,' he chirped, sarcastically, as Keaton stooped to close the door. With an exchange of waves and two beeps of his horn, he pulled away.

Keaton watched and waved until the tail lights of the Saab turned the corner at the far end of the road and were out of sight. The street fell quiet, with only the ticking claws of an urban fox breaking the silence as it crossed the road, the only audible sound to spoil the purity of silence.

Keaton watched the animal a while with an appreciative smile before ambling towards her front door, feeling like the whole, strange experience had been a bizarre, stomach-knotting fever dream.

She drew her keys from her pocket and slid them into the lock, wondering why she didn't feel the guilt she knew she should. She shouldered the door aside and stepped into the warmth and familiar scent of the entrance hallway.

She nudged the door shut with her hip and attempted to smile through what she knew was wrongdoing, her legs still feeling like Nitrile rubber.

'Penny?' she called, dropping her keys into the bowl and opening the door to the living room.

She wandered through into the warmly lit room, stooping to drop her bag behind the settee and stood again. Then she stuttered, rocking back on her heels at the sight that met her eyes.

Penny's body was sat on the sofa facing the television, looking unnaturally stiff but strangely serene. What appeared to be a bullet hole had perfectly pierced the centre of her forehead, with a neat stream of dried blood dissecting her expressionless face.

'What a touching display of affection from Daddy,' a voice behind her said.

Keaton shuddered at the sound of the voice and stumbled around to find it.

Masterson's large frame stepped from behind the door and swung it shut, grinning with all the knowing of a high court judge.

'*Goodnight, sweetheart*… such an endearing sentiment, and under the circumstances, thoroughly apt,' he said, aping Gutteridge's parting words, before suddenly lunging forwards and grasping her ponytail in his muscular hand, jamming the

sharp end of a taser into the side of her neck. With an angry
crackle that filled her head, Keaton blacked out...

TWENTY-NINE

GUTTERIDGE NAVIGATED the warren of roads leading from Keaton's house and suddenly remembered his phone was still on silent from their time at the gym.

He leaned an arm back and fumbled in the footwell behind his seat and drawing it from the side pocket of his holdall. He switched the sound back on and checked the screen for messages. There was just one WhatsApp message and twelve missed calls, all from DS Stanton.

He frowned and opened the message to quickly scan it, not fully able to read the contents as he was driving, but the words looked urgent.

He tapped to return the call, selecting the hands-free option and slipping the device into its cradle. With a pop, the phone linked to the car's Bluetooth and the sound of ringing filled the cabin. Stanton answered.

'Sir. You got my message?'

'I did – *well*, kind of. I haven't had an opportunity to read it properly yet. I'm driving. What's the matter?'

'It might be worth you pulling over. I've WhatsApp'd you screenshots of Masterson's credit card records – you might want to take a look.'

'He's still using his credit card?' Gutteridge muttered. 'Shit, he really *is* going for broke. So what's on them, anything of interest?'

'Well, mostly what you'd expect: food, petrol, clothes, the usual… and one interesting purchase made from a company called Hide and Seekers. That's why I've been calling.'

'And what's that? Did you look them up? Who are they?'

'They make a few, niche products, but their main stock in trade are small, stowable, battery-powered tracking devices. You know the sort of thing – to track a bag, or a briefcase, or your business's fleet of delivery vans – or even, *a car!*'

Gutteridge spied a parking bay up ahead and pulled in, absorbing the ramifications of that particular snippet of information.

'He's bought a tracker?'

'Well, I *believe* so. It's nearly 18:30, so of course, they're closed for business now, but the amount taken from his card tallies with the listed cost off their website of their flagship model plus next day delivery.'

'When? *When* did he buy it?' he asked, now leaning into the call, his voice taking on an air of urgency.

'Roughly one week before Kerry Marston's body turned up at *your* house!' she revealed, now sounding as knowing and urgent as Gutteridge.

Gutteridge spun in his seat, looking about the car for signs of displaced interior trim. 'Battery life?' he barked.

'Three years!'

'*Christ*,' he fizzed. 'He probably knows everywhere I've been.'

'He very well might,' she agreed.

'Fuck. I've got to go,' he snapped. 'I need to let people know.'

'Okay, sir. If there's anything I can do, just call and I'll be on it. I'm still at the station and I won't be going anywhere anytime soon.'

'Okay. I will, but I'll have to get back to you. Just hang tight.'

Gutteridge quickly ended the call, sitting listening to the thrum of the car's engine, trying to assemble anything remotely resembling a plan of action. He ran through all the places he'd been since the Kerry Marston body dump.

The intimidating words written on the note that had been pinned to the receptionist returned to him:

> *the next one, though, she will be a loved one. Perhaps the most loved of them all?*

He quickly scrolled to Jackson's number, frantically stabbing an impatient finger at the thumbnail.

It started to ring and Gutteridge sat listening in pregnant silence. 'Come *ooooon*… Come *ooooon*…'

With a click, the phone answered and Asha's happy voice chirped down the line. 'Well, hello, handsome.'

'Asha. Is Toby there? I need to speak to him. It's urgent!'

Asha stuttered on the end of the line, confused by the out-of-character tone to Gutteridge's voice. 'Erm… okay. I'll just get him.'

He heard the synthetic creak of the mouthpiece being covered and the confused, muffled tones of exchanged conversation.

The creaking intensified then the sound turned bright and roomy again, before Toby Jackson's quizzical voice lit the earpiece. 'Pat? Something wrong?'

Gutteridge suddenly felt the shame of visiting further problems upon those he already had, those he now called friends, but fought through the awkwardness. 'Toby. I'm so sorry.'

'What is it, friend? Is this about the Ferrari? Did you find it?'

'Ferrari?'

'Yeah. I had it delivered to your place today. It should be there now. Is it that?'

'No. I-I've not been home yet. Listen, I, *we*, think Masterson's had a tracker on my car. We've discovered a purchase for one on his credit card statement.'

'A tracker? On your car – the *Saab*?'

'*Yes*. My Saab.'

Gutteridge could sense Jackson thinking through the earpiece.

'So… he probably has a mapped log of everywhere you've ever been since he installed it?'

Gutteridge sighed a chestful of his considerable embarrassment. 'Right!'

Without pause or complaint, Jackson's technical mind erupted into action. 'Okay. Listen, I'll WhatsApp you my plans, but we have a retreat – a weekend away sort of thing. We'll go there, now. We'll be out of the door in less than an hour.'

'I'm so utterly sorry,' Gutteridge pleaded.

'Forget it, pal. We can worry about that stuff later. Right now, what's most important is getting Eve, *and* us, away from here and to safety. I think I'll take the Range Rover, that's always locked away in the rear barn, so there's little chance anyone could have had access to that. I'll make sure we're not followed.'

Gutteridge allowed himself a moment for the sense of relief to settle. 'Look, Toby,' Gutteridge said. 'You may never want to talk to me ever again after all this has blown over, but right now, you're as good a friend as I've ever had.'

'Aren't I just,' Jackson joked. 'Listen, do you want a quick word with Eve? She's right here.'

'Please.'

'I'll go and start getting packed up, Asha's already on it. I'll message you, and don't worry – it's actually really quite exciting.'

The creaking returned, then a moment later Eve's sweet, Polish voice warmed Gutteridge's ear. 'Patrrrick? Is everything alright?'

Gutteridge closed his guilt-ridden eyes and pressed his phone to the side of his face, using it as a physical extension of his adoring wife's lovely face, caressing his cheek against her crystalline skin. 'Sweetheart. I'm so, so, sorry. You have to move again. Just do everything Toby says, okay?'

'Why? What's happened? Are you in danger? Am *I* in danger?'

'No, it's… it's not like that. It's going to be okay. I just don't have time to explain right now. Toby will explain everything, *once* you're on your way. I just need you to trust me and do everything Toby asks you to. Would you do that for me?'

A pause. 'Of course – of course I will,' she whispered. 'But I'm *worried* about you… and I miss you,' she added.

Gutteridge shut his eyes tighter to block out his guilt. 'And I miss you, too, sweetheart. So very, very much! And please, there's nothing to worry about.'

'When will I see you again?' she asked, her voice sounding heart-crushingly forgiving in light of his recent infidelity.

Gutteridge thought about Bryant's imposed deadline. 'Soon. I'll be seeing you real soon, I promise. I have so much making up to do.'

Eve pondered the possible connotations behind this last statement, sensing a strange air of regret in his voice, but decided to let it go – at least for now. 'I love you,' she whispered.

A tear broke rank from Gutteridge's eye, rolling down

his cheek. *'Kocham cię...* I love you, too,' he whispered in response, before lowering his wife's voice away from his ear and touching his forehead to the screen affectionately, before ending the call.

He sat motionless, pausing for a beat to let his guilt dissolve into the clouded waters of desire to be a better husband. His attention then returned to his phone.

Gutteridge contemplated his mother's situation. She was at least a long distance away from the main hub of Masterson's recent activity, and housed somewhere with buzz-doors and a reception area that was manned by staff 24/7. Her identity was also camouflaged within a sea of other forgotten souls and lost memories. But still, a call seemed necessary and proper.

He found the number and tapped it. The phone answered almost immediately.

'Radcliffe Manor Care Home, Felicity speaking,' chirruped the girl on the other end.

'Hi, I... erm... I'm calling to check on my mother. Margaret Gutteridge?'

'And you are?'

'Her son. I'm... I'm her son... Patrick.'

'Ah yes. You were here just the other day. I'll check her notes...' The phone fell silent for a moment, giving Gutteridge time to contemplate other places he'd recently visited: the gym, the station, Masterson's rented house *and* his Buxton home, the Quays' carpark, Jane Keaton's house... He paused to let that last one land... Jane Keaton... could Jane be in any danger?

The phone crackled back into life and he heard the receptionist's voice again. 'Hello? You still there?'

'I am.'

'Okay. The log says she ate all of her dinner, choosing the mushroom pasta and sticky toffee pudding. Then she requested to look out of her favourite window where she had a bit of a sleep. She's now propped up in her bed with the television on, with a cup of tea and a biscuit.'

Gutteridge found the list of mundane activities screamingly ordinary, but strangely comforting in comparison to the world he was currently being forced to occupy. He suddenly hankered for his own, personal moment of boredom.

'That sounds great,' he said down the phone. 'Would you give her my love when you next drop in on her, please?'

'Of course,' said the girl. 'I'll go and do that right now. I could do with stretching my legs a little.'

'Thank you,' Gutteridge said. 'Have a good evening.'

'I will,' the girl sang. 'Same to you. Goodbye.'

The phone clicked off, leaving Gutteridge sitting in solitude again.

Rain began spattering the screen, muddying the view ahead and diffusing the streetlights. He flicked on the wipers and opened Keaton's contact details to call her, *knowing* he was being overly cautious, but still.

Her phone began to ring. He listened, an apology for the interruption poised at the ready.

The phone continued to ring without response, until it went to answering machine.

'This is Detective Sergeant Jane Keaton. Please leave a message, and I'll return your call at my earliest opportunity.'

The answer phone beeped and Gutteridge rang off, sitting waiting for the return call and probably an explanation along the lines of: *I was just on the loo and couldn't get to the phone in time,* but it never came.

He tried again. Again the phone rang, but still there was no answer. His heavy brow and whole troubled demeanour darkened, something didn't *feel* right, but was it just the cancer of paranoia that had been growing inside him for the past week, or something more sending alarm bells?

He checked the mirrors and throttled out of the lay-by, drifting in the road to head back towards Keaton's house.

THIRTY

GUTTERIDGE HOOVERED PAST Jane Keaton's home. The lights were on, the curtains closed, and things didn't – on the face of it at least – look out of place, they just felt it.

He turned the car around at the end of the road to pass again and pulled up next to her driveway. He rose into the night, leaving the engine running. There was another car parked outside the property – a silver Ford Fiesta. *Was that the babysitter's car?* he wondered.

He leaned into his own car to turn off the ignition and wandered to the door, lifting a hesitant hand to knock, and that's when he noticed the door hanging open a crack. His whole face washed over with concern.

'Jane?' he called through the opening. 'Are you there? I… I called, but you didn't answer,' he said, but nothing came back.

Tentatively, he opened the door a little way, stepping inside and listening for tell-tale sounds of everyday living: a flushing cistern, a hissing shower, jangling cutlery or clacking plates, the creaking of weight-loaded floorboards. But, again, nothing.

'Jane?' he called again, this time louder and more vehement, as he gingerly opened the door to the living room.

His eyes hardened at the sight of the babysitter's body posed on the settee, clocking the ribbon of blood that cleaved her blank expression in two. She looked to be young, possibly only in her late teens.

Gutteridge stumbled backwards until his shoulders thumped against the wall. Then saw it, the note – *another* of those dreaded notes.

'*JANE!*' he yelled, lunging forward from the wall and pacing the house. 'Are you here? Oh God, *speak* to me!' he screamed until his lungs pained to the force of his desperation. But he knew enough about the Masterson's to believe his cries were pointless.

He spun panicked looks about the room, searching and listening for signs of his son, but there was nothing. He began to sob, biting at the side of his hand. His vision swam behind the veil of tears that cascaded down his face – images of every single mutilated body he'd had to face during his whole time chasing this fucking maniac flashing through his paralysed thoughts.

Reluctantly, he relented and tentatively crossed the room to retrieve the note from the babysitter's breast. With damp eyes full of dread, he opened it and began to read.

Hello again, Patrick.

If you're in any doubt, I have her, the love of your life.

Amazing what you can learn from earwigging in restaurants – and how the simple act of shaving prevented you from recognising me.

Boy, she's a beauty! She looks like a sleeping baby lying here, unconscious.

I wonder what part of this incredible body I'll be keeping? Her arms? Her lovely neck? Those perfectly formed feet? And do I stop here, knowing that there are others still in the land of the living that you care for? Or will slaughtering the mother of your child be enough? Hmmm… it's a difficult one.

Oh… I have the baby, too, by the way. I might raise it as my own until it's old enough to know the value of life, then kill it?

Welcome to my world, Gutteridge – to my pain, to my torment. Crippling, isn't it?
M

Gutteridge scrunched the note in his frustrated fist and drove it hard against the wall, smashing a hole through the plasterboard. His hoarse sobs turned to a roar of infuriated rage as his paralysed mind attempted to recall the facts of the case – trying to entice anything of worth that might lead to even the vaguest of ideas about what to do next.

Jane Keaton's smiling face invaded his tumbling thoughts: her beautiful eyes, her smiling lips, and his son – Joshua – a face full of pure innocence beaming up at him from the crook of his cosseting embrace.

He began pacing the room again, attempting to ignore the corpse posed upon the settee, going over anything and everything they'd encountered to date that might be of relevance…

After a minute, Gutteridge stopped pacing, reflecting on a moment of possible significance. 'Keys?' he said. 'Where were the keys?'

He shut his eyes tight around the memory to aid thought, recalling fumbling through the spill of Kerry Marston's handbag detritus.

'They weren't there,' he muttered. 'Why weren't they there?'

Gutteridge thundered from the house and sprinted to his car, snapping the door open and dropping inside.

He spun the ignition on then stopped, looking around the interior, recalling the tracker that DS Stanton had called to draw his attention to. He realised that Masterson could probably follow his every move.

Alighting the car again, he ran back inside and began looking around for the babysitter's bag, or a loose set of Ford keys, but nothing.

'*Fuck! Fuck! Fuck! Fuck!*' he spat, before suddenly remembering his call to Toby Jackson. He turned and ran from the house again, this time remembering to shut the door in an effort to preserve the scene, then jumped back in the car and sped away.

Gutteridge turned the nose of his Saab into the gravelled driveway of his cottage, the sweeping glow of the headlights landing on a gleaming, blood-red Ferrari that looked screamingly modern in front of his antiquated, cot stone home.

He quickly exited the Saab and made for the front door, keys held out at the ready. His phone began to buzz in his pocket; he drew it out and answered it. The voice on the end of the line was a woman's.

'Sir? It's DS Stanton. I'm just checking in to see if there's anything you need me to do. I'm still here, at the station.'

Gutteridge stopped, wondering how much to let on. He had a hunch, but knew if a whole squad of police cars arrived to confront a terminally ill serial killer with a grudge and little or nothing to lose, Masterson would likely slaughter Jane Keaton, *and* his son.

He selected his words with care. 'Can you send a team over to DS Keaton's home address? It should be somewhere on file. There's a body there, at the location.'

He heard a sharp, stuttered intake of breath on the end of the line.

'No! It's not Jane,' he added, quickly. 'It's someone else. Look, I can't explain right now and I *can't* be disturbed for a time. There's something important I need to do and I need to keep the line clear. Just get a team over there ASAP to secure the scene.'

He shut the call down before Stanton could even reply and slid the key into the lock of his door. It swung open and he began looking around the unlit mat for anything resembling a Ferrari key-fob.

His phone rang out again, causing his heart, in his agitated state, to lurch from his chest.

He swiped a frustrated finger at the screen to answer it. '*Listen* – I asked you not to call me…'

The other end of the line remained strangely silent… 'I have no recollection of that,' said a voice on the other end, but it did not belong to DS Stanton. It was a man's voice: cold, calm, and deep in tone.

Gutteridge recognised it – a voice he hadn't encountered in a little over twelve years.

'*Masterson?*'

'Hello, Gutteridge. Long time no see. Well, if we're being picky, *I've* seen you – *seen* you plenty. You just haven't noticed me. Some detective you turned out to be.'

Gutteridge briefly lost his ability to speak, faltering in the moment.

'What's wrong? Cat got your tongue,' Masterson said.

'W-where's Jane?' Gutteridge stuttered.

'She's here, with me, sleeping like a baby. A veritable little family scene we've got going on here. Me, your partner, and of course… your child. Such a shame I'm going to have to kill them both – it really is quite the picture of domestic bliss.'

'P-please, Terry, you don't have to do this. You're not the man your brother was, you're *better* than that. Always *were* a better man than him.'

Laughter erupted on the other end of the line, then subsided. 'Is that what you think? Is that the conclusion that *you*, with your brilliant, detecting mind, have made? My God, you really are incompetent.'

Gutteridge's arid lips were briefly lost for words. 'Terrence... please... you—'

'You really *should* stop calling me that. I'm beginning to find it deeply offensive – besides, I must go now, things to do, people to kill.'

'*No!*' Gutteridge barked, before the line went dead.

He began frantically stabbing at his phone to return the call, but it went straight to voicemail. He tried again, but the attempt was met with the exact same result.

He wanted to cry, then spied an envelope at his feet, stooping to retrieve it, heard keys rattling inside.

The phone chimed again. Gutteridge frantically scrambled to answer it, then noticed Carl McNamara's name on the screen. He swiped to answer it with an impatient hand. 'Carl – not now. This isn't a good time.'

'Pat!' came the response. 'You have to listen! That body, the one we discovered at Terrence Masterson's Buxton residence. The DNA results have come back – it's *not* Jerry Masterson!'

Gutteridge hung in his doorway, stunned. 'What? But... the wallet?'

'I know, that threw me too. But we *did* get a match, from forensics taken on your original case. That body, it's *Terrence* Masterson. His brother! Jerry must have killed his brother and assumed his identity, living life as him. The man we've all been assuming was Terrence Masterson, is in fact *Jerry* – the Shropshire Ripper!'

'Oh dear Jesus,' Gutteridge whispered, absorbing the ramifications of such a horrifying snippet of information. 'How could I have had it so wrong? It was Jerry. All along it was Jerry… and now that fucking psychopath has Keaton!'

'*What!?*' Carl hissed.

'Oh, shit! Nothing. Look. I need you not to have heard that, at least for now, for the sake of Jane. She's in danger and if we screw this up, she's as good as dead. Do you understand me?'

'Y-yes, but—'

'*No.* You have to work with me on this. I think I might know where she is, where *they* are, and if a squadron of cars turns up with lights flashing and sirens screaming, we'll have done little other than sign her death warrant. Do you understand?'

The phone went silent… 'O-okay… but I can only give you a head start, else I'll lose my job. Tell me where it is you're going, and I'll hold off raising this for fifteen minutes.' Carl could hear Gutteridge thinking about his offer. 'Listen, it'll take time to get a team together, so that will give you at least half an hour head start, *probably* more.'

Gutteridge reconsidered the offer while he tore the keys from the envelope. 'Okay, old friend, I can work with that,' he agreed. 'I think he's holed up at Kerry Marston's home. The address will be somewhere on file, but it's in Staunton, north of the city. I've been there before, so I think I can probably still find it.'

'Okay, old friend,' Carl said. 'Go safe. And good luck…'

It had taken Gutteridge a deeply frustrating minute – which in the light of his panic, had felt like an eternity – to recall how the paddle shift gearbox in Jackson's Lamborghini worked, after discovering that the Ferrari 430 sat on his drive was fitted with a similar system.

He was now speeding down the dual carriageway towards the Over Roundabout at the northern end of the city's perimeter, the hollow, metallic howl of the engine singing its

269

flat-plane-cranked harmony. It was an experience that he dearly wished he could be enjoying, but all his mind could focus on was *save Jane Keaton*.

He had the Glock 17M from his Saab's glovebox sat on the passenger seat beside him. He leaned to place a comforting touch to its muzzle as he neared the junction.

He thundered onto the roundabout and took the first exit, dropping a gear with a flick of the left paddle and gunned the throttle. The back-end of the Ferrari stepped sideways, its engine wailing as the tyres lit up the tarmac. He caught it with a twitch of the wheel and the tyres bit, slamming him into the seat and began reeling in the moonlit horizon.

'Holy shit!' he blurted, terrified by how easy it was to shatter the speed limit in this thing.

He took a few moments, while negotiating the winding roads to Staunton and Corse, trying to recall the layout of Kerry Marston's property. He'd only ever visited three, or was it four times? During a period of his life when the police and the press had placed their differences aside and agreed to cooperate on a distinctly carnal level. He recalled her impressive Victorian property being set back from the main road at least a good hundred yards, with a narrow lane just one and a half cars wide to access it.

Then he remembered the sign – a road sign warning of a concealed junction that he would use to earmark the location of the approaching turn into Marston's driveway. It was positioned just before the crest of a hill, and the turning was a short way after.

Gutteridge suddenly coloured uncertain about his hunch. What if they *weren't* at Kerry Marston's, what then? But he *knew* Jerry, knew him well, and having the sheer audacity to set up shop at one of his victim's homes was precisely the kind of warped thing he would do.

Gutteridge eventually neared the property and spied the concealed entrance sign fifty yards ahead, allowing the Ferrari to slow to a crawl.

He'd been searching out the button he knew to be in these types of vehicle – the one that diverts the pipes through additional silencers to quell the engine noise. He pressed it and the howl of the engine instantly turned muted as he continued to slow.

He saw the entrance ahead and distant lights from windows of the house through the trees surrounding the property – lights that, under the circumstances, shouldn't be on. His racing heart skipped a few beats. He'd been hunting down Jerry Masterson for fifteen years of his life and now, he was mere yards away from where he suspected he now was.

He clocked a narrow, dirt lay-by thirty yards past the turning and made for it, shutting the lights off and coasting to a halt. Grabbing the Glock from the passenger seat, he rose into the night, nudging the door shut with his knee. It was just beginning to spit with rain again as he trotted back towards the entrance to the driveway, keeping low, meandering towards the house, using the corridor of trees as cover.

He couldn't recall the drive being tarmacked when he last visited, but he had a feeling that it used to be gravel underfoot. Either way he was glad for it now, as it aided him passing undetected. He saw a mustard-yellow panel van parked up outside the main entrance as he neared the house. He began hoping, *praying*, that they were all inside and that he wasn't too late.

The thought that Jane Keaton could already be dead terrified him – if she was, he was sure he'd put a bullet straight through Masterson's sick, deranged brain and gladly wear the consequences, feeling entirely justified in the severity of his response.

271

The curtains downstairs were shut tight, but they were thin ind glowed warmly from the light inside. He made his way around to the back of the house, his wide, frosty eyes addressing every window and unlit corner, looking for cameras that could alert those inside to his presence.

He reached the back door and crouched, allowing a moment for his shredded nerves and racing pulse to settle.

The rear gardens were partially illuminated, looking to Gutteridge like the kitchen blinds must be open, spilling light outside, so he stretched up to peer through the window. He could see no one, but the house undeniably looked occupied.

He sank down again, contemplating his options, noticing a cat-flap in the door ahead of him.

Gutteridge dropped to his knees and carefully pushed his fingertips against the clear plastic screen. It swung inwards and he presented an ear to the opening, listening for sounds that would suggest occupancy. He heard a voice, a *man's* voice: *Masterson's*.

He almost laughed with what he knew to be premature relief. If Masterson was talking, he wasn't alone – and if he wasn't alone, Keaton might still be alive, *mustn't she*?

He pushed the flap in again and listened some more. The voice sounded moderately distant and he knew from memory that the house was impressively large and cavernous inside. He stretched up an arm and carefully tried the handle. It turned, but didn't give – it was locked.

'*Shit!*' he fizzed, raising up to peek through the keyhole. He could see a key, sitting in the lock on the other side.

Gutteridge twisted down and extended his arm through the cat flap, reaching up to try and retrieve it. At full stretch, his fingertips could just about kiss the lock's surround and the fob dangling from the key – but his arm wasn't quite long enough to withdraw it.

'Bollocks!' Gutteridge seethed, wondering whether to take the risk and simply kick it through.

Looking around, he spied a circle of slender canes in an adjacent flowerbed, looped in twine to support a wilting wallflower. He leaned across to snap a few inches off the end of the nearest one.

He listened at the flap again to check the coast was clear, but all inside had gone disconcertingly quiet.

Gutteridge paused in his uncertainty for a moment, wondering what risk it was wise to take and running through all the scenarios he might encounter as well as his possible responses to any of them.

'Fuck it,' he muttered, stretching up and presenting the section of stick to the lock. He extended his other arm back through the cat flap, and with a shove, caught the key.

His cold, wet cheeks winced as he gingerly threaded the key back into the lock. It was raining hard now and, with two hands to try and quell any tell-tale sound, he turned it…

The lock withdrew with surprisingly little commotion. Gutteridge retrieved his pistol from the mat beneath his feet and made his way inside…

He quietly pushed the door closed enough to stop any draughts that could give his arrival away, slipping his shoes off so that he could navigate the space undetected.

He darted across the white tiled floor of the modern kitchen to a door that he recalled led to the farthest end of the entrance hallway. He clocked the mutilated remains of a cat, dumped by its food bowl, before rolling a look around the frame towards the front door.

He could hear movement from the stair-end of the long, door-lined corridor, plus a sound like someone shaking something. Then he heard what sounded like muffled sobs – high-pitched and definitely female.

Gutteridge hoped upon hope that it was Jane, because if she was sobbing, she was alive – and if she was alive, there was hope. He steeled himself and, with the gun raised, slinked around the doorframe and made his way towards the sound.

The grand staircase rose to the house's upper levels from the opposite end of the hallway on his left. It climbed from the front door facing him – a familiar layout that so many Victorian properties seemed to possess.

Carefully, he negotiated the long sliver of wood-tiled flooring, his back pressed hard up against the under-panelling of the staircase. He slid past a door that he remembered led to a wine cellar below. The undetermined sounds of shaking and the sobs were getting louder the further down the passageway he got and, for some reason – self-preservation, perhaps – he began readying himself for the worst.

He caught a fleeting glimpse of someone's arm reflected in a mirror mounted on the opposite wall of the hallway. It looked to belong to a man, who seemed to be sitting in a chair facing the stairs.

Gutteridge took a preparatory breath, stepping back, crouching slightly to clear himself of the mirror's reflection. He began micro-lunging a few stealthy looks into the mirror to assess the lay of the land.

He caught sight of Jerry Masterson, the man he'd thought dead for over a decade, sitting in a chair at the base of the staircase facing the treads. He seemed to be looking at something out of Gutteridge's limited field of vision, sat reclined in a buttoned leather seat, caressing his genitals.

The wooden floorboard beneath Gutteridge's tentative steps suddenly creaked and Masterson sprung from the chair, pulling up his jogging bottoms and rabbiting up the staircase.

Gutteridge sank to the floor, hesitating, panic flooding his limbs with adrenalin. He steeled himself, then rose to his feet and darted to the far end of the hallway, slamming his back against the front door and swinging the muzzle of the Glock up the stairwell.

The subtle smell of petrol fumes hit his nose and then he saw Keaton – naked, her hands tied behind her back. She was sat partway up the stairs on the seventh or eighth tread, watching him, her mouth gagged with tape, eyes maroon from weeping.

His heart, soul and stomach sank down to his shuffling feet. Keaton's pleading expression was a mixture of relief and blind panic at seeing him suddenly materialise – that's when he noticed Masterson lurking in the unlit stairwell behind her, holding a length of cord that seemed to drop from the landing above. Then he saw it – a necklace of razor blades threaded through another length of line, wrapped around Keaton's exposed throat.

Gutteridge raised his hands and aimed the Glock at Masterson's head.

'Ah, ah, ahhh – I wouldn't be so quick to shoot if I were you, unless you don't care about the health and wellbeing of this lovely creature sat here,' he sang, looking self-assured and smug. 'You see, the minute I let go of *this*,' he said, indicating the line he was holding, 'the cast iron weights up there will drop, ripping this beautiful angel's delicate throat out.'

He stroked Keaton's cheek with his free hand, bowing to smell her hair. 'I'm sure you wouldn't be wanting that, now, would you? Lover boy.'

Gutteridge shuffled forwards towards Masterson. 'I-if you do, I'll—'

'You'll *what*?' Masterson spat, his voice aggressive and threatening. 'You'll do nothing – *that's* what you'll do. I have the upper hand here. So lower the gun and do your piece-of-fluff-on-the-side here a big fucking favour!'

Gutteridge faltered, knowing it was a stalemate. The only alternative option he could see open to him was to try and shoot through the cord rising from Keaton's throat – but if he missed, he knew it would be game over.

His eyes met Jane's. They both began to weep. 'I'm so utterly sorry,' he mouthed, his brows wilting.

'Aww, how touching,' Masterson mocked, stooping down behind Keaton and using her as a shield, leaning out just far enough to tie the line he was holding to one of the barley-twist balustrades.

He stood again, now holding the blade of a Karambit knife to the tether, looking like a tiger's talon. He retrieved a can of lighter fluid from his pocket and began spraying it onto the line, splashing some over Keaton for good measure. She screamed through the tape, and shook at the icy sensation of the petroleum on her skin, the smell of the fumes making her panic.

With a deft flick of the wrist, Masterson struck up a zippo lighter and presented it to the cord. The flame caught, climbing the line to the landing above with frightening speed and illuminating the entire stairwell. The whole scene looked like some description of Hell from the *Book of Revelation*.

'Gotta go,' Masterson said, briefly touching the flame to Keaton's shoulder, before sprinting up the staircase as fast as his aging legs could carry him.

Gutteridge took aim and contemplated firing but saw the fluid that glazed Keaton's naked body catch and begin spreading rapidly. He knew the flames would burn relatively cold for only a few seconds before her skin began to smoulder. He tossed the gun aside and ran to her aid, grasping a jacket from a hook by the front door and using it to douse the flames, careful not to catch the necklace of blades still looping her neck in his haste.

With the flames finally out, he threw the jacket aside and

turned a look up the stairwell towards the landing. Masterson was nowhere to be seen, and there were two, cast iron, Olympic-sized barbell plates dangling from a line high above them. The line ran through an intricate series of pulleys, looking every bit like the sword of Damocles.

Gutteridge turned his attention back to the necklace of blades, trying to see if he could untie it – but it was knotted too tightly to undo with his shaking fingers. He darted another look up to the flaming tether, which now, had nearly burned through.

He lunged towards the base of the staircase and scrambled desperately on his knees for his gun, grasping it in his panicked fingers and turning to take aim at the line rising from Keaton's neck.

He fired off a few shots, the third bullet clipping the line and making it skip to the side. He adjusted his aim, and fired off two more shots, the second slicing through the fibres of the rope.

The necklace around Keaton's neck went slack and Gutteridge dropped the gun again, lunging forward and grabbing her feet, dragging her unceremoniously down the treads just as 90lbs of cast iron sheered the burning cord and crashed against the step she'd been perched upon.

They both heard the door of the panel van outside slam shut and the engine start, before it pulled away.

Gutteridge took up his gun again, struggled to his feet and ran to the door, fumbling with the locks before flinging it open and firing the remaining rounds in the clip in the direction of the van's vanishing tail lights. He watched as they bled away into the trees, noticing the van make off in the direction of the M50, before turning back to Keaton.

He took another coat down from the hook by the door and wrapped it around her nakedness, trying to preserve her dignity.

'I'm so very sorry,' he whispered, wrapping his arms around her and placing tender kisses on her sweat-soaked scalp, before freeing her of her restraints and the tape across her mouth.

Liberated, she began to cry, her weeping strained and softly vocal.

Gutteridge carefully stroked the hair from her face. 'He'd been tracking us,' he explained. 'I didn't know. I'm so utterly sorry this happened. But you're safe now.'

Jane Keaton began to sob uncontrollably, curling into a ball within Gutteridge's affectionate embrace.

He suddenly remembered the penknife he had in his back pocket, reaching back to retrieve it. He thumbed it open and used it to carefully cut the blades away from her neck.

She had a ring of micro-slashes around her throat, some bleeding, some only appearing superficial – but none looking deep enough to leave long-term scarring.

He finally managed to remove the blades and tossed them aside. She held him, tightly. Gutteridge could see bite marks on the sides of her ribcage and around her waist, cupping them in his hands.

'I'll call backup and get someone over here, but I'll have to go. I can't let him get away,' he said, his words making Keaton cling to him even tighter, sticking to him like a limpet. Gutteridge closed his eyes and wrapped himself around her, again. 'I *need* to chase him, Jane, before he manages to get too far.'

'I-I'm coming with you,' she said. '*Please*… don't leave me alone.'

Gutteridge leaned back out of the embrace, caressing her quivering cheek, considering his options.

Keaton continued to plead. 'I want to come, b-be by your side. Help you catch him. I-I'm okay. I promise. I'm okay…' She delivered a look of supreme concern up into his eyes. 'He has our baby.'

In the confusion, Gutteridge had forgotten all about their child. 'He has Joshua? Where?'

'I think he left him in his truck – he said as an insurance policy.' She began to weep. 'Pat, he has our child! He has our baby!'

Gutteridge felt momentarily paralysed, as though held in checkmate. Then he forced a temperate smile, if only to try and calm Keaton's soul. 'Okay. It's okay. You're coming with me. Just let me find you some clothes...' Gutteridge took a few moments to make sure she was covered over, then quickly stood to search for her suit.

'Where are we going?' Keaton asked.

Gutteridge turned to face the question, looking lost and deep in thought, giving him a strange look of serenity. 'North,' he replied. 'He'll go north...'

THIRTY-ONE

KEATON SAT CURLED UP in the passenger seat of the Ferrari, wearing jogging bottoms and a sweater that had once belonged to Kerry Marston. It felt strangely sacrilegious to be clothed in a dead woman's belongings, but her own clothes had been – as Gutteridge had so politely put it – 'used'.

Gutteridge rang off a call, the cabin alive to the wail of the V8 engine.

'That was Wainwright,' he said. 'They're putting a team of surveillance on Masterson's Buxton address. I also spoke to my old boss in the Shropshire division – they're doing the same for both the old Masterson family home, and Jerry's previous property. There are people living there now, of course, but they're being relocated to temporary accommodation and replaced with armed officers who will sit in wait.'

Awkward silence filled the air for a mile. 'Are you okay?' Gutteridge asked, his voice gentle and understanding.

Keaton sat thinking about the answer. 'I will be.'

Guilt hit Gutteridge again like a kick to the gut. He loaded his next repugnant question. 'And... did he...?' he asked, nodding towards Keaton's lap, the question tailing off.

Keaton shook her head. 'No. He didn't... well, I... I don't

think so? I was unconscious for a lot of the time, but... I don't feel he has,' she mewed, sliding a hand to her groin. 'He touched me... and, *bit* me, but – no...'

The relief that engulfed Gutteridge was overwhelming, feeling almost biblical in its sheer force.

'So where is it that we're going?' Keaton asked, her voice meek and vulnerable.

Gutteridge huffed a sigh. 'First, I need to get my mother out of that care home and move her to my cousin's place. They won't be on Masterson's radar.'

He turned to look at Keaton again. 'Are you sure you don't want me to drop you at a hospital?'

'*No!*' Keaton snapped. 'I want... *need*, to be with you. To catch this wanker! To get our son back!' She paused in her thoughts, the tears threatening to run free again, before directing a look of dread across at him. The most horrifying of questions was sat poised on her lips. 'Is he going to kill him? Is he going to kill our baby?'

Gutteridge gave the repugnant notion his very real consideration, drawing on his extensive knowledge of who, or more accurately, *what*, Masterson was. 'No, I don't believe so. He's deranged – but he's no paedophile. His perversions and triggers always seemed to relate exclusively to women – they *always* have. The young and the beautiful, for sure – but *never* children.'

He turned and looked confidently at Keaton, in an attempt to cement the truth he believed to be in his words. 'A male, infant child would hold little interest for Jerry Masterson – sexually, at least. He is, however, a solid gold bargaining chip. Something with which to negotiate. So *no*, as long as we play this right, there's every chance he won't be killed.'

The tears finally came to Keaton's sore eyes. 'God, I hope you're right.'

Gutteridge smiled, eyes soft, regretful, but understanding. 'So do I...'

He changed lanes and indicated onto the slip-road signposted M5 North, gunning the throttle and thrusting them both into their seats, reeling in the horizon to a thrashing cacophony of reciprocating machinery and howling tailpipes.

Gutteridge searched out and pressed the button to switch the Ferrari's gearbox to automatic, then extended a comforting hand to take hold of Keaton's.

*

The waspish buzzer made the girl manning the reception at Radcliffe Manor House Care Home jump. 'Jesus!' she slurred, checking the time on her phone, not used to receiving visitors this late.

She quickly checked the log... There were no out-of-hours visitors booked in and the nightshift changeover had already happened. She buzzed the outside door to let whoever it was enter, standing to watch as a heavily built man, obscured by a bouquet of flowers, negotiated the air-locked foyer doors.

The visitor kneed the second door aside and stepped into the warmth, smiling kindly, wiping his feet on the mat before approaching the desk.

'Hi there,' he breathed, looking around the reception with notable interest. 'I have a delivery, forrrr...?' he began, consulting a slip of paper held in his hand, 'a Mrs Margaret Gutteridge?'

The receptionist smiled. 'Oh yes. She's one of our residents.' She outstretched her arms to take the flowers from the man.

'No,' the new arrival said, pulling them out of her reach. 'I... I have to give them to her personally.'

The receptionist's amiable front turned regretful. 'I'm

282

sorry, but I'm afraid we don't let members of the public onto the premises, unless they have relatives staying here.'

The man looked put out and more than a little exasperated. 'But, I'm supposed to sing to her. I'm an opera-gram, see. I sing Puccini's "Nessun Dorma". I've been booked by… hang on, it's here somewhere…' he consulted the slip of paper again. 'Mr Patrick Gutteridge? I think it might be her son?'

The girl's face lit up. 'Oh, wow, how fun is that. I didn't even know that was a thing. Nessun Dorma. What a brilliant idea. Erm… hang on a mo,' she said, colouring strangely excited and stepping through into the rear office to scan the day room. 'Yes, she's still in there – I can see her, sitting by her favourite window.' She turned back to address the visitor. 'I don't know what she can be looking at, it's pitch black outside,' she giggled. The receptionist then turned thoughtful. 'Could I possibly ask you to wait just a few minutes while we bring a few more of our residents through? I know it's getting quite late, but I'm sure they'd really enjoy hearing something like that?'

'Of course,' said the visitor, seeming eager and happy to oblige. 'So… she's in there, is she?'

'Yes,' the girl said, turning and pointing towards the bank of rear windows. 'She's just there – at the back, red dressing gown.'

She turned to face the visitor again and found herself staring down something cylindrical that was being held out towards her.

There was a sharp, cracking pop that shattered the calm and the receptionist's head snapped backwards, sending skull fragments spinning into the office. Her body dropped to the ground like a wet blanket and Masterson rounded the counter, feeling beneath the lip for a button. He found and pressed it, hearing the buzz and clunk of the door's locks releasing.

Masterson trampled over the dropped flowers and made his way inside.

'What was that?' an orderly said, rushing from one of the corridor of suites wearing a frown.

'Oh, a bookcase fell – through there,' Masterson said, swinging an outstretched arm in the direction of the reception area.

The orderly rushed past him to help, then slowed. 'And... who are you? Are you visiting one of our residents?' the orderly asked, turning to face Masterson.

'Seems that way,' Masterson said, raising his gun to the man's throat and firing.

A pluming mist of crimson ejected from the back of orderly's neck and he stumbled backwards, sinking to the ground, still alive but paralysed.

Masterson hurried into the day room, guided to the window by a shock of white hair and the blood-red of his mark's dressing gown.

He crossed the room and crouched down before the old lady, seeing the moment as a shadow from his past, wishing it were his own mother he was there to see.

Margaret Gutteridge averted her attention to observe the new face looking up at her. 'What was that sound?'

Masterson smiled. 'Just something falling.'

'Oh,' the old woman said. 'Is it broken?'

Masterson gave a solitary laugh. 'I think he probably is.'

The old woman's face morphed into confusion. 'And who are you?'

Masterson took her papery hand in his. 'I've come to collect you. I'm going to take you away from here – to somewhere nice.'

The old woman's expression flickered. 'Patrick? I-is that you?'

Masterson's brow briefly darkened, then lit up like a dawn morning. 'Yes... yes, Mum. It's me... it's your Patrick.'

THIRTY-TWO

THE M42 EVENTUALLY BLENDED into the A42, but the needle of the Ferrari remained relentlessly wavering either side of 110.

They'd both felt encouraged by the increasing regularity with which they were encountering signs for Nottingham, a sure indicator they were drawing near. But there was also no denying that the knowledge that their child was at the mercy of a psychopath was a very real, and wholly unwelcome distraction.

'I can't believe we haven't got a squadron of cop cars on our tail,' Keaton said, leaning a glance over at the speedometer that was now kissing 130.

Gutteridge's brows flashed at the statement. 'I can't deny, I'm glad the traffic cops around here do seem to be a bit shit,' he said, his face remaining stern and alert, eyes locked on the meandering road ahead. 'We don't need the fanfare of their involvement slowing us down.'

Gutteridge's phone buzzed again, like both his and Keaton's had been doing for the past hour, but they'd been clocking the names of those calling and purposefully ignoring them.

Keaton glanced at the screen and her brow furrowed. 'This one's got an 0115 area code?' she said.

Gutteridge also frowned. 'That's the area code for Nottingham,' he said, his expression turning to one of concern. 'Answer it!'

Keaton quickly swiped at the screen. Gutteridge extended a hand to take it from her. 'Patrick Gutteridge.'

Keaton watched as her partner listened. 'Yes,' he said to whoever was on the other end of the line. 'She is. She's my mother?'

Gutteridge suddenly stamped on the brakes and pulled the car over to the side of the road, causing passing motorists to lean on their horns and Keaton to nearly scream.

Gutteridge clamped the phone hard to his ear and listened, intently. 'What! When?' he fizzed, sitting motionless, absorbing the information being relayed to him. 'Oh fuck!' He sat shifting in his seat, breaths unsteady and staccato. 'He did *what*? Oh dear God!'

He swapped the phone to his other ear and clamped it even tighter, now rocking in his seat. 'That man,' he said. 'His name's Masterson. *Jerry* Masterson. He's wanted for multiple murders. A case I'm – *we're* – currently working on.' He listened some more. 'And, do you know where he might have taken her? I mean, is there CCTV or anything at all indicating the direction which he left?' He continued to listen, Keaton watching his face morph through a series of horrified expressions. 'A van? Was it yellow? Like, you know, a mustard colour?'

Keaton could just about hear the responses over the hollow burble of the engine. It all seemed to be getting very serious very quickly, and she wasn't so sure that Gutteridge's decision to keep Bryant and the team's involvement at arm's length was the best option anymore. She allowed her attention to return to Gutteridge, whose expression seemed now to have relaxed into some revelant form of comprehension.

He expelled a long, resigned breath. 'I think I might know where he's taking her,' he said into the phone's mouthpiece, seeming to be talking more to himself than whoever it was on the other end of the line. He erupted from his analytical torpor. 'I have to go, there's something I need to do – but I'll be back in touch to give an official statement.'

He curtly rang off, quickly opening the phone's settings menu and switching to do not disturb.

He then quickly opened the map function, typed a name into the app's search engine and hit 'directions'.

Gutteridge pressed the drive button on the Ferrari's gearbox and pulled away, Keaton watching his actions from within the bubble of timidity that her terrifying ordeal had placed her within.

The phone instructed them to make a U-turn, while Gutteridge's wandering hand searched for a place to prop the device.

'Here,' said Keaton, taking it from him and glancing briefly at the screen, before turning the map to face him. 'Lake Vyrnwy? Where the hell's that? W-why are we going there?'

Gutteridge spun the car in the road and accelerated away, looking strangely detached and distant. 'Jerry Masterson...' he said. 'He has my mother.'

Keaton lifted a hand to her mouth.

'He's killed two of the attendants at the care home, shot them, and he took her.'

Tears filled Jane Keaton's eyes, tumbling down her tremulous cheeks. The nightmare only seemed to be intensifying, with no option to wake from its barrelling horrors.

'Don't you think we should call this in?'

'*No!*' Gutteridge snapped. 'If we do that, he'll kill them both for sure.' He turned his now waterlogged eyes to face hers. 'I know this man. I know what he's capable of and I also know the way he and his fucked-up mind works. You have to trust me on this. He's taking them to Lake Vyrnwy.'

'But… why? Why there?'

'Because that's where his mother took her own life. And I think that's where he means to deprive me of mine.'

THIRTY-THREE

THE UNDULANT ROADS rolling through the bleak and deserted regions of Powys were just visible through the van's flat windscreen and held no surprises for Jerry Masterson. He'd made sure to visit this area every year, religiously, ever since his mother's passing – some skewed, unhealthy form of pilgrimage, a journey made without fail ever since the day she took her own life. Ever since the day that bastard had killed her!

He had his gun sat in the door-pull pocket at the ready. One of the headlights had gone out making it hard to see, but if he got pulled over, he would have to dispatch the interfering policeman involved – or, if he was lucky, *policewoman*. And if she was in any way attractive, who knows – there might even be some impromptu fun to be had...

The old woman sat quietly beside him, seemingly happy to just stare out of the window. She'd said surprisingly little considering the magical mystery tour she now found herself being taken on.

'Where are we again?' Margaret Gutteridge asked for what felt to Masterson like the hundredth time.

'Wales, Mum. We're in Wales.'

'Oh, that's right, you did say. Silly me,' she chirped in her fragile voice, touching a jaunty hand to his knee.

He recoiled from the unexpected moment of tactility, unnerved by the tenderness in her action.

She leaned into her side window again and peered through the veil of fog that her breath had deposited onto the chilled glass.

'There aren't many houses, are there?' she said. 'Where do people live, in caves?'

Masterson allowed himself a snigger, then fought to quell it. As cold-hearted as he knew he could be, having realised a long time ago he was a psychopath, he couldn't afford to allow any fondness for the old bitch to permeate his sociopathic personality.

'There *are* houses, you just can't see them in the dark. It's late, Mum – people are in bed.'

Margaret Gutteridge turned her not inconsiderable interest towards him again. 'Then why are *we* up?'

'Because we're going somewhere very special. It's a secret. Something I've organised *just* for you.' He turned to look at her and smiled.

The old woman clapped her papery hands together and beamed, the swaying of the van and the chattering rasp of the diesel engine only adding to the air of adventure.

She started peering about the utilitarian interior, looking bemused. A brief moment of recollection crimped at her eyes – moments that, due to the worsening dementia, were growing rare.

'Are you still a policeman?' she asked, her swinging interest refocussing on Masterson, his face underlit red by the dashboard lighting. She narrowed her inquisitive stare. 'You look different. What have you changed? Is it your hair?'

Masterson turned his face away a quarter turn, glancing

290

down at the bottle of chloroform and the rag sitting in the door pocket.

'Yes, Mum. It's my hair. I've changed my hair.'

The bleating sounds of the baby in the back once again began drifting through the thin sheet metal of the bulkhead. The old woman attempted to turn and look, confused – like they *hadn't* heard it at least four times already during the time they'd been together.

'What was that? Is that a baby?'

Masterson's patience was slowly fraying aagin. '*Yes*, Mum – it's a *fucking* baby.'

A scolding look from the old woman met his words. 'I did *not* raise you to use that kind of language, young man!' she attempted to bark in her cracking voice.

Masterson pulled the van over to the side of the road, popped the door and grabbed the bottle of trichloromethane and the rag from the side pocket.

'Give it a fucking rest, Mum,' he spat, dropping off the seat into the damp night air, the rumble and clatter of the side door cutting through the silence.

The baby's crying grew louder as the door slid open, briefly intensifying, then a beat later, fell eerily silent.

Masterson pulled the door shut again and re-pocketed the chemical sleep. He stood staring through the opening at the frail old woman, rag still in his hand. He contemplated silencing the inquisitive old bitch for the rest of the journey, but decided against it, feeling his spent patience coming off the boil.

He climbed back inside and impatiently threw the van into gear, pulling away again. He leaned on the wheel and gazed out into the night.

'Why don't we have peace and quiet for a bit?' he muttered. 'Shut your eyes. We're not too far away now, I'll wake you when we're getting close, then our fun can begin…'

291

THIRTY-FOUR

THE SCREAMING FERRARI thundered along the B4393 towards Llanwddyn. Gutteridge and Keaton leaned into the screen, watching the flora flanking the narrow lanes flash past the side windows at break-neck speed, illuminated by the violent swing of the headlights.

'Fuck me this is quick!' Keaton fizzed, allowing the resulting adrenaline rush a moment to distract her from her concerns for her baby, before allowing it to gestate again. She turned a worried look Gutteridge's way.

'What if we're wrong? What if he *isn't* there, at this lake?'

Gutteridge shook a repudiating head, not willing to allow such doubts to take root. 'I can't think of anywhere else he'd go. Everything he does or has *ever* done has reason – some warped form of logic for sure, but logic all the same. No... he's taking them to the lake, I'm certain of it.'

They suddenly thundered past a sign for Lake Vyrnwy – they were drawing close.

'How far, now?' Gutteridge asked, not daring to tear his eyes from the road.

'It says eight minutes,' Keaton replied, consulting the phone, 'But I think the rate we're going, it might be more like six!'

They howled through the small village of Abertridwr, sliding around a sharp, left-hand bend and past a convenience store – the only shop of any description they'd seen for miles.

The tyres scrabbled for purchase, caught, and the car lunged forward towards the next section of rapidly approaching horizon.

'Where the fucking hell are people around here supposed to buy food?' Gutteridge asked. But Keaton's awareness of the increasing geographical closeness to her baby was robbing her attention.

Gutteridge hadn't been to this region for well over a decade, not since the original investigation, but he was surprised by how much of the layout he still recognised.

'I reckon we'll be coming up on the dam I described at the southern end of the lake, soon. It should appear on our left. There's a narrow road that crosses it but, if I remember correctly, there used to be a couple of parking spaces on this side. I reckon we should park there and cross on foot, else he might hear us approach.'

'Hang on,' Keaton said, opening a satellite image of the area on the map. She swiped around the image. 'No,' she said, shaking her head. 'I think the whole area must be much bigger than you're remembering. That slipway you spoke of – I think you said it was at the canoe rental paddock, yes?'

Gutteridge nodded. 'Yes.'

She scrolled around some more. 'I can see it. I think you should cross the dam, turn right at the end, then there's a parking area about half a mile further along on the left. We could run from there. It's still a bit of a trek, but it's doable.'

She lifted a finger towards the dashboard. 'If you do that thing where you mute the exhaust, he'd probably just shrug us off as passing locals.'

Gutteridge thought about what she'd said, tallying it with

his own faded memories, and nodded. 'Okay. I'll put my trust in your judgment.'

He flicked a glance her way. 'Are you going to be okay? You know, with everything you've been put through?'

She nodded, looking meek and decidedly more vulnerable than Gutteridge had ever seen her before. Yet, by the same token, she appeared determined and unwaveringly resolute.

'I'm fine,' she said, sounding adamant. 'I'm not going to say this won't mess with me – but, right now, I just want my baby back.'

Gutteridge held eye contact, then nodded in solidarity.

Keaton squirmed in her seat. She could still feel the bite marks along her back and down her sides – once again, feeling the indignity of being used as pornography for Masterson's diseased and debauched fantasies. But despite that, at this *very* moment, none of it mattered – all her concerns were focused exclusively on her one and only child and, of course, Gutteridge's mother.

Gutteridge continued to turn the occasional look in Keaton's direction, watching the mixed emotions visible on her face. He forced a smile that – retrospectively – felt inappropriate, then through the corner of his eye, noticed sporadic flashes of heavy slate-stone blockwork peeking through the canopies of the trees that lined the road. They'd finally arrived and he didn't know what they were going to find.

He reached for the mute button again and pressed it, strangulating the engine and, more importantly, the eager howl of the V8.

They slowed until the trees cleared the blockwork dam, its impressive architecture brutal in its Victorian extravagance.

'We're here,' he said, as he turned onto the narrow road that crossed it, contemplating flicking his lights off, but deciding against it, knowing that it would look suspicious if noticed.

'Okay, drive across and turn right at the end,' Keaton said, for some reason whispering. She allowed herself a moment to absorb the impressive landscape blanketed under a veil of light mist. 'There's a lay-by on the left. Pull in and we can travel the rest of the way on foot.'

She peered across at Gutteridge, her face a picture of uncertainty. 'Oh God, Pat. I hope they're here.'

He grasped her hand, giving it the tightest squeeze he could muster. 'Me too…'

THIRTY-FIVE

MASTERSON WAS LEADING THE OLD WOMAN by her withered hand, the canoe rental paddock just visible a hundred yards ahead, their pathway illuminated by the single headlamp of the panel van which sat abandoned in the lay-by behind them.

'This way,' he said, supporting her elbow, watching her slippered feet shuffle along the road.

'Where are we going?' she asked again, her incessant, repetitive questioning beginning to make Masterson's temper fray.

'We're going for a boat ride, you'll *enjoy* it,' he snapped. 'I *told* you that already.'

For a second time, the old woman look disgruntled. 'Isn't it a bit dark to be going out on boats? And it's awfully cold.'

Masterson didn't answer immediately. He was growing impatient, but fought to quell it for the sake of his plan.

He had a coil of old rope with a dumbbell weight threaded through it hanging from his shoulder and it was banging into his leg, irritating him even further.

'We're not going to be out for very long, for Christ's sake. There's a jacket in the boat for you to put on and a cup of tea in one of those mugs.'

The old woman smiled at that lie, and appeared to speed up her soporific walk.

Masterson suddenly stopped and turned to look behind them, thinking he heard an engine. He hung still in the drifting mist, listening, gazing out into the obsidian darkness...

'What is it?' the old woman asked.

'*Shhhh!*' he hissed, wafting an impatient hand towards her face as if trying to swipe the sound of her voice away.

He stood for a while longer, motionless, listening... but nothing.

Slowly, brows still heavy, he turned back. The old woman's face looked quizzical. 'It's nothing,' he said. 'I just thought... it's nothing.'

He took the old woman's skeletal hand in his again. It felt cold. He towed her towards the paddock and clambered over the white-painted railings, dropping off onto the other side.

'Come on,' he said, 'come here.'

Masterson leaned over the railings and hooked the old woman's featherweight frame in his arms, the iron weight clattering against the cold steel of the bars, sounding deafening in the stillness of night. He lifted her over the railings like a child.

Unnerved by the sounds he thought he'd heard, he decided to carry her the rest of the way down the shingled path to the water's edge.

His thoughts turned to his own mother, alone with her regrets, filling her clothes with gravel, there only to prematurely end her time in this world.

He placed the old woman down again, ignoring the adoring looks she seemed to be giving him. Masterson un-shouldered the weight, dumping it onto the frosted grass at his feet then trotted up the path to retrieve a small row boat they'd passed. He heaved it onto his broad back and carried it back down to the slipway. With a shrug, he flipped it off his shoulder and it splashed into the lake.

'What's that for, Patrick?' the old woman asked, indicating the weight.

'Oh. It's erm… it's an anchor, you know, to stop us drifting, if we felt like stopping a while to watch the stars.' He smiled to waylay the old woman's concerns.

Her sepia eyes turned to the heavens, then he stepped to the bank opposite the water's edge to secure a pair of oars from a stockpile.

He carefully laid them along one side of the boat, grabbing the weight from the ground and dropping it in too, before turning to help Gutteridge's mother into the craft.

'Go on,' he said. 'Get in. In you go…'

She darted him a dubious look. 'Can we not do this another day, when the weather's nicer?'

'Will you just get in the *fucking* boat?' he snapped, his patience dangerously close to spent, looking around nervously before manhandling the old woman towards the bobbing hull.

She suddenly coloured afraid, reluctantly shuffling down the slipway, water licking at the cloth of her slippers. She fumbled her feet over the lip of the craft, unsteadied by her advancing years, stumbling as the boat rocked beneath her. She lost her footing, tripping over one of the thwarts, and fell into the crook of the keel.

The chilled night air shocked to the bright snap of the old woman's fragile wrist. She screamed as loud as her desiccated vocal chords could still manage, making Masterson clamber into the hull behind her and clamp a hand over her mouth.

'*Shhhhhhh…*' he hissed, his mouth now an inch from her ear. 'You have to be quiet. No noise, you hear me?'

He wrapped her tiny frame in his other arm and lifted the

simpering old woman to her feet, before sitting her down on one of the wooden seats, his hand still covering her mouth.

Masterson used his free hand to thread the oars into the crutch of the rowlocks, then sat down opposite and gradually allowed his hand to slide from the old woman's mouth.

'Are you going to be a good girl, now, and make no noise?' he asked, his tone threatening.

She peered across at him as he leaned back and began to row, clutching her shattered wrist. 'Who are you?' she muttered, cold, shivering, the skin on her hands beginning to turn blue. 'Y-you... you're *not* my son?'

'No,' Masterson said with a grin. 'No, I'm not.'

THIRTY-SIX

KEATON AND GUTTERIDGE could see the tail lights of the mustard-yellow transit ahead, advancing – what they hoped was undetected – behind the blinding glow of the van's single headlamp.

Keaton peeled off to check the vehicle, noticing the driver's side door hanging wide open. She trotted to the rear quarter panel and took a calming breath, then with her back pressed flat against the side of the payload bay, slid towards the opening.

She darted a few looks around the door jamb and could see the cab was empty. She stepped in and peered around the inside, desperately looking for sight or sound of a tiny life – but there was nothing.

Keaton began to panic again, quaking, wondering if the child she'd carried inside her for nine months was already gone.

She clocked the handgun in the door then, turning, noticed a sliding door on the side of the payload bay. Gingerly, she leaned on the handle and grasped it tightly, lightly tugging on it until it popped.

Slowly, she began sliding the rumbling door open, taking great pains not to make a sound that would alert Masterson to their presence, but at the same time, dreading what horrors she might find in the back of a serial killer's truck. But as the door unveiled the stark interior, all she saw was her baby, lying deathly still on the hard, unforgiving surface of the plywood decking.

She put her hands over her mouth and began biting at her fingers, letting out a snort as she began to weep. The baby looked dead. The stillbirth of their failed attempt to save its tiny, innocent life. A last, final indignity to crown her day of shame and humiliation.

Then she noticed Joshua's chest rise, ever so slightly, and ever so slowly, but movement all the same. Keaton quickly leaned in and gathered him up in her arms, stepping back and placing him gently on the soft, damp grass beneath her feet, hoping the cold would shock his system awake. Tears dripped off her nose onto his tiny body as she dropped to her knees, still heavily bruised from being tasered unconscious. She pulled Joshua's mouth open and began exhaling into his tiny lungs in desperation, to aid his own weakened efforts to draw breath.

She could taste the remnants of trichloromethane on his skin, mixed with the salty tears of her own anguish. She continued to deliver CPR until the child finally began to stir, his movements weak, but gradually increasing along with Keaton's soaring levels of relief.

Gutteridge finally reached the boundary fencing of the rental paddock. He could hear voices, quiet and distant, but still close enough to at least give him a modicum of hope.

Despite the time he'd had for contemplation during the journey there, he realised he hadn't formulated any kind of plan – he'd been far too focused on his driving to have given the situation any real thought.

'Shit!' he hissed into the mist, realising that in his haste he'd left his Glock in the footwell behind the seat of the Ferrari.

He contemplated running back to retrieve it, but he could hear his mother's voice growing distant, sounding quiet, fragile and afraid. He daren't risk leaving her at the mercy of that demented psychopath.

Silently, he climbed over the fencing and crouched in the frozen grass, then set off, trotting in the direction of the voices.

Looking around, he recognised the space, recalling the moment when divers had extracted the bloated corpse of Jodie Masterson from the lake. He also remembered how much he'd like her, warmed to her, pitied her during interview – and how the look of loss and pain in her eyes had saddened him. In retrospect, it was easy to see the way things were going to go for her; the life-ending decision she was eventually going to make. But did that in fact make him culpable for her death, as Masterson had always felt?

He reached a bank of trees and could just see a boat through the layer of mist that blanketed the water, drifting at the core of expanding ringlets of ripples at least fifty feet from the shoreline.

He ducked down and peered around one of the trunks. He spotted his mother first, then Masterson, fiddling around with something or other, still drifting slowly away from the shoreline.

His eyes widened at the sight – it was one he'd been fully expecting to be confronted with, but actually seeing it made his guts feel like they were melting through his body. He kept low, trying to assess his dwindling options, attempting to push his fears aside to court clarity.

The moon was almost full and hanging in a sky with very few clouds, offering Gutteridge good visibility for his observations. Still, he was unarmed and, at that very moment, clueless.

'What are you doing that for?' asked Margaret Gutteridge, watching as the stranger tied a rope to her ankle.

'It's to keep you safe, so you can't fall out of the boat,' Masterson explained, his voice curt and abrupt.

'My wrist really hurts, can we go back now?' she whimpered, cradling the hand that was now swinging from her arm, blood dripping from the protruding bone.

Her words continued to test Masterson's rapidly fraying patience. He tugged the last knot tight then spun and grasped her face in his huge hand, squeezing it hard. '*Shut*, the *fuck*, up!' he seethed, deliberately allowing his inflamed annoyance to germinate. It would assist him in throwing the daft old bitch over the side, a woman who – in so many ways – reminded him of his own dearest, darling Mummy. This fact, he knew, would only make his job that much harder.

For a brief moment, he considered knocking her out and simply dumping her over the side. But ideally, he wanted her to be aware of *everything* that was happening to her – the way his own mother had been.

Masterson thrust her pained expression away from him, leaning a look over the side of the boat into the waiting, watery grave – mesmerised by the onyx sheen of the lake's calm surface. The reflection of the wispy, cloud-covered moon high above him looked almost like a face watching him within the swirling waters – the face of his precious mother, smiling up at him, urging him to send the old woman in to join her.

He suddenly noticed other ripples passing over the water's reflection, colliding with those emanating from the boat – ripples that seemed to be expanding from the shoreline behind them.

His eyes quickly darted to the side and he clambered around behind the old woman, turning to look and noticing Gutteridge waist-deep in the water. He was edging down the slipway towards them, his large frame barely visible in the darkness.

'Don't even think about it!' Masterson snarled, struggling to lift the iron weight from the bobbing hull and holding it out over the side.

Gutteridge stopped, his hands held out. 'No! Please, don't. O-okay…'

'I-is that you, Patrick?' his mother said, recognising his voice, her failing eyesight struggling to see him in the gloom.

Masterson shuffled to the other side of the boat, still holding the weight over the water and reaching for one of the oars with his free hand. He had to try and row further out but, in his haste, he knocked it and it slid from its rowlock and splashed into the lake.

'*Fuck!*' he spat, eyes remaining locked on Gutteridge. He shuffled back behind the old woman again – this was the second stalemate he had found himself in that day with Gutteridge.

A crippling pain suddenly expanded from Masterson's left lung, firing through his body like a bolt of electricity, making him crane in agony. It was the cancer sinking its large, remorseless teeth into him, setting up the moves for its final endgame. The pain lingered, spearing his decaying organs with its cruel fingers, then as quickly as it had come, it dissipated into his racking body.

Taking a few breaths to recover, Masterson began shuffling the old woman to the side of the boat, the cancer reminding him that he had nothing left to lose and not long left to live.

'Why are you doing this?' Gutteridge asked, taking the opportunity to edge in further, cloaked by Masterson's frantic activity. 'What is any of this *really* going to accomplish?'

Masterson finally managed to manhandle the old woman to the side of the craft. 'Don't go reading too much into it, Gutteridge,' he said. 'It's purely revenge. Eye for an eye.'

'Haven't you taken enough from me, already? How many lives is going to be enough?'

Masterson spun around and gnashed through the thickening fog towards his pleading. 'It'll never be enough,' he growled. 'As long as I have breath in this fucking failing body of mine, it'll never be enough.'

Gutteridge took another tentative step into the freezing lake. 'I know about the cancer and I know it's inoperable,' he said. 'Why don't you show the world you have a heart? As your last action on this earth, why not show them all how wrong they were about you?'

Masterson finally stood and leaned over the bewildered old lady, jabbing the cast iron weight towards Gutteridge's pleading in rhythm with his rebuke. 'Nice try, but I'll kill, and I'll *keep* killing,' he seethed, 'and I won't rest until everyone who ever meant anything to you is in the fucking soil, rotting like the body of my mother. My mother that you—'

A sudden crack that echoed around the basin of hills surrounding the lake shattered the stillness of the night. A shot fired from the shore, the bullet fizzing past Gutteridge's left ear and scything through Masterson's outstretched arm. He screeched, the weight dropping from his fingers and clattering onto the boat, a look of ultimate shock emblazoned across his grimacing face and he stumbled, overwhelmed by the searing pain.

A second crack flashed from the shoreline ahead of them, the bullet smashing through Masterson's gritted teeth and embedding itself in the back of his throat, followed by a third, which sliced through his right eye, dragging shards of bone and brain matter through the exit wound at the back of his skull. Suddenly, and gracefully, like a felled tree, he toppled from the boat into the icy waters.

The coil of rope was tangled around his foot, dragging the cast iron plate over the side with him.

Gutteridge saw his mother's leg hop the lip of the craft,

as slowly, she was dragged into the liquid death sentence with him.

'*Nooooo!*' Gutteridge screamed, wading in towards his mother's flailing arms.

Keaton stepped out from the bushes, Masterson's gun held in her shaking hands.

Gutteridge pushed off the slipway, making a lunging dive towards his mother, frantically swimming to where he last saw her before she slipped under the surface. He reached the side of the drifting boat, swinging his legs through the freezing water, trying to make contact with anything soft and organic – but nothing.

He sucked in a full breath and dove beneath the frigid surface, his skin stinging at the cold, his rapidly numbing arms pulling him deeper into the gloom of the lake.

Keaton hovered on the shoreline, feeling helpless, watching as the ripples on the surface slowly dissipated, wondering what – if anything – she could do.

Gutteridge tried opening his eyes, but it was too dark to see anything, the cold sending needles of pain shooting through his vision. He swam further down into the charcoal blackness, trying to find his mother, the arctic chill deadening his ability to feel.

Then his hand hit something drifting in the turbulence, not a body as whatever it was felt hard but flexible. He reached towards it again and clipped it – it was the rope.

His arms swung around desperately in the darkness until he managed to grasp hold of it, and he began reeling it through his fingers until he came to what felt like a foot – a foot clad in something heavy, thickly-soled and undeniably made of leather. It was a boot, a man's boot – and that's when the coppery taste of blood began filling his mouth.

He panicked, nearly gagging on the taste, ejecting the

contaminated water from his mouth. His breath was beginning to run out and he knew his mother's would be too. Gutteridge began running the rope back through his hands the other way, then remembered the penknife he still had in his pocket. He grasped the rope in his teeth, trying to ignore the metallic tang on his tongue. Taking pains not to drop it, he retrieved the knife from his pocket and fumbled the blade out of the handle.

He started sawing frantically at the fibres of the rope, feeling the increasing pressure being exerted on his body, aware that the weight was dragging them all down to the bottom of the lake.

The rope finally relented to his efforts. Gutteridge had to make absolutely certain not to drop the wrong end, else he would lose his mother forever to the obsidian depths of the huge expanse of water – the final, indignant act of a shitty son.

He wound the cut end of the rope that he still had hold of around his wrist and, not truly knowing which way was up, swam towards the lightest part of his swirling vision. Eyes stinging, limbs numb, he hoped upon hope it was the moon he was swimming towards, as he held his lips tightly closed and tried to thwart his body's instinctive desire to draw breath.

Keaton padded about on the shore. It had been over two minutes and the compulsion to cry was growing ever stronger. Her jaw began to chatter – part cold, part grief – then, with a splash, Gutteridge erupted through the surface of the lake like Poseidon.

With a sucking gasp that felt like rebirth, he inhaled a whole chestful of air, his pluming breath billowing white into the frigid air around him.

His arms clawed at the water, dragging the dead weight of the woman who'd raised him towards the bobbing surface and the shoreline.

Keaton noticed the rope wrapped around Gutteridge's hand, but the body of his mother hadn't yet surfaced – she realised that probably meant her lungs would be filled with fluid. She prepared herself and waded into the water to intercept his arrival, taking the rope from his frozen hand and continuing to reel it in.

The shadow of two legs emerged through the black umbrella of the water, breaching the surface like driftwood. Keaton grasped them in her shaking hands and dragged them towards the shore, the old woman's paperweight body creating little to no resistance.

Keaton heaved her lifeless body onto the ridged surface of the concrete slipway, rolling the old woman onto her side and using her fingers to clear her airways. She lay her flat against the concrete again and pinched her nose to begin administering CPR.

Gutteridge crawled from the water, exhausted, close to succumbing. He knelt on the slipway, watching as Keaton worked to save his mother's life, his fatigued limbs shivering with the early onset of hyperthermia.

Keaton thumped, pounded and breathed her best efforts for what felt to Gutteridge like hours, thrusting her desperation to save a life down upon the old woman's brittle ribcage, her barked, breathy counting only seemed to mark the increasing length of time that the old lady had been unconscious for. Nothing resembling life crossed the limp body of Gutteridge's mother, her emaciated limbs scattered across the concrete, skin purple, lying precisely where Jodie Masterson's body had lain twelve years earlier.

With three, last, hope-starved thrusts on the old woman's sternum, Keaton ceased her efforts. Exhausted, she sat back on her heels, the cold teeth of the midnight air making the bite marks on her skin tingle.

'I'm so sorry,' she said. 'She's gone. I couldn't...'

Gutteridge reached out a shaking hand, and placed it on Keaton's back. 'I know. I... I know. You did what you could,' he said, his voice cracking. 'And... Joshua?' he asked.

Keaton slouched, and felt strangely guilty for smiling inside. 'I found him. He's fine... he's going to be fine.'

THIRTY-SEVEN

GUTTERIDGE HANDED KEATON another envelope, hovering awkwardly in the middle of her freshly decorated living room. He glanced down at the new settee, memories of discovering the babysitter's body still strong in his mind.

Eve was sat outside in the car, bags packed for a week away.

'There's a little extra in there, this week,' he said, with a soft smile, looking – as he always did during what had become regular handovers – mildly guilty.

'You didn't have to do that,' Keaton responded with a curious smile.

Gutteridge's shoulders hopped a carefree shrug. 'I know. But if you saw the cheque I just received from Toby Jackson, you'd probably be asking why it isn't more.'

Keaton's expression brightened, her sky-blue eyes igniting and Gutteridge could see her fighting the question he knew she desperately wanted to ask. 'Go on?' she relented, with a dip in her voice.

Gutteridge hesitated, toying with her eagerness. 'Just shy of £137,000.'

'You… are… *fucking* with me!'

Gutteridge huffed a muted laugh. 'Nope!' he chirped,

before turning to look down at Joshua who was sound asleep in the cot beside them, with not a care in the world.

'I've opened a separate account for this little one,' he announced. 'You know… for college funds, emergencies, that sort of thing.'

Keaton looked strangely shocked and taken aback. '*Really?*'

'Yeah,' Gutteridge smiled. 'Of *course* I have.'

Keaton held her ruminative stare, then stooped to place the envelope gently on her new coffee table. She stood again to face him, raising tentative arms. 'May I?'

Gutteridge laughed. 'Of course.'

Jane Keaton stepped in, if a little hesitant, and wrapped her gratitude around him.

Gutteridge shut his eyes, absorbing the embrace. 'It's the sex we have to abstain from,' he whispered. 'But I guess we're still allowed to hold each other. You *are* the mother of my son.'

Keaton paused in that thought. 'What about kissing?' she responded, aware she was pushing her luck, her soft voice vibrating through his shoulder. 'I miss kissing you.'

Gutteridge squeezed her tightly in his arms, his chin resting on her head. 'Cheeks, yes. On the lips, 'fraid not.'

She eventually released him and lifted her arms to grasp his shoulders, stroking her petite hands along the length of his triceps. 'I'm going to miss these,' she said, cupping his delts in her slender fingers, before dropping a hand away and sliding the Yazoo T-shirt she had on clear of her stomach. '*And* I've been purposefully hitting my abs at the gym to try and reel you in.'

He pulled the T-shirt down again. 'Behave,' he smirked.

Keaton's irreverent expression turned serious. She cocked an inquisitive head. 'How did the tribunal go?'

He rolled his eyes. 'It was basically just a wrist-slapping exercise for going rogue. But I think they actually understood

311

my reasoning – however off-piste it may have seemed.' His expression turned softly serious and thoughtful. 'I think anyone with half a brain would understand that I cut the team off for the sake of the wellbeing of the potential victims – you, Mum, *Joshua…*' he said, darting another look down at the cot beside them.

Keaton gave a pensive smile, her eyes locked on his. 'Good. I'm glad,' she whispered, lifting an affectionate hand to cup his ear. 'The funeral was lovely by the way, really tasteful.'

'Thank you,' Gutteridge whispered. 'And *you*? Is the therapy helping?'

Keaton flashed a subtly pessimistic brow. 'A bit, I guess. But the leave I've taken certainly is. Time the healer – isn't that what they say?'

Gutteridge smiled weakly and reciprocated her gesture, touching a hand to her face. 'It can be,' he agreed. 'Hell of a thing to go through, though. It's bound to mess you up a bit. But you're safe now, and that's all I care about – and *all* that matters,' he added. He sucked in a deep breath to extricate himself from what was fast becoming a dangerously tender moment. 'Well, I'd better get going. Eve's waiting for me outside.'

Keaton followed him to the door. 'Where are you two going again? And how long is it you're away for?'

'A week. Just to reset,' he said, stopping short of the door and turning to face her. 'We're going to a place near Chester – The Hollies. I've booked us a log cabin in the woods. You know the sort of thing – log fires, exposed timbers, tree-lined rambles through idyllic forests.' He smirked, seeming to almost ridicule the notion but making sure to remain positive. 'I just think me and Eve need some time together, *alone*, to regroup. I also feel that I'd like to rediscover the gentleman in me that I know has got a bit lost lately, a bit swamped. I liked him better.'

He turned reflective, dropping his attention to the ground between them. 'I remember we once raided a den of iniquity on Barton Street, a few years back now. You know the kind of thing – whips, chains, shackles, gas masks. There was even one guy dressed as a fucking baby – some fine, upstanding, local business man!' He attempted to smirk through his concerns. 'I just don't want to risk ending up like one of those freaks, just because I let life get to me.'

Keaton had to stop herself from laughing. 'Lightly clamping a mouth to heighten someone's orgasm is *hardly* the same thing.'

'Isn't it?' he questioned.

Keaton slow-blinked and flashed doubtful eyes. 'Well *I* don't think so...'

Gutteridge considered her dissent. 'Anyway, as I say, the break's really more for me *and* Eve, to help us to start over.'

Keaton attempted not to look pained, but failed.

Gutteridge noticed and sagged. 'Look...' He sighed. 'You know I love you, always have and I *always* will. But perhaps it's more the *caring* kind of love. The *compassionate* kind? I don't know.' He cupped her shoulder with an affectionate hand. 'And *you*... you're so beautiful, inside *and* out. And I've said it before, there are *so* many men out there who can't help but notice. Men better than me.'

Her sad expression began to dampen again, as tears broke free of the confines of her electric-blue eyes, cascading her cheeks and baptising her lips.

'No one's better than you,' she whispered.

He caressed her cheek, his temperate smile sad but appreciative of her words, however in error he considered them to be. 'Yes – they are.'

*

Gutteridge dropped into the seat of the Ferrari and joined Eve as they waved their farewells.

'Everything alright?' she asked.

'Yeah,' he said and smiled, sounding less than convincing. He clipped into his belt and fired up the engine.

'Are you sure?' Eve added, having to raise her voice a little to contradict the angry hum of the V8.

Gutteridge ceased his preparations, turning a look towards her questioning. 'Of course, everything's fine... Why wouldn't it be?'

She mirrored his fixed stare, searching for truth behind his eyes, then broke from it with a flickering smile. 'Okay...'

With a final, parting wave, they pulled away, the skies around the estate alive with the belligerent howl of the Ferrari's flat-plane-cranked engine.

Eve sat looking distracted, actively compiling her thoughts, checking and rechecking dates in her mind. She loosed a resigned sigh as some sort of opener to a conversation she'd rather not be having...

'I know you've been through a lot, lately,' she said, 'and I guess it's also fair to say, you've been through a lot throughout your entire life. *Because* of that, and *because* I love you, and care for you, and yes, because I *need* you. Because of all those things, I'll probably never leave you. But...' she paused, her whole demeanour sagging, 'you *really* need to be there for that child,' she said, her eyes dropping away to her lap. 'He needs a father, needs *you* to be a father – the father that you are. You should be there to help guide him through his life. A man guiding a man.' She looked apprehensive and fearful of the response she may receive. 'Just prrromise me it's over?'

Gutteridge's stomach sank through his seat; he felt like his soul had left his body. 'H-how long have you known?'

Eve allowed herself a tainted smile. 'Since the very first time I saw him.'

314

Gutteridge felt a wave of shame wash over him, mortified, his regrets reignited. 'It was just a mad moment,' he muttered. 'A mad, confused moment that both of us dearly wish had never—'

Eve cut him off with a gentle hand to his arm. 'It doesn't matter. Not now, and I don't want to know the details,' she said, seeming to deflate. 'I don't think I could handle the details – I know it happened before we were married but, still, it happened, and nothing anyone can do will change that.' She sighed. 'Besides – I've had the results of tests through, tests I had a while ago. Tests I didn't tell you about.' Her cheek winced at the irony. 'I'm unable to have childrrren, Pat,' she announced, looking emotionally impotent and decidedly tearful. 'Something to do with my ovaries and the shape of my womb,' she added. She seemed reluctant, circumspect, broken.

She straightened in her seat, fighting the feelings of shame and inadequacy that were only natural for a woman to feel. 'So… I guess that's where we are. I can never give you a child, *if* you actually ever wanted one – you know – *with* me,' she muttered. 'So I suppose what I'm saying is – if you can be accepting of that, I guess I can be accepting of Joshua. Of the son you already have, albeit, with another woman.'

She slowly turned a hope-filled look across the car at him and his inflamed ignominy, seeking answers in his frozen body language, answers that she dearly hoped to find.

'I love you, Patrick. I always will. I just can't give you children… and I can't be sharing you, either,' Eve said. She cocked her head, her expression uncertain, but inquisitive. She shrugged. 'So… how about it?'